TOUCHING
EVIL

Also by Kay Hooper
in Large Print:

Out of the Shadows
Hiding in the Shadows
Stealing Shadows
Elusive Dawn
Eye of the Beholder
It Takes a Thief
On Her Doorstep
Rafe, the Maverick (Shamrock Trinity)
Return Engagement
After Caroline

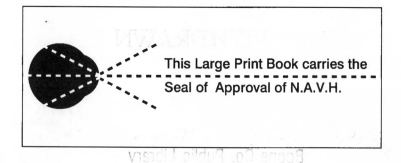

TOUCHING EVIL

KAY HOOPER

Thorndike Press • Waterville, Maine

Published in 2002 by arrangement with Bantam Books, an
imprint of the Bantam Dell Publishing Group, a division of
Random House, Inc.

Thorndike Press Large Print Americana Series.

The tree indicium is a trademark of Thorndike Press.

The text of this Large Print edition is unabridged.
Other aspects of the book may vary from the original edition.

Set in 16 pt. Plantin by Minnie B. Raven.

Printed in the United States on permanent paper.

Library of Congress Cataloging-in-Publication Data

Hooper, Kay.
    Touching evil / Kay Hooper.
       p. cm.
      ISBN 0-7862-3718-X (lg. print : hc : alk. paper) —
      ISBN 0-7862-3719-8 (lg. print : sc : alk. paper)
      1. Police artists — Fiction. 2. Seattle (Wash.) — Fiction.
    3. Women — Crimes against — Fiction.
    4. Large type books. I. Title.
    PS3558.O587 T68 2002
    813'.54—dc21   2001053449

For My Family
As Always

PROLOGUE

It was cold.

She could feel the wind tugging at her hair, hear it whining around the eaves and rattling what sounded like a loose piece of tin somewhere. The cold, moisture-laden air left her skin clammy and chilled her all the way to her bones.

She supposed she was in shock. It was an odd sensation, shock. A curious sort of limbo where nothing disturbed her very much.

So it must have been instinct rather than concern that prompted her to move, to pull herself forward despite the pain. The unevenness of the floor was both a help and a torture, providing fingerholds even as it cruelly scraped her skin and gouged her body.

She felt one of her fingernails tear painfully and was conscious of dirt and crusted blood underneath the few that were left undamaged. *I'm probably corrupting evidence or something. Probably really screwing things up.*

But that didn't seem important either. She focused on what was. Just keep reaching out, one hand at a time. Hold on to something, no matter how much it hurts. Pull yourself forward, no matter how much it hurts.

It became automatic, mechanical. Reach. Grab. Pull. Reach. Grab. Pull. There went another fingernail. Damn. Reach. Grab. Pull.

When her reaching fingers abruptly encountered thin air, it took her several minutes of fumbling exploration to realize she was at the top of the stairs.

Stairs.

Just the thought of her aching body bumping down rough step after rough step made her shudder, and she heard a thin sound of dread hardly louder than a whimper escape her swollen lips.

It was going to hurt like hell.

It did.

Somewhere near the bottom, her strength gave out, and she slid over the last few steps in an agonizing rush that left her sprawled, limp and sobbing quietly, on the ancient tile floor that smelled of dirt and cooked cabbage and urine.

She might have slept a while, or maybe just lay unconscious, because her body refused to go on. But eventually the same instinct that had driven her this far insisted she begin moving again.

I have to. I have to.

Yes. You have to.

That was peculiar, that other, alien voice in her head. She thought about it for a while, curling into a fetal position on her side even though the position was more painful. It was getting harder and harder to breathe. *Broken rib, probably.*

Three broken ribs. And a punctured lung. Listen to me, Hollis. You have to keep moving. Someone will be passing by in just a few minutes. If you aren't outside by then, you won't be found until tomorrow.

How strange. The voice knew her name.

Tomorrow will be too late, Hollis.

Yeah, she thought it probably would be too late.

Do you want to live?

Did she? She thought she did. Not that it would be the life she'd had before. In fact, it might not be much of a life at all. But . . . dammit . . . she wanted it. If only to live long enough for . . .

Vengeance?

Justice.

Hollis turned painfully back onto her belly and began the methodical effort of inching forward once again. She thought she was making progress, at least until she encountered a wall.

Damn.

Listening, she thought she could hear faint traffic sounds; that was her only clue to the whereabouts of a door that would allow her to escape the building. She began to feel her way along the wall toward the sounds.

It was getting colder. The wind that had whistled through the building during her entire agonizing journey downstairs was blowing in her face now. She guessed the building had long ago lost most of its windows and doors, so the wind found easy passage, stirring the dust and mold of many long years of neglect even as it cut into her shivering body.

Just a little farther now, Hollis.

She wondered why the voice didn't just call 911 but thought that was probably too much to ask of a figment of her imagination.

There's the doorway. Feel it?

She felt the threshold under her sore fingers, ancient weather stripping or something that was mostly rust. Beyond it was the broken concrete of a stoop or walkway. Hollis prayed there weren't any more steps.

Grimly, she pulled herself across the threshold and out of the building, shivering as the full force of the cold wind out there cut into her. There was one painful step down, then a walkway that seemed to be more rocks and gravel than concrete. It hurt like hell to pull herself across that jagged surface; the only saving grace was that it continued to guide her toward the street.

She hoped.

Not long now, Hollis. You're almost there.

Almost where? she wondered. Out in the street so a car could run over her?

He's near. He'll see you any minute now.

Before Hollis could wonder who was supposed to see her, she heard a male voice utter a shocked exclamation, then hurried footsteps coming toward her.

"Please," Hollis heard herself say in an unfamiliar, thickened voice. "Please help . . ."

"It's all right." The man's voice, near now, sounded nearly as thickened as her own had been. And shocked and horrified and compassionate. He touched her shoulder gently with a warm hand, then said, "I don't want to move you until EMS gets here, but I'm going to cover you with my coat, okay?"

She felt the blessed warmth and murmured a thanks, allowing her weary head to fall so that it rested on her forearm. She was very tired. Very tired.

Sleep now, Hollis.

She thought that was a good idea.

Sam Lewis checked her pulse just to make sure, then took a couple of steps away from her and spoke urgently into his cell phone. "For God's sake, *hurry!* She's — she's in bad shape. She's lost a lot of blood." His gaze followed the startlingly bright smeared trail of blood that marked her progress across broken concrete all the way back to the gaping doorway of the long-abandoned old house.

He tried to listen to the professionally detached voice in his ear, but finally cut off the 911 operator's questions by saying sharply, "I don't know what happened to her, but she's bruised and cut up and bleeding — and naked. Maybe she was raped, I don't know, but — but something else happened to her. She's . . . Her eyes are gone. No, dammit, not *injured*. Gone. Somebody's cut her eyes out."

CHAPTER
ONE

"She's not going to like this." Andy Brenner's voice was more unhappy than worried.

John Garrett stepped past him into the small, bare room. "I'll take the flak," he said, his gaze already fixed on the large two-way mirror that dominated the far wall and offered them a secret view into another small room.

This mostly bare room contained a scarred wooden table and several chairs. Three women sat at the table, the two facing the mirror sitting close together in a posture that suggested they were clinging to each other even though they weren't touching. The younger of the two wore very dark, heavy-rimmed sunglasses and sat rigidly in her chair, while the older woman watched her worriedly.

Sitting at right angles to them at the table, her back to the mirror, was the third woman, her face hidden from the watching

13

men. It was impossible to guess her shape, since she wore a bulky flannel shirt and faded jeans, but a rather wild cloud of long, dark red hair made her appear slight.

Andy sighed. "It's not flak I'm worried about. The chief likes to pretend Maggie works for us on our terms, but the rank and file know better; what Maggie wants, Maggie gets — and she wants total privacy when she's interviewing a victim."

"She'll never know we're here."

"I keep trying to tell you, John — she'll know."

"How? I push this button, and we can hear what's going on in the room but they won't hear us, right? We see in, they don't see out. So how will she know we're here?"

"Beats the hell out of me, but she will." Andy watched the other man move closer to the window and stifled another sigh. Anybody else and he would have stuck to his guns, but John Garrett was a hard man to say no to. Andy tried to think of an argument he hadn't used yet, but before he could come up with anything, John pushed the right button, and a quiet, curiously pleasing voice reached them clearly and without any of the tinny, hollow characteristics that were usual with an intercom.

". . . how difficult this is for you, Ellen. If

I could, I'd far rather wait and give you more time to —"

"Heal?" The woman wearing the sunglasses laughed, a brittle sound holding no amusement. "My husband is sleeping in the guest room, Miss Barnes. My little boy is afraid of me. I can't find my way through my own house without knocking over furniture and bumping into walls, and my sister has to cook for my family and help me dress every morning."

"Ellen, you know I'm happy to help," her sister protested, her soft voice half pleading and half weary. "And Owen wouldn't be sleeping in the guest room if it wasn't what you wanted, you know that."

"I know he can't bear to touch me, Lindsay." Ellen's voice was tight, a bare note away from shrill. Her hands were clasped together on the table, and her long, pale fingers writhed. "And I don't blame him for that. I can't blame him. Why would he want to touch me after —"

Maggie Barnes reached across the table and covered Ellen's hands with one of her own. "Listen to me, Ellen." Her voice remained quiet, but there was a new note in it now, an oddly soothing, almost hypnotic rhythm. "What that animal did to you can never be undone, but you can't allow it to

15

destroy you. Do you hear me? Don't give him that power over you. Don't allow him to win."

Listening, John unconsciously tilted his head to one side, trying to focus on the strangely compelling undercurrent he heard in her voice. It was almost . . . it was as if he knew that sound, as if it was something he only half remembered, like a song from his childhood or the last faint notes of music from a dream chased away by morning. Haunting.

Ellen didn't attempt to free her hands, and her rigid posture seemed to ease a bit, just a bit. "I don't want to remember," she said, low, almost whispering. "Don't ask me to remember."

"I have to." The regret in Maggie's voice was achingly genuine. "I need your memories, need every scrap of information you can give me. I need you to remember everything you can, Ellen. Every sound, every scent, every touch."

Ellen's shudder was visible. "He touched . . . I can't bear to think about how he touched me. Please don't make me . . ."

"Don't make her." Lindsay's face twisted, and she put a hesitant hand on her sister's arm.

"I don't have a choice," Maggie said.

"The police can't catch this animal without some idea who he is, what he looks like. We can't even warn other women to watch out for him. Ellen, some detail you remember may help me put a face on him. I —"

She turned her head suddenly, and John actually started in surprise at the abruptness of the movement — and the fact that he had the unsettling feeling she was looking directly into his eyes, even through the two-way mirror. She had very light brown eyes, the only unusual feature in a face that was pleasant but unremarkable.

And those pale eyes were looking right at him, he was sure of it. He felt it.

Behind him, Andy murmured, "Told you."

Hardly conscious of speaking aloud, John said, "She sees me. How can she —"

"X-ray vision. How the hell do I know?" Andy sounded as disgruntled as he felt. He hated it when Maggie was mad at him — and she was definitely going to be mad at him.

Maggie turned back to face the other two women and spoke gently. "I'm sorry, but there's something I have to do. I'll be right back."

Lindsay gave her an accusing look, then

leaned closer to her sister as though in support. Ellen didn't say a word, but she had the appearance of someone poised on the brink, frozen, as if unable to move forward or back.

John turned his back to the mirror as Maggie left the interview room. "She must have heard us," he said.

"No," Andy said. "She didn't hear us. This room is soundproofed, I told you that. She just knew, that's all."

The door of the observation room opened and Maggie Barnes stepped inside. John was surprised at how tall she was — at least five-ten, if he was any judge. But he hadn't been mistaken in thinking her slight; she wasn't unnaturally thin, just one of those very slender, almost ethereal women. He wondered if she dressed in the bulky layers out of some need to have more weight or substance.

When he looked at her face, John decided he'd been wrong in thinking it unremarkable. Graced with very regular features, not quite pretty but pleasant, it was saved from plainness by those slanted, catlike golden eyes and something stamped into her expression, innate to it, that was more than compassion and less than pity, a kind of empathy for the feelings of others that he knew was far more rare and valuable than high cheekbones or a perfect nose.

She looked at him briefly, a head-to-toe glance that missed nothing along the way and left him with the disconcerted realization that he had been very accurately weighed and analyzed.

Andy did his best to melt into the woodwork before she looked at him but obviously felt pinned to it instead when those catlike eyes fixed on him. He held his hands out, palms up, and offered an apologetic shrug.

"Andy?" Her voice was very gentle.

"Sorry, Maggie." He shifted uncomfortably, ruefully aware that he probably looked for all the world like a scolded schoolboy.

John stepped toward them. "It's my fault, Miss Barnes. I asked Andy to bend the rules. My name is —"

"I know who you are, Mr. Garrett." Her gaze was direct, her voice matter-of-fact. "But some rules apply to you too, whether you like it or not."

"It wasn't a question of rules not applying to me. I have special permission to observe the investigation." He only just managed not to sound defensive, which surprised him.

"And that includes watching and listening like a voyeur while a shattered woman forces herself to remember a nightmare you can't even begin to imagine? Is that the observing you were given permission to do?"

John stiffened, but her accusation struck a nerve and left him at least momentarily silent. Maggie didn't wait for a response but went on coolly. "How would you feel, Mr. Garrett, if two strange men had watched and listened in silence and secret while someone you cared about relived the entire horrific experience of being brutally raped and maimed by an animal?"

That struck more than a nerve. He drew a breath and let it out slowly. "You're right. I'm sorry."

Andy said, "Sounded like you were reaching her there for a minute. The interruption won't help things, will it?"

"No. No, it won't help things. I'll try again, but she may not be willing to talk to me anymore today."

John felt the reproach, even though she wasn't looking at him. "I'm sorry," he said again. "I didn't intend to interfere. That's the last thing I want to do."

"Fine. Then you won't mind leaving." She stepped back, holding the door open in a clear invitation — if not a command — for them to leave.

Andy wasted no time in obeying, but John paused in the doorway and met her gaze steadily. "I would like to talk to you, Miss Barnes. Today, if possible."

"If you want to wait around, suit yourself." Her tone was indifferent, but the steady golden eyes never left his. "I may be a while."

"I'll wait," John said.

Hollis was awake but didn't move or make a sound to indicate that. For the first few moments it was always like this, tension and terror until her scrambling mind left nightmare and caught up with reality.

Which was also a nightmare.

The bandages over her eyes — over where her eyes had once been — were becoming a familiar weight. She didn't yet know how she felt about the fact that beneath those bandages were now someone else's eyes. An accident victim who had lost her life but left a signed donor card behind.

The surgeon, proud of his groundbreaking work, had been surprised and rather aggrieved when Hollis's only question had been one he obviously considered unimportant.

"What color are they? Miss Templeton, I don't think you understand the complexity —"

"I understand, Doctor. I understand that you believe medical science has advanced to the point that I'll be able to see with this poor woman's eyes. And I understand that it'll be days at least, possibly weeks, before we find out if you're right. In the meantime, I'm asking what color my . . . new . . . eyes are."

Blue, he'd said.

Her old ones had been brown.

Would she be able to see? She didn't know, and she suspected that her doctor, for all his confidence in his abilities, was unsure of the surgery's outcome as well. The optic nerve was a tricky thing, he didn't have to tell her that. And then there were all the other nerves, the blood vessels, the muscles. Far too many tiny connections to be certain of anything. They didn't think her body would reject the new eyes, and antirejection drugs would probably make certain of that, but nobody seemed nearly as sure what her brain might do.

Vision was as much the mind's interpretation of images as it was anything else, after all. With the intricate connection between organ and mind severed and then painstakingly rebuilt, who really knew what her brain's response might be?

Hell, maybe it was no wonder she hadn't even been able to decide how she felt about it.

Most of the other physical injuries had been surprisingly minor, given everything she'd been through. The broken ribs were healing, though she still breathed carefully, and doctors had repaired the puncture in her lung. A few stitches here and there. Scrapes and bruises.

Oh — and she'd never be able to have children, but what the hell. No kid needed to be saddled with a probably blind, certainly emotionally wrecked mother anyway, right? Right.

I know you're awake, Hollis.

She didn't move, didn't turn her head. That voice again, quietly insistent, as it had been virtually every day of the past three weeks. She'd asked a nurse once who it was that came to visit her and sit by her bed hour after hour, but the nurse had said she didn't know, hadn't seen anyone except the police officers who came regularly to ask gentle questions Hollis didn't answer.

Hollis had so far refused to question the voice, just as she refused to speak to the cops or say any more than absolutely necessary to the doctors and nurses. She wasn't ready to think about what had happened to her, far less talk about it.

You'll be able to leave soon, the voice said. *What will you do then?*

"Stepping in front of a bus might be a good idea," Hollis said calmly. She spoke aloud to remind herself that hers was really the only voice in the room. Of course it was. Because that other voice was just a figment of her imagination, obviously.

If you really wanted to die, you never would have crawled out of that building.

"And if I wanted rational platitudes from a figment of my imagination, I'd go back to sleep. Oh, wait — I am asleep. I'm dreaming. It's all just a bad dream."

You know better.

"Better that it happened? Or better that you aren't just a figment of my imagination?"

Instead of answering either question, the figment said, *If I handed you a lump of clay, what would you make, Hollis?*

"What kind of question is that? One of those inkblot questions? Is my figment psychoanalyzing me?"

What would you make? You're an artist.

"I was an artist."

Before, you created art with your hands and your eyes and your mind. Whether or not the surgery is successful, you still have your hands. You still have your mind.

The figment, Hollis realized, didn't believe she'd be able to see with these borrowed eyes either. "So I should just turn myself into a sculptor? It isn't quite as simple as that."

I didn't say it was simple. I didn't say it would be easy. But it would be a life, Hollis. A rich, creative life.

After a moment, Hollis said, "I don't know if I can. I don't know if I'm brave enough to start over."

You'll have to find out, then, won't you?

Hollis smiled despite herself. So her figment could offer more than knee-jerk platitudes, after all. And the challenge was unexpectedly bracing. "I guess so. That or go looking for that bus to step in front of."

"Miss Templeton? Were you speaking to me?" The day-shift nurse was a bit hesitant as she approached the bed.

Hollis was learning to read footsteps, even the nearly soundless ones of the nurses. This nurse feared for Hollis's sanity; it wasn't the first time she'd caught the patient talking to herself.

"Miss Templeton?"

25

"No, Janet, I wasn't speaking to you. Just talking to myself again. Unless there's somebody sitting in that chair beside the bed, of course."

Warily, Janet said, "No, Miss Templeton, there's nobody in the chair."

"Ah. Well, then, I must have been talking to myself. But don't let it worry you. I did that even before the attack." She had learned to refer to it that way, as "the attack." It was the phrase the doctors used, the nurses, the cops.

"Can I — can I get you anything, Miss Templeton?"

"No, Janet. No, thank you. I think I'll take a nap."

"I'll make sure nobody bothers you, Miss Templeton."

Hollis listened to the footsteps recede and pretended to be asleep. It wasn't difficult.

The hard part was keeping herself from asking aloud if the figment was still here. Because it couldn't be, of course.

Unless she really was crazy.

"We're no further along than we were when you were here six weeks ago." Luke Drummond, the lieutenant in charge of detectives in this division of the Seattle P.D.,

26

was accustomed to reporting to his superiors, but he disliked being obliged to divulge details of an ongoing investigation to a civilian, and his hostility showed. Especially since he couldn't report any progress.

"There've been two more victims since then." John Garrett kept his voice level. "And still no evidence, no clues to lead you any closer to identifying this bastard?"

"He's very good at what he does," Drummond said.

"And you aren't?"

Drummond's eyes narrowed, and he leaned back in his chair, deceptively relaxed. "I have a very skilled and experienced squad of detectives, Mr. Garrett. We also have some damned good forensics experts on the payroll, and state-of-the-art equipment. But none of that is much good when there's no evidence to study or witnesses to question and when the victims are, to say the least, traumatized and unable to give us much to go on."

"What about Maggie Barnes?"

"What about her?"

"She hasn't come up with anything useful?"

"Well, as everybody keeps reminding me, what she does is an art — and apparently it can't be rushed." He shrugged. "In all fairness to Maggie, she hasn't had much more to work with than the rest of us. The first two victims are — well, I don't have to tell you. But neither gave us anything much to go on right after the attacks. The third is just now well enough physically to sit down and talk to Maggie. And the fourth is not only still in the hospital but so far hasn't been willing to answer even the simplest question from any of us. All the shrinks tell us that if we push these women we'll lose any chance we might have of gaining any relevant information from either of them."

"Why haven't you called in the FBI?" John demanded.

"Because there's nothing they can do that we can't," Drummond replied tersely.

John wasn't so sure about that, but he knew he was on the edge of alienating Drummond completely and dared not push any harder. Pulling the right strings had gotten John access to the investigation, but if Drummond wanted to, he could make that access fairly useless.

Holding his voice level, he said, "So the consensus is that Maggie Barnes is your best bet to get something useful from the victims?"

"If anybody can guide those women

back through the hell they experienced without hurting them even more, it's Maggie. Whether she gets anything we can use is something else. We'll just have to wait and see." He watched John Garrett shift in his chair almost unconsciously and for the first time felt a genuine pang of sympathy for the other man. He might be a pain in the ass at the moment, but his motives were certainly understandable, and Drummond could hardly blame him for muscling in on the investigation. In Garrett's place, Drummond thought he'd probably do the same.

Assuming, of course, that he had a billion or so dollars and a shitload of political influence to make both the chief and the mayor practically piss their pants in their eagerness to be cooperative.

Luke Drummond would have loved to have at least that political influence; he intended to sit in the governor's mansion one day. He hadn't made any secret of his political aspirations and, despite not being an elected official, tended to react to any situation as a politician rather than a cop, but to date that hadn't hurt either his present career or his ambitions. He was enough of a cop to be able to do his job and do it well.

At least until this damned psychopath had turned up.

At the moment, however, Drummond had neither Garrett's political juice nor his money, so it was in the cop's best interest to be at least courteous to the man.

"Maggie needs time to interview the two surviving victims," he said evenly. "We have to be patient."

"He attacked Hollis Templeton a little more than three weeks ago; how much longer do you think he'll wait before he acts again?" John heard the edgy tension in his own voice, but he was beyond being able to hide it.

Drummond sighed. "According to the shrinks, he could grab another woman tomorrow — or six months from now. So far, he hasn't established any kind of time pattern we can identify. There were two months between the first two victims, but he grabbed the third only two weeks later. Then he waited nearly three months to strike a fourth time."

"No pattern," John echoed.

"And nothing else to hang our hats on. No blood evidence other than the victims', and he was smart enough to wear condoms, so there's been no semen found. Nothing under the fingernails of the vic-

30

tims, no hair or fibers found on them or anywhere near them, nothing to identify where he might have held them. They're always dumped someplace else afterward, a remote or at least unoccupied building. Ellen Randall remembers being transported inside something, the trunk of a car, she thinks, but since he stuck to pavement we didn't find any tire tracks."

"How was Hollis Templeton transported?"

"We don't know, not yet. I told you, she's not answering our questions. Her doctors say Maggie can try talking to her in a few days. That's if she's agreeable, and she probably won't be, since she hasn't been anxious to talk to us so far."

"What then?"

"I don't know." Drummond sighed again. "Look, Garrett, I'm sorry as hell, but there's nothing more I can tell you, at least not at the moment. We're doing the best we can. And that's all."

Andy was waiting for John around the corner from Drummond's office and offered a wry "Told you so."

"I can see I'm going to make myself real popular around here," John said.

"Oh, don't mind Drummond. He's a nice enough guy, for a politician."

"I'd rather he were just a cop."

"Yeah, so would most of us. But we comfort ourselves with the certainty that he won't be around long, just long enough to get a secure toehold to boost himself higher up the food chain. In the meantime, however, we're stuck with him."

Andy led the way to his own corner of the bullpen, snagging two cups of coffee as they passed the pot.

"Jeez, Andy, take it all, why don't you?" a nearby younger cop grumbled. "You could at least make another pot."

"I made the last one, Scott. Your turn."

John sat in Andy's visitor's chair and accepted one of the cardboard cups. He took a sip, grimaced, and said, "This is really lousy coffee, Andy."

"Usually is, no matter who makes it." Unoffended, Andy took a healthy swallow of his own and shrugged. "You going to wait around for Maggie?"

"Do you think she'll talk to me?"

Andy thought about it. "Well, you pissed her off, so it's hard to say. Just what is it you're hoping she'll tell you, John?"

There was no easy answer to that, and John let the silence build for a few moments before he finally replied with a question of his own. "Why are all of you so convinced she's your best chance of catching this bastard? What is it that's so special about Maggie Barnes?"

Andy leaned back in his chair until it creaked in protest, and took another swallow of coffee. He studied the man across from him, wondering how much to say. Wondering how much would be believed. John Garrett was a hardheaded, hard-nosed businessman who'd made a fortune by understanding the cold logic of finance; Andy hadn't known him long, but common sense told him John wasn't the sort of man to easily accept anything he couldn't see with his own eyes or hold in his hands.

"Andy?"

"Maggie has . . . a knack, John. You can call it exceptional skill, or talent amounting to genius, or amazing empathy, but whatever you call it, the result is that she talks to shattered victims of crimes and from the little they're able to tell her she manages to give us a face we can look for."

"I didn't think police even used sketch artists anymore. Isn't there a computer program just as good?"

"Not as good as Maggie."

"She's that talented?"

Andy hesitated, then sighed. "Talent's

only part of it, though she has that in spades. She could make a fortune as a real artist, but instead she spends her days sitting in cramped interview rooms listening to horror stories I hope you never have to listen to. She listens, and she talks to those people, and somehow she helps them relive a nightmare without letting it destroy them. And then she comes out and starts drawing and nine times out of ten gives us a sketch so accurate the guy could use it on his driver's license."

"Sounds like magic," John said dryly.

"Yeah. It does, doesn't it? Looks like it sometimes too. I don't know how she does it. Nobody here knows how she does it. But we've learned to trust her, John."

"Okay. Then why doesn't she have a sketch of the rapist yet?"

"Because not even Maggie can work with nothing. The women haven't *seen* anything. And besides that — the first victim died before anybody could talk to her, the most recent one is still in the hospital, and you saw what kind of shape Ellen Randall's in."

"You didn't mention Christina," John forced himself to say.

Andy gazed at him steadily. "I didn't think I had to. She did the best she could for us, but she didn't see anything either."

"Maggie Barnes talked to her, didn't she? That's what you told me, what the report said."

"Yeah, she talked to Christina."

"Without witnesses?"

Slowly, Andy frowned. "Without anybody in the observation room, if that's what you mean."

"Then maybe she can tell me something none of the rest of you can tell me."

"Like what?"

"Like why Christina killed herself."

CHAPTER
TWO

As she'd expected, Maggie quickly found that Ellen Randall had withdrawn again into her frozen shell. Pushing her would only make matters worse. So Maggie didn't protest when Lindsay announced she was taking her sister home, and she didn't try to arrange another meeting.

Even though she could hear the clock ticking away in her head. Time was running out, she knew it. She felt it. And every day that passed with the police no closer to catching the animal the newspapers had begun calling the Blindfold Rapist brought them closer and closer to another victim.

Another life ruined.

Another soul marked.

Worse, Maggie knew that he would only become more violent as time passed. It would take more cruelty to satisfy whatever unnatural hunger drove him to do what he did. Soon, very soon, he would begin killing his victims. And when that happened, when the police were denied even the shaky recollections of living victims, then they would have no chance at all of stopping him — unless and until he made a mistake.

So far, he hadn't made a single one.

Maggie glanced into the bullpen and saw John Garrett sitting at Andy's desk. She didn't want to talk to Garrett, not now. Not yet. She retreated to an unoccupied office near the interview rooms and sat down with her sketch pad open before her.

There was very little on the page. Just the vague shape of a face surrounded by hair so long that Maggie suspected he'd worn a wig. At their first meeting a few days before, Ellen Randall had given Maggie that much. Longish hair, she'd felt it brush her skin when he bent over her.

But no other useful details, nothing for her to build on. Maggie had no feeling for the shape of the face, whether his forehead was high or low, his jaw strong or weak, his chin jutting or receding. She didn't even know if his complexion was smooth or rough; both Ellen and one other victim thought they remembered the touch of cool, hard plastic covering his face, as though he'd worn a mask.

Just the possibility disturbed Maggie, on a level as much instinctive as it was analytical. What man would be so wary of discovery, of being identified, that he would wear a mask even after blinding his victims? Of course, criminals seldom wanted to be identified, but Maggie had talked to the cops working on the investigation, and all of them agreed that this particular criminal was going to unusual extremes to protect his identity.

Why?

Was there something about his face even a blinded victim could recognize when it touched her? Scars, perhaps, or some other kind of deformity?

"Maggie?"

She didn't look up and swore silently at him for disrupting a mental musing that had often, in the past, produced results for her. "Hey, Luke."

He came into the office and sat down in the visitor's chair across from hers. "Any luck?"

"No, unless you count bad luck." She closed the sketch pad with a sigh. "Ellen froze up again. We were . . . interrupted, and it broke the connection I was trying to establish. I'll have to wait a few days and then get her back in here."

"I just talked to Hollis Templeton's doctor," Drummond said. "She's doing even better than he'd hoped, physically at least. He's hopeful the surgery was a success. If it was, if she can see again, then maybe . . ."

"Maybe what?" Maggie looked at him steadily. "Maybe she'll be a little less traumatized and able to help us?"

"It's possible, Maggie."

"Yeah. Yeah, I know it is. It's also possible she noticed things the other victims wouldn't have. Since she was an artist, I mean."

"Would you go try to talk to her? She hasn't said shit to any of us, but she might talk to you."

"I'd rather wait until she leaves the hospital. The atmosphere there isn't exactly conducive to the kind of conversation I need."

"I know, but . . . there's a lot of pressure, more every day. The newspapers, citizens' groups, the mayor. There's a panic building out there, Maggie, and I can't stop it. Get me something I can use to stop it."

"I can't work miracles, Luke."

"You have before."

She shook her head. "That was different. This guy is determined his victims will never testify against him. He's not letting them see him, he doesn't speak to them, he makes damned sure they don't get their hands on him. The only sense left is smell, and so far all I've got is that he smells like Ivory soap. Deliberately, of course. He's using the scent of the soap to block anything else they might smell."

"Yeah, I know he hasn't missed a trick so far. But, like you said, his most recent victim was an artist, and I'm told artists are trained to use their senses differently from most of the rest of us. Hollis Templeton might be able to give you more to go on. Try, Maggie. Please."

She had stopped wondering if he had any idea what he asked of her, of the victims. He didn't. Luke Drummond was a fair cop, an able administrator, and a good politician, but he didn't have much in the way of imagination or empathy, not when it came to victims.

Did he even guess she was as much a victim as the women she talked to? No, probably not.

"I'll go over there tomorrow," she said. "But if she won't talk to me, I can't press her, Luke. You know that."

"Just try, that's all I ask." He got to his feet, visibly relieved. She could almost see him silently deciding what he was going to tell the chief of police and the mayor. He wouldn't mention her by name, of course, just say that they were "pursuing a good lead in the investigation."

It wasn't that Luke Drummond didn't want to share the credit, it was just that he mistrusted what he didn't understand, and he didn't understand how she did what she did. He wouldn't have understood even if she had explained it to him — and she had no intention of doing that.

"I'll try," Maggie said, because there was nothing else he would hear.

"Great. Hey — have you talked to Garrett yet?"

"No, not yet."

"He's waiting out in the bullpen, I think."

"Yeah, I know."

Drummond looked down at her with a little frown. "Don't tell him any more than you have to. He might have the mayor and the chief in his hip pocket, but I don't like civilians being handed all the details of an ongoing investigation."

"Such as they are," Maggie murmured.

"You know damned well we're holding back a few things publicly. Like the Ivory soap bit. I'm just saying I'd rather we kept that stuff within the unit — to rule out copycats, if nothing else. I'm serious, Maggie."

"I know you are. Don't worry. John Garrett doesn't want to talk to me about things like that."

Drummond had started to turn away but paused as his attention was caught by what she'd said. "I thought you hadn't talked to him yet."

"I haven't."

"Then how do you —" He broke off and frowned. "Oh, yeah. I guess it makes sense he'd have only one thing on his mind, at least when he's talking to you. You were the last one to talk to Christina Walsh, weren't you?"

"So they tell me."

"I read the report," he said unnecessarily. "Garrett read it. I don't know what the poor bastard thinks you can tell him."

"I don't know either," Maggie said, lying.

"Tread lightly, Maggie. He can cause us a lot of trouble if he wants to."

She nodded but didn't say anything else, and Drummond left her alone in the office. Pushing John Garrett from her mind, at least for the moment, she opened her sketch pad again and stared down at the vague outline of a man's face.

"Who are you?" she murmured. "Who are you this time?"

Andy said, "I doubt Maggie knows the answer to why Christina killed herself, John. She hasn't mentioned it, and I think she would have."

"Maybe not. If it had nothing to do with your investigation, she might have kept it to herself."

Carefully, wary of what he knew was still an open wound, Andy said, "John, after what happened to Christina, suicide was probably the only option she felt she had left."

"His other victims didn't kill themselves."

"He didn't do to them what he did to her, you know that. The bastard was apparently still experimenting with ways of blinding his victims, and that acid did more than take her sight. Jesus, John — I know a lot of strong men who would have taken the same way out under those circumstances."

"Not Christina." John's voice was level with the sort of control that was about as stable as nitro. "As bad as things were, it would have taken more, much more, before she gave up. She was one of the stron-

43

gest people I've ever known. I'm absolutely certain of that, Andy."

"Okay. But everybody has a breaking point, and none of us can be that sure of somebody else's. I'm just saying, don't expect too much from Maggie."

"All I expect is the truth."

Andy grimaced. "Well, I'm pretty sure you'll get it from her. If she talks to you at all, she'll tell you the truth as she sees it. But . . ."

"But?"

"If you want my advice — and you probably don't — you'll be careful how you ask. Maggie's very independent, John, and I mean on the prickly side. From what I've seen, she doesn't take any shit from anybody, no matter who they are. I don't think you could piss her off to the point that she'd walk away from her work here, but I'd rather not take any chances. She's committed to helping us, and I'd like to keep it that way."

"Why?"

"Why would I like to keep it that way?"

"Why is she so committed to helping you? You said yourself she has to listen to horror stories, that she could make a fortune as an artist. So why does she do this instead?"

"I don't know."

"You've never asked her?"

"Sure I have. So have some of the others. But whatever her reasons are, they're obviously private. This time, take my advice — and don't go there."

It wasn't in John's nature to accept being warned off, not when he was curious. And not when he was feeling an unaccustomed sensation of frustrated helplessness about this entire situation. But all he said was "I'll keep that in mind."

Andy knew when he was being humored. "Yeah, yeah. Look, you want more lousy coffee?"

"I just want to talk to Maggie Barnes."

"I saw Ellen Randall and her sister leave a little while ago, so Maggie's probably free. But I don't know —"

"I'm free," Maggie said from just behind John's left shoulder. "You wanted to speak to me, Mr. Garrett?"

He got to his feet quickly. "If you can spare me a few minutes, I'd appreciate it."

"Drummond's office is empty right now," Andy offered. "He's headed across town for a meeting."

"With who?" Maggie asked.

"Dunno, but probably another citizens' group. He's catching a lot of heat, Maggie."

"He told me."

"Yeah. I'll just bet he did."

Maggie shrugged. "Can't really blame him for pushing. Or for not understanding he didn't have to."

Andy sighed an agreement.

Maggie turned away, clearly assuming John would follow her as she led the way to Luke Drummond's office. When they went in, she took one of the visitor's chairs in front of the desk, shifting it so that it faced the other one. After closing the door behind them, John took the other one and turned it as well.

The closed door would keep them from being overheard, but that was the extent of privacy; the partitions between this office and the bullpen were glass from the waist up, and though there were blinds, all were wide open. John was aware of several curious stares directed their way, but Maggie didn't seem to notice.

"I don't know what you expect to learn from me, Mr. Garrett," she said. "There's nothing I can tell you that isn't in any of the numerous reports I'm sure you've read."

He caught himself listening to her voice more than what she said, trying to identify that elusive sense of a half-remembered song. "I know what's in the reports."

She nodded and looked down at the sketch pad in her lap. "Then you know it all." She really didn't want to talk to him like this. She didn't want to have to answer the question she knew he wanted to ask her.

"Miss Barnes —" He shook his head. "Look, I'll be around until this bastard is stopped, even if I'm not officially part of the investigation, so why don't we drop the formality? My friends call me John."

She made herself look at him and nod again. Tried to distract herself with an artist's automatic inventory. He was a good-looking man, in a commanding sort of way. Big, broad-shouldered, athletic — or at least worked to stay in good shape. Though he was undoubtedly both impressive and formidable in a business suit, the more casual jeans and black leather jacket lent him a slightly dangerous air that was probably, Maggie thought, not the least bit deceptive.

His hair was very dark, but she knew there'd be a hint of red in the sunlight. Eyes an unusual shade of blue-green, and deep set beneath brows that flared slightly upward at the outer corners so perfectly an artist might have drawn them.

He'd look mean as hell when he scowled,

she thought idly. Probably *be* mean as hell mad. But there was humor in the curve of his mouth, in the laugh lines fanning out from his eyes, and more than enough intelligence and self-control in those eyes to mitigate whatever temper he had.

Most of the time, anyway.

"Okay, John it is. I'm Maggie," she said, wishing she hadn't been here today or he hadn't. Anything to postpone this conversation a little longer. "But I still can't tell you anything about the investigation that you don't already know."

"That isn't what I wanted to talk to you about. At least, not directly." He drew a breath. "There's something I wanted to ask you."

She hadn't intended to, but Maggie found herself nodding. "Yes. About Christina."

"I guess it's not so surprising that I'd want to ask you about her," he said after a moment.

"No. But there's nothing I can tell you." Until that moment, Maggie hadn't known what she would say. She hadn't known she would lie. It required an effort to keep meeting his eyes steadily.

"You were the last person to see her. The last one to speak to her before she died."

"I interviewed her. Just the way I interviewed Ellen Randall today. Asked her questions, asked her to relive what had happened to her. It was painful for her."

"So painful she decided to kill herself twelve hours later?" John demanded, his voice suddenly harsh.

Maggie didn't blink or flinch. "It wasn't our first interview. We were going over what we'd discussed before, there was nothing new. No new impressions from her, no new questions from me. She seemed . . . the same as always when I left."

"You left her alone."

She did flinch at that. "The nurse had always been there, in the next room. I assumed she was there that day, even though I hadn't seen her. I didn't find out until later . . ."

John relented, uncertain in his own mind whether it was because he knew she wasn't to blame or because that haunting voice of hers affected him in a surprisingly powerful way. "You couldn't have known what she'd do. She was always . . . a very good actress." He gazed into those strange cat eyes and had the sudden realization that here was another woman entirely capable of hiding her thoughts. But before he could do more than wonder if he wanted to pursue that, she spoke again in the same level tone.

"In any case, there's nothing helpful I can tell you. I'm sorry you wasted your time."

"I didn't waste it. I've wanted to meet you since Andy first told me they had a uniquely talented sketch artist working on the investigation. I'm curious about how you work — which is why I barged in on your interview today. I really am sorry about that, by the way."

She didn't respond to the apology, other than with a brief nod. "There's nothing extraordinary about the way I work. It's the way sketch artists have always worked. I talk to victims, ask them questions, gain impressions, and then I draw what I think they saw. Sometimes I get lucky."

"According to Andy, it's more than luck. And more than just sometimes."

Maggie shrugged. "Andy's a friend. He's biased."

"And is the police chief also biased? He was singing your praises to me yesterday."

She dropped her gaze briefly to the sketch pad in her lap, then said in a matter-of-fact tone, "His niece was abducted from her school playground about five years ago,

50

and I helped them find the guy before he could hurt her."

"With a sketch? There were witnesses?"

"The other kids. The oldest was only nine, so it was . . . difficult. Kids tend to elaborate, to invent details using their imaginations, so we had to weed through what they said they saw to get at the truth."

"How were you able to do that?"

Maggie hesitated only an instant. "I listened to them."

"And you knew truth from an elaboration — how?"

"I . . . don't know. I mean, I don't know how to explain it. Andy calls it intuition, instinct. I guess that's as good a word as any. I've been doing this a long time."

Surprised, John said, "It can't have been all that long. You're — what? — twenty-five?"

"Thanks, but it's thirty-one. The first time I sketched a face for the police I was eighteen. So I've been doing this almost half my life."

"Isn't eighteen awfully young to work for the police?"

"I wasn't working for them then, not officially." Maggie sighed. "I happened to witness a crime and I was the only one present who saw anything. I also happened to be able to draw. One thing led to another, and by the time I was in college I was also officially on the police payroll."

John had more questions, but before he could ask them Andy knocked on the door and opened it to say, "Sorry for the interruption, but — Maggie, we just got a call. Hollis Templeton says she'll talk to you Saturday afternoon at the hospital."

Maggie got to her feet. "She called us?"

"Yeah. After ignoring us for weeks."

"Did she say why?"

"No, but . . ."Andy shifted his weight the way he did when he was uneasy. "You two haven't met, right?"

"Right."

"Know each other by reputation?"

"I don't know her work. Don't see how she could know mine. Why?"

"She asked for you by name, Maggie. Said she'd only talk to you."

John got up. "Why is that strange?" he asked.

"Because," Andy said, "none of us has told her Maggie's name. And there's been no publicity about her being our sketch artist; we keep that quiet. So Hollis Templeton really shouldn't have known who to ask for."

The hotel room in Pittsburgh was like every other hotel room he'd ever stayed in, and Quentin Hayes wondered idly if there was a hotel decorators' association and they met secretly two or three times every year to decide what all the hotel rooms in America were going to look like. Because surely it was beyond coincidence that they all used variations of the same floral-print bedspreads and drapes and hung the same bland landscapes on the walls. And arranged the furniture in the most unreasonable way so that there was never an outlet where one was needed and it was always necessary to unplug a lamp in order to plug in a computer or fax machine.

No, it was obviously a conspiracy. He expressed that opinion to his companion, and she gave him a wry response.

"You've been on the road too long," Kendra Eliot said.

"That does not," Quentin said, "negate the probability I'm right."

Kendra typed another sentence into her report, keeping her gaze on the laptop even as she said, "A vacation, that's what you need. A nice, long one. A couple of weeks spent *not* chasing after bad guys or coming up with imaginative reasons to explain how you know the things you know."

"How can you talk and type at the same time? If I try that, I end up typing what I'm saying."

"My uniquely flexible mind. I'm telling Bishop you need a break."

"A change of scene is what I need." Quentin lay back on the bed and clasped his hands together behind his neck, resting his blond head against the headboard. "I'm tired of this place. It's going to snow tonight."

"According to the weather reports?"

"No. It's going to snow."

She glanced at him, then continued typing. "Well, we should be able to get out before the bad weather moves in. Right?"

"Mmmm."

"And maybe our next assignment will be someplace warm and sunny."

"Mmmm."

Kendra stopped typing, this time turning in her chair to study him. He appeared to be looking at the ceiling, but she knew that inward-turned gaze, the utter stillness, and waited patiently.

Finally, softly, Quentin said, "Shit."

"Trouble?"

He sat up, raked his fingers through his rather shaggy hair, and swore again beneath his breath. He looked at his cell phone lying on the nightstand, and five seconds later it rang.

Kendra lifted an eyebrow but went back to her report.

Quentin answered the phone. "Hey, John."

"I wish you wouldn't do that," John Garrett said.

"Answer the phone? It rang, so I answered it. That's what they're for, you know."

"I know what they're for, and you know what I meant. Even if you do know it's me calling, I wish you'd pretend otherwise."

"But that would be denying my deepest self," Quentin said solemnly.

John sighed.

Quentin grinned, then said, "Okay, okay. But it's just so much fun to poke holes in your certainties."

"Oh, is that what you've been doing all these years?"

"It's what I've been trying to do. Without visible results. One of these days, my friend, you're going to admit that there are more things in heaven and earth than you can find in those balance sheets of yours."

"I never denied that."

"No, you just deny precognition."

"How can you see something that hasn't happened yet?" John demanded.

"I don't *see* anything, I just know what's going to happen before it happens."

"Bullshit."

"I knew you were going to call."

"Lucky guess."

Quentin laughed. "Yeah, I just guessed it'd be you calling on a Friday morning in November when we haven't talked for more than a month. Use that hard head of yours and admit the paranormal exists."

It held the sound of an old argument, and Kendra tuned out Quentin's side of it until something he said a couple of minutes later caught her attention and made her realize the friendly debate was over.

". . . again? So it's four victims now?" He shook his head. "I had no idea, John. We've been caught up in something in Pittsburgh for the past few weeks, and I've barely looked at a newspaper. They're sure it's the same guy?"

"They're sure. He's still blinding his victims, for one thing. And I've got a hunch there are a few more similarities they haven't put in their reports. At least, not the reports I've seen."

"You said the detectives handling the investigation were good."

"Not good enough. Quentin, they don't know a bit more than they did when Christina died, and that was three months ago. Two more women have been maimed for life, and the cops don't even have a decent description they can broadcast so the rest of the women in Seattle know who to be wary of. It isn't a real fun time to be a man in this city, I can tell you that."

"You're staying out there?"

"For the duration."

Surprised, Quentin said, "I know all those companies of yours practically run themselves these days, but is it wise for you to spend so much time away from L.A.?"

"I can fly down if I have to. I need to be here, Quentin."

"Okay, but the cops there may not be happy to have you breathing down their necks, John. Why don't you back off and give them room to work?"

"They can't work when they have nothing to work *with*." John drew a breath. "If you're really convinced that this new FBI unit you're with can get results using . . . unconventional methods, then now's the time to prove it. The usual five senses aren't accomplishing a goddamned thing."

Quentin frowned. "Have you persuaded

the lieutenant in charge to call us in?"

"Not exactly."

"By *not exactly,* do you mean he's wavering? Or do you mean this is all your idea?"

"The latter."

"Oh, hell, John."

"Look, I know it should come through official channels, but the lieutenant in charge is stubborn as a mule and he's not going to yell for help until he's up to his ass in outraged citizens. So far, he's handling the flak and pushing his own people to work harder. But with nothing to go on, all they can do is sit around and wait for this bastard to make a mistake. That means more victims, Quentin."

"I know what it means. But this is out of our jurisdiction, you know that. And without an official request for help made through official channels, the Bureau is not going to send us in. We're walking a tightrope as it is, bending over backward to be careful as hell every time we *are* called in so the locals don't get the peculiar idea that we use witchcraft to solve their crimes."

"I won't let you be burned at the stake."

"Very funny." Quentin sighed, and looked across the room to find Kendra watching him with raised brows and her patented don't-do-anything-you'll-regret expression. He sighed again. "You've still got political juice there, right? Can the mayor or governor put pressure on the chief of police to call us in?"

"They're reluctant. The lieutenant has some juice of his own, and he wants his team to handle this."

"Because he's a good cop and sure of his team?"

"No. Because he wants to sit in the governor's mansion himself one day."

"Shit."

"Yeah. I just don't think he's going to ask for help, Quentin. At least not officially."

"I knew you were going to say that."

"Then you know what I'm going to say next. You've probably got vacation time coming." John's voice was persuasive. "Spend some of it here. You haven't been home except for flying visits in years. I'll pay the tab — send the jet for you, best hotel suite, you name it."

"Best hotel suite, huh?" Quentin gazed around at the repressively unoriginal decor of the room he was in.

Kendra murmured, "Oh, God."

John was saying, "Absolutely the best. Say the word, and I'll send the jet. Where did you say you are?"

"Pittsburgh."

"Why?"

Quentin almost laughed at his friend's astonished tone. "I told you, we had a case. Unfortunately, it was here."

"Is the case over?"

"Yeah. We won in overtime."

"Good. Then you most certainly need a break."

"I'll agree with that much — but I'm not sure I can take one right now, John. It all depends on whether there's another assignment waiting for me. Let me check with the office and get back to you."

"All right. Call me on my cell."

"I'll let you know something by this afternoon, I hope. Talk to you then, John." Quentin turned off his phone and set it on the nightstand.

Patiently, Kendra said, "We aren't supposed to work unofficially, Quentin, you know that."

"I know that."

"Bishop won't like it."

"I know that too."

Kendra sighed. "Seattle, huh?"

He smiled slowly. "Seattle."

"Because he's your friend?"

"Yes. And because his sister was."

CHAPTER
THREE

Since she was forced to wait until Saturday afternoon to see Hollis Templeton and knew better than to try arranging another interview with Ellen Randall so soon, Maggie found herself at loose ends on Friday. Her small house was too quiet and the bright studio where she painted held no appeal, so late in the morning she picked up the sketch pad that went virtually everywhere with her and drove across town to another small, rather shabby house.

She went around to the back door that was never locked, pushing it open and calling out a hello.

"Studio," he called back.

Maggie picked her way through the usual clutter of books, magazines, newspapers, and half-finished craft projects to the studio, an addition to the house that was in stark contrast to the rest. Not only was it roomy and very bright due to numerous windows and skylights, it was also extremely neat and well organized, with paints and brushes stored precisely and canvases stacked in wooden bins. Various props and materials for drapes were kept ready on shelves between the windows, and the assorted chairs, lounges, and tables often used for backgrounds were arranged simply to comfortably furnish the large room.

In the center of the room an artist worked at an easel on a nearly completed canvas. The subject was a woman, and though she wasn't present in the flesh it was clear from the charcoal sketches pinned to another easel nearby that she had posed more than once for the artist.

The artist himself was about thirty, a tall and lanky man with the face of an angel — or so Maggie had always thought. She'd never seen an angel, but she had seen traffic literally stop and mouths drop open when this man walked by, and she figured he was about as close to heavenly perfection as earthly mortals were likely to get. He had long, wheat-gold hair he wore tied back at the nape of his neck, and his faded jeans and work shirt were, as usual, flecked with paint.

"Half a minute," he said without looking at her, his attention fixed on the careful shading beneath his subject's left ear.

"Take your time. I was tired of my own company and just came by to visit," Maggie said.

He sent her one quick glance from very pale blue eyes that were almost unnervingly discerning, then continued with his work. "Not like you to be bored," he said.

Maggie sat down at a clean but scarred wooden table and watched him. "Not bored exactly. Restless. I'm supposed to go talk to the most recent victim tomorrow, and until then there isn't a whole hell of a lot I can do. It's very wearing on the nerves, just sitting around waiting for the next attack."

"I warned you," he murmured.

"I know you did. But why didn't you also warn me that Hollis Templeton would ask for me by name?"

He stopped working and looked at her steadily. "Nobody told her your name?"

"No."

"What do you know about her?"

Maggie shrugged. "She's an artist, but she's new in Seattle and I think the work she did on the East Coast was mostly commercial stuff, so we wouldn't have heard of her. Late twenties, single. From the photo I saw, she was attractive before the attack. I don't know about now."

"He took her eyes."

"Yes. Removed them — very neatly, according to her doctors. No acid this time. He used a knife or scalpel and seems to have known what he was doing. Little damage to the optic nerve, to the eye socket and eyelids. Which is why they decided to try the transplant."

"Was it successful?"

"You tell me."

He smiled slightly and turned back to his painting.

"I hate it when you do that," Maggie told him.

"Do what?" His tone was innocent.

"Ignore a question. I start really dreading it when you don't want to answer."

"Whether Hollis Templeton sees again is entirely up to her."

"Well, that's cryptic enough. Did they teach you to talk like that at seer school?"

"I didn't go to seer school."

"Prognosticator's school, then."

He chuckled. "That either."

When it became clear he wasn't going to say anything else, at least for the time being, Maggie sighed and opened her sketch pad. For several moments she stared at the vague outline of a rapist's face, then swore beneath her breath and closed the pad again.

"I really hate this, Beau," she said.

"I know you do. I'm sorry."

"But not sorry enough to be a little less cryptic."

"Being sorry has nothing to do with it."

"Free will."

He nodded and stepped away from the easel to begin cleaning his brushes. "Free will. You have to make the decisions and choices facing you of your own free will."

Maggie watched him broodingly. "And yet you know what those decisions and choices are going to be. Which argues that fate is set, my destiny planned — and there is no such thing as free will."

"Then let's call it the illusion of free will."

"You can be very maddening sometimes, you know that?"

"You tell me so often enough." Beau disappeared into the kitchen for a few minutes and returned with two canned soft drinks. "This stuff is very bad for us," he said vaguely. "I read it somewhere." He handed her a can and sat down across from her to pop the top of his own.

Maggie followed suit. "You swear to me you can't tell me who the rapist is?"

Beau frowned. "There's no sense of identity, and I can't see his face. That's something I would tell you if I could, Maggie, believe me. There's nothing in the seer's handbook about protecting monsters."

"He is that, you know. Inhuman."

"I know."

"I have to stop him."

"You mean you have to try."

"Yes. Yes, of course that's what I mean."

"You're helping, Maggie."

"Am I? I don't have a sketch yet."

"Maybe not, but you're helping those women. If they have any kind of a life when this is over, it'll be largely due to you."

"Then why don't I feel better?"

Quietly, he said, "Because you've let yourself get too close to them. You won't be able to do this much longer if you don't back away a bit. Try to stop feeling everything they feel."

"Teach me how to do that and I'll give it a shot." She laughed, but the sound held no amusement. "We're running out of time. It's only going to get worse from here on out, Beau, we both know that."

"Even so, stop trying to carry all of the load yourself. You can't do this alone, I've

66

told you. You have to trust someone else to help you."

"Someone other than you."

"I'm . . . outside the loop. My job is to offer cryptic warnings, remember?"

"Yeah, right."

Beau smiled slightly, but it was sympathetic rather than humorous. "I wish I could do more."

"Then do more, dammit."

"The seer handbook, remember? We all have to play by the rules, Maggie. Putting one foot carefully in front of the other, testing the ground, feeling our way, studying the signs. So wary of doing something that might make things even worse. You've been doing that too. Otherwise you would have told them the truth a long time ago."

"And how am I supposed to tell them the truth? Andy, the other cops? How will they ever understand? Hell — how will they even believe me?"

"When you don't quite believe it yourself," he murmured.

"It isn't an easy thing to believe, to accept."

"I know."

"You could be wrong about it," she said, more of a question than a statement.

"I really wish I was, Maggie. For your sake." He watched her for a moment in silence, then said, "Is Garrett here yet?"

"Yes. He was at the station yesterday. Wanted to talk to me about Christina."

"Did you tell him?"

"The truth? No. I lied. I looked that man in the eye and lied to him about his sister's death."

"Why?"

"Because . . . I don't know why. Because he wouldn't suffer less for knowing the truth. Because he'd blame himself for something he did, or failed to do. Because Christina wouldn't want him to know. Because he wouldn't believe me." She lifted her drink in a mocking salute. "Or maybe just because I'm a coward."

"I don't think that was it."

"Don't you? I'm beginning to wonder. I'm afraid, Beau. I'm scared to death."

"Of the future?"

"Of now. What if I'm not strong enough? Or smart enough, or quick enough? I wasn't before."

"You will be this time."

"Is that from the seer? Or just from you?"

"From me."

Maggie sighed. "That's what I thought."

She brooded in silence for several minutes, then said abruptly, "Garrett. You're wrong about him."

"Am I?"

"Yes."

"Well," Beau said affably, "I've been wrong before. Not often, mind you, but it has been known to happen. Time will tell, won't it, Maggie?"

"Yeah," she said. "Yeah, time will tell."

Andy Brenner had been a cop almost fifteen years. He loved the work, even though it had cost him his marriage — which wasn't exactly an unusual price for cops to pay. Half the guys in the department were either divorced or trying to make a second marriage work better than the first one had. And the female officers didn't seem to have it any easier.

Like most of the spouses, Andy's had hated the long hours and lousy pay, the stress of knowing her husband waded in filth virtually every day and might not come home except in a flag-draped box. But, even more than that, Kathy had hated his commitment to his job.

Well, Andy could hardly change that. Hell, he couldn't even apologize for it. A cop wasn't much good to anybody if he wasn't dedicated, was he?

No.

Which was why he was staying late yet again on this Friday night. Going over files he'd already studied so many times the information was practically embedded in his brain cells. Only now there was nobody waiting for him at home, pacing the floor or drinking too much wine after a supper alone.

"Andy?"

He looked up. "I thought you left hours ago, Scott."

Scott Cowan shook his head. "No, Jenn and I were just in the back digging through some of the old files." He was holding a dingy gray folder in his hands.

"What the hell for?"

"Just following up on a hunch."

"A hunch about what? The rapist?" Not, Andy thought, that there was much chance it was about anything else; the case possessed all of them these days.

"Well, yeah."

"So? Let's hear it."

Scott hadn't been a detective long enough to have a lot of faith in his hunches, and he reddened a bit under Andy's gaze. "Well, I know we fed all the information we've got on this rapist

70

through the computer to look for similar crimes, but Jenn and me were talking today and we started wondering about the old files. Some of those files go back fifty years and more, and none of the info is in the system."

Patiently, Andy said, "I doubt our rapist was attacking women fifty years ago, Scott. That'd make him — what? — seventy-five or eighty now? Not even a little blue pill could help a geezer like that get it up."

"No, that's not the way we're thinking. Something the shrink said at the meeting yesterday. She said this rapist seemed to have his rituals well established, as if he'd been at this much longer than the six months we know he's been active. So we thought he might have found himself some ready-made rituals, copying a much older string of crimes."

"Taking the information right out of our old files?"

"Not necessarily. Jenn checked, and some of this stuff has been written up in books over the years, especially the un-solved crimes. It's a popular subject, Andy, you know that. And it's at least a possi-bility that our guy could be following somebody else's game plan, isn't it?"

"Anything's possible." Andy pursed his

lips for a moment as he considered the idea. "Not bad, Scott. It's an angle we haven't considered. Find anything yet?"

"We're not sure."

"Something else interesting?"

"Something peculiar. At least we thought so. Maybe you can say different." He opened the file and extracted a yellowed sheet of paper, which he handed across the desk. "Just for the hell of it, we started with the really old files, those from more than fifty years ago. Specifically from 1934. Jenn found this in one of them, among some case notes of a murder investigation."

Andy stared down at the sketch and felt a sensation he'd never felt before, as though a cold finger had trailed slowly up his spine. The heart-shaped face and delicate features, the long dark hair . . . "Who is this? I mean — who was she?"

"She was the victim, Andy. A young teacher, stabbed to death in an alley. Apparently she was pretty beat up, so much so that they used an artist to sketch her the way they figured she looked uninjured, just so they'd have something to show around while they tried to identify her. They found out who she was, all right, but . . . the case was never solved."

"It must be a coincidence," Andy muttered. "The artist got it wrong, guessed wrong about how she really looked. Or some kind of family tie. What was her name?"

Scott opened the folder again. "Her name was . . . Pamela Hall. Spinster, twenty-two. No family in Seattle, at least not that the cops could discover."

"Was she raped?"

"Yeah, she was. In those days, though, rape was seldom reported and never investigated, at least as far as I can tell. It was just mentioned by the doctor in his postmortem notes; the cops treated it like a murder, pure and simple. They weren't looking for a sexual predator."

Jennifer Seaton joined them at Andy's desk in time to hear that, and said, "I don't think that term even existed then." She shook her head, more in weariness than anger. "They still thought rape was a forceful act of sex — and nothing more."

"Have you found any other attacks around the same time?" Andy asked.

Jennifer shook her head again. "Not yet. But this one happened early that year, and there are more files we can go through. We just thought we should check with you before we go any further. It wasn't the attack itself that caught my attention — lots of women were killed in Seattle around that time. It was the sketch I couldn't get past."

Andy drew a breath. "I see what you mean. Shit. If this sketch is accurate, she was the image of our first victim, Laura Hughes."

"That's what we thought."

Andy propped the sketch against his phone and stared at it. Probably just coincidence. Hell, it had to be. Still . . . "Look, it's late, you two should go home. But when you come back on duty, you might want to keep digging in those files, see if you turn up anything else."

Scott nodded, eager to participate more fully in an investigation where, so far, he'd been more of a glorified gofer than anything else. "Sure, I can do that. Jenn?"

"Gladly. Beats the hell out of sitting at my desk taking call after call from panicky citizens."

Scott said, "Hey, Andy, you think we might have something here? Maybe this guy is copying old crimes by hunting for look-alike victims?"

"Maybe," Andy said. "But let's not get too excited just yet, okay, guys? One sketch doesn't mean much, except maybe that all of us have — or had — doubles in the world. Just keep digging, and bring me anything you find."

"You bet, Andy. Want us to leave this file for you?"

"Yeah." Andy accepted the file and wished the younger cops a good night. They walked out together, talking, and he wasted a minute or so wondering if they were sleeping together. Not very surprising, if so, and they wouldn't be the first pairing in the department. But he hoped they were smarter than that.

When he was alone again, he stared at the sketch of a young woman long dead and gone. Hell, *twice* dead and gone, or at least that was how it looked. Pamela Hall, stabbed to death in 1934 after being brutally raped; Laura Hughes, brutally raped and beaten in 2001, blinded, dying days later of her injuries.

The two women didn't just resemble each other — they were virtually identical, right down to the little mole at the left corner of their mouths. But an artist had drawn this sketch with only the battered face of the victim as a guide, and Andy reminded himself that artists were hardly infallible.

Except for Maggie, anyway.

Andy combed through the file, but it

held precious little information. From the sound of their notes, the investigating cops had been saddened by the murder of this young woman but not surprised; she had been found in the bad part of town, and it was clear they considered it her own fault that she had placed herself in the path of danger. Still, they had investigated methodically for a while — and then moved on to the next crime demanding their attention.

The postmortem notes were no more helpful. The victim had died of blood loss and shock; there was evidence of *forcible sexual activity,* and she was beaten and bruised. It was the opinion of the doctor that she had fought her attacker, evidenced by the injuries to her arms and hands, but her strength had, clearly, been no match for his.

Andy went back to studying the sketch. Were Scott and Jennifer right in their speculation? Was their modern-day serial rapist choosing his victims from old unsolved cases?

It was, of course, ridiculous to base an assumption such as that one on a single example, but Andy couldn't help doing a little speculating himself. So far, they hadn't been able to find any pattern in the means or reasoning their rapist had used to choose his victims. Since one of the women had been abducted from a crowded shopping mall and another from her high-security apartment building, they had ruled out simple ease of access, which meant he was picking his victims some other way and quite deliberately.

Could he be using old unsolved investigations? And if he was, had he found the information he sought in books? Or in the actual files themselves?

If he was, Andy hoped it was the former. He really hoped so. Because he was pretty sure that the only people who could have gained access to the old files without attracting notice were cops.

SATURDAY, NOVEMBER 3

Maggie wasn't terribly surprised to find John Garrett at the hospital when she arrived to talk to Hollis Templeton shortly after two o'clock. She also wasn't terribly happy about it.

"The interview will be private," she told him.

"I know that. I just thought we might be able to get a cup of coffee somewhere afterward. Talk."

She didn't bother to explain that interviews such as this one was likely to be usually left her feeling something less than sociable. "I doubt I'll have any new information," she warned him instead. "The first interview with a victim seldom produces anything we can use."

"I understand that. I'd still like to talk. And — there's someone I'd like you to meet."

Maggie was curious enough about that to nod and say fine, that she'd meet him at the waiting area near the elevators when she was finished with her interview. Then she went on to Hollis Templeton's room, braced herself as well as she could, and knocked quietly before going in.

"Miss Templeton?"

"Yes?" She was sitting by the window, her face turned toward it even though bandages covered her eyes. She was dressed in jeans and a bulky sweater, much as Maggie was dressed herself — even to the comfortable running shoes. Her brown hair was short and styled for a casual look and ease of care, nothing at all fussy about it.

Maggie crossed the small room to stand by the empty chair apparently awaiting her. "I'm Maggie Barnes."

"I see." Her face turned toward Maggie, and lips that bore a healing cut moved in a smile. "Well, I don't, really. Have you ever stopped to think about how many things we say using words like *see* and *look,* when we don't actually mean to describe doing anything visual?"

Maggie slipped into the chair. "I've thought about it a lot lately," she answered.

Hollis smiled again, her face seemingly unmarked except for the healing cut — and those bandaged eyes. "Yes, I imagine in speaking to blinded victims you find verbal minefields all over the place. I'm Hollis, by the way. A ridiculous family name. My father tried to shorten it to Holly when I was small, but I hated that even more."

Maggie had talked to too many victims of violent crime to find the conversation in any way strange; some victims had to discuss irrelevant things first, partly to delay reliving the pain of what had happened to them and partly to at least attempt to establish a feeling of normalcy. So she was able to respond easily and without impatience.

"Most people think Maggie is short for Margaret, but it isn't. I've always been Maggie."

"It's a good name. It means *pearl,* did you know?"

"Yes."

"Hollis means *lives by the holly trees.* What kind of name is that for a grown woman?" She shook her head, adding abruptly, "Dumb subject. And trivial. Sorry, I don't mean to waste your time."

"You aren't, Hollis. I'm glad you called us."

"Us." She nodded as though a private thought had been confirmed. "So you do consider yourself one of the cops, huh?"

"I guess so."

"It can't be a fun job, listening to horrible stories about . . . man's inhumanity to man."

"No, that part of it isn't fun."

"Why do you do it?"

Maggie studied the other woman, noting the stiff posture, the hands still bearing faint scratches and fading bruises gripping the arms of the chair tensely. Slowly she said, "I . . . have a knack. I listen to disparate details and manage to put them together to form a picture. A face."

Hollis tilted her head slightly. "Yes, but why do you do it? Were you a victim once?"

"No."

"Somebody you cared about?"

Maggie almost shook her head, then remembered Hollis couldn't see her. It was an odd surprise; she could almost feel a gaze, feel attention fixed on her so completely that it was as if the other woman *could* see her. "No," she murmured, answering the question even as she wondered if what she felt was her imagination — or something more.

"Is it pity?"

If Hollis was expecting a swift denial, she didn't get it. Calmly Maggie said, "I imagine that's part of it. Pity, sympathy, whatever you want to call it."

Hollis smiled. "You're honest. Good."

"I try to be."

A little laugh escaped Hollis. "And truthful enough to know it isn't always possible to be completely honest with other people."

"A lesson sadly learned."

"Life is full of them." Abruptly, Hollis said, "I know I'm the fourth victim. I remember reading in the newspapers that the first two were dead."

"Yes."

"But he didn't leave them dead. They died later."

"Laura Hughes died of her injuries.

Christina Walsh killed herself about a month after she was attacked."

"Did either of them have kids?"

"No."

"What about the third woman?"

"She has a little boy."

"I hadn't even decided if I wanted kids. Now it's a decision I don't have to worry about anymore."

Maggie didn't offer platitudes. Instead, she asked, "Is that the worst of it for you? That there won't be any children of your own?"

"I don't know." Her lips moved again in that small, brief smile. "I guess it might depend on whether the transplant was a success. The doctor's confident, but . . . I don't know what you learned in art school, but one of the things they taught us is that the eyes, like the spine, are hardwired into the brain. That's why there hasn't been a successful transplant before now. They can transplant corneas, of course, but not the eyeball — or at least that's conventional medical wisdom. My doctor intends to become a pioneer."

"You'll be one too," Maggie reminded her.

"I'm not so sure I want to be. But I do want to see again, so I signed the papers.

Any chance is better than none, right?"

"I'd say so."

"Yeah. But nobody really knows what might happen. My body doesn't seem to be rejecting the eyes, but the odds against them working the way they're supposed to are pretty long. The funny thing is . . ."

"What?"

She drew a little breath. "They say when you lose a limb, you get phantom sensations — that you still feel the limb attached to you, moving. Hurting."

"I've heard that."

"I asked my doctor if it was the same way with eyes. I don't think he quite got what I meant until I asked him if I should be able to move them. Because that's the kind of sensations I feel, that the eyes are moving under the bandages, behind my eyelids. Like now, when I think about looking toward the door . . . I can feel them move."

"What did your doctor say?"

"That it was probably phantom sensations, there hadn't been time for the muscles and nerves to heal. That was just after the operation, so I guess he was right. But it still feels the same to me, those sensations."

"When will they take the bandages off?"

"Another week or so. Until then, all I can do is sit here . . . and wait. I never was very good at waiting."

"Is that why you called us?"

"Maybe. If I could do anything to help them catch that . . . monster . . . then I want to do it." She paused and swallowed hard. "At least, that was the plan. Now I'm not so sure I can talk about it yet. I'm sorry, but —"

"Hollis, it's all right. You have to do this in your own time and way. Look, why don't I come back tomorrow, and we'll talk again. We'll talk about anything you want for as long as you want. Until you're ready."

"If you don't mind."

"I don't. I'll see you tomorrow afternoon, okay?"

"Thank you, Maggie."

Hollis didn't move after the door closed behind her visitor. She turned her face back toward the window, thinking vaguely that if she'd been back in New England she might have felt the sunlight on her face even in November. But the nurses had told her it was a typical Seattle day, overcast and dreary, with no sunlight to be had. They hadn't understood why she'd wanted to sit by the window anyway.

You should have talked to her, Hollis.

"I did talk to her."

I told you that you could trust her.

She laughed under her breath. "I don't even know if I can trust you."

You know.

"All I know is that I'm creeping out the nursing staff by talking to someone who isn't there."

I'm here. And you know I'm real.

Hollis turned her head so that she faced the chair across from her own. "If I could see, would I see you?"

Perhaps.

"And perhaps not. I think I'll make up my own mind who to trust, if it's all the same to you, figment."

Make up your mind soon, Hollis. We're running out of time.

CHAPTER
FOUR

"I couldn't push her," Maggie said. "I can't push her. We just have to wait until she's ready to talk about it."

"And when will that be?" John asked. He sat back to allow the waitress to serve their coffee, wondering if Maggie had suggested this coffee shop across from the hospital because she liked it or because she wanted to spend as little time with him as possible.

"My guess is a few days. She's coping better than I expected, maybe because she has the hope of seeing again. But her emotional condition is still . . . very fragile."

"Did you ask her how she knew to ask for you by name?"

"No. I didn't want to ask anything that might have been interpreted as . . . suspicious."

"Bad for the rapport?"

"That's one way of putting it. If I can't establish a strong bond of trust, then she won't confide in me. Especially as long as she can't see."

John didn't lack imagination, and it was not difficult for him to at least try to understand the terror of being suddenly locked away in darkness, especially as it applied to dealing with others. "No visual clues," he said slowly. "We use our eyes so much when it comes to weighing other people and judging the worth of what they tell us."

A little surprised, Maggie said, "Exactly."

He smiled but didn't comment on her surprise. "So you didn't learn how she knew about you. Anything else? Do you think she saw anything before he blinded her?"

"I don't know. She has something on her mind, but I have no way of knowing what that might be." If she hadn't been gazing directly at his face, she wouldn't have seen his instant of hesitation — and the decision to say what was on his mind.

"So what we need," he said lightly, "is a good psychic."

"Have a few on the payroll, do you?" Her voice was matter-of-fact.

"Not on my payroll, no. At least, not that I know of. But I have a friend who might be willing to help. Assuming he can, of course."

"You doubt his abilities?"

"I," John said deliberately, "doubt the entire concept, if you want the truth. I have a hard time believing in the so-called paranormal. But I've seen Quentin find answers when no one else could, and even if I'm not sure how he does it, at least his way is another option. Especially in a situation where there is so little information and so much need for more."

Maggie sipped her coffee to give herself a moment to think, then said, "I'm pretty sure Luke Drummond would balk at having one more civilian officially involved in the investigation."

"I'm positive he would. Which is why Quentin can only be involved *un*officially."

"Which means access to the investigation is going to be a problem. Is that why you're telling me? Do you expect me to get him access to the victims?"

John immediately shook his head. "I wouldn't put you in that position *or* ask those women to talk to yet another stranger, especially a strange man. No, I'm telling you because from everything Andy's said about you, my hunch is that you're going to be at the center of this investigation for the duration — and I don't mean sitting in an interview room downtown."

"What do you mean?"

"Andy says you've walked the areas where the first three victims were found. True?"

She nodded slowly.

"Why?"

Maggie couldn't think of a simple answer and finally shrugged. "To gather impressions, I suppose. I told you, a lot of what I do is intuition."

"According to Andy, you always immerse yourself in an investigation. You don't just interview victims and witnesses or just study the crime scenes. You read all the reports, talk to the cops, comb through files, even hit the streets following up on your hunches. You talk to family and friends of the victims and construct your own diagrams of crime scenes. Andy swears he believes you have a filing cabinet tucked away somewhere at home with your own personal files of the investigations you've participated in."

Maggie only just stopped herself from flinching. "Andy talks too much."

"Maybe so, but did he lie?"

She laced her fingers together around her cup and stared down at it for a long moment before finally meeting his gaze again. "Okay, so I get involved. What does that have to do with you and your friend? I won't share confidential details of the investigation."

"I don't expect you to. Look, I can get most of the information on the formal investigation myself, as least as much as Andy can give me. What I'm asking you to do is to work separately — independently of the official investigation — with Quentin and me."

Maggie frowned at him. "You're planning to run an independent investigation?"

"Why not? I have resources the police can't begin to match. I can go places they can't go, ask questions they'd be damned for asking."

Steadily, she said, "As the brother of a victim?"

His jaw tightened, but John nodded and replied calmly, "As the brother of a victim. Nobody will be much surprised that I'm trying to find answers on my own, and most people will be sympathetic. We can use that if we have to."

"Ruthless," she noted.

"Practical," he disagreed. "There's nothing cold-blooded about this, remember. That bastard destroyed Christina. He murdered her as surely as if he killed her with his own hands. I intend to see to it that he pays."

"I don't think much of vigilante justice."

"That isn't what I have in mind. If we get even a whiff of a viable suspect, we'll hand the information over to the police immediately. I don't want to do their job, Maggie, I promise you that. But I do believe the investigation needs a fresh start, a new slant. It's been six months since the first victim was attacked; do you believe the police know much more today than they did then?"

Reluctantly, she said, "No, not much more."

"Neither do I."

"Okay, but what makes you think you — we — can accomplish any more working independently?"

"Call it a hunch."

She shook her head. "For a man who denies belief in the paranormal, you're putting a lot of faith in a hunch."

He smiled. "No, I'm putting a lot of faith in Quentin. And in you. And . . . I can't keep just waiting around twiddling my thumbs, Maggie. I have to at least *try* to find some way of putting this bastard behind bars before he attacks again."

She understood that drive all too well, but his plans still made her uneasy. Stalling for time, she said, "Don't you have a business empire to run?"

"What I need to do I can do by phone, fax, or modem. I've spent the past six weeks arranging things so I could take time off for this."

"And you expect me to take time as well?"

"I expect you to go on doing exactly what you would have done anyway — but with sometime companions." John leaned forward a bit. "Useful companions; I wasn't kidding about having resources. But even more than that, we can help you with the legwork, case notes, research — whatever is needed. Quentin and I can share the load."

. . . *stop trying to carry all of the load yourself.*

Maggie didn't have to wonder if it was a coincidence that Beau had used the same phrasing; there were few coincidences anywhere in his orbit. She drew a breath. "And when Andy and the other cops find out I'm involved in a private parallel investigation? Just how long do you expect it to take for them to slam the door in *all* our faces?"

"They won't do that — if we've made progress. And I expect us to make progress."

She swore under her breath and stared

down at her coffee again.

"You're going to investigate on your own anyway, aren't you?"

Not yet ready to admit that she'd already started, Maggie shrugged.

It was John's turn to swear, just as softly as she had. "If I thought money motivated you, I'd ask your price. But it doesn't. So what does motivate you, Maggie? What can I say to convince you to help me?"

She finished her coffee and set the cup down, meeting his gaze with a sense of inevitability. "You just said it." And before he could question her apparently sudden capitulation, she added, "You're right, I'd investigate on my own anyway. Might as well make it a team effort."

He reached across the table and covered her hand with his. "Thank you. You won't regret it, I promise you."

The physical contact caught her off guard, and for just that unprotected instant before she could shut it out, she felt his determination as well as his conviction that she could help him. And she felt something else, something warm and very male and disturbingly familiar.

She sat back, gently drawing her hand away under the pretext of pushing her coffee cup to one side. "What's the game plan? I assume you have one."

John frowned briefly, as if something he couldn't quite define puzzled him. "The beginnings of one, anyway. Andy said you hadn't yet walked over the area where Hollis Templeton was found."

"No, not yet."

"That's as good a place as any to start. I've asked Quentin to meet us there."

As much as she hated to admit it even to herself, Maggie had put off that chore because she dreaded what she knew awaited her there. What she wasn't sure of was whether having companions on the visit would make it better — or worse.

Still . . . maybe it was time to show John Garrett a glimpse of her "magic." Time for him to at least begin to understand.

"We don't have much daylight left," she said, keeping her tone brisk. "I'm ready if you are."

"Well," Jennifer said, "we definitely have something. But I'll be damned if I know what it is."

"It's gotta be coincidence," Scott said. "It's gotta be coincidence, right, Andy?"

Andy didn't blame either of them for being bewildered. What they'd found, by mid-afternoon on Saturday, were three more files concerning murder investigations in 1934. All three victims were young women, all three had been brutally attacked, raped, and left for dead, and all three murders had gone unsolved.

In two of the three folders they had found something more than scanty case notes. They had found sketches of the victims, sketches the police had used in identifying the women, again because their faces had been so badly battered — obvious in the grainy crime-scene photos. One of the sketches was rather inexpertly done and had not, in fact, helped the police to identify the dead woman; she had gone nameless to a pauper's grave.

But the second sketch was a good one and had been backed up later once she was identified by a photograph. The victim had been the daughter of a local businessman, and not only had her reputation been spotless but she had apparently been attacked not twenty yards from her own back door — in the best part of town. Her name was Marianne Trask.

And according to the sketch, she bore an uncanny resemblance to Hollis Templeton. The same medium-brown hair and strong, attractive features, same oval face, same slender neck.

"Not identical," Jennifer noted. "But damned close. And if you read the descriptions of the other victims, even without sketches to go by, they sound a lot like Christina Walsh and Ellen Randall. Coincidence? I guess it could be."

"It's arguable," Andy said. "Four women attacked, and each case matches up with one of ours — at least as far as the description of the victim is concerned. But there are differences."

"Yeah. All the 1934 victims died within hours." Jennifer sighed and reached into her pocket for a cinnamon-flavored toothpick; she'd recently quit smoking and claimed chewing the toothpicks soothed her oral fixation. It was a mark of the respect in which she was held by the men that not one of them had ventured a lewd response. At least not out loud.

"That's not all," Andy said. "There's no mention in the case files of any of them being blinded."

Scott offered, "That could be our guy's own personal twist. I mean, maybe he's trying to find look-alike victims but making damned sure they can't look at him."

"In 1934," Jennifer pointed out, "leaving them for dead did the trick, so that killer didn't have to worry about his victims even trying to identify him."

"Why doesn't our guy kill his victims?" Scott asked, directing the question to Jennifer. "He goes to such pains to blind them; wouldn't killing them outright be a hell of a lot easier?"

"Why ask me?" She shifted the toothpick to the other side of her mouth and added, "If I had to guess, I'd say he just hasn't been quite ready — so far — to cross the line into outright murder. But I'm no expert, and if you want my opinion that's what we need on this case. Our shrink's good, but she's no profiler."

Andy grunted. "Drummond won't call in the FBI, and you know how the chief feels about the officer in charge of an investigation making that decision."

"If we can't solve this, he'll have to," Jennifer objected.

"You don't know our Luke," Andy said sourly.

Jennifer rolled her eyes. "Oh, yes, I do. I just keep hoping I'm wrong, that's all."

Scott made a rude noise not quite under his breath.

"I wouldn't mind being wrong about that," she told him mildly.

"Let's stick to business," Andy said. "Four victims. That's it for the year?"

"Well, we aren't sure about that." Jennifer traded looks with Scott and shrugged. "Files are missing, Andy."

"What the hell do you mean, missing?"

"I mean that from June — just after the fourth victim was killed — through the end of that year, there are no files. And the box is so packed it's hard to say if files have been removed or were never there."

"They had to be there, Jenn, at least in 1934. Crime doesn't just stop in June to take a vacation."

She shrugged again. "Well, they aren't there now. Jeez, how many times since then do you figure the file boxes have been moved around? This isn't the original site of the investigating station, and even this building has been rebuilt or remodeled at least three times. As the city grew, the districts multiplied; police records for Seattle are probably scattered over a dozen different buildings or more."

Scott sank down in Andy's visitor's chair and groaned. "I never thought . . . But you're right. Every station probably has file boxes in its basement or storage rooms."

"And none of it on computer," Jennifer reminded them. "It's taking all the manpower we can muster to get the modern records on computer for comparison; if the old stuff is ever part of the computerized record it won't be anytime soon."

Andy sat back in his chair and stared at the two sketches propped up against his lamp. "Two pretty conclusive matches," he said slowly, "and descriptions of two more that sound close enough to be strong maybes. Four victims closely matching our four victims. You know, guys . . . I'd really like to see the files for the rest of that year, maybe the year after."

Jennifer got it first. "In case there are more rape–murders. You think if there were more victims then — we'll have more now. And maybe a shot at identifying would-be victims?"

"Hell, I don't know." Andy scowled. "Even with sketches and photos we don't have much hope of finding look-alikes in a city this big. But more files may give us more information, and God knows we could use it, so I say we look for them."

"I just had a creepy thought," Jennifer said. "What if this bastard is just yanking our chains, copying old crimes or picking look-alike victims only as long as we don't catch on?"

"How could he know we'd caught on?" Scott objected.

"If we manage to identify a potential victim, say."

"One nightmare at a time," Andy told them. "You guys want to get on the phone and try to track down those missing files?"

The building where Hollis Templeton's bleeding body had been dumped wasn't precisely in the bad part of town, it was just somewhat isolated from the buildings nearest it and in very bad shape. Intended for demolition so that a modern new apartment complex could rise in its stead, it had stood empty for at least six or eight months.

Maggie got out of her car and stood on the curb, absently hugging her sketch pad to her breast as she waited for John to park his car and join her. It was chilly, a restless wind whining around like something lost and alone, and the overcast sky was allowing darkness to approach even earlier than usual.

Maggie hated this. She hated this lonely place, hated being here with darkness creeping ever closer. She hated the cold fear writhing in the pit of her stomach and the dread that made her skin feel prickly as though the nerves lay rawly exposed on the surface.

"Maggie?"

She started despite herself and tore her gaze from the broken rubble walkway leading to the building to find John standing beside her.

"Are you all right?"

She nodded quickly. "Yes, of course. Just . . . woolgathering. Where's your friend?"

"Well, since there's a rental car parked across the street, I'd say he's already here." He studied her face, not quite frowning but clearly bothered by what he saw. "Are you sure you want to go in there?"

"Want to? No. But I'm going in."

He smiled faintly. "Determination, or just plain stubbornness?"

"Is there a difference?" Maggie didn't wait for him to answer but walked steadily up the walkway to the building.

John walked beside her. "I've always thought so. Do you have a set pattern for going over crime scenes, or is every one different?"

"I suppose each is different. And this isn't really a crime scene, anyway. She was left here but not attacked here."

He paused with her just a few feet from the doorway and looked down at her. "But her attacker was here, if only long enough to leave her inside. Is that what you hope to pick up on . . . intuitively?"

As tense as she was, Maggie had to smile. "You really are uncomfortable discussing intuition, aren't you?"

"The way you and Quentin appear to use it — yes."

"I'm not psychic."

"Sure about that?"

Before Maggie could answer, a tall blond man appeared suddenly in the doorway and offered a cheerful greeting.

"I hope somebody brought a flashlight. Because unless we're damned quick in here, we're going to end up in the dark."

"I thought they taught you to always be prepared," John said.

"That's the Boy Scouts. I wasn't a Boy Scout. Wasn't a marine either."

John didn't question the latter statement, just sighed and said he had several flashlights in his car.

"I knew you would. That's why I didn't bring any."

"Don't start with me. Maggie, this is Quentin Hayes, who claims to know things before they happen." There was no scorn in his voice, merely a sort of amused mockery, and he left her to make what she would of the introduction while he returned to his car for the flashlights.

"So you're a seer?" she asked.

102

"Not in the true sense of the word, meaning one who sees. I don't, actually. No visions." He shrugged. "I just know things. Sort of the way most people tune in to memory or bits of information they've learned. The difference is that when I tune in, it's often to the knowledge of something that hasn't happened yet."

"That must be unsettling."

"It took some getting used to." He eyed her thoughtfully. "I hear they call what you do nothing short of magical."

"That's not what I call it."

"Oh? What do you call it?"

"An ability I've practiced nearly half my life to perfect. I happen to be able to draw. I also happen to be able to listen to people describe what they've seen and then draw it. Nothing magical about that." It was virtually automatic by now, this reasonable explanation of her abilities.

"When you put it like that," Quentin said affably, "it does sound perfectly normal, doesn't it?"

"Only because it is."

John returned to them then, handing out flashlights. "Quentin, how long have you been here?"

"Half an hour, maybe a little longer. I went upstairs for a bit, following the path she took when she dragged herself out of here."

Maggie said, "It's still visible, isn't it? The blood." She gripped the flashlight tightly with one hand and held her sketch pad close with the other.

Quentin looked at her, and for just an instant she felt as if he'd reached over and touched her physically with a warm hand — even though he hadn't moved. But the moment passed, and he nodded, sober now.

"I'm afraid so, at least in places. Dried and brown now, but still there. Those of us with vivid imaginations — or something more — can even smell it. I'm sorry, Maggie."

She wasn't certain if he was expressing sympathy or apologizing for something, and she decided not to ask. Instead, she said, "I want to see where he left her."

"This way." Quentin turned, and they followed him into the building.

Maggie was so accustomed to guarding herself that it usually required a conscious effort to open the barriers inside and let all her senses probe her surroundings. She didn't like any of the sensations but by now at least knew what to expect when she reluctantly dropped her guard.

With all the broken windows in the place, there was light enough to see, if not very well. Stairs rose upward along the right side of the foyer. A hallway stretched past the stairs toward the rear of the building, with doorways lining it, most of them gaping open because of missing or severely damaged doors. Peeling paint covered the woodwork, and stained wallpaper dangled in ragged strips from the walls.

Fixtures such as doorknobs and lights had been removed and all else of any possible value long ago carted out of the building either legitimately or by vandals. Beneath their feet, creaking floorboards were barely covered by ancient linoleum, and the place smelled of dirt and mold and many years of cooking and living.

And blood.

Heavy, coppery, the stench rose up, threatening to choke her. All she saw on the floor was the faint brown trail Quentin had described, but what she smelled was something still warm and wet and sticky.

Maggie tried to unobtrusively breathe through her mouth. Could Quentin really smell that, or had he only known that she could?

"According to the reports," John said, switching on his flashlight and shining it around them, "the police found nothing here. At least nothing they considered evidence."

"Just like his other dumping places, right?" Quentin's voice was as matter-of-fact as John's had been. He turned on his own flashlight and led the way to the stairs, walking beside the intermittent brown trail of dried blood.

"So they told me. Drummond claims to have a very efficient forensics team, and they have a solid reputation. According to their reports, they went over this entire building and searched a block in every direction. Nothing."

Nothing, Maggie thought, but Hollis Templeton's blood. She concentrated on turning on her flashlight, on walking up the stairs behind Quentin and ahead of John, all of them avoiding the dried blood trail. She could feel the familiar inner quivering, the cold weight in the pit of her stomach, and her legs felt stiff, awkward as they moved. At first distantly, she became conscious of twinges of pain and dull aches that slowly intensified until they throbbed inside her.

The darkness came in flashes that lasted only a second or two, and Maggie climbed steadily without outwardly betraying the fleeting moments of blindness.

The smell grew stronger.

She had hoped that more than three weeks would have made it all feel more distant and unreal, that she could get through this without exposing her pain to these two men, but that seemed increasingly unlikely.

At the top of the stairs, Quentin pointed his flashlight toward the rear of the building, down a hallway. "She was left in a room at the back of the house. Odd, really. Why carry her upstairs at all? Why not just dump her downstairs?"

Softly, hardly aware of speaking, Maggie said, "He wanted her to have to drag herself all that way."

Almost as softly, Quentin asked, "Why did he want that?"

Maggie walked past him, only dimly aware of the question. She followed the blood trail down the hallway, her light pointed at the floor, until she found herself in a room. Like the rest of the place, it was peeling paint and ancient wallpaper and not much else. A broken window allowed light into the room, though it wasn't much light. She walked to the center of the room and pointed her flashlight to one of the rear corners, where the blood trail ended and a roughly rectangular shape of less dusty floor hinted that something had lain there for a while.

"There was a mattress," John said, his voice low but nevertheless startling in the silence. "It's where he left her. The police don't believe he brought it here, just found it here. They have it now, of course."

Maggie stood there stiffly for a long moment, wanting to fight everything she felt but trying not to. It came at her in waves, the stench of the blood, the warm stickiness of it that clotted and chilled with the icy wind touching it. And the pain, all the degrees of it, sharp jolts and dull aches and the swelling agony that was as much emotional as physical. And the intermittent flashes of darkness that lasted seconds now, horrible darkness filled with terror and panic and loss, such loss . . .

She had forgotten her companions and started when John grasped her arm. She was coughing. When had she started coughing?

"Maggie?"

"I have to . . . get out of . . ." She jerked her arm free of his grasp and lurched toward the door, almost stumbling.

John started after her, but Quentin caught his arm to stop him.

"Jesus," the other man murmured softly.

Staring at him in the dim light, John was surprised to see something that looked like awe on his friend's mobile face. "What?" he demanded. "What is it? What was wrong with Maggie?"

"Wrong? I don't know if I'd call it wrong." Quentin drew a deep breath. "But I don't envy your Maggie, I'll tell you that."

John didn't question the possessive. "Why?"

"It explains a lot," Quentin mused. "How she's able to establish such a strong bond with victims, how she's able to so accurately draw what they see. Christ, no wonder it looks like magic to those around her."

"She's psychic?"

"It's not quite that simple, John. There's psychic . . . and then there's gifted. Or cursed. Did you see her face just now? She was in agony. Actual physical pain."

"Why? What was hurting her?"

"He had hurt her. The rapist. He attacked her, raped and beat her, took her eyes — and left her here to suffer." Quentin shook his head. "John, that's what Maggie was feeling. She was feeling everything Hollis Templeton felt in this room more than three weeks ago."

CHAPTER
FIVE

Jennifer Seaton was a good cop. But even more, she was an intuitive cop who had learned to trust her hunches. So while Scott worked the phones attempting to track down those missing files, she got on her computer, connected to the Washington state library system database, and conducted a different kind of search.

She hit possible pay dirt before Scott did, but since it was very late on a Saturday afternoon it took her another half hour just to track down a library still open for business.

"I understand the request, detective," the head librarian said, the confusion in her voice belying the words, "but we're locking the doors in ten minutes, and —"

"Police emergency," Jennifer said, ruthlessly misusing her authority. "If you'll hold them for me until I get there, I'd appreciate it. I'm leaving now."

As she hung up the phone and rose to her feet, Scott said sourly, "Oh, yeah, leave me with this, why don't you?"

"Any luck?" she asked, pausing by his desk and digging into her pocket for another cinnamon-flavored toothpick.

"All I've got so far is a growing list of stations with old files stored in their basements. Nobody really knows what they've got, and nobody's volunteering to go down and check, especially on a cold Saturday afternoon. And I can't say that I blame them." He raked fingers through his hair and peered up at her. "Calling it a day?"

"No, I'll be back in about an hour. I may have found a shortcut for us — or at least another source we can use."

"Well, bring me back a snack, will you? I missed lunch, and there's nothing here but stale sandwiches and some *really* stale donuts."

Jennifer nodded. "I'll see what I can do. Where's Andy?"

"Beats me. He was at his desk a minute ago."

"If he gets back before I do, ask him not to leave for the night until he talks to me, okay?"

"Sure."

Jennifer left the station and made her way to the side lot where her car was parked. The streetlights had come on even though twilight made it easy to see, and she paused beside her car to look around, uneasy for no reason she could explain to herself. Being intuitive didn't make her overly imaginative, so she was surprised to realize that she definitely had the creeps.

It was a sudden sensation, a chill that crawled slowly over her body and raised the hair on the nape of her neck. What her mom had sometimes referred to as "somebody walking over my grave." It wasn't a commonplace feeling, and Jennifer had learned to pay attention and be wary, because she had come to realize that it invariably meant her subconscious had noted something important and/or dangerous that her conscious mind was as yet unaware of.

A cop's instincts, Scott called it.

So what was it? The scene she studied was perfectly normal, a few cops moving in or out of the building, a couple of civilians walking briskly past on the sidewalk, not much else. A slight wind stirred the nearby trees, their bare limbs scratching against one another while the last dead leaves clinging to them rattled dryly.

Jennifer shivered and zipped her jacket all the way. "You're getting jumpy, Seaton," she muttered to herself. As if she could possibly be in danger here in the parking lot of the police station. It was absurd. But she couldn't help looking back over her shoulder as she unlocked her car, and she was careful to check the backseat thoroughly before she got in.

There was nobody there, of course. But as she put the key into the ignition, Jennifer saw a folded piece of paper lying on the dashboard. Something that definitely hadn't been there when she had returned alone from lunch and locked the car up. She was wearing gloves, as usual this time of year, so didn't hesitate to carefully unfold it.

Block-printed on the paper in a faint and rather unsteady hand were two numbers. Dates?

1894
1934

Jennifer sat staring at the paper for a long time, her mind working. The 1934 date — always assuming it was a date, of course — corresponded with the date of the murders in their incomplete files, and that couldn't be a coincidence.

Could it?

Was the earlier date another year during which other similar crimes had taken place? *Was* their brutal rapist copying crimes from long ago, choosing his victims to closely match doomed women some other monster had attacked and left for dead, adding only his own personal touch of blinding them?

If he was, why? What twisted motivation compelled him to at least partially re-create old, unsolved crimes? Because they were unsolved? Because he believed he, too, could commit his crimes and walk away undiscovered?

Could it be so simple?

That possibility was unsettling enough; what really disturbed Jennifer was the certainty that someone had placed this note inside her locked car while it had been parked mere yards from the police station. Someone who seemingly knew a lot more about this series of brutal rapes than the police had yet discovered.

Who? And was this note an effort to help the police?

Or was it a direct and mocking challenge from an animal more hunter . . . than hunted?

"She's gone," John said as he rejoined Quentin in the chill, empty room at the top of the stairs.

"Told you she would be." Quentin moved slowly around the room, his flashlight pointed at the floor. Most of his attention seemed focused on what he was doing, but his voice was matter-of-fact. "Fight or flight. She couldn't fight, so she ran. I imagine she has a place she feels safe and reasonably secure. Home, probably. She'll be there. She'll need to be there, at least for a while."

John frowned as he watched his friend. The room still wasn't quite dark, and he could see Quentin fairly well. "Is that why you stopped me when I would have gone after her? Because she needed to get somewhere she felt safe?"

"And because I knew you'd push her."

"What are you talking about? Push her how?"

"Push her to tell you whatever information she might have gained in this room, information that could help us find answers. You're convinced she can help us find those answers, and your tendency will be to press forward without any loss of time, just the way you would in business. And I'm telling you that's the wrong tactic with Maggie. Like it or not, you're going to have to be very careful with her. She'll help us in her own time and her own fashion —

and that's the way it's going to be."

"Why? Because she's *gifted?*"

"Pretty much, yeah. John, living with this sort of thing, most of us develop defense mechanisms to cope. If we have . . . understanding or at least sympathetic family and friends, the defenses tend to be simple ones. But if we feel too alone, too isolated and different from those around us, especially for most of a lifetime, then the defenses can be major and complex. I'd guess your Maggie belongs in the latter group."

"Isolated? She's surrounded by people who admire what she does," John objected. "Not one of the cops I talked to showed anything but respect and gratitude toward her. Hell, it was almost awe."

"I'm sure they are grateful. And I'm sure they respect her for her ability to help them catch bad guys. But that *awe* you were picking up on can be read another way. Fear. You can bet most of those cops don't understand how she does the things she does, and when there's no understanding there's often fear. Especially of something that looks like magic. You can also bet that Maggie knows exactly how they feel."

"It doesn't seem to bother her," John said. "At the station, she was very sure of herself, not at all hesitant."

"She would be — there. My guess is that while she's probably strongly empathic with people and able to bond with them fairly easily when she wants to, where she really connects is at a scene of violence. Like this one." Quentin hunkered down for a moment to more closely examine the area of floor where a mattress had lain.

"How is that possible?"

"Well, one theory is that thoughts and emotions contain an actual electrical signature, a form of energy that may linger in objects, in an area, especially if what was experienced in that area is particularly intense or violent. If you think about it, it'd explain a lot of the so-called ghostly sightings of things like battles and soldiers. Hell, there are places in Europe where some people swear ancient Roman soldiers still march."

"You don't believe in ghosts?"

"If you mean do I believe the dead have an existence beyond the flesh, yes, I do. But I'm also convinced that what most people believe are ghosts are actually those electrical signatures I'm talking about. Violent things happened in some places, and some of those places — for reasons we don't yet understand — retained that energy. It wouldn't be visible to most people, because people tend to use their senses in only the simplest and most limited way. But some people would be sensitive to it, able to feel and possibly interpret the energy. As a rough comparison, think about static buildup on a cold, dry day; it isn't apparent until you touch something and are able to discharge the energy."

"Are you saying Maggie's a conduit?"

"More or less. If electrical energy *can* permeate objects, then it's reasonable to assume the energy would remain for at least a while, until it could dissipate naturally or could be discharged through some kind of contact."

"You make it sound like a logical equation."

Quentin straightened and absently flexed cramped muscles. "In a way it is. Stop thinking of it as something magical or unnatural; take what you know is scientific and push it a little further, extend it to the next logical step. On the most basic level, our thoughts are nothing more than electrical energy interpreted by the brain. True?"

"True."

"Okay. Then it's perfectly reasonable to suppose that just as there are incredibly gifted musicians and scientists, people who seem born with amazing knowledge and abilities, some people could also be born with an unusual sensitivity to the kind of energy we're talking about. Just another talent or ability, perfectly human even if rare. Where you look at this room and see dirt and stains and peeling wallpaper, people especially sensitive to the electrical energy of thoughts and emotions might see a lot more."

John shook his head. "Even assuming I can accept that, it still doesn't explain Maggie and what she seemed to be going through. You seriously expect me to believe that she has the ability to feel — physically experience — what happened to another person here in this room weeks ago?"

"You saw the same thing I did," Quentin reminded him.

"Yeah, but . . ."

"But you didn't believe it."

"I believe she's sensitive enough to have . . . imagined . . . what Hollis Templeton must have gone through here in this room, but to say she actually, physically *felt* it — no. I don't believe that. I can't believe it, Quentin."

"Which is another reason I told you not

to go after her." Quentin completed his examination of the room and returned to John. "One of the hardest things to deal with when you know you can do something beyond the abilities of most other people is the disbelief and often fear of those around you. Nobody quite calls you a liar — but the doubt is easy to see. And feel. Especially when you can't really prove what you can do. She can't prove to you that she's an empath any more than I can prove to you I know some future events before they happen. Even though I keep trying." Quentin studied his friend with a faint smile. "We've laughed and joked about it for nearly twenty years. And in all that time, you've ascribed my ability to tell you what's going to happen before it happens to luck, to intuition, to inspired guesswork or a logical sequence of events — to everything except what it is. Precognition. Clairvoyance. Knowledge before the fact."

"You've been right more than you've been wrong," John admitted.

"Thank you," Quentin said dryly.

"But how is it possible to know something before it happens? Explain *that* by taking what we know to be scientific and extending it to the next logical level."

"I can't. The truth is, I have no idea how I'm able to do it. If I understood it, I could probably control it. I could say to myself, Quentin old buddy, how will the stock market look by, say, the end of the year? What lottery numbers are going to come up winners? Which one of the dotcom companies is *really* worth an investment? Who'll win the Super Bowl?" He shrugged. "But it doesn't work like that. I wish it did — but it doesn't."

"Which is why you can't tell me if the police are going to catch this rapist."

"Which is why. I only know what my wayward mind chooses to tell me — and that isn't something I've been told. So far, at least. Sometimes, once I've got involved in a situation, I've been able to pick up facts related to the future of that situation — but my control could best be described as erratic as hell."

"That's not much help."

"Tell me about it. You know, my boss says that if a psychic is ever born who can totally control his or her abilities, the whole world will change. He's probably right. He usually is. Dammit."

John stirred slightly. "And speaking of Bishop — how long before he shows up here with blood in his eye?"

"Never, I hope." Quentin sighed. "Realistically, I figure I've got maybe forty-eight hours or so until the case he's on breaks or he has a spare minute or two to realize I should be back at Quantico by now. I was going to ask Kendra to run interference for me, but I figured we'd need her here. She's a crackerjack profiler and researcher as well as an adept, and we may well need all her abilities."

"She's at the hotel?"

"Yeah. On the computer, tapping into every database we thought might be helpful. And I suggest we go back there. This place is giving me the creeps."

"Professionally, or psychically?"

"Both. Not being empathic, all I get is a sense that the bastard picked his dumping place very carefully — but I don't know why. The cop in me sees the signs that other cops went over this area with a fine-tooth comb. I won't find anything they missed. You have the forensics report?"

"A copy, yeah." By mutual consent, both men turned and began making their way out of the abandoned building. "I have no way of knowing, of course, how complete it is. But I'm betting Drummond has given orders to hold back on at least some information."

"Probably. It's standard procedure to keep some facts within the investigating unit — to weed out copycats and more quickly zero in on similar crimes, if nothing else."

"Maybe, but I figure this is personal."

"Don't get paranoid."

"It isn't that. I've weighed enough competitors across boardroom tables to know when someone is out to beat me. Drummond wants his people to find this bastard, and he wants it bad. He isn't above keeping some information out of my hands just to make sure I'm handicapped."

"His political aspirations?"

"Partly. And he's the competitive sort by nature."

"Well," Quentin said, "we can work around that. Hopefully. You do realize we're going to have to be very, very careful not to do anything to impede the official investigation?"

"I realize that."

"And that your Maggie is going to have to walk a very fine line while she works to help both us and the police?"

"After what happened here, I'm not at all sure she'll be willing to help us," John said.

"Willing," Quentin said, "has little to do

with it. Unless I miss my guess, Maggie Barnes feels she has to help us. She simply doesn't have a choice."

"I don't like it," Andy said. He stared down at the scrap of paper now sealed in a clear plastic evidence envelope, feeling as grim as he looked. "Jenn, you're *sure* this wasn't in your car when you got back from lunch today?"

"Positive. So somebody put it in there while my car — my locked car — was parked in a police lot. Lousy security around here, Andy."

He looked across his desk at Jennifer, not misled by the flippant tone. And he didn't blame her for being shaken. He was pretty damned unnerved himself. "Assuming this is useful information and not just a couple of random numbers, *and* assuming it's even connected to this particular case, I suppose somebody might have been trying to help us. Or it could have been some enterprising member of the press, maybe trying to get a reaction out of us," he speculated. "It's at least conceivable that one of them might have stumbled onto the 1934 murders."

Scott, sitting across from Jennifer in Andy's other visitor's chair, said reluctantly, "Isn't that a bit of a stretch? I mean, even supposing a reporter dug up the similar murders, why tell us — and anonymously? Why not just run with the story?"

"Yeah, it's a stretch," Andy admitted. "The truth is, I can't think of a reason why anybody'd do this. Except for our perp, that is."

Having given the matter a lot of thought, Jennifer shook her head. "I don't see that. He's gone to a hell of a lot of trouble to hide from us — why step out into the open and do this? If he wanted to taunt us, I figure he'd do it another way. Maybe leave something on the victim or change his M.O. suddenly. But notes left in a cop's car? No, I don't think it's him."

"Then who?" Scott demanded. "You and I stumbled into this just tossing around ideas because we were frustrated there wasn't more we could do. How likely is it that somebody else took the same turns and reached the same possibility?"

"Not very," she admitted. "Besides which, if this note was intended to be helpful, then why give it to us anonymously and make damned sure there were no prints on it? Why not come forward and explain themselves?"

Slowly, Andy said, "Unless whoever it is knows there's a connection because he — or she — knows or suspects who the rapist is. It wouldn't be the first time a family member or suspicious wife or girlfriend knew just enough to worry about it but was too afraid or ashamed of their suspicions to come forward openly."

"A good possibility. But why the hell did they have to pick my car? And how'd they unlock and then relock the doors without leaving signs, dammit?"

"Maybe it was a locksmith," Scott offered, only half joking.

Andy shrugged. "Hell, maybe it was just somebody who knows cars well enough to be able to get into yours, Jenn. Or had an electronic key that worked. In these days of glorified electronics, it's getting easier rather than harder to jack cars, so why not? Anyway, until we find out who left the note, there's no way of knowing."

"I really hate not knowing," Jennifer said gloomily.

Andy picked up the scrap of paper and studied it more closely. "Do any of those books of yours have murders listed for 1894?"

"Nothing like what we have here, or at least I don't think so. I might be able to find other books, but when I found these they seemed to be all the ones available on local unsolved crimes."

"That means we'll have to depend on our own police files. And we'll have to look all the way back to 1894."

Scott groaned. "Shit. I can already tell you that either we do the legwork ourselves, going into the basements and storage rooms of the other buildings to dig into the files, or else somebody's going to have to make it a priority request to get us some more willing hands. Andy, I've been pretty cagy about asking so far — I haven't wanted to say what case it is, not when all this is so . . ."

"Iffy?" Jennifer supplied dryly.

"Weird," Scott corrected. "Call a spade a spade. Anyway, without something more solid to go on, I didn't really want to tell file clerks in the other divisions why I was interested in the old files. And I sure as hell wouldn't want to talk to the detectives about it — at least not until we're sure there's a connection."

"Not even then," Andy ordered after only a moment's thought. "We keep this among ourselves for the time being. If our guy is a copycat and we've managed to find his playbook, I sure as hell don't want to show our hand. The last thing we need is anybody outside the team discovering what we've found and broadcasting the info."

"That means we do the legwork." Jennifer didn't appear to be nearly as daunted as Scott was. Her eyes were very bright and she was smiling a little. "We'll need some kind of excuse, Andy, if we don't want the other cops to start wondering what we're up to. I mean, how often do we need to dig up files over a hundred years old?"

Andy pursed his lips as he considered that, his mind turning over various possibilities. Then he smiled. "I've got it. Everybody knows Drummond is ambitious as hell and always coming up with this theory or that plan to improve police efficiency so the political powers that be will take notice. So we tell anybody who asks that he's got a new bee in his bonnet and has us hunting down records of past crimes in order to do a comparative study. As long as it's one of you asking and not me, I don't see anybody tying it to a current investigation, and most especially not this one."

"Because we're glorified gofers," Scott said, sighing.

"No," Andy corrected, "because I've had

TV cameras shoved in my face as the lead detective on this investigation; the rest of our team is thankfully invisible to the public — and to most cops outside this division. Just keep your requests casual and try to sound completely bored with the whole thing."

"Are you going to tell Drummond about this?" Jennifer asked.

"Not yet. Not unless and until we have some very solid connections between past victims and present ones."

Voicing a reluctant thought, Jennifer said, "What if we do all this work and still end up with information that doesn't help us stop this creep? Knowing how many women he plans to attack won't help us identify possible victims before he gets them. Records this old, we're lucky to get sketches and reasonably accurate descriptions of the victims, and we can only connect those to crimes he's already committed."

"So what good will it do us to find all the files?" Scott echoed.

"It might do us a lot of good," Andy said. "Think about it. If this bastard is copying past crimes, he has to have a source for his information. And if we're lucky, it'll either be books like those Jenn found — or our files. Either way, we may be able to find something — a name on a library card or notation by a police file clerk that a certain file was checked out for research purposes by whoever. Anything that might point us in his direction."

"Would he have been that careless?" Jennifer wondered.

Andy smiled. "Careless? What possible fact or lead would have caused us to look a hundred years into the past for clues? The very idea is absurd."

Across town in his studio, Beau Rafferty worked on the painting that was his latest commission, using an exceptionally fine brush to get the most painstaking detail exactly right. He was a perfectionist. Always had been.

And he had an ever-present sense of his surroundings, a built-in radar that told him whenever someone was near. Even when they didn't make a sound opening his front door or moving through his house to the studio.

"One of these days, I'll have to start locking that door," he said without turning around.

"That might be a good idea. These are dangerous times."

"The times are always dangerous. People never change." Beau glanced back over his shoulder at the visitor. "Is that why you're here?"

"Don't you know?"

Beau returned his attention to the painting and very carefully shadowed a character line in the lovely face. "No. I didn't see you. I probably should have, I guess. You're usually around when bad things start happening."

"Bad things have been happening here for quite a while."

"Yes. So what brings you now? Maggie?"

"Would that surprise you?"

"No, not really. You were back east when it started, weren't you?"

"Yes."

"They never put it together when it started." Beau shook his head. "Not so surprising, I suppose. He's always more lucky than he is careful. And he's very careful."

"He doesn't want them to see him."

Beau turned at last from the painting, frowning as he began to clean his brushes. "But Maggie will see him. Sooner or later. She's determined to. The only question is, will she see him before he sees her."

"I know."

"I want to help her."

"I know you do. But you can't."

"I could at least tell her what to watch out for. Who to trust."

"No. You can't do that, and you know it. Free will. You've already told her too much."

Beau put his brushes away and studied his visitor wryly. "I haven't told her about you."

"I appreciate that."

"Do you? I wonder." Beau shook his head. "Never mind. I don't think I want to know after all. Is there a particular reason you came to see me today?"

"Yes. I wanted to talk to you about Christina Walsh. And why she died."

CHAPTER
SIX

MONDAY, NOVEMBER 5

Gazing around the large, spacious room, Quentin said, "There are hotel rooms and then there are hotel rooms."

Without looking up from her laptop, Kendra said, "That's the third time you've said something like that. Keep it up, and John will think the FBI makes its agents stay in backstreet dives crawling with roaches and rats."

"I never said it was that bad." Quentin went into the kitchenette to pour himself a fresh cup of coffee, then came back into the parlor. "But you must admit — this is much, much better than our usual digs."

Kendra did look up then, rather absently glancing around the spacious, airy parlor of their two-bedroom suite. It was a room geared to business functions, with half the space taken up by a generous desk containing every modern technological amenity — including a multiline phone, a fax machine, and a computer supplied by the hotel — and a conference table that seated eight. On the other side of the room, a sitting area grouped around a large television promised relaxation, conversation, or entertainment.

It was a luxurious space in the sense of true luxury, nothing ornate or gilded, but beautiful, well-made, and comfortable furnishings and fixtures, and muted but tasteful decorating. Not exactly surprising for the best hotel in the city.

She smiled slightly as she watched Quentin contemplate with satisfaction the oil painting hanging over the desk, but said mildly, "With your taste for luxury, I don't know why on earth you ever joined the Bureau."

"I don't have a taste for luxury, I just enjoy being in a room that isn't a carbon copy of every other room in the place."

Pretending as always that she hadn't noticed him neatly evade the implied question about his past, Kendra said, "Well, while you're enjoying that, could you please hand me the forensics file? Once I get the last of that fed into our personal-investigation database here, we'll have everything the police *say* they have."

"You're as paranoid as John is," he told

her, taking a file from the stack on the desk and handing it across the conference table to her.

"I resent that," John said, coming out of Quentin's bedroom, closing up his cell phone. His leather jacket was hanging over a chair in the sitting room, and he slid the phone into a pocket before joining them at the conference table.

"You should never resent the truth," Quentin said. "Did you get hold of Maggie?"

"I got her voicemail. Asked her to drop by here in the next couple of hours if possible or to meet me at the station at four." John gave Quentin a wry look. "I was very polite and low-key. No pressure, no demands, just a pleasant request."

Seriously, Quentin said, "There will come a time for demands, John, believe me."

"What do you mean?"

It was Kendra who answered, her gaze remaining on the files whose information she was feeding into the laptop's database; her fingers flew even as she spoke. "In this sort of investigation, the emotions of everyone involved tend to grow more powerful and erratic as time goes on. Naturally. Not just for the victims, but for the investigators as well. It'll be hard on all of us, but particularly on an empath. At some point, Maggie's natural instincts for self-preservation will demand that she distance herself from all the pain around her."

"And that's when we make demands?" John asked, watching Kendra in unconscious fascination. It was his first encounter with Quentin's usual partner, and so far he wasn't having much luck in figuring her out. A quiet, contained woman with rich brown hair and soft brown eyes, she was pretty without being in any way extraordinary — except that she obviously was.

"That's when we'll have to. Always assuming she's a help in the investigation and not a drawback."

"Why would she be a drawback?"

"Powerful emotions tend to cloud the mind and affect judgment, among other things. Worse for an empath, naturally. Maybe she's learned to handle that, or maybe not. If not, feeling her own and everyone else's pain could drive her to do things she wouldn't ordinarily do."

"For instance?"

"She could get careless with her actions or incautious in sharing information. Get obsessed with a particular line of investigation to the exclusion of all else or, conversely, have increasing difficulty in even remembering things from one day to the next. She could strike out at those around her."

Quentin murmured, "That would be us."

Kendra nodded, but added, "She could also feel driven to resolve the situation as quickly as possible, whatever the cost to herself."

"You said her instincts for self-preservation would protect her," John objected.

"Eventually, yes. But from all we've been able to find out, Maggie's been doing this for some years, which means she has to be strongly motivated to see it through. But this is quite probably the worst investigation she's been involved in, given the depth and scale of the sheer human suffering. Rape is bad enough for any woman to just have to imagine; feeling that physical and emotional trauma even at second hand has got to be sheer hell. When you hurt badly enough, you'll do almost anything to stop the pain as quickly as possible."

"She could do that by walking away."

"Could she?" Kendra glanced up, her fingers pausing only an instant, then continued with her work and continued speaking calmly. "Whether or not you believe she's an empath, John, you can't deny that for anyone to deliberately expose themselves on a regular basis to the worst pain and trauma experienced by other people argues an incredible amount of resolution and dedication. She's driven to do this out of some deeply felt motivation, and whatever it is, it won't allow her to just walk away."

"So she'll stick it out as long as she can bear it," Quentin said. "Deliberately opening herself up to pain and emotions none of us would choose to feel — if we had a choice. Fighting herself and her own instincts harder than she'll ever have to fight anyone or anything else."

"In other words, she's a loaded gun," John said.

"More like nitroglycerin in a paper cup."

John sighed. "But she can help us?"

Quentin nodded. "Oh, yeah, you were right about that. She can help us. She might even be able to help herself, by the time this is over. But the duration is apt to be . . . painful for everyone concerned."

"I buried my sister a few months ago," John said steadily. "More painful than that?"

Quentin hesitated, traded a quick glance with Kendra, then said, "Could be, John. I know that's hard for you to believe, but the truth is that when new pain follows old pain, the weight of the whole tends to be a hell of a lot heavier than any individual wound."

Her eyes once again on the forensics file, Kendra said, "Four victims so far, and the rapist has left us virtually no hard evidence to consider. Nothing even remotely objective for us to concentrate on. That means our investigation is going to have to focus on the people involved. Victims, their backgrounds, friends and families. People in pain, all around us. Frightened, angry, grieving, hurting people."

John looked from one to the other of them with a frown. "Are you two trying to persuade me to leave Maggie out of this?"

"We never attempt the impossible," Quentin said.

"Almost never," Kendra corrected.

Quentin considered that, then shrugged and said to John, "Anyway, what we're trying to do is warn you that things are likely to get a lot worse before they get better, even for you."

"How could things get worse?"

Wincing, Quentin replied, "Never, never

ask that question. Things can always get worse — and usually do. We've got a vicious madman roaming around out there, and he hasn't exactly left us a trail of bread crumbs to follow in order to stop him. We have four victims so far and no sign whatsoever that there won't be more. We don't know how he's choosing said victims, who appear to have virtually nothing in common except that they're female and white — which gives us about half the population of a major city to worry about. We have a police lieutenant with political aspirations in charge of a police department that seems to have just about reached the limits of its resources. We have a frightened city, an increasingly militant press — and we have to walk on eggshells while trying to investigate this because we're not supposed to be involved."

Quentin drew a breath, traded another glance with Kendra, then finished, "How could things get worse? Jesus, John — how could they not?"

"All right, point taken."

Quentin didn't press it. "When Kendra finishes our database, we'll run a comparison with everything the Bureau has on unsolved aggravated rape cases; even though most such seemingly isolated crimes aren't technically FBI territory, we've begun in recent years keeping track of as many as possible simply because sexual predators tend to grow more and more violent the longer they remain at large. And they usually have a history — if we can find it and track it."

"What do you mean?"

"He's been active here in Seattle for about six months, as near as the police can estimate. But his ritual is too well-established for him to be that new at it."

"I thought you weren't a profiler."

"I'm not the best at it. But I work with a few of the best, and I've picked up a thing or two. Kendra agrees with me on this. Our guy is no rookie."

"So he's been . . . active . . . somewhere else?"

"Probably."

"Wouldn't the police have checked for that?"

Quentin nodded. "Sure. According to the reports, they did. But in checking NCIC and VICAP and various other sources, it looks like they only listed the most obvious similarities between these attacks: that he blinds and maims his victims, never speaks to them, dumps them somewhere else in a fairly isolated place when he's finished with them. Not nearly enough specifics and similarities to provide for a thorough search of all the available files, in our experience."

"What other similarities are there?"

It was Kendra who replied. "He goes to extraordinary lengths to make certain these women can never identify him, yet it's clear he watches them for at least a period of time before he grabs them. He has very specific reasons for taking the women he takes, and it has nothing to do with how easily he can get his hands on them. He's varied his methods of blinding, becoming arguably more adept and skilled at it, which indicates it's a fairly recent part of his ritual. He may well have begun by simply blindfolding his victims or knocking them unconscious before raping them: a possibility that must be noted. The fact that he blinds them now could be a natural evolution and escalation of his ritual — or it could be because at least one victim in his past saw him and was able to identify him."

After a moment, John said, "You mean this bastard might have been caught at some point? Jailed?"

"Possibly."

"And — what? Escaped?"

"Maybe. Or maybe served his time. I'm estimating he's between thirty and forty now, so he certainly could have served time in prison at some point."

"Do you believe he did?"

Kendra paused in her typing long enough to turn to a new page in the report she was studying, then replied, "No, somehow I don't think he's seen the inside of a jail. I think he moves around, changing location after some specific period of time or specific event or point of transition in his ritual."

"So," Quentin said, "we'll run all the information — and educated guesswork and skilled speculation — we can muster and compare it to the Bureau files drawn from police departments all over the country. If we're very lucky, we just might find enough to be able to build a history on this bastard. And with a history we can study, there's a better chance of figuring him out, of knowing where and how to look for him."

Kendra said, "Once the database is set up, it'll probably take a day or two to run the comparison, at least with the information we've got, and that may only give us a long list of possibles we'll have to narrow down."

John looked at Quentin. "How does she do that? Type and talk at the same time?"

"Her uniquely flexible mind," Quentin murmured.

"It's a little scary," John noted.

"Yeah. I think she does it just to unnerve me."

Kendra smiled but didn't look up from the file. "It would also probably be wise to check in with the police and find out if they have anything new."

"That's why I asked Maggie to meet me at the station," John said. "Not that I expect them to have anything new, but Andy would sure as hell start to wonder if I didn't keep turning up there to ask every day or two." He was looking at Kendra, but when she stopped typing suddenly and looked at Quentin, he followed her gaze and felt an odd little chill.

Quentin didn't seem to be looking at anything in particular, except perhaps something only he could see. His eyes were unfocused yet curiously fixed, unblinking, and he was very, very still.

"Quentin?" Kendra's voice was quiet. "What is it?"

He didn't answer immediately; it was a full minute of silence before he stirred and looked at them, saw them. His expression hadn't changed, but there was something bleak in the depths of his eyes. Slowly, he said, "The police will have something new, John. Any minute now."

Hollis knew that Maggie was relaxed; she could hear that in the other woman's casual tone. It was an interesting voice, oddly compelling for something so soft and pleasant, and as deceptively benign as the surface calm of a deep pool. But what lay beneath the surface? Something always did.

"We can talk about anything you like," she was saying. "Just like when I came back yesterday. Pick a topic. The weather, sports — cabbages and kings."

Hollis smiled. "My favorite quote was always the one about believing six impossible things before breakfast. That always seemed like a good attitude to have."

"I know what you mean. The way the world is these days, it's almost incomprehensible how anyone could have a closed mind. It seems like most every day there's a story in the news about one of our certainties being turned on its ear."

"Maybe that's what it means to be human," Hollis offered. "Forever questioning our certainties."

"Maybe," Maggie agreed. "It's as good a definition as any other, I guess." She paused, then said, "Only a few more days until the bandages come off. How do you feel about that?"

"You sound like the hospital shrink," Hollis noted, neatly avoiding an answer.

"Sorry. Occupational hazard, I suppose; I spend so much time asking people how they feel about one thing or another. But I am curious. If the operation was successful and you can see again, do you think that will help you to get past this and move on with your life?"

Hollis didn't really want to answer but heard herself answering anyway. "In some ways, sure. If I can see, he won't have . . . destroyed everything. I'd still have my art, and still in the same way, so that'd probably help. Give me something to concentrate on."

"But your art is going to be different no matter what," Maggie said. "Nobody experiences violence without coming out of it fundamentally changed."

"You mean the dreams?" Hollis asked the question jerkily.

"Yes." Maggie's voice remained quiet, easy, as if nothing she said was at all unusual. "Your dreams have become more violent and far more vivid, with nightmares common. You wake up often in the night, suddenly, even without nightmares. Most of your senses have become sharper, and you'll be quicker to react to them. And it'll be a long time — if ever — before you feel completely safe again."

"You're more blunt about it than the shrink was."

"I don't see any reason to soft-pedal it. You're an intelligent woman, and you've had plenty of time to think these last weeks. To wonder. To ask yourself what is and will be different now. Your art will be. I don't have to know what you drew or painted before to be certain of that."

"Yeah, I know." Hollis gripped the arms of the chair, her fingers clenching and un-clenching restlessly. "But how will it be different?"

"There's no way to be sure until you find out for yourself. I'd guess that if you paint you'll discover a tendency toward starker images, more vivid colors. You may choose subjects you avoided before, or even fixate on one or two images to the exclusion of most others."

"Images like the scalpel he used to take my eyes?"

"Maybe. Or some other image that represents violence or loss to you. It might have no connection at all to what happened to you — at least to all appearances. But it will be connected. And you'll know how or will have to figure it out. The images won't leave you alone until you deal with them." Maggie's voice remained matter-of-fact but was not without compassion or understanding.

Hollis drew a shaky breath. "My mind was always preoccupied with images before this. But how will there be images, visible images, from this? What happened to me was all . . . darkness. I never saw anything at all."

"Your other senses will fill in the blanks. What you heard and felt, what you smelled, what you touched and what touched you."

"Evil touched me. How will I paint that?"

"I don't know. But you'll know. Eventually, you'll know. And you'll have to paint it or somehow give it form. That's what artists do."

"Is that what you do? Give evil form?"

"I . . . suppose I do. Or at least try to give it a face."

Hollis half laughed under her breath. "You know what's most ironic about all this? I came out here for a whole new start. I inherited enough money to be able to quit my crass commercial-art job and spend a few years finding out if I had enough talent to be a real artist. And I'd barely got my studio set up when this happened. Fate just loves to kick us in the ass."

"Yeah, I've noticed." Maggie paused, then added, "I suppose it's useless to ask you if you remember anybody watching you before the attack. Following you."

"I don't remember anything out of the ordinary. So if he was watching me, I never saw him. Which is a very, very creepy thought. Why did he — do you know why he picked me?"

"The police haven't found a helpful common denominator among the victims. Different physical appearances, different jobs and lifestyles, a fairly wide range of ages — though he does seem to lean toward women in their twenties. It was probably nothing you did, Hollis, and it certainly wasn't your fault. You just fit whatever requirements he's put together in his twisted mind."

"Do you think . . . he'll do it again? Attack another woman?"

"Yes."

The immediate, calm answer made Hollis hesitate, but only for a moment. "Until he's stopped. Yes, of course. But why? Why is he doing this?"

It was Maggie's turn to hesitate, but then she replied slowly. "I'm sure a psychologist or profiler could develop all sorts of motivations. And I'm sure they'd be right. There are always reasons, at least explainable — if not understandable. Even for monsters."

"But there's only one real reason, isn't there? One real motivation behind his acts?"

"Yes. There's always a single driving motivation behind a predator like this one."

Hollis tilted her head, listening to that voice, the steady calm that was so deceptive. She wondered what it was she could almost hear moving about in the unseen depths beneath Maggie's tranquillity.

Something . . . cold. No, not really cold. Chilled. Something dark and chilled.

Fear? Knowledge? Understanding?

For some reason, Hollis was unwilling to ask aloud. Maybe because she didn't know Maggie well. Maybe because she was half convinced she was imagining way too much in the darkness behind her bandages.

Or maybe just because she was afraid of the answer.

She forced herself to concentrate on the subject of a monster's motivation. "What is it? Why does he do this to us, Maggie?"

"Because he wants to. Because he likes it."

Hollis drew a breath. "Yes. I . . . felt that. The way he touched me. As if the very texture of my skin intrigued him somehow. The way he . . . smelled me."

"He enjoyed your scent?"

"Must have. Or wanted to remember it later. He kept . . . sniffing. I'd feel his breath on my skin, then hear him sniff. My arm, my throat, breasts. All over. I'd stopped . . . begging . . . by then." Hollis heard her own voice as though it belonged to someone else, the words coming faster and faster, almost spilling out of her.

"I was tied up, unable to move. When I'd come to the first time, it was to realize he'd taken my eyes. I struggled then, fought him. Cursed him. But it was no use; no matter how loud I screamed or how hard I struggled, it didn't seem to affect him at all. He . . . did what he wanted to do. Raped me. And after that, after I'd stopped screaming and cursing, he . . . beat me — almost methodically. It seemed to take all

151

my will to deal with the pain without screaming. I didn't want him to hear me scream from the pain. Didn't want him to . . . have that satisfaction. So I didn't make a sound, just concentrated on listening to him."

"What else did you hear, Hollis?"

"Him. Breathing. He was very quiet, but once or twice I heard him humming to himself. Not a tune I recognized, although there was something familiar about it. Not even a tune, really. Just humming. And . . ."

"And?"

"There was something else, but . . . I can't remember. I know I heard another sound, a sound that bothered me somehow. Because I recognized it, or thought I should have. Something. But I don't remember now."

Hollis knew Maggie leaned toward her, and didn't start when a cool hand covered one of hers.

"You'll remember when you can, Hollis."

"I remember everything else. I remember every goddamned thing he did to me. I remember the way his breath smelled in my face, like spearmint chewing gum. The way *he* smelled of Ivory soap. The way his skin felt against mine, hot and slick with sweat. The way he . . . grunted in the back of his throat while he raped me. I remember . . . everything. Except that. Why not that?"

"There's a reason. There's always a reason."

"You mean my mind doesn't want me to remember? But why that? All the horrible things he did to me — and I can't remember a sound? Just a sound? Why?"

"I don't know. But we'll figure it out. I promise you, Hollis, we'll figure it out." Maggie drew a little breath, and Hollis thought she heard a catch in the sound, but the other woman's voice was steady when she said, "Can you start from the beginning? Can you tell me everything that happened from the moment he grabbed you?"

"Yes," Hollis said. Her hand turned and gripped Maggie's tightly. "I think I can now."

Hollis Templeton's room was around a corner and near the end of an unusually quiet corridor on a quiet floor of the hospital; her doctors felt she would be better off not disturbed by the hustle and bustle common in most of the building. So when

John got off the elevator and passed the silent waiting room, he found himself half consciously walking more quietly down the deserted hallway so as not to intrude upon the peaceful atmosphere.

He turned the corner having seen no one and stopped abruptly when he did see someone. Maggie. She was outside Hollis's room, leaning back against the wall beside the closed door. She was hugging her sketch pad with both arms, her head bent, long hair falling forward to mostly hide her pale face, but even from this distance John could see her shoulders shaking and hear the muffled but wrenching sobs.

Before she could see or sense him there, John stepped silently back around the corner and retreated to the doorway of the waiting room, more shaken than he wanted to admit to himself.

Magic. No, it wasn't magic, what she did. Whether her ability was paranormal as Quentin insisted or merely an overdeveloped sensitivity to the feelings of others, the undeniable fact was that Maggie suffered right along with the victims of violence she tried to help. He wondered if he had the right to ask her to put herself through that. If anyone did.

And, not for the first time, he wondered

why she did it. He had considered having her background investigated, certainly something he could have done, but it wasn't his habit to acquire information about people that way. Especially people he wanted to work with. Digging into somebody's past without so much as a by-your-leave was hardly a good first step to induce trust and cooperation.

Both Quentin and Kendra had adamantly stated that Maggie's motives had to be both powerful and deeply felt, and John could see that clearly enough. To willingly put herself through what she did, her reasons would *have* to be strong ones.

So what were they? What could possibly drive a sensitive woman, with the intelligence and artistic talent to be anything she wanted, to torture herself this way?

John shoved his hands into the pockets of his jacket and waited there, leaning beside the doorway, all too aware that only Maggie could answer that question. And nobody had to tell him it wasn't something she would willingly discuss, especially with a virtual stranger.

Both the question and that reluctant answer were difficult to accept, and he thought about both, so preoccupied that he didn't hear her approach until she spoke.

"What are you doing here?" Except for a faint redness around her eyes and a hint of strain in her face, there were no lingering signs of that storm of emotion John had briefly witnessed.

"I called the station. Andy said you were probably here talking to Hollis Templeton. He said he'd tried to call you."

"I turned off my cell phone. I usually do during interviews." Maggie frowned slightly. "But I got your message; I was planning to meet you at four."

He nodded, accepting that. "Yeah, well, it might be a good idea if we go there now."

"Why?"

He didn't want to tell her, but there was no choice. "The police think there's been another attack, Maggie. A woman was reported missing a couple of hours ago. Her husband just returned from a business trip and discovered her gone and the front door literally standing open."

Maggie was very still, staring up at him. "There's something else, isn't there? What else?"

He really didn't want to tell her.

"John? What is it?"

"She's pregnant. More than six months."

Hollis remained in her chair by the

window, but only because she felt too drained to move. Talking about the attack, telling Maggie all the horrible, painful details, even those she hadn't dared think about, had exhausted her. But not nearly as much as she had expected it to.

And her emotional state was much better than it had any right to be, she knew that. She felt peculiarly calm, almost . . . at peace.

Because of her.

"Because of Maggie?" By now, it seemed almost normal to discuss things with her figment. Reassuring, even.

Yes.

"Why? Just because she listened? Because she was sympathetic and understanding?"

No. Because she took some of your pain.

Hollis frowned. "What do you mean?"

She took it away. Took it into herself, so that you wouldn't hurt so much.

"You don't — surely you don't mean she actually *physically* absorbed what I was feeling?"

She has a unique gift. It's why I wanted you to talk to her. So you could begin to heal.

"But . . . she felt it? All the pain?"

Yes.

Hollis was horrified; she wouldn't have

wished that on anyone, and for Maggie to have suffered so when she was only trying to help . . . "Dammit, why didn't you warn me?"

I couldn't warn you. Neither could she. We both knew you'd fight not to inflict such pain on another. We both knew you wouldn't tell her the things she had to know if you had been warned it would hurt her too.

As upset as she was, Hollis had a realization then, one she was surprised hadn't occurred to her before. "You know her, don't you? You know Maggie."

Yes. I know Maggie. I know her very well.

CHAPTER
SEVEN

"The forensics team is going over that house inch by inch, but so far nothing. I've got people canvassing the neighborhood, but on a busy Monday with most at work or at school, the area was all but deserted — today, anyway."

"How long was the husband away?" John asked.

"From last Thursday. He says at a business conference on the East Coast, and I don't expect to find anything different; he arrived at Sea-Tac this morning, sure enough. And I'd bet my pension he's half out of his mind with worry, so I'm not looking at him as a suspect. He says he talked to her late last night when he called from his hotel; records confirm he certainly called the house and there was a lengthy conversation, so we're probably looking at about a twelve-hour window during which she might have disappeared. According to friends and family, she wouldn't have run away . . ."

Maggie tried to concentrate on what Andy was telling them, but it wasn't easy. The interview with Hollis, productive though it might turn out to be, had drained her; the pain and anguish of the other woman, dragged out into the light of day and sanity for the first time since the attack, had been virtually an open wound. Maggie needed to recover from that. Unfortunately, she hadn't been granted the time or seclusion necessary.

So she was faking it. Or trying to.

". . . the husband says you'd never know she's pregnant. One of those women who hardly show at all right up to delivery, apparently."

"*He* knows," Maggie heard herself say.

Andy frowned across his desk at her. "The rapist? If she isn't showing, how could —"

"He's been watching her. He would have seen her doing things to prepare for a baby."

"Things?" John asked.

Maggie didn't look at him. "Doctor visits, shopping, decorating. It's a first baby. There'd be a lot to do."

Andy said, "But he might not have realized how far along she is."

"Maybe not. I wouldn't bet money on it, though."

Andy grimaced and rubbed the nape of his neck. "No, me either. Is this supposed to be a fun new twist for the bastard? Christ. If it turns out that Samantha Mitchell was taken by the rapist, this city is going to come apart at the seams."

Maggie drew a breath and fought to keep her voice steady. "You realize she's not likely to survive."

"You could have gone all day without saying that."

"It's true and you know it. Hollis says he beat her almost methodically and violently raped her at least three times. She was so damaged internally she'll never be able to have children. Add to that the sheer physical and emotional shock of being blinded, and the odds are that neither a pregnant woman nor her child could survive the attack."

Andy shook his head, his face grim, but said, "Did you get anything helpful from the interview with Hollis?"

"I don't know. Maybe. Details, but not the sort to help the police, at least not yet."

"Such as?"

Maggie drew a breath and let it out slowly, trying not to sound as tired as she felt. "He used spearmint-flavored gum or breath mints. He hummed to himself sometimes, but not a tune Hollis recognized. He was fascinated by the texture of her skin and her scent."

John moved slightly in his chair, and under his breath muttered, "Son of a bitch."

Maggie sent him a quick glance of apology. It had to be hell for him, hearing this sort of thing and knowing that his sister had been held and tortured by the same animal. In situations like this one, an informed imagination could be a lot worse than an ignorant one.

For the first time, Maggie realized that he probably slept no better than she did and that his nightmares undoubtedly grew more vivid with each brutal fact he learned about what his sister had actually gone through.

Andy, more adept than either of them at not letting his emotions sidetrack him, said to Maggie, "Those don't even sound like the sorts of details that might help you. Are they? Are you beginning to see this guy?"

"Every detail helps me see him. Eventually." Every detail, every throb of agony and anguish she had felt right along with Hollis. And Ellen. And Christina.

"Do you have a sketch yet?"

"No. Not yet."

John said, "Andy, I know your boss would hate it, but is there any way we can see the Mitchell house today?"

"We?"

"Maggie and me."

Maggie wanted to protest but bit back the words. She had so far managed to hide from Andy her reaction to actual scenes of violence or suffering and intended to keep it that way if she had any choice. It was difficult enough to do what she did without having to also cope with the increased uneasiness or even fear she knew most of these cops would feel if they saw one of her little . . . performances.

She had no idea what John thought of what he had witnessed on Saturday, but she didn't doubt he and his friend had discussed her. His supposedly psychic friend.

She felt cold. And worried. Was she moving too fast? Could she afford not to? It was so desperately important that they stop this monster before he destroyed more lives, but what would be the price demanded if she chose the wrong path? And who would have to pay it?

"Maggie, are you up to it?" Andy asked.

She nodded. "I'm fine." A lie, but she thought it was probably a pretty convincing one.

"I know Maggie usually walks the scene eventually," Andy said slowly, "but why you, John?"

Because he wants to watch me. But Maggie didn't say that, of course. She just waited silently.

"I suppose," John said, "because I'm trying to . . . immerse myself in the investigation. To see everything. And who knows, Andy — I may see something all you cops miss. I may not be trained in police work, but I usually don't miss many of the details when I turn my mind to something."

It was the truth, Maggie thought. But not all of it.

Andy drummed his fingers on his desk for a moment, eyeing John intently, then shrugged. "I'll okay it. I wanted Maggie to walk it anyway, and you might as well go along, although I doubt you'll find anything we missed. The forensics team should be just about finished up by the time you can get to the house, and Mitchell has given us permission to do whatever it takes to find his wife, so I don't imagine he'll object. If he even notices, which is doubtful."

Maggie got to her feet when John did, but paused to ask Andy, "Is there anything else? Anything new?"

Only someone who knew him well would have seen the hesitation before he replied, "No, nothing. At least until we have the forensics report later today."

Maggie pretended she didn't know him well and nodded as she turned away. She'd have to come back here later and corner Andy, try to find out what was going on. Unless it was her, and not John Garrett, he didn't want to tell.

She didn't much like this. If it came down to it, where would her loyalties have to lie? With the police or with John? That shouldn't have been a question, but it was. And she knew why it was.

Pushing those troubling thoughts aside for the moment, Maggie followed John from the station. He didn't speak until they were on the steps, and then it was to make a wry request.

"Would you mind if we went together in my car? I'll bring you back here afterward to get your car." He grimaced slightly when she looked at him quizzically. "I don't know if you've noticed, but these days any unaccompanied man moving around the city tends to draw quite a few suspicious stares, especially in a neighborhood such as the one we'll be visiting. Aside from disliking the way it makes me feel, I'd just as soon avoid the undue attention."

Maggie half nodded and went with him to his car, and it wasn't until they were on their way that she said, "It's the not knowing, of course. As far as most of the women in this city are concerned, any man they don't know could be the rapist — and sad to say there are probably far too many women who aren't even sure of the men they do know."

"That is sad. It must be hell to look at someone you believed you could trust and realize you aren't completely sure anymore. And hell to be on the receiving end of that doubt."

"I imagine so."

He glanced at her. "Imagine? Can't you feel it? When they do, I mean."

"Why ask when you don't believe it's possible?" Maggie made her voice a little dry but still casual. "Is that why you wanted me to go with you to the Mitchell house, by the way? So you could watch another . . . performance and explain it away?"

John was silent for a moment, then said, "I hate it when Quentin's right. He said you'd probably lived with doubt and disbelief most of your life."

"He'd know, being a seer. Not that you believe that either." She realized abruptly that they weren't heading for the address of the Mitchell house Andy had provided but in another direction entirely. Where —

"That's an old-fashioned term for it, isn't it? Seer?"

Maggie shrugged, feeling a slow little chill crawl over her skin. "I suppose. Anyway, he said he didn't see things, just knew them."

"And you?"

"What about me?" She clung to casual disinterest and fought the rising panic.

John drew a breath and said softly, "When you walk through a place where something violent happened, do you see things? Know them? Or feel them?"

Repeating her earlier answer, Maggie said, "Why ask when you don't believe it's possible?"

"I never have believed it's possible, but that doesn't mean I can't change my mind, Maggie. Not long before I called Andy and found out about the Mitchell woman, Quentin told me another woman had been taken. He knew."

"I'm sure you explained that away. It could have been a lucky guess." She knew where they were going now. Damn. *Damn.*

"It could have been. But if so, there've been a lot of lucky guesses over the years, too many times he knew things before he should have. And then there's you."

Stolidly, Maggie said, "I'm just overly sensitive, that's all. With a vivid imagination."

"I guess you've heard that a lot during your life."

"Enough."

"Okay. But at least I'm trying to have an open mind. Give me that much credit."

After a moment, she said quietly, "I'm sure you use calculators and computers and other machines in your business affairs; do you really have to understand the nuts and bolts of how they work in order to be satisfied with the information and answers they provide?"

"No. But I have to trust that the information they provide is accurate and reliable, and sometimes that requires at least some level of understanding. And you're not a machine. I really do want to understand you, Maggie."

Deliberately, Maggie half turned in the seat to look at him steadily. "If your friend Quentin hasn't convinced you in years of trying to, then what hope do I have? At least the things he tells you can be verified, predictions backed up by fact when those predictions turn out to be true. But what I do? What I do isn't backed up by anything, really. It's all subjective. Besides, I don't have the spare energy to jump through hoops for you, John. Just tell yourself I have a peculiar skill honed by half a lifetime of working with the police, and let it go at that. I can't prove anything to you."

"Can't you?"

"No."

He pulled the car over to the curb and stopped, then looked at her, his jaw tight. "I know a way you can."

She didn't have to look to know where they were. "No. I can't."

"Because the interview with Hollis took too much out of you?"

She had to be honest. "No."

"Because you have to save your energy for the Mitchell house?"

"Partly."

He nodded as if an inner belief had been confirmed. "But not completely. So what's the rest of the answer, Maggie? Andy told me you never walked through Christina's apartment after she died. Why not?"

Maggie drew a short breath. "I have my reasons." Reasons he wouldn't understand, let alone believe.

"What reasons?"

"Private reasons."

"Maggie —"

"John, I'm not going to walk through Christina's apartment. Not today."

"And you won't tell me why."

She shook her head slightly in a brief but final negation.

"I'm trying to understand this," he said, his voice slow, as though he chose his words carefully. "Because it's such a simple question, Maggie — why did my sister kill herself? I think you could answer that question, so I have to wonder why you won't even make an attempt. Am I asking so much? Just walk through her apartment and tell me what you see. Or know. Or feel."

Andy hung up his phone and scowled at Jennifer as she approached his desk. "Please tell me you have something," he begged.

She sat down and said, "We didn't expect forensics to find anything, especially not this quickly. So something else must have put you in a bad mood. Or somebody. Drummond?"

If anything, Andy's frown deepened. "I don't know whether to look forward to the day he's sitting in the governor's mansion or dread it. He'd be mostly out of my hair — but God help the state."

"Let me guess. Samantha Mitchell or her husband has a Very Important Friend in government?"

"Hell, they know everybody. At least according to Luke. And *everybody* is yelling at him to find the lady, pronto."

"I guess you told him we're trying to do that."

"I mentioned it, yeah."

Jennifer smiled. "Well, here's something else to brighten your day."

He braced himself visibly. "What?"

"While Scott's trying to track down those missing files, I've been taking a closer look at that book I got from the library. There aren't a lot of specific details on the series of murders in 1934, but there was one very interesting thing. It turns out the cops were undecided whether to call it six victims — or eight. Six was the official verdict, but there was a lot of doubt, apparently, among the investigating officers."

"What kind of doubt?"

"They were positive the first six victims were killed by the same man because of the similarities. The women were always raped and killed somewhere else and their bodies dumped later in remote or deserted spots, he always beat them up badly, the women always bore defense injuries, and he never tore their clothing."

Andy blinked. "Never?"

"No. The bodies were always discovered dressed, all the buttons fastened and nothing ripped. Which is interesting in several ways. For one thing, the women were always found without underwear. No bras or panties, no girdles or stockings or slips. Just their outer dresses. And there was usually very little blood or dirt on those dresses."

"So he stripped them — and then dressed them afterward, but without their underwear. Kept the underwear as trophies, maybe?"

"Maybe. But think how difficult just the mechanics of it had to be. By the time he finished with them, the women were either dead or dying. And instead of dumping them somewhere, naked, which would certainly have been the easiest and simplest thing to do, he takes the time and trouble to dress them in their outer clothing. Almost as if . . . he was trying to protect their modesty."

"You been talking to the shrink?" Andy wanted to know.

"No, but I've listened to her talk about this sort of thing before, so I feel safe in making a semieducated guess about it. I think the detail is important, Andy. It could be something as simple as the fact that the 1934 killer lived during a more . . . modest time. Or a quirk of his psyche — he'd defile them in every way possible, but it was for his own enjoyment. When other men saw the women, they had to be decently covered."

"Sounds like the sort of quirk entirely likely in one of these twisted bastards. Okay, it makes sense to me. It definitely sounds like those six women were killed by the same man. But there was doubt about two more victims?"

"Uh-huh."

"Why? The M.O. was drastically different?"

"Two young women found in remote places, having obviously been raped and killed somewhere else, badly beaten, with defense injuries, and wearing their virtually undamaged outer clothing all neatly fastened."

"Sounds like the same guy."

"Yeah, except for one addition."

"Which is?"

"Their eyes were missing. Cut out —

with absolutely no finesse."

Andy stared at her a moment, then drew a short breath. "Shit."

"Yeah. Knowing what we know now about the escalation and evolution of this sort of sick predator, I say those last two victims belong with the first six. He had just grown more violent, and more creative. Which means eight, Andy. Killed within the space of about eighteen months."

"Which may or may not mean we could have a year and four — or three — more victims to go."

"If our guy is copycatting earlier crimes, yeah. The killings that started in 1934 sure sound familiar. All of our victims survived the attacks, and only one actually died of her injuries, but that could be as much luck as anything else; they were found before they could bleed to death, unlike the women in 1934. We have naked victims, but that may just be because our particular monster has fewer hang-ups than his predecessor did. Or a better knowledge of forensics."

"He certainly has that," Andy said heavily. "And it does sound more and more like he studied at least some of these earlier crimes. For inspiration, goddamn his soul."

"He doesn't have one," Jenn declared.

Andy grunted an agreement. "What about the earlier date, 1894?"

"Nothing so far, at least in that book. And we haven't found any files from that year — not here and not at any other station. It was a long time ago, Andy."

"Tell me about it." He sighed. "All we can do is keep looking. What else have we got?"

Jennifer sighed and got to her feet. "Yeah, you're right. By the way — I know we're keeping this to ourselves for the time being, but are you going to tell Maggie?"

"I haven't decided yet. What do you think?"

"I say tell her."

Andy leaned back and looked at her curiously. "Why?"

"Because Maggie works best when she has all the information we can give her. And because . . . she's very good with intangibles, Andy. Victims give her subjective impressions and feelings and pain — and in all that confusion, Maggie finds a face we can search for. As far as I can tell, with her it's all instinct and emotion. She comes at this differently than we do. Maybe she'd have an idea or observation we'd never have."

"Yeah." He nodded slowly. "Yeah, maybe."

"You going to tell Garrett?"

"I don't know that yet either."

"It might give him a focus other than his sister's death."

"It might. And we might need the resources he can tap. I don't know. We'll see how it goes."

"I'm glad it's your decision and not mine," Jennifer told him with a casual salute, then returned to her own desk.

Andy wished it was somebody else's decision. He was a good cop, and maybe it was that inborn instinct that warned him uneasily that this particular case was somehow beyond his experience. Not just because this bastard was torturing his victims the way he was and going to such elaborate extremes to hide his own identity, but because of the chillingly methodical way he went about satisfying his twisted needs.

Andy would have loved to hand the whole mess over to somebody else. But he couldn't do that. It was his mess, and he had to find his way through it. Which meant Jenn was right and he'd have to tell Maggie about these latest puzzle pieces.

Even more, he might just have to break the rules and ignore Drummond's orders and bring John Garrett fully into the investigation. He needed all the resources he could get his hands on, and with Drummond's stubborn refusal to call in the FBI, John could provide a wide and willing conduit to virtually every database and source of information available.

Maybe even some sources that could take them all the way back to 1894.

Maggie wondered if he had any idea at all what he asked of her and thought that he had at least an inkling. But not belief. Because if he believed, he could never have asked her to go to the apartment where a despondent, tormented woman had died and allow those emotions to seep into her. At least . . . she hoped he couldn't ask that of her.

"Even if I did, it wouldn't be proof," she said flatly. "Because Christina isn't here to verify whatever I'd say."

"I'll know if it's the truth."

"Will you? And how will you know that? Because you were her brother? You've lived in L.A. for the last ten years, and she moved back to Seattle more than five years ago; did you know so much about her life? I'd bet not. I'd bet you didn't know much at all."

"Maggie —"

"She volunteered at a day-care center in her neighborhood, did you know that? And at the local animal shelter. She still woke up in the night and reached for her husband, even though it had been nearly two years since he'd died. She talked to her plants, even sang to them sometimes. She was learning to use a computer for the first time; with Simon gone, she no longer felt she'd have to compete with his genius in that area. She watched old movies in bed at night, and just before the attack she'd been in the middle of a wonderful series of mystery novels."

Maggie drew a breath. "Did you know that? Did you know any of that?"

John stared out through the windshield, a muscle moving in his tight jaw. "No," he said finally. "I didn't know any of that."

Looking down at the sketch pad in her lap, Maggie consciously loosened her grip on it. She really needed to stop clinging, she thought vaguely. It was a very bad sign. "John, if I believed, really believed, that I could help you by going up to Christina's apartment, then I would. But nothing I could find out by doing that would help you in any way." *Assuming I survived to tell you.* But she didn't add that, of course.

Quietly, she said, "We should try to get

to the Mitchell house while the cops are still there."

Without a word, John put the car in gear and pulled away from the curb.

Maggie didn't sense any hostility coming from him, so she didn't worry about his silence. Instead, she used the time granted to her to do her best to shore up what few defenses she had. Not that she ever had many, except for a fair ability to master her expression and what Beau referred to as her prickly touch-me-not posture.

So she worked on those, at least for the ten minutes or so until they reached the Mitchell house. The police had tried to keep this disappearance as quiet as possible until they knew whether Samantha Mitchell had been abducted by the serial rapist, but the press had found out at least part of it and were milling about just beyond the long drive, where several uniformed officers were holding them at bay.

Andy had sent word of their clearance, so they were waved through and pulled into the driveway with barely a pause. But with enough of a pause, unfortunately, for one photographer to get a picture.

"Shit," John muttered.

Maggie, who had done her best to make certain her face wouldn't be visible, said,

"You'll make the papers tomorrow. I wonder if Andy realized that seeing you here would pretty much confirm the reporters' suspicions about this woman being the latest victim."

"It won't be an official confirmation, so all they can do is speculate. That isn't what's bothering me."

"Then what?"

"Drummond." John sent her a wry look. "He wasn't happy I was granted access to the investigation, and I more or less promised to keep my involvement low-key."

"Ouch."

"Yeah." Without saying anything else about that, John parked the car and they got out.

It was a big Spanish-style house in an upper-middle-class neighborhood where virtually every house had its own unique style. Manicured lawn, exquisite landscaping. Maggie glanced around as they made their way through the tangle of police vehicles clogging the upper part of the driveway and murmured, "Wouldn't you think a stranger would be noticed in this neighborhood?"

"I'd think so, yeah. Unless he was dressed as some kind of maintenance or service person. Hiding in plain sight."

Maggie knew the cops had undoubtedly made a note of that possibility; neither Andy nor any of his people was stupid. But it nevertheless struck her as distinctly odd that a rapist who went to such lengths to hide his identity from his victims could allow himself to move openly in neighborhoods and shopping malls where he was almost certain to be noticed — even hiding in plain sight.

The cop at the door said they'd been okayed to go through the house, and since the forensics team was packing up now, they could come in whenever they wanted.

"Where's Mr. Mitchell?" Maggie asked.

"He's in the kitchen with a couple of detectives."

Maggie nodded and stepped past him into the foyer. Several equipment boxes standing open and closed on the polished wood floor of the area attested to the presence of the forensics team, and an occasional voice could be heard from upstairs. It appeared they had finished their work downstairs.

She was momentarily highly conscious of John standing just behind her but forced herself to concentrate on what she was here to do. It was difficult to prepare herself for the painful and disturbing invasion even after all these years, especially when she could hear the forensics team. One of the reasons she always tried to delay a walk-through of the scene until after everyone else had finished their work and gone was because the emotions of other people could affect what she was trying to do.

One of the reasons.

"There's no blood trail here." John's voice was matter-of-fact. "So where do you start?"

She glanced at him, wishing she didn't have to prove herself to him this way. But if he couldn't accept and believe this, how would he ever be able to accept and believe the rest? And no matter which way it went, he'd have to believe the rest.

Wouldn't he?

Making up her mind abruptly, Maggie abandoned the I'm-just-an-overly-sensitive-person mantra. "I'm a human divining rod for violence," she said, matching his tone. "If there was any here, I'll find where it happened."

He was completely expressionless. "I see."

"I doubt it." Maggie hugged her sketch pad like the security blanket it virtually was and walked into the living room on her left. She didn't look at the comfortable and expensive furnishings or pay any attention to the decorating scheme but just stood in the center of the room, closed her eyes for a moment, and reluctantly opened the inner door to that unnerving sixth sense.

As always, it was a peculiar feeling, at first a distant murmur accompanied by flashes of scenes, like a strobe projector flickering images in her mind's eye. Then she caught the whiff of wine, the acrid smell of wood smoke, cologne or after-shave. Heard voices raised suddenly in an argument, felt her hand sting as if she'd slapped someone. Then hands gripping her wrists and a mouth coming down hard on hers . . .

Maggie took a jerky step backward to physically break the connection and under her breath muttered, "Shit."

"What?" John was watching her intently, a tiny frown between his brows.

She glanced at the fireplace, where no fire burned today, then looked at the apparently very comfortable couch and sighed. "There's violence — and then there's violence. Dammit. I hate being a voyeur."

"Maggie, what are you talking about?"

"Nothing was done in this room against

anyone's will, John. I just picked up on . . . Well, let's just say the Mitchells have an active and . . . energetic sex life."

He glanced at the couch as she had done, then looked quickly back at her face. "Oh."

Maggie didn't try to read his face or his emotions or waste time wondering if he believed her; she was reasonably sure he didn't. Instead, she moved into the next room. She didn't stop now but walked slowly, looking around her but allowing that inner sense to be the one seeing. And hearing. And feeling.

She caught the flicker of another marital argument in the den that seemed to be about, of all things, a parrot, another scene of rather violent lovemaking in the sunroom, and knew someone had been cut — oddly enough by a broken mirror — in the breakfast room. In Thomas Mitchell's study, many business arguments had taken place, the most recent of which had been between Mitchell and his father-in-law.

Maggie reported each event calmly and without looking at John, speaking aloud as much to keep herself grounded as to supply him with information. She was holding on to her control with all her will, determined not to allow herself to be lost within the emotional turmoil of these people's lives.

It was getting more and more difficult to keep herself separate and apart from what she sensed, and that frightened her more than a little. *Could* she actually get lost in the violence of past events? And if she did . . . would she ever be able to find her way out again?

They bypassed the kitchen, where they could hear the murmur of voices, and moved on to the other ground-floor rooms. There was nothing of interest to report in a powder room or exercise room, a butler's pantry or laundry room.

Maggie was beginning to wonder if everybody had got it wrong and Samantha Mitchell had walked out of this house of her own free will, when they reached the game room. Maggie walked into the fairly dark room and was staggered by an overwhelming wave of absolute terror.

It was as brief as it was fierce, just cold terror and iron arms around her and the bitter bite of chloroform — and then darkness so intense it was as if she had fallen into an abyss.

"Maggie."

She came out of it abruptly, shaken. It was John's arms she felt around her then, holding her upright, and the terrifying darkness receded, leaving only the bone-deep cold behind. And the terrible certainty.

"He's got her," she whispered.

CHAPTER
EIGHT

In what had once been an ordinary conference room of a New Orleans police station, now transformed by bulletin boards and computers and stacks of files into the base of operations for a very unique task force, Special Agent Tony Harte refilled his coffee cup and then returned to brooding over the photographs pinned to the center bulletin board.

"I just don't see a pattern," he announced.

"Look again."

Tony sighed. "Boss, I've looked so often and so hard my eyes are starting to cross."

Special Agent Noah Bishop looked up from the laptop where he'd been working and said dryly, "Maybe you'll be able to see better that way."

"Personally, I think we've been hexed."

Bishop lifted an eyebrow.

"Hexed," Tony insisted firmly. "That source of yours down in the Quarter talked about voodoo, and I think we should pay attention to her."

"I think you need a vacation, Tony."

"Oh, come on — is it so much easier to believe in telepathy and precognition than in hexes?"

"Yes."

"Why?"

"Telepathy and precognition don't involve fashioning a doll out of burlap and human hair and sticking pins in it."

Tony pondered that for a moment. "I don't know, boss. I've seen some pretty weird things since I started working for you."

"Next you'll be seeing zombies."

"I could state the obvious," Tony observed, eyeing his boss pointedly. "But I won't."

Bishop didn't rise to the bait. "Hand me that file on the banker, will you?"

Tony handed it across the conference table. "Anyway, if you and Miranda could just have a vision and help us out a little, I'd really appreciate it. Try, why don't you?"

The words were barely out of his mouth when Bishop paled and closed his eyes, an in-drawn breath hissing between his teeth.

Tony watched him intently and had to wait at least a minute or two longer than was customary before the other man's unusually penetrating gray eyes opened. Hopeful, he asked, "About our case?"

"Shit." Bishop massaged his temples briefly, then raked his fingers through his black hair, slightly disarranging the vivid white streak over his left temple. He looked decidedly grim. "Who the hell gave Quentin permission to go to Seattle?" he demanded.

Tony blinked. "Not about our case, then. Beats me. I thought his and Kendra's last assignment was in Pittsburgh."

"It was. But they aren't there now, typing up their reports like good little agents. They're in Seattle, and up to their asses in trouble." Bishop looked toward the doorway, and an instant later a tall, raven-haired, and strikingly beautiful woman appeared. She was absently massaging one temple with her fingers, and her startling blue eyes went instantly to Bishop.

"Out loud," Tony requested automatically.

She looked at him, sighed, then came to the conference table and sat down. "We can't go out there," she reminded Bishop. "Not yet, anyway."

"I know."

"He can take care of himself. Kendra too. You trained them well."

189

"Maybe. But this . . . Jesus Christ. Why do I put up with him, can you tell me that?" Bishop asked.

"Because he's good. A good investigator and a strong psychic. Too good to lose even if he does sometimes try your patience."

Bishop shook his head grimly. "Be that as it may, Miranda, it's taken us years to get this unit on its feet and earn enough respect from law enforcement *and* the Bureau to be taken seriously. Far from gaining the autonomy we want, one major public screwup and we'll find ourselves chained to our desks doing background checks for security clearances. And any time we stick our noses in where they aren't wanted, we run a huge risk of political fallout as well. Quentin knows damned well we don't get involved unofficially in ongoing investigations."

She smiled slightly. "You mean like the one you got involved in a couple of years ago in Atlanta?"

"That was different."

"Was it? Kane's your friend. John Garrett is Quentin's friend. We should have expected it, you know. Once Garrett's sister became a victim out there, it was only a matter of time before Quentin had to get involved — officially or unofficially."

Tony, who had been listening intently, decided he was up to speed at last and ventured a comment. "That serial rapist? Lots in the papers about the case."

Miranda looked at him, still smiling. "And what are you doing reading the Seattle newspapers?"

Caught, Tony grimaced and said "shit" under his breath, then tried to brazen it out. "Look, I didn't know for sure what was going on, it's just that Kendra had made a modem request for some data, and the return tag said Seattle, so I figured . . ."

"And you didn't think we'd be interested?" Bishop demanded. He shook his head. "Jesus, Tony, you're as bad as Quentin is. Keeping you two even marginally under control is like trying to herd cats."

Tony grinned. "Maybe you should stop trying, boss."

"They do tend to land on their feet," Miranda observed. "Although what I can't figure out is how either of them believes they can hide anything for long in a unit run by a telepath."

"Eternal optimists, both of us."

"Um. And you're both convinced you

can charm your way out of trouble."

"Only because we usually do," Tony said guilelessly.

Bishop groaned.

"Don't waste your energy," Miranda advised him, still amused. "You'll never fit either of them into any kind of FBI mold."

"I wasn't going for that," Bishop confessed, staring at Tony. "I seldom hope for miracles. Just something reasonable, like occasional obedience to my so-called authority. Not very much to ask, I'd think."

"Would it make you feel better," Tony inquired, "if I said I'd always considered you an authority figure? I mean, I do call you boss, after all."

"Only to remind yourself that's what I *am*. Otherwise, you'd never remember."

"Hey, you're the one who always says psychics are a prickly, independent lot, prone to go it alone more often than follow the rules or the regs. Can I help it if Quentin and I fit your definition to a T?"

"You could at least pretend to follow the rules every once in a while."

"Oh, I do. Every once in a while." Tony's smile died, and he added quietly, "Okay, you've both done a dandy job of trying to lead me away from asking about your vision."

"Not so dandy," Miranda murmured.

"I'm also tenacious," Tony reminded her. "So what is it you're trying very hard *not* to tell me?"

Miranda exchanged a glance with Bishop, then said, "We need you here, Tony."

"I know that. I won't go haring off after Quentin and Kendra no matter what you tell me. Like you said — they can take care of themselves." But he could feel tension seeping into his muscles, and when he looked at Miranda, he had the sudden, disquieting idea that she *knew*. And if she knew . . .

It was Bishop who said, "They're into something a lot more complicated than they realize."

"A fairly common trait of investigations we get involved in," Tony said, trying not to think about how much both of them knew about things he would have preferred to keep to himself. "So what did you see?"

Miranda said, "Sometimes visions are as clear and distinct as if they're scenes from a movie, a story with a beginning, a middle, and an ending. But sometimes they aren't. Sometimes they're flashes of stop-motion images, out of sequence, all jumbled together. Even worse, instead of presenting a single prediction, they can be — variations on a theme. Possible outcomes to a complex, fluid situation."

Tony scowled. "Meaning you don't know exactly what's going to happen out there, but at least one possible outcome is a bad one?"

"No," she said softly. "Meaning only one possible outcome is a good one. The deck's stacked against them this time, Tony. Against all of them."

"We have to warn them." Tony spoke before he considered and wasn't surprised by Bishop's response.

"You know better than that. In the kind of situation they're in, any foreknowledge, especially from outside, could trigger the very events we want to avoid. We can't help them by telling them what may or may not happen. They have to make their own choices, their own decisions, based on what's happening at any given time and based on their own abilities — paranormal and otherwise. Anything else is virtually guaranteed to only make things worse."

"Then what the hell good is it to even be precognitive?" Tony demanded.

Bishop smiled wryly. "Who told you it was a good thing? You've been listening to fairy tales again, Tony."

"Shit." Tony drew a breath. "So we say nothing? We leave them to . . . fate?"

Miranda said, "Fate's a very big player in this one, and some things really do have to play out as they're meant to. So, yes, we leave them to fate. We don't have a choice."

Tony looked from one to the other of them, then said with forced lightness, "I guess this is where I demonstrate my ability to obey orders and follow the rules, huh?"

"I'm afraid so," Bishop said.

"Okay. Well, then, if you two don't mind, I think I'll go see how Sharon is coming with that autopsy." He didn't wait for approval but left the conference room briskly.

Bishop said, "You know he's rattled when he voluntarily observes an autopsy. He hates them."

"Yeah. This isn't going to be easy for him." Miranda hesitated. "Are we right to keep him away?"

Bishop sighed explosively. "Hell, I don't know. You saw the same thing I did. That whole situation's so damned precarious, one player too many turns it into a bloodbath. Quentin and Kendra are involved now, there's nothing we can do to change that. Pull them out, and we could make

195

things immeasurably worse. Go in ourselves and the same thing could happen. And, like you said — this one's about fate. We'll have to leave them all to find their destiny."

They'll make it, Miranda said through the telepathic link they shared.

I hope so. But I've found fate to be a . . . brutal master. Even if they do make it, they'll never be the same again.

Her hand reached across the table, and their fingers twined together in a gesture neither of them had to comment on. No matter how intimately minds touched, sometimes the only real comfort to be found was in the warmth of flesh touching flesh.

Maggie turned off her cell phone and returned it to her pocket. "Andy said he'd have the forensics team go over the game room again, just to be sure. Apparently they didn't find much the first time, but he said they were figuring she was grabbed in the kitchen or front hall."

"So he believed you when you told him Samantha Mitchell was attacked in that room?"

"Yes, he believed me. Experience has taught him to trust my . . . instincts."

They were sitting in John's car, still parked in the drive of the Mitchell house, and he made no move to start the engine. Instead, turned slightly in the driver's seat, he watched her intently. "You haven't shown him what you've shown me, have you? Why not?"

Maggie was trying very hard not to shiver visibly, but the cold weariness she felt was getting harder and harder to ignore. She just wanted to go home and soak in a hot tub, maybe listen to some peaceful music and simply try to *forget* for a while.

"Why not?" John repeated.

"Because it wasn't necessary," she answered, almost too tired to think. "All Andy ever needed from me was sketches, and he could believe what I gave him without questioning where it came from, because I'd proven he could believe it."

"So I need more from you?"

For a moment, Maggie was tempted to tell him what a loaded question that really was. Instead, she abruptly opened her sketch pad and turned to a certain page and stood the pad up on her lap so he could see the sketch.

John caught his breath.

It was a sketch of Christina as she'd been before the attack that had ruined her face

197

and destroyed her life. This face he stared at was, John realized dimly, more than simple pencil lines on ivory paper. Much more. The pale brown hair, straight and cut casually mid-length, surrounded a delicate oval face that was unusually pretty, with large sparkling eyes and a beautiful smile with a deep dimple on one side . . .

It was his sister as he remembered her, so vividly alive he expected her to laugh suddenly or cut her eyes sideways at him the way she always had when she found him amusing or he tried her considerable patience when he was, as she put it, "being big brother."

"Jesus," he murmured.

Maggie tore the sketch neatly from the pad and handed it to him. "If this was all you needed from me, you wouldn't have to believe anything beyond what you understand. I knew your sister, I drew her likeness — there it is. I'm an artist, it's what artists do. Nothing paranormal about it."

"I'm not so sure," John said, handling the sketch carefully. "But thank you for this."

"You're welcome. Do you mind if we leave now? I know you wanted me to go with you to talk to your friend Quentin at this command post you guys have set up, but I need to be home for a while first. I'm a little tired."

John looked at her for a moment, then nodded. "Quentin said you probably needed to spend time at home alone whenever one of these . . . events . . . tired you."

"Quentin was right."

He got his briefcase from the backseat and secured the sketch carefully inside before starting the car. It was several miles before he spoke again, and then it was to ask a slow question.

"So what more do I need from you?"

She didn't hesitate. "Answers."

"About Christina?"

"About all of it. You want to know why she killed herself, but more than that. You want to find the man who destroyed her life. And . . ."

He frowned. "And?"

Maggie stared out through the windshield. Was Beau right about this man? He was usually right. And if he was right — she had to be very, very careful.

"Maggie?"

"And . . . you want him to pay for what he did. You may not fully believe there's anything paranormal about my work, but you do believe I can help you find this rapist."

After a moment, he said slowly, "Why do I think that isn't what you were originally going to say?"

She was silent.

"Okay, then tell me this. How is it you're so sure Samantha Mitchell was abducted by the serial rapist? Abducted I'll buy, but how can you know it was him?"

Maggie hesitated, then said deliberately, "Because it felt like him."

"You . . . don't mean felt emotionally, do you?"

"No. It physically felt like him. When he grabbed her from behind, the feel of his arms around her, his chest against her back, the way he . . . rubbed himself against her as she struggled, were all just the same as with the other attacks."

"You felt that because they did?"

"Yes."

"When you interviewed them? When they relived those memories?"

She nodded.

"Did you go to the places the other women had been abducted from?"

"Only one of them. Laura Hughes was abducted from her high-security apartment building, so I was able to do a walk-through there. But the others were grabbed either in very public places or places where there had been far too many people around later. It would have . . . muddied the impressions."

"Impressions?"

Dryly, she said, "What do you expect me to call them — psychic vibes?"

"You flatly denied being psychic just the other day."

"Yeah, well, that's always the safe thing to do — at least until I get to know whoever's asking."

He shot her a quick look. "Is that why you're finally being honest with me?"

"Well, I thought it might avoid a game of twenty questions. Obviously, I was wrong."

That surprised a laugh out of him. "Okay, point taken. It's just that I really do want to understand, Maggie."

"And believe?"

He barely hesitated. "And believe. It's just so far outside my experience that I know virtually nothing about it."

"You don't like not knowing, do you?"

"No, I don't. So I ask questions."

Maggie waited until he turned the car into the police lot where she'd left her own to say, "I really don't mind questions, John. But my brain isn't working too clearly at the moment, and I'd rather postpone them, if it's all the same to you."

He pulled into the slot beside her car. "Will you come to the hotel later? I still think we should sit down and go over everything with Quentin and his partner, come up with some kind of game plan from here on out."

"Partner?"

John swore under his breath, wondering if Maggie's apparent psychic abilities included being able to make him say things he had no intention of saying. "Yes, his partner."

"He's a cop, isn't he?" Maggie had one hand on the door handle but was waiting, brows slightly raised. "Quentin's a cop."

"He's here unofficially, Maggie."

"Uh-huh. What kind of cop?"

"Federal," John answered reluctantly. "FBI."

"Oh, lovely. And if Drummond finds out?"

"Then everything hits the fan. But I'm hoping he won't find out — at least until we have something to help his people put this bastard behind bars for the rest of his miserable life."

Maggie shook her head. "You do like to live dangerously."

"Maybe. Will you come to the hotel later?"

She didn't think there was a maybe

about it but was too tired to worry much about it at the moment. "Look, I'll see how I feel in a couple of hours and let you know, okay? I still have your cell number."

He nodded but turned the car off and got out when she did, saying, "I want to talk to Andy for a few minutes."

Maggie unlocked her car door and said calmly, "Do you want me to write down the stuff I told you at the Mitchell house so Andy can try to verify it for you?"

John stood on the walkway a few feet away, staring at her. "Shit. Was I that obvious?"

"Let's just say I'm beginning to understand the way you think."

He smiled slightly. "Is that a good thing or a bad thing?"

"I'll let you know."

He half laughed. "Fair enough. No, you don't have to write anything down. As it happens, I have a very good memory."

"Now, that doesn't surprise me at all. See you later, John." She got into her car and closed the door. She started the engine, watching him walk toward the station, and muttered under her breath, "FBI. Great. Just great."

Andy hung up the phone and frowned

across his desk at John. "Okay, I checked. And, as you heard, an understandably bewildered Thomas Mitchell confirmed. He and his wife *did* have an argument in their den about a parrot last week, his wife *did* cut herself on a hand mirror in the breakfast room the week before that, and he and his father-in-law *did* have a rather loud 'discussion' about business in his study just the other day. Now I've left the poor bastard wondering if somebody's got him bugged. I'm wondering too."

John tried to head him off. "I've got to know more about the parrot. Why'd they fight about that?"

"Samantha Mitchell wanted one as a pet," Andy answered impatiently. "John —"

"Who won the fight?"

"She did. The bird's on order. John, how the hell did you know about this stuff?"

He hesitated, but only briefly. There really wasn't another explanation and, besides, John had a hunch that if any one of these cops could accept Maggie totally no matter how bizarre her talents seemed to be, it would be Andy.

"I know," he answered finally, "because Maggie told me. While she was walking through the Mitchell house."

Andy didn't even blink. "So she is psychic, huh? Well, I always thought so."

"I'm still not a hundred percent convinced," John said, "but I have to admit she's been pretty damned impressive. I was just a step behind her when she walked into the Mitchells' game room, and I'll swear whatever she was experiencing nearly knocked her to her knees. She says the attacker *felt* a certain way, his arms, his body behind her. And she claims to have felt those same physical traits when the victims she interviewed relived their attacks."

"Jesus," Andy murmured. "If she felt that . . . then she must have felt the rest. All that pain and fear. I knew she was strong, but I had no idea just how strong."

John studied him. "You don't doubt that, do you? That she really feels what she says she does."

"No, I don't doubt it." Andy drew a deep breath and let it out slowly. "About two years ago, we had what looked like a simple case of a runaway teenager. Normally, I wouldn't even have been involved, but the parents were political players in the city, and the chief wanted his best people looking for their fifteen-year-old daughter.

"So we interviewed dozens of her

friends, trying to establish when and how she might have run away. Maggie sat in on the interviews because the chief asked her to, but she never asked a question, just listened. When we were done, none of us had a clue where that girl might be, but everything — and I mean *everything* — pointed to her having simply packed up some things and left home. Even the shrink agreed."

"So what happened?"

"We'd spent the better part of two days interviewing the friends, and afterward Maggie asked if she could walk around the girl's house and the yard. Well, we'd been all through the house, forensics had been over it, and I didn't hold out much hope Maggie could find something all of us had missed. I think they call that hubris, don't they?"

John smiled slightly. "She found something?"

"You could say that. I knew by then, of course, that she preferred to walk a scene alone, so I was keeping my distance. I was standing out near the garage and hadn't realized she'd come back outside until I saw her near the patio. She was walking very slowly, apparently not looking at anything in particular. When she got to the edge of the yard, she just stood there for the longest time. I didn't realize at first that she was crying, but it eventually dawned on me.

"I figured she was just upset about the missing girl, and I didn't want to embarrass her by calling attention to it, so I went to the car and waited. She came back a few minutes later, and except for a little red around her eyes, she looked the same as always. I asked if she'd found anything and she said no. Then, about halfway back to the station, she started talking about the interviews. She said something about one of the older boys bothered her. Nothing she could put her finger on, mind you, just a hunch. Wondered if I'd mind calling him back in for another talk, if maybe she could ask him a question or two.

"I wasn't looking forward to telling the chief we had squat for leads, so I said sure, why not. The boy wasn't a suspect, and since he was eighteen we didn't have to interview him in the presence of his parents, but we did tell him he could have a lawyer if he wanted one. He didn't. I asked him a few questions, then Maggie started talking to him. Just talking to him, quiet and gentle. About his school and his parents. About the girl."

When Andy fell silent, John said, "She got him to confess."

Andy nodded. "Took nearly an hour, and by the time he finally told the truth he was bawling his eyes out. The girl was supposed to meet him in the woods for what had become a regular session. Only that night she'd had a fight with her parents and decided to run away. To him. So she'd packed a bag, left a note for her parents, and there she was, expecting him to take care of her.

"He hadn't bargained on having a fifteen-year-old hung around his neck for life, and he panicked. They argued, and at some point he shoved her. When she fell, she hit her head on a rock. She didn't get back up. He had a shovel in his car. The gardeners had been doing landscaping around the yard and the ground was soft, covered with a dense layer of pine mulch. It was all too horribly easy, he said, to bury her and her little suitcase right there."

Andy sighed. "Right there — not ten feet away from where I watched Maggie stand and cry. She knew. She knew exactly what had happened to that girl. There wasn't a sign to be seen, a clue to be found. But she knew."

"You never told her what you'd seen?"

"No. Figured if she wanted me to know, she'd tell me. It seemed to me it was the sort of thing that would be difficult to live with, so I guessed she was used to coming up with . . . other explanations for the things she knew." Andy looked at the other man steadily. "It was fine by me. I'd learned to trust her by then, and to be perfectly honest I don't give a damn if she reads tea leaves or peers into a crystal ball. In five years and hundreds of tough cases, I've never known her to be wrong."

"Never?"

"Never. Oh, there've been times when she was no closer to an answer than we were, but whenever Maggie got one of her *hunches* I knew damned well the case was about to break."

John shook his head slightly. "I don't know what I believe, except that whatever Maggie experiences is obviously very real to her. So why does she do it? Why does she put herself through this kind of trauma, this kind of suffering?"

"You asked me that last week, more or less. I don't know the answer, John, but I'm willing to bet that if you ever find out what it is, you'll have the key to understanding Maggie Barnes."

CHAPTER
NINE

Despite what she'd told John, Maggie hadn't intended to go back out on Monday evening, not after the day she'd had. But a couple of hours' rest, a hot bath, and hot soup all combined to make her feel much more like herself. And restless.

She was used to being alone, more or less. Her father had died before she was born, and Beau's father had departed the scene not long after his birth; Alaina Barnes Rafferty had not been an easy woman to be married to. Or to be the offspring of, come to that.

Neither Maggie nor Beau bore her any malice; she had loved them both, something they had never doubted. But her artistic gifts had caused her more pain than pleasure, demanding much of her time and energy and leaving little for her children. Which was probably why they were so close as adults: growing up they had only had each other.

Still, with differing careers, she and Beau

sometimes went weeks without seeing each other, and since virtually all of Maggie's friends were cops who worked difficult hours, she found herself alone often enough to be accustomed to it. Usually, anyway. But not tonight.

She went into her studio, thinking it might help to work for a while, but since she didn't have a commission at the moment and didn't feel particularly inspired, instead found herself staring broodingly at the single canvas propped on her working easel — blank except for the vague outline of long hair and the indistinct shape of a face.

Unidentifiable.

"I'm losing it, that's the problem," she muttered.

The image was a virtual duplicate of the one in her sketch pad, a few uncertain lines too tentative to provide any sense at all of an individual. She didn't even know for sure that he had long hair, just guessed that he did because both Hollis and Ellen Randall had felt something like that brush against their skin.

Maggie had felt it too.

She shivered and turned on the small stereo system she kept in the studio, filling the silence with quiet, pleasant music. It was dark outside, but the lighting in the studio was excellent, and the music made the room feel warm and . . . safe.

At least for now.

Frowning, Maggie moved the canvas off the easel and put a clean blank one in its place. She went to her worktable and chose brushes and tubes of color, mixing the latter on her palette without really thinking about what she was doing.

When her tools were ready, she stood before the easel and gazed at the blank canvas for a moment, then took a deep breath and closed her eyes. Beau said she could do this if she tried, if she could trust in her own abilities enough to let go of her conscious control. It wasn't an easy thing to do, and so far Maggie had resisted every attempt.

But as she stood there with her eyes closed, listening to the soft music and keeping her mind as blank as possible, a strange thing began to happen. It was almost as if she drifted away, almost as if she fell asleep and began dreaming. The dream was peaceful, with soft music in the background and the sound of her own steady breathing up close, and all she could see was blue sky stretching forever, the expanse broken only intermittently by fluffy white clouds. She seemed to be far away, and getting farther away moment by moment, and yet she could still hear the music, hear herself breathing, smell the familiar scents of her studio.

It was a very peculiar feeling. It seemed to last only a moment or two, yet she had the strong sense of the passage of time, and when she opened her eyes abruptly with an odd, jarring sensation of shock, it was to find herself standing at her worktable with her back to the easel. Her palette lay before her, covered with gobs and blobs of paint she didn't remember selecting.

When she looked at her hands, it was to see more paint, bright and dark flecks and smears of color on her skin from wrists to fingertips and, even more, heavily spattered on and completely ruining her sweater. As if she'd been working hard, and for a long time. When she touched the paint on her sweater hesitantly, most of it felt nearly dry to the touch. She was using acrylic paints rather than oil, but still . . .

Her fingers felt stiff, cramped, and there was an ache between her shoulder blades, the sort of ache she got only after hours working at her easel.

There was no clock in the studio.

Maggie fumbled to push up the paint-encrusted sleeve of her sweater to see her watch and was deeply disturbed to see it was after midnight.

Hours. She'd been in here for hours.

She gripped the edge of the worktable, conscious now that her breathing was no longer steady, that she was acutely aware of the canvas on the easel behind her. She could feel it there, whatever it was she had painted in a state of virtual unconsciousness, almost as if it leaned toward her, reached out for her . . .

She was terrified to turn around.

"Paint on canvas," she whispered. "That's all it is. Just paint on canvas. Probably not even a recognizable image. How could it be, when my eyes were closed, when I wasn't thinking of anything in particular?" Maggie drew a deep breath. "There won't be anything there, except paint on canvas. That's all."

But even with those reasonable words said aloud like a mantra, it took all the self-command Maggie could muster to force herself to turn around and look at what she had done.

"Jesus," she whispered, staring in horror at what was unquestionably the best work she'd ever done.

The painting, all too hideously complete, was done almost entirely in slashes of black and flesh tones and scarlet, yet for all the limited use of color the central image looked so lifelike that it might have breathed.

If it could have breathed.

The woman lay sprawled against a dim, indistinct background, her wispy dark hair fanned out around her head and visible only because of the blood streaking the strands. Her head was slightly tilted and turned so that she seemed to gaze at the watcher in a mute plea for help that had never come.

Between her open, bruised, and puffy eyelids, more darkness peered out because her eyes were gone, the empty sockets seeping blood that trickled down her temples.

Her sensitive mouth was slightly open, the delicate lines of her lips misshapen by swelling and bruising, and another thin line of blood trailed down over her chin and jaw. On the other side of her face, an ugly bruise marred the high cheekbone.

She was naked, her body so petite it almost seemed childlike with its small, high breasts and gently rounded belly. But there was nothing childlike about what had been done to her. The breasts bore more horrible bruising and one nipple was missing, the ragged wound showing the unmistakable marks of teeth. The rounded belly had also been sickeningly mutilated, laid open from the sternum to the pubic bone in a single deep slash agape in wet scarlet.

Her legs were splayed wide, knees slightly raised, and more blood streaked her thighs and had pooled between them in a congealing puddle of crimson and maroon.

Around one delicate ankle was a thin gold chain from which dangled a tiny gold heart.

It was that final poignant detail that shattered Maggie's frozen horror. She dropped to her knees, fighting to keep from retching, unable to tear her eyes away from the painting, from the dreadful image of a dead woman she had never seen before in her life.

TUESDAY, NOVEMBER 6

It was something of a joke around the department that Luke Drummond was proud of the fancy conference room in his station, proud of the wide, polished table that could seat more than twelve in nicely comfortable chairs and provide them lots of elbow room in which to . . . do whatever it was he pictured them doing in the room. Nobody had ever been quite clear on what that might be.

The truth was, the room had never been used for anything more than an occasional hand of poker when the late shift got bored. Until now, anyway.

Andy decided it was high time the conference room was actually used for something remotely resembling police work, and since both the usual investigatory methods and Scott and Jennifer's work were beginning to pile up paper they needed to keep handy and in some kind of order, it seemed logical to use that space. So Andy commandeered the room and within a couple of hours that morning had efficiently shifted the bulk of the files and other paperwork on the investigation from various desks in the bullpen to the conference room.

The room had at least been set up to facilitate such a move, so it was a simple task to have the switchboard reroute relevant calls to the multiline phones in there, and Andy pretty much rerouted himself to the room on a semipermanent basis.

"We also have a bit more privacy in

here," he told Scott and Jennifer when they gathered there shortly before lunchtime. "I won't declare this room off limits to those not actively involved in the investigation, but I will make it known that anything in here is to be considered confidential."

Jennifer shifted a cinnamon toothpick to the other side of her mouth and said, "And by doing so we can hope that they won't think we're nuts or, if they do, that they won't talk about how nuts we are."

Andy shook his head. "I doubt anybody's going to think we're completely nuts, not with this." He nodded toward the bulletin board they had just finished setting up. "We have sketches, photos, or descriptions of four victims in 1934 closely matching four of our victims. That has to be more than coincidence, and it has to mean something."

"Yeah, but what?" Scott wondered.

"That's what we have to determine. Which means we'll use every source we can until we figure it out."

"Does that mean you're telling Garrett about this?" Jennifer asked.

"Yeah. Drummond insisted we keep some of the crime-scene and victim details confidential, but he didn't say a damned thing about our speculation and lines of research. Garrett's smart, and he has sources we can use. So I'm telling him. Maggie too. I'll try to get them both in here this afternoon."

Jennifer tapped the folded newspaper lying on the table before her. "Well, since Garrett got his picture in the paper today and the reporters are hotly speculating that he's *assisting* the police because of his sister being a victim, I imagine you'll be hearing from an unhappy Luke any time now."

Andy sighed. "Yeah, I know. What the hell was I doing letting a civilian into the Mitchell house when our forensics team was still working there, for Christ's sake. I know what he'll say. And if he doesn't like the way I'm running this investigation, he can run it himself."

Jennifer grinned. "Aw, he won't want to do that. Might ruin his nice manicure or get blood on his shoes. If you lean on your acting talents and make like you want to dump it all in his lap, he'll probably make himself scarce for at least the rest of the week."

"It's a thought," Andy said, brightening.

Scott laughed, but said, "Well, we should have plenty to keep us busy. Even running into dead ends takes time."

"No sign of the rest of the files from 1934?" Andy asked.

"Nope. But I haven't stopped looking. If the damned things exist, I'll find them."

"In the meantime," Jennifer said, looking at Andy, "anything new in the search for Samantha Mitchell? Since we've been in here trying to get organized this morning, I hadn't heard."

"No, nothing new. I've got teams out canvassing the neighborhood and every patrol in the city keeping their eyes peeled for that lady. It's like she dropped off the face of the earth."

"What about Maggie's hunch? Did forensics get anything from the Mitchell's game room?"

"A couple of things, yeah. They picked up chemical traces of chloroform on one spot in the carpet not too far from the door, as well as a few strands of Mrs. Mitchell's hair. And there are some very faint signs that he got into that room through a window. There was a short in the security net that the system didn't pick up for some reason."

"A short he caused?" Scott wondered.

"Could be. The really interesting thing is that Mitchell insists his wife never — but never — stayed alone in the house without having the system on. So if the attacker knocked her out with chloroform —"

"Then who deactivated the system at the front door?" Jennifer finished.

Andy nodded. "Exactly. It *was* deactivated at the control panel by the front door, so he either knew or was somehow able to obtain the security code. And it wasn't one even a hacker could figure out just by using the predictable numbers — phone numbers, anniversaries or birthdays, and so on. Our resident electronics wizard says our guy is either very, very good or very, very lucky."

Jennifer said, "And since we already know he beat a top-notch system in order to snatch Laura Hughes, we can assume he's very, very good."

"That would probably be a safe assumption."

Scott said, "How come Maggie tumbled to it being the game room Samantha Mitchell was abducted from? I mean, how come our guys missed it the first time through?"

"I asked them that," Andy said. "They had lots of reasons, but what it all boiled down to is that they concentrated on the expected points of entry like the front and back doors. Needless to say, they won't make that mistake again."

Jennifer smiled slightly. "I'll bet. You can tear the bark off a tree with that temper of yours when you're really pissed, Andy."

"I was really pissed."

"I'm not surprised."

Scott said plaintively, "But how did Maggie know?"

"Instinct," Andy answered promptly. "And she's got enough sense to check the unexpected as well as the expected. Just like you two. Keep it up, will you?"

Scott nodded, faint puzzlement still lingering on his face.

Andy decided he'd make a lousy poker player.

Jennifer said, "The other victims were found within forty-eight hours of being abducted, so if it is our guy, we should know something by tomorrow."

"Yeah," Andy said. "Question is, will Samantha Mitchell be a living victim or a dead one?"

To say Maggie hadn't slept well was an understatement, and she was feeling unusually raw and edgy when she went to Beau's house on Tuesday morning. She let herself in and made her way to the studio, calling out hello as she went.

Beau glanced up from the portrait he was working on and said immediately, "Have some coffee."

The pot was already on the worktable, along with two cups and the milk Maggie preferred.

"So you knew I was coming," she muttered, pouring herself a cup and sitting down.

"I thought you might be, yeah."

"Yeah?"

"Yeah. Call it a hunch."

"Goddammit, Beau!"

He smiled slightly. "Okay, it was more than a hunch."

"I could really dislike you sometimes, you know that?"

"I know. I'm sorry, Maggie."

She sat in silence for some minutes, drinking her coffee and watching him paint. Then she sighed a bit raggedly. "She's dead, Beau. Samantha Mitchell is dead. And her baby with her."

He paused to wipe off one of his brushes, gazing at her soberly. "I'm sorry about that too. Have they found her body yet?"

"No. But they will."

"When?"

"You tell me." She stared at him challengingly.

He returned to his painting but after a moment said, "Tomorrow, I think. Early tomorrow. Or maybe late tonight. Hard to tell."

"Do you know where?"

Beau was silent.

"Maybe I was wrong. Maybe she's not dead yet. If we could find her as soon as possible —"

"It wouldn't make any difference," he said softly. "She's dead already, Maggie. You know she's dead already."

Maggie knew, but she'd been hoping . . . After a long moment, she said, "Yesterday at her house, while I was walking through, I felt her. And when he grabbed her . . . she was so scared. So scared. For herself. For her baby. She knew neither one of them would survive. From the instant he grabbed her, she knew."

Beau painted for a moment, then asked, "Did she know who he was?"

"The same way I know who he is. Not a face, not a name. Just evil. Just evil alive and walking around pretending to be human. I have to stop him. I have to."

"Yes."

"And there isn't much time left. I feel that too. More and more with every day that passes. If I don't stop him soon, it'll be too late. It's my last chance, Beau."

"You don't know that."

"Do you?"

"No."

She laughed without humor. "If you did know, would you tell me?"

"Probably not."

"Free will again."

"Yes. Free will." Leaving his painting finally, Beau cleaned his brushes and palette, then fixed himself a cup of coffee and joined her. "You're doing the best you can, Maggie. It's all you can ask of yourself."

"It isn't enough."

"It will be. Trust yourself. Trust your abilities and your instincts."

She looked at him steadily. "Yesterday was a real . . . bitch of a day. First interviewing Hollis and then walking through the Mitchell house. And it got worse. It actually got worse. I painted something last night. I closed my eyes and cleared my mind the way you told me to, and I painted something horrible. It was inside me, Beau. That image, dark and bloody, was in my head, a part of my soul. I could almost . . . feel her die."

He didn't look surprised and merely nodded. "I told you it would probably happen."

"Not like that. You didn't tell me it would be like that."

"You're an artist, you think — and feel — in images. It's natural."

"*Natural?* What's natural about painting the corpse of a tortured, mutilated woman? A woman I've never met, never even seen?"

His voice remained calm. "You have to try to distance yourself, Maggie, or this is going to destroy you."

She drew a breath and struggled to keep her voice level. "I told you once before that I was afraid. It's . . . blinding me, I think. I don't know what to do next."

Beau hesitated, then said, "It isn't your fight alone, you have to remember that. Stop trying to do it all yourself, Maggie. Let them help you. Let him help you."

After a moment, Maggie nodded. "I'll try." She pushed her cup away and got to her feet.

Gazing into his coffee cup, Beau said almost absently, "You might want to show Garrett the painting."

Just the idea made Maggie feel even more raw. "Why? Why should I show him . . . that . . . in me?"

"Call it a hunch," Beau said.

". . . So that's what we have so far."

Quentin frowned at the stacks of papers and files spread out on the conference table in the parlor, then looked at Maggie again. "Not a whole hell of a lot, but probably as much as the investigating officers."

Kendra said, "He didn't mean that the way it sounded."

Quentin lifted his brows. "How did it sound?"

"Arrogant," she explained. "We've only been here a few days, and we're claiming to have as much info as the cops who've been on the case for months. Use your head, Quentin."

"You're a lot more fun when you're typing something," he told her.

"And you wouldn't rattle on like this if you didn't have a dozen cups of coffee in your system. I keep telling you, caffeine is not your friend."

"I am *not* wired."

"Want me to point out how many times you paced the length of the table while you talked?"

John said, "Ignore the byplay. Apparently, it's their way of working together."

"Yeah, I got that," Maggie said. She was sitting at the far end of the conference table near the windows, chin in hand. "But could we call a truce, guys? Andy wants

John and me back at the station this afternoon, and it'd be nice if I got all this clear in my mind so I'll have my story straight just in case any awkward little questions come up."

Quentin grinned at her. "Walking both sides of the street beginning to bug you?"

"Let's just say I'd feel a lot happier if Andy, at least, was in on this parallel investigation of ours. For one thing —" She broke off, wondering irritably if she had any hope at all of keeping things straight.

"For one thing," John finished calmly, "he and his detectives do have — or think they have — something new. Something he's told neither you nor me."

Maggie looked at him. "So you caught that?"

"For a cop, Andy has a very readable face. Either that, or he wanted both of us to guess there was something and press him to find out what it is."

She thought about it, then nodded slowly. "Maybe. Without Luke Drummond holding him on a leash, I think Andy would use just about any resource he could get his hands on to cage this animal."

Quentin said, "So given his druthers, he'd grant you two complete access?"

"I think so, yeah. As a matter of fact, I

don't think he'd have too much of a problem with a couple of FBI agents working quietly behind the scenes to help."

"He wouldn't think we were stepping on his toes?"

Maggie shook her head immediately. "Not Andy. Unlike Drummond, Andy's not the least bit political, and he doesn't give a damn who breaks a case or gets the credit for it, just as long as the bad guys get put away. He's a cop to his bones."

"The best kind," Quentin said.

"Yeah. Which is why I don't think he'd protest too much if he found out about you two. With Drummond breathing down his neck and hell-bent not to call in outside help, the fact that you guys are here unofficially is all to the good, as far as Andy's concerned."

John said, "And if Drummond does somehow find out, I'll take the flak. He's already pissed at my interference, and today's newspapers won't make him any happier. I might as well make him good and mad while I'm at it. He can get royally pissed at me for acting without authority and he won't have to blame any of his people for going behind his back."

Quentin glanced at his partner, then said

to John, "It's up to you two, of course, but if this detective is likely to be open to our involvement, we say let's tell him. In all honesty we'd prefer at least one cop on the inside and in a position of authority to know we're involved. It would certainly make sharing information easier and more profitable — and it'll undoubtedly make our little jaunt out here more palatable to Bishop."

Maggie frowned slightly. "Bishop?"

"Our boss," Quentin explained. "Bishop leads our unit at Quantico."

If anything, Maggie's frown deepened. She studied Quentin for a moment, then turned her gaze to Kendra. Abruptly, she asked, "You wouldn't happen to be psychic too, would you?"

Without a blink or a hesitation, Kendra said, "What I am we usually term 'adept,' used more to mean skilled than expert. I'm very mildly telepathic, but I tend to be able to pick up more from objects than people."

"And this unit of yours is entirely made up of . . . adepts?"

Quentin also didn't hesitate. "More or less. We have some support people who barely qualify as adepts, but most of the field agents are. Varying abilities and strengths. We use our abilities as just another tool to investigate crimes. Needless to say, it's something we generally keep quiet about, at least publicly."

Kendra murmured, "You understand why, of course."

Maggie smiled. "Oh, of course. It's not exactly something the Bureau would want to advertise, especially with its other public-relations nightmares of recent years."

"Exactly."

"And then there's the whole believability factor. Telepathy? Precognition? Not what they usually teach in Criminal Investigation Techniques 101. You're not just using unscientific methods, you're practically out in the ether."

Quentin grinned. "Sometimes even further out. One day I'll have to introduce you to a young medium we know — who talks to the dead."

"I can hardly wait."

"She's convincing, believe me. But for now, yes, traditional cops tend to frown on what they don't understand, even with a solid success record like ours. So even though we're billed as using 'unconventional investigative methods,' we tend to stick to traditional police work as much as possible."

"Mmm. So you generally pretend to be

conventional agents with . . . a few lucky breaks and a little intuition? I'll bet you guys have a hell of a time coming up with reasonable explanations for how you know the things you know."

"It can be challenging," Quentin admitted.

"Yes, I imagine it can. And you're letting me in on it because I am — presumably — psychic as well?"

"We wanted all our cards on the table," Kendra said. "In our experience, psychics outside our unit become much more comfortable working with us once they understand that *we* understand what they've been going through."

Maggie glanced at John, who was expressionless, then lifted a brow at Kendra. "And do you understand?"

"Frankly, you're a bit outside even our experience, Maggie. We have an empath in the unit, but he's nothing like as strong as you seem to be."

"Or as . . . uniquely focused," Quentin added. "Is it only violent experiences you pick up on?"

Unlike the two of them, Maggie did hesitate before replying, but finally shrugged and said, "That's strongest, maybe because that's where I've had to concentrate all these years. Places where violent events have happened, people who've experienced trauma and violence. I can usually sense other emotions when I try, but more dimly, and they don't . . . affect me . . . the way violence and pain do."

Matter-of-fact but not without sympathy, Quentin said, "Not only is there actual pain and all the traumatic emotions, but it drains you just the way it would if the event had actually happened to you."

She nodded. "Sometimes I just get a little tired, but other times I seem to need to sleep ten or twelve hours before I feel normal again."

"And it's all the senses, isn't it? You feel what they did, see what they did, smell what they did — everything."

Again, Maggie nodded, very conscious now of John's silent attention. He'd told her that Andy had confirmed what she had picked up at the Mitchell house the previous day, but he hadn't said whether the confirmation made any difference to him. And in the presence of the two agents she was guarding herself, so she had no idea what he was feeling.

Kendra said, "It's the same when you bond with victims? When they relive what happened to them?"

"More or less. Sometimes their own minds have . . . dulled the sharp edges of the pain, and it isn't so intense. Other times their emotions nearly overwhelm me, and I can barely concentrate to ask them questions or listen to their answers." She drew a breath. "Not a lot of fun."

Deliberately, Quentin asked, "So why do you do it? Why do you put yourself through that kind of ordeal, Maggie?"

"Why do you?" she challenged.

He smiled faintly. "My abilities don't hurt me, generally speaking. I don't suffer. But you do. So why do you keep opening yourself up to that kind of suffering?"

Before Maggie could even begin to answer, John's cell phone rang, and she felt his gaze on her as she muttered not quite under her breath, "Saved by the bell."

John said hello, then listened for a moment. His face hardly changed expression, but something in his voice warned them when he said, "All right. We're on our way."

It was Quentin who asked, "What's happened?"

"Andy wants us at the station now." John kept his gaze on Maggie. "Thomas Mitchell just received what appears to be a ransom note from the man who kidnapped his wife."

CHAPTER
TEN

Andy greeted them at his desk but led the way immediately to the conference room, where two more detectives rose to meet them. Or, rather, to meet John; Maggie obviously knew both and murmured hello to Jennifer Seaton and Scott Cowan and then took a seat at the long table while they were being introduced to John.

He wasn't so preoccupied by meeting new people that he didn't notice Maggie had isolated herself, choosing a chair between two others that each held large file boxes. When the introductions were over and everybody sat down, he deliberately moved one of the file boxes and sat beside Maggie.

She sent him a quick glance but otherwise kept her gaze fixed on the blank bulletin board placed several feet away from the other side of the table. He didn't have a clue what she was thinking, but he knew stress when he saw it and he saw it in Maggie. From the moment she'd shown up at the hotel this morning, he'd been absolutely certain that something else had happened, something that had shaken her badly.

Was this it? Had Maggie realized somehow that she'd been wrong in saying Samantha Mitchell was in the hands of the Blindfold Rapist? Or was it something else?

"I have three more detectives on the case full-time," Andy told them, "but right now they're out trying to find out if this note is legit. Since the rest of us are here, I thought now would be the time to go over a few things." He pushed the plastic-bagged piece of paper toward John. "I want to know what you two think about this."

The note was block-printed on what looked like an ordinary sheet of notepaper torn from a pad, and the message was chillingly simple.

IF YOU EVER WANT TO SEE
YOUR WIFE AGAIN
IT'LL COST YOU 100K

There were three smears on the paper — two that looked like black fingerprint powder, and one that looked like blood.

"Prints?" John asked.

"Yeah, couple of real clear ones. One of my guys was with Mitchell when he got the note, so it was handled properly. The prints likely belong to whoever sent it. We're checking the state and federal fingerprint databases. So far, no matches, but we just got started looking."

John slid the note over to Maggie. "Is he stupid, or just an amateur?"

"Well, that's part of the problem we're having with this whole kidnap thing. Mitchell, he's all ready to pay the so-called ransom, but we've got quite a few questions. I'm sure you can guess what they are."

"Why a kidnapper would have asked for such a ridiculously small sum from somebody like Mitchell," John said. "Why he would carelessly put his own fingerprints on the note. How somebody that seemingly incompetent could have beaten a first-class security system in order to snatch Samantha Mitchell out of her own house, leaving virtually no evidence behind. How am I doing?"

"Full marks," Andy said. "That's pretty much what we thought."

Maggie pushed the bag away from her and murmured, "But?"

Andy nodded. "But. That is blood on the note, and the type matches Samantha Mitchell's. We can try for a DNA match, but that'll take weeks. My hunch is the situation's going to get resolved long before we'd get the results."

"How was the note delivered?" John asked.

"Just stuck in his mailbox on top of the regular mail. Nobody saw anyone near the box except for the usual mail carrier, and she swears she didn't put it there. I'm inclined to believe her, especially since she's been at her job for fifteen years without so much as an unauthorized sick day."

John thought about that. "Nobody saw anyone . . . I assume we're talking about the press? Don't they still have the house staked out?"

"Yeah. And tried to interview my guys instead of answering the questions, damn them. But the bottom line is, they didn't see anything unusual. Not especially surprising. With a bunch of them milling around near the end of the driveway — and the mailbox — it wouldn't have been too hard for somebody with a camera around his neck to wander past the box and pause for a half a minute without being noticed."

Maggie stirred slightly. "Andy, do you believe Samantha Mitchell was kidnapped and is being held for ransom?"

"Can't say that I do. Everything we know about her disappearance matches the M.O. of our guy, and if I'm certain of anything, it's that he doesn't give a flying fuck about money."

Jennifer said, "Scott and I agree with Andy. We think the rapist snatched her, and he's not going to get all helpful and leave us his fingerprints at this late date. So the question is, who sent the note?"

"Somebody who knows the rapist?" John suggested. "Or, hard as it is to believe, somebody who read all the news reports and decided to try to cash in on a disappearance?"

Andy grimaced. "That last is the most likely, we think. Helluva world we live in."

"What about the blood?" John asked.

Scott shrugged. "The guy could have pricked his own finger and just got lucky with the blood type. I mean, except for the way he left the note without being seen, he isn't coming across as too bright, is he?"

"There's another possibility," Maggie said. She wasn't looking at any of them but gazing at the bagged note. "The blood could be hers. Whoever sent the note . . .

239

could have found her body."

Andy looked at her steadily. "You think she's dead?"

"Yes. I think she's dead."

John was also watching her face, and as she spoke he felt a little chill of certainty. Maggie didn't just think Samantha Mitchell was dead.

She knew it.

Kendra slipped back into the passenger side of the car and said, "Let's go — before one of those guys back there decides to ask for a closer look at my I.D." She removed the camera strap from around her neck and returned the camera to its case.

Quentin pulled the car smoothly away from the curb half a block up from the Mitchell house. "That I.D. is designed to stand up to scrutiny, you know."

"Even so, no reason to push it."

"Okay. So, did you get anything useful?"

"The reporters all bought the kidnapping story — at first. But whether because the Blindfold Rapist is better copy or somebody just reasoned it out, now they're pretty much agreed that it's probably just an attempt to cash in on the disappearance."

"Mmm. Any ideas on who might be making that attempt?"

"None they were willing to share with me."

"You mean your charm had no effect on them?"

"Not so you'd notice."

"Or your big brown eyes?"

"I suppose they all prefer blue."

"Or your uniquely flexible mind?"

"That barely impresses you." Kendra pulled a small black address book from her shoulder bag and began turning the pages. "What we need is someone who knows the disreputable side of Seattle a lot better than we do."

"You forget — Seattle was my childhood home."

"I didn't forget. But you've been away from here — what? — twenty years?"

"About that, but I come back for regular visits."

"Still, I imagine things might have changed around here since your childhood."

"Sure, which is why I keep in touch with people who have a very firm finger on the pulse of this place. Joey, for instance. Joey is a living testament to the adage that only the good die young. Because if the bad died young, Joey would have dropped in his crib."

"You think he might have sent that note?"

"No, figuring out and executing a plan of any kind would take Joey longer than a few hours. Give him a few weeks, and he might come up with something, but not a few hours. I think he might know who did come up with the kidnapping idea, though. If anybody would know, it would be Joey."

"And do you know where we can find him?"

"Give me ten minutes," Quentin said.

It turned out to be an optimistic estimate, but knowing her partner, Kendra was ready for that. In a distinctly seedy neighborhood, she waited patiently at the end of a long alley Quentin had disappeared into, keeping one eye on their car while standing ready to back him up if need be. For the half hour or so he was gone, she politely refused three invitations for a "date" and not so politely warned off an interested pimp.

When Quentin reappeared abruptly, she said, "You picked this corner deliberately, didn't you?"

He grinned. "Still a busy place for the trade, huh?"

"Bastard," she said without heat.

"Well, I knew you could take care of

yourself. Think of it as a compliment."

"Yeah, right." She eyed him and waited.

"Okay, I've got to know," he said. "What was the top offer?"

"You seriously expect me to tell you what several lonely men offered for my body?"

"Several?"

"Don't push it, Quentin."

He grinned again. "Who knows when we might have to go undercover in the trade, and I'd need to know your street worth, that's all."

"Go to hell," she said politely. "Did you or did you not find out where Joey is?"

"I did."

"Then let's go."

Five minutes later, sitting beside him in their car, Kendra said, "Five hundred."

Astonished, Quentin said, "As much as that? Jeez, either the streets around here have changed since my day, or inflation must be a real factor."

"Bastard!" she said, this time with considerable heat.

John closed the folder containing the forensics report on the Mitchell house as well as case notes and a photograph of the missing woman, lifted a questioning brow at Maggie, and when she shook her head pushed the file back across the table to Andy. "Thanks for letting me take a look," he said. "Not that I see anything helpful."

"That's the way it always is with the disappearances. Not a damned thing to go on. And not much more when the women are found."

She knew it wasn't a pointed reference, but Maggie nevertheless said, "I wish I could give you a sketch of this animal, Andy. But he's been so careful, none of the victims have been able to remember any helpful details."

"I know that, Maggie."

"I should try talking to Ellen Randall again. I wanted to give her a few days to calm down after —"

"After I intruded and messed things up," John finished. "I really am sorry about that."

Maggie nodded. "I know. She probably wasn't ready to talk to me then anyway. And I doubt she'll be able to give me anything useful. But I have to try. I'll call her this afternoon, find out if she'll meet with me, maybe tomorrow."

"Here?" Andy asked.

"I think I'll leave it up to her. She might be far more comfortable at home."

"Well, let me know if you'll need an interview room."

"Okay."

Andy tapped the Mitchell file with one finger. "So that's where we stand," he said. "On the Mitchell investigation, at any rate. I've got people out trying to find out what they can about this damned note, and I've got people looking for Samantha Mitchell — dead or alive. Since there's not much more we can do in either case, at least for the time being, there's something else we wanted to discuss with you two."

John glanced at the two younger detectives, then looked steadily at Andy. "I had a feeling there was."

"I wasn't keeping anything back because of orders but because this is . . . pretty farfetched, John."

"In what way?"

Andy leaned back and gestured slightly toward the other cops, clearly inviting them to explain.

Jennifer said, "We were sure this guy was picking particular women, but with all the varied descriptions of them and where he grabbed them, nothing pointed to how, to any sort of common denominator. And even though we're pretty sure he's been active only for six months or so, we kept hearing from the shrink that his ritual was too well established to be so recent. So Scott and I started wondering if maybe he was getting his ideas from somewhere specific. Like maybe accounts of old, unsolved crimes."

"I wouldn't call that far-fetched," John commented. "In fact, it sounds pretty reasonable."

"It is reasonable — except for what we found when we started digging through files."

"Which was?" Maggie asked.

John glanced at her quickly, suddenly aware of another of those odd little certainties; this was something else she knew.

"Which was a little creepy," Jennifer said. "What we found was a very similar string of rape–murders that took place here in Seattle in 1934. Six women for certain, though possibly eight in all, killed within an eighteen-month period."

"So he is copying earlier crimes," John said.

"Here's the creepy part." Jennifer rose from the table and went to flip one of the bulletin boards so that they could all see the other side. Under the heading 2001, four photographs were pinned in a vertical row, pictures of Laura Hughes, Christina

Walsh, Ellen Randall, and Hollis Templeton. Beside that row and under the heading 1934 was another row, this one containing three sketches and two photos.

"You'll notice," Jennifer said, "that the first sketch done in 1934 shows a woman virtually identical to Laura Hughes. The second sketch is pretty amateur and didn't help them I.D. the victim, but it and the description of her taken together closely match Ellen Randall. The third sketch is backed up by a photograph, and as you can see, this victim resembled Hollis Templeton. We only have a crime-scene photo of the fourth victim, but the description matches Christina Walsh."

Maggie said, "He's picking look-alikes."

Andy said, "I doubt it's coincidence that these women just happened to be attacked in much the same way as their virtual doubles were almost seventy years ago."

John said, "So he has access to police files?"

"Maybe. But there've been books written about unsolved crimes here in the city, so we can't be sure he would have had to use police files."

Jennifer said, "And there's something else." She told them about the note found in her car, finishing, "Needless to say, we don't know who wrote the note, how they got into my locked car, or why they picked me. We also don't know if he, she, or it was trying to be helpful or is bent on leading us on a really big wild-goose chase."

"But," Andy said, "we have to assume the 1894 date could be important, at least until we prove otherwise. Problem is, we've had no luck running down any files at all from that year. Not really surprising, since Seattle was only founded a few decades earlier."

Maggie said, "Maybe it's . . . some other place. Some other city."

"Maybe," Andy said. "But if it is, I don't see how we have a hope in hell of figuring out where."

Kendra hadn't really pictured Joey in her mind, but she was definitely surprised when they ran him to ground in a crowded backstreet poolroom. It was a disreputable place by and large, where the other patrons scrupulously minded their own business when Quentin strolled up behind a hulking redhead who was pocketing his winnings from a game and tapped him on one meaty shoulder.

"Hey, Joey."

Joey swung around, his fierce expression a neon warning to any sane person.

Quentin, of course, didn't so much as step back. He just smiled that curiously sweet and wholly deceptive smile of his and added, "How've you been?"

Kendra didn't draw her gun, but she kept a hand near it; she had a lot of faith in her partner's abilities, but despite Quentin's height and undoubted strength, Joey was taller and looked as though he could have lifted an all-pro tackle over his head and heaved him across the room.

But it was Joey who backed up a step, a funny little grin twisting his lips. "Oh. Hey, Quentin. Long time no see."

"Oh, it's just been a few months," Quentin said cheerfully. "Still, we have so much to catch up on. What say we step into your office and talk about old times, okay, Joey?"

Without protest and with rather astonishing meekness, Joey turned and led the way to a back hall and an incredibly filthy men's room. Kendra did her best not to touch anything and wondered vaguely if she could throw her shoes away the moment they got out of here; there was something crunching underfoot and she really didn't want to look down and see what it was.

Joey didn't object to her presence, which was hardly surprising since he didn't take his eyes off Quentin.

"You back for good?" he asked, hoping transparently for a negative response.

"Nah, just visiting, as usual. You keeping your nose clean, Joey?"

"Sure I am, Quentin."

Quentin lifted a disbelieving brow.

"Okay, I mighta been in a little trouble here and there, but nothing major."

"You haven't killed anybody else, have you, Joey?"

"No, I swear."

"I can find out if you're lying to me. You know I can."

Joey's lips twisted again in that sick little grin. "Yeah, yeah, I know. Honest, Quentin, I been good. Ask anybody."

"I'll do that, Joey. In the meantime, I'm looking for a little information."

"Okay, sure. Shoot."

"You know about the disappearance of Samantha Mitchell?"

Joey frowned for a moment, gears almost visibly turning, then nodded. "Oh, yeah. S'posed to be another one grabbed by that rapist."

"That's right. But now somebody's claiming to have kidnapped her. And that somebody wants her husband to cough up a ransom."

Joey shifted uneasily. "It ain't me, Quentin."

"Then who is it, Joey? What sorry son of a bitch decided to take advantage of that poor lady's misfortune?"

"I dunno, Quentin, honest."

Gently, Quentin said, "I want you to find out for me, Joey. And I want you to find out fast. Understand?"

Joey nodded. "Okay. Okay, Quentin, I can ask around, sure. Guys owe me some favors, somebody's bound to know what's going on."

Quentin produced a card and handed it to Joey. "The underlined number is my cell phone. Use that to call me as soon as you find out what I want to know."

Joey accepted the card gingerly. "Right. Gimme a couple hours, and I'll see what I can dig up."

"Don't make me wait any longer than that, okay?"

"Sure, sure."

"Call me quick enough, and I might not have time to ask around and find out what you've been up to, Joey."

Once again, the gears turning behind Joey's round blue eyes were almost visible, and his hopeful understanding definitely was. "Yeah. Okay, yeah, I got it. I'll call, Quentin. Count on it."

They left him there, his back literally pressed up against the grimy wall between two disgusting sinks. He showed no inclination to follow them out and, in fact, when Kendra glanced back as they were leaving the poolroom, he still hadn't come out of the bathroom.

"That is one very nervous incredible hulk," she commented as they got in the car. "I'd swear he was terrified of you."

Quentin smiled as he started the car but didn't respond to the comment.

Kendra eyed him, then said, "So Joey's an old childhood pal, huh?"

"More of a childhood acquaintance, you could say."

"Uh-huh. I don't suppose you'd want to tell me about this interesting childhood of yours?"

"Oh, it's not interesting. Boring, really."

"Really?"

"Sure."

"Mmm. Somehow I doubt that. But never mind — for now. Who did Joey kill?"

"I think that's 'whom,' " he said thoughtfully.

"Stop correcting my grammar and answer the question."

"Yes, ma'am. Joey killed his father. Shotgun blast full in the face."

"Jesus. And he's running around loose? Our judicial system sucks."

"Not so much in this case. Joey was eleven when it happened, and his old man had just beaten his mother into unconsciousness for about the hundredth time. Joey walked in on it, took one look — and something snapped. He very coolly went into the bedroom, found and loaded the old man's gun, then came back and blew him away."

Kendra turned slightly in her seat to study her partner. "That was his story?"

"Well, his story for the record was that he got the gun only to defend his mother and that when his father charged toward him with murderous rage in his evil face, Joey acted purely in self-defense."

"The evidence backed him up?"

"It didn't contradict his version of events. Especially with a witness testifying on his behalf."

"A witness?"

"Yeah. A classmate had come home with him to borrow a schoolbook. That was back when Joey actually showed a glimmer of turning into something better than his old man. Anyway, the witness backed him up, and Joey got probation and therapy."

"The therapy doesn't seem to have done him much good, if he's been in trouble since then."

"No, and he dropped out of school as soon as he could outrun the truant officer. Given his genetic heritage and environment, not so surprising. His father really was one of those pure evil bastards life sometimes produces, and I hear his grandfather was worse. But Joey got enough of his mother's blood — and her influence — to make him a lot more manageable. He'd con you six ways from Sunday and pick your pockets if he found you unconscious or dead, but he's terrified of his own strength and temper; he doesn't want to turn out like his old man. To his credit, he usually manages not to turn violent."

Kendra nodded. "So why is he wary of you? Afraid you'll tell the truth after all these years?"

Quentin smiled faintly. "I wouldn't. But the possibility does help me keep Joey in line."

"Even from the other side of the country?"

"Well, I try to come back here at least

once a year or so. And I always look him up, find out what he's been into." He chuckled. "Ever since I joined the Bureau, Joey's kept his nose pretty clean. I think he's seen one too many Hollywood distortions of the power of the FBI."

"So your badge helps keep him in line as well."

"So far. Joey's down as a one-time impulse killer, and I'd like to keep it that way. It's the difference between being bad and crossing over into being evil."

"Mmm." Kendra studied him a moment longer, then said, "Why do I get the feeling your enigmatic past contains a number of stories like Joey's?"

"Probably your vivid imagination."

She sighed, unsurprised. "That was a filthy place you dragged me into."

"Sorry about that."

Kendra turned her gaze to the windshield. "You owe me a new pair of shoes."

With their questions left hanging unanswered in the air but providing a definite spur, both John and Maggie volunteered to stick around for a few hours and help go through the file boxes in search of more information about the earlier crimes. Within an hour, they had files stacked on every available chair but nothing else to show for their efforts.

It was nearly one when Scott and Jennifer left to bring back a late lunch for them, and John took the opportunity to tell Andy about Quentin and Kendra.

"Shit," Andy said, though clearly more startled than angry. "FBI agents — and unofficial? I didn't know the Bureau did anything unofficially."

"They belong to a fairly new unit of investigators and have a bit more autonomy than most. They're very good, Andy, and completely trustworthy. And they aren't interested in taking any credit no matter who breaks the case."

"It was damned officious of you, John."

"I know. And I'll apologize if you want me to — not for calling them in but for not telling you I was going to."

"Gee, that's big of you."

John chuckled.

Unwilling to relent just yet, Andy gave Maggie a hard stare. "You knew about this too?"

She met his gaze squarely. "I don't much care who gets the credit either, Andy. Or who helps. Just as long as we get this animal in a cage where he belongs."

"Drummond's going to shit a brick."

Andy sighed. "He's already blasted me once today, John, thanks to you. Do me a favor and keep that famous profile of yours off the front page from now on, will you?"

"I'll do my best. And none of us wants Drummond to find out too soon, believe me. If and when he does find out, it'll be me who called them in — not you or anyone under Drummond."

Andy eyed him wryly. "You got a death wish?"

"I can handle Drummond." John smiled. "I've been handling men like him for fifteen years."

"He's got a lot of juice in this town, John."

"So have I. I just haven't used much of it yet."

"Okay, okay. As long as you understand he will *not* be happy. And as long as none of my people gets the blame."

"They won't."

"In that case — when do I get to meet these agents of yours? I like to know who I'm working with."

"We can meet up at the hotel whenever you like, but Quentin and Kendra are out now trying to find out all they can about this supposed kidnapping. They didn't think it was any more likely than your people did, but like Maggie said — whoever sent that note might know something about Samantha Mitchell, and we need to find out what that might be."

"Think they can find out something before my people can?" It wasn't — quite — a challenge.

John smiled. "Well, let's just say I've learned never to bet against Quentin. One way or another, he usually finds what he goes looking for."

CHAPTER
ELEVEN

Andy decided to strictly limit who in his department would know of the FBI agents' involvement, choosing to tell Scott and Jennifer, but not the other detectives.

"All my people have busted their asses on this case," he told Maggie and John, "but these two kids took some initiative *and* thought outside the box. Besides, I know for a fact they'll be happy about it — and not everybody would."

Scott and Jennifer were definitely pleased, especially when John told them of both the agents' profiling expertise, Kendra's computer skills, and the full range of databases available to them with federal authority.

"Maybe they'll be able to track down why the 1894 date is important. If it is," Jennifer said. "In the meantime — Andy, if it's okay with you, I'm heading over to the Central precinct. Their file clerk isn't *absolutely* sure, but there might be some really old file boxes in their storage room. I want to check them out, see if I can find those missing 1934 files or possibly some from 1894."

Andy looked at the stacks of files on the conference table and sighed. "Yeah, go ahead. Nothing in this mess is helping us."

Scott asked, "Jenn, want me to come along?"

She grinned at him. "Oh, no, pal. You get to put all these useless files back where they belong and then try to find out what happened to the ones the North precinct clerk *swears* were lost in the move to their new building."

With a grimace, Scott said, "It is not fun being the low man on the totem pole." But he seemed cheerful enough as he picked up a file box and followed Jennifer from the room.

"They need to be busy," Andy told Maggie and John with a sigh. "Neither one of them has been a detective long enough to be comfortable with the realization that seventy-five percent of police work is sitting around — either going through papers, trying to piece together a jigsaw puzzle of facts, or just trying to talk through the problem until it starts to make sense."

"Sometimes I think most of life is like that," John offered wryly.

"I don't blame them for being restless," Maggie said, her brooding gaze fixed on the bulletin board. "It's hell just sitting here waiting. Wondering when the phone is going to ring."

When it did at that moment, Andy lifted a brow at her and scooped it up. He said, "Brenner," and listened for several minutes, and didn't have to mutter, "Oh, Christ," for everyone in the room to know the news was bad.

As soon as he hung up, John guessed, "Samantha Mitchell?"

"No," Andy said heavily. "The bastard's having a busy week. We've got another missing woman."

In the storage room of the Central precinct station, Jennifer found a lot of files. A lot of old files, some going all the way back to the 1890s. But she didn't find anything of interest for 1894; there had been relatively few murders reported in Seattle around then, and none that even came close to fitting their criteria.

Worse, there was absolutely no sign of any more files for 1934. For that entire decade, as a matter of fact.

After more than an hour of fruitless search, she was dusty, irritable, and had

261

three paper cuts and a headache. She was also inclined to appreciate computers a lot more than she had before all this had started. Those machines had their bad points, but at least they didn't get dust up her nose or slice up her fingers.

She made her way to the station's lounge and sat down with a soft drink, glumly considering her options. They weren't promising. Maybe Scott could track down those files lost in a move to a new building, but it didn't seem likely. Unless she wanted to physically visit every storage room and basement of every station in the city — and she did not — then she had to accept that this particular trail might well have dead-ended.

Jennifer hated dead ends.

She had been so *sure* that something useful would be found in the old files. Oh, she'd been offhand about it with Scott, but from the moment she had seen that first sketch from 1934, the adrenaline rush had been intense. All her instincts had been screaming at her. Finally, after all these months, a break in the investigation.

Except that it wasn't, of course. Dammit.

"Hey, Seaton, what're you doing in our neck of the woods?"

She looked up and managed a faint smile for Terry Lynch as he joined her at the table. "Slumming, of course."

He eyed her consideringly, his deceptively open face as friendly and guileless as always but his gaze sharp. "There's a smear of gray dust on your nose."

"Because you have a filthy storage room," she told him, using a paper napkin to dab at her face.

"I wouldn't be at all surprised. Looking for anything interesting?"

Jennifer gave him an abbreviated version of the Drummond's-got-us-digging-through-old-files speech, perfectly aware that Terry wasn't buying it. Not easy, she reflected silently, to lie to an old partner. Or an old lover.

But he nodded gravely, only his wry blue eyes telling her he knew she was bullshitting him. In a chatty tone, he said, "You guys any closer to getting that rapist?"

"Not so you'd notice."

"Just heard there's another woman missing."

"Oh, shit. Do we know it's him?"

Terry shrugged. "I think your boss is checking it out; any woman goes missing in the city, you guys get the call, you know that."

Jennifer frowned. "If it is him — he's moving a hell of a lot faster."

"Looks like."

She barely hesitated. "Are you hearing anything on the streets, Terry?" He was a patrolman, having failed the detective exam Jennifer had passed with flying colors; the blow to his ego hadn't ended their relationship, but her transfer to another precinct nearly a year ago had.

He wrapped both hands around his coffee cup and hunched his shoulders in the thinking posture she recognized with a pang. "Not really."

"Not really? So you did hear something — but aren't sure it means anything?"

His smile twisted. "Still reading me like a book. Yeah, there was one thing. I was going to call you, but . . . hell, Jenn, it sounds so screwy."

"In this case," she told him dryly, "screwy is beginning to be the order of the day, Terry. What is it?"

"Well, we picked up a transient day before yesterday, got him for creating a disturbance outside a store. You know how it is. Anyway, the guy was mostly drunk and not making a whole lot of sense, but he did say something that caught my attention."

"Which was?"

"Said he'd seen a ghost."

"Oh, come on, Terry — he was drunk and babbling. Probably had the DTs."

Terry nodded. "Yeah, I thought the same thing. But, see, there were a couple of odd things. For one, he didn't sound as crazy as he should have, somehow. And it turns out this guy used to be some hotshot computer expert. Apparently, he had too many problems being bipolar to hold on to his job and ended up on the streets."

"Sad," she commented. "But sadly not so unusual."

"No. But here's the other odd thing. We found him about two blocks away from where that last rape victim was found — Hollis Templeton? And he was staring toward that building while he was babbling about having seen a ghost a few weeks before. So I wondered."

Jennifer wondered too. "Terry . . . is he back on the streets?"

He grimaced. "Afraid so. But my guess is, he'll still be in the area. There's a mission near where we picked him up where guys like him can get a bed and a meal. You might try there. I don't have much of a description to give you — he was so filthy it was hard to say what he looks like. White male, maybe forty, six feet, not more than a hundred sixty, brown and brown." He pulled out his notebook and jotted down the name and address of the mission as well as the man's name, then tore out the sheet and handed it to her.

She accepted it but didn't get up right away. Instead, she said wryly, "You told the file clerk to suggest I just might find what I was looking for here, didn't you, Terry?"

He smiled. "You know how fast word gets around, Jenn. Especially with Scott Cowan calling every station, too innocently asking about old files. So I figured one of you'd show up here sooner or later. I just asked Danny to hint we might have the files you wanted here."

"And then let you know I was coming?"

"Like I said — I was going to call you about it. But I figured you might think I was just using it as an excuse and refuse to even take my call."

"You might have told me all this *before* I spent so much time in your filthy storage room."

"Yeah, I might have."

She got to her feet, smiling. "So you weren't using it as an excuse?"

"Well, not entirely."

"I would have taken the call, Terry."

"Yeah?"

"Yeah." She saluted him casually and left the lounge. It wasn't until she was in her car and looking at the note he'd given her that her smile faded. Another dead-end lead? Would she discover only a poor, damaged man with a damaged mind playing tricks on him?

Or something else?

Maggie wasn't especially eager to walk through the home of the most recent missing woman, but she knew only too well that time mattered; the sooner they could determine with certainty whether Tara Jameson had been abducted by the Blindfold Rapist, the better. So when Andy suggested she and John go along and check out the apartment while he talked to the fiancé who had reported her missing, she agreed.

"Another high-security place," John noted as they stood before the apartment building.

"The bastard seems to like them," Andy agreed sourly. "Our department shrink says it's some kind of challenge, that maybe he goes out of his way to take the women from supposedly secure locations even though he could get them a lot more easily when they went out to grocery shop or something."

"A challenge," John mused.

"Yeah."

"This is an older building, isn't it? I remember it being here twenty years ago."

"Yeah, but it's been updated, at least as far as security goes."

Maggie, who was silently marshaling her energy and trying to narrow her focus in order to retain at least some kind of detachment, only half listened until they entered the building, checked in at the security desk, and Andy asked her where she wanted to start.

"The fiancé is waiting in her apartment with one of my people," he added.

Maggie looked around the bright lobby. "This is awfully public. Is there a service elevator?"

"Yeah, down that hallway there, and it's the only one goes to the basement. It was checked out, even though the security videotapes for both here and the basement access door don't show anyone the guards didn't okay in the areas, and nothing at all suspicious." He nodded toward the security desk and the two guards who were watching them warily.

"Still, it's the most likely way for him to get her out of the building, right?"

"I'd say so."

"Then I want to start there. Go up to her floor in that elevator."

"I'll go with you," John said.

Maggie didn't object, just nodded.

"Eighth floor," Andy told them. "Apartment 804. I'll be there with her fiancé." He headed off toward the regular elevators.

"Are you sure you're up to this?" John asked her abruptly.

"Why wouldn't I be?"

"Maggie, you were upset when you got to the hotel this morning, and you're still upset. When you went home last night, you were more tired than anything else. So I can't help wondering what happened later."

She was only a little surprised; either his perception was sharpening where she was concerned, or else she wasn't hiding her tension very well. "It was . . . a nightmare, that's all. I didn't sleep well."

John had the feeling she had evaded the subject and yet hadn't really lied to him, which made him all the more curious to find out the whole truth. But all he said was "You don't have your sketch pad today. It's the first time."

"So? I don't always carry it."

"I think you usually do, especially during an ongoing investigation."

Maggie shrugged. "Usually — not always."

"So why not today?"

"Maybe I forgot it."

"Did you?"

"No."

"Well, then?"

She looked at him for a moment, then shook her head. "Never mind. The only thing I'm thinking about right now is whether Tara Jameson is or isn't the sixth victim."

John followed as she moved toward the service elevator. "You know, you could just try saying it's none of my business," he commented mildly.

"I guess I could," she murmured.

He decided to take a chance and push just a little bit. "Unless maybe it is. I think you're too honest to lie about that. So is it my business, Maggie? Is there something you're not quite sure you should tell me?"

She glanced at him, then drew a breath and said calmly, "Several things, actually. But not here and not now. Okay?"

Bearing in mind Quentin's warning, John got a grip on his curiosity and nodded. "Okay."

A flicker of gratitude crossed her face, which made him glad he'd agreed. It also made him wonder even more what could have upset her so much; clearly, she wasn't looking forward to telling him about it.

Maggie paused in the hallway a few feet from the service elevator and visibly braced herself.

John was hardly given to premonitions, but a sudden uneasy impulse made him say, "Maybe this isn't a good idea."

She looked at him gravely. "Why not? Because I might *imagine* something terrible? But my own imagination can't hurt me, can it, John?"

He chose his words carefully. "After what I saw in the Mitchell house, I know it's more than imagination, Maggie. I just . . . I don't want to see you hurt like that again."

Maggie almost reached out and touched him, wanting to reassure him, needing to, but stopped herself with an effort she hoped didn't show. Steadily, she said, "If Tara Jameson is the sixth victim, she's the one hurting right now. Whatever I feel is . . . temporary."

"That doesn't mean it hurts any less."

Instead of denying that, she merely said, "I'll be fine." She didn't give him a chance to protest again but went to the service elevator and pushed the button.

The doors opened almost immediately, and before she stepped inside, Maggie cautiously allowed her inner senses to reach in and probe the innocent-looking cubicle.

The elevator was well used, and at first all she got was a jumble of images and flashes of emotion, mostly irritation and low-level anxiety. Not unusual, she knew, for a building in which often harried, stressed people lived and visited.

Then, on the extreme edges of her awareness, she felt something . . . alien.

Dark. Hungry. Cold. So cold . . .

It grew stronger, pressing in on Maggie until she found it difficult to breathe. The darkness was black, viscous, slimy like an oil slick, and it wrapped around the hunger that was cold and grotesque in its twisted urgency.

"Maggie?"

She blinked and looked at John, at his hand gripping her arm, and wondered vaguely what her face looked like to make him feel so much concern. As if a door had closed — or opened — all she could sense right now was him, his worry about her, and other, less defined but no less powerful emotions. "I'm fine," she murmured.

"Are you? Then why did you say that?"

"Say what?" She didn't remember saying anything aloud.

"You said, 'deliver us from evil.' Almost as if you were reciting the prayer."

After a moment, Maggie pulled her arm gently from his grasp. "Funny. I'm not even religious." She tried to focus again, recapture that cold, dark presence, but all she could feel right now was John, even without the physical contact. As if that door that had opened refused now to be closed. And a very large part of her wanted to burrow in and surround herself with him, luxuriate in the warmth and strength that was more familiar and yet more tantalizing than anything she could remember feeling before.

"Maggie, what is it? What did you sense?"

She wondered if he was even aware of the term he had used, but didn't ask. She stepped into the elevator and watched him follow, watched her own finger push the button for the eighth floor. Only when the doors closed did she ask a question of her own. "Have you ever wondered about the nature of evil?"

He was frowning at her, still disturbed. "I don't know that I have. Why? Is that what you felt — evil?"

Maggie nodded. "Evil. Him. He was here. In the elevator. It's . . . the first time I've been able to feel him like that." And she didn't even try to explain how horribly unnerving that was.

"How can you be sure it was him?"

"His . . . desire . . . wasn't normal. The hunger he was feeling."

"Christ," John muttered.

"I'm sorry, but you asked."

His mouth tightened. "What do you sense now?"

"Nothing, really." *You.* "It was just a flash, maybe what he was feeling right before he left the elevator."

"Did he have her with him?"

Maggie frowned, only then realizing. "I don't think so. I mean, I don't think he had her here in the elevator. But I'm certain he'd taken her, because he was . . . anticipating . . . what he would do with her."

"But he didn't take her down in the elevator?"

"No."

As the elevator doors opened on the eighth floor, John was saying, "Then how the hell did he get her out of the building?"

"I don't know."

They both looked around as they moved down the hall toward Apartment 804, John silently gesturing toward the security camera positioned to get a clear view of the entire hallway. It didn't seem possible that anyone could have carried an unconscious woman from any of the apartments without being observed — and taped — by security.

"Somehow, he must have tampered with the system," John said. "But that still doesn't explain how he got her out of the building."

Maggie stopped suddenly, getting another flash of that darkness, as well as a sense of determination, of effort. "It was . . . difficult," she murmured. "It took more strength than he expected."

"What did?" John asked quietly.

"Getting her out of here."

"How did he do that, Maggie?"

Her head turned slowly as she scanned the hallway. Other apartment doors. A few tall green plants and occasional tables and framed prints and mirrors providing pleasant decoration. Fire extinguishers and glassed-in fire hoses placed strategically here and there.

. . . *nearly rusted shut* . . .

Her gaze fixed on a large, gilded mirror halfway between the elevator and Tara Jameson's apartment, and she walked toward it slowly. She was disconcerted when she saw her own reflection, wondering idly why she was so pale and why her eyes looked so peculiar, the pupils enormous. Then John came up behind her, and she stared at his reflection, briefly confused by what she saw.

No, that wasn't right. He was —

. . . *nearly rusted shut* . . .

"Maggie?"

"It's behind the mirror," she said.

He moved her gently aside and used his handkerchief to avoid leaving fingerprints as he carefully pulled the heavy mirror far enough away from the wall so he could look behind it.

"Son of a bitch. An old laundry chute. A big one."

"It was almost rusted shut," Maggie said. "But he got it open."

John eased the mirror back into place, his face grim. "So that's how he did it. Dropped her in this, probably with some kind of cart waiting underneath the chute opening in the basement to catch her. Then took her out."

"That's how he did it. Though I still don't know how the cameras missed him." She swayed slightly and felt John's hand grip her arm. "Sorry. I seem to be a little tired."

"I'm taking you home," he said.

"But I should —"

"Maggie, do you have any doubt that Tara Jameson is the sixth victim?"

"No."

"Then you don't need to go into that apartment."

"Yes, I do. John, what if I can sense more of him in there? What if I can get something that could tell us who he is?"

"You haven't been able to before."

"No — not until the elevator. Not until now. So I have to try."

John muttered a curse under his breath but didn't try to stop her when she moved toward the apartment. He also didn't let go of her arm.

Expecting them, Andy had left the apartment door ajar, and as soon as they crossed the threshold they could hear him just beyond the foyer, talking to Tara Jameson's fiancé.

Maggie eased her arm free of John's grasp and took a step away from him, trying to concentrate, to focus. And this time it was with an almost brutal suddenness that knocked the breath out of her that she felt the wave of terror, the iron arms holding her from behind, the bite of chloroform. And something else.

That cold, dark, twisted hunger. And . . . familiarity.

"Maggie?"

She found herself once more supported by John, his touch bringing her out of it and wrapping her in warmth and worry. Through a throat that felt strangely constricted, Maggie said, "He knows her, John. He knows her."

Hollis?

She came awake abruptly, riding out the usual first moment of panic, of wondering why it was dark and what the weight across her eyes was. Then she was awake, aware. Napping in her chair in front of the window.

Hollis.

"Yes, I'm awake. Why am I awake?"

Hollis, we're running out of time. I've tried, but I can't — she won't let me in.

"Who? Who're you talking about?"

Hollis, listen to me. And trust me, you have to trust me.

"I don't even know your name."

Is that important?

"Well, yes, I think so. If I keep on calling you figment, somebody's going to hear me talking to you and lock me away. At least with a proper name, I can claim you're my imaginary friend. That's probably what you are anyway."

All right, Hollis. I'm — my name is Annie.

"Annie. That's a nice name. Okay, Annie — now, why should I trust you?"

Because you're the only one I've been able to clearly reach. And because you have to help me.

"Help you do what?"

Help me to save her. And there isn't much time. He's seen her now. He's seen her, and he wants her too.

Hollis felt a chill crawl up her spine. "Do you — do you mean the man who attacked me?"

Yes. We have to try to save her, Hollis. I can't reach her. But you can. You have to warn her.

Hollis sat there for a moment longer, her fingers gripping the arms of her chair tightly. But then she swallowed and said, "I'm a blind woman, Annie. What can I do?"

Will you help me?

"Just . . . tell me what you want me to do."

It took hardly more than fifteen minutes to drive to Maggie's small house in a quiet suburb of the city. Since it was dark by the time they arrived, John didn't bother trying to form an impression of the house, just followed her inside.

Almost as soon as they crossed the threshold, he saw her shoulders shift slightly, as though throwing off a burden, and he thought, *Quentin was right again. This place is her sanctuary.*

The living room they stepped into was very much Maggie, he thought. Nothing fancy but obviously good quality, the furniture was comfortable and casual, and the slight clutter of books and magazines combined with the riotous growth of numerous green plants gave the room a cozy, lived-in feeling. There were several framed paintings on the walls and one impressionist-style work propped on the fireplace mantel that struck a vague cord of familiarity in him.

"Nice place," he commented.

"Thanks." Maggie shrugged out of her flannel shirt and tossed it over a chair, and the close-fitting black sweater she wore underneath was a startling reminder to him of just how slender she was.

All that hair and the layers of clothing she invariably wore were both deceptive, he decided. And he had a shrewd hunch she used the camouflage quite deliberately.

"I could use some coffee," she said, pushing her hair back away from her face with both hands in an absent gesture. She was still too pale and obviously tired. "You? I'd offer something stronger, but since I don't drink I usually don't have anything on hand."

"Coffee's fine." John knew he should leave her alone to rest, but he was reluctant to leave her at all.

"Coming up. Make yourself at home." She headed off toward the kitchen.

John followed, saying, "Mind if I keep you company?"

"No, not at all." She gestured toward the three comfortably wide and strong-looking stools on one side of the big center work island and moved toward the sink on the other side. "Have a seat. When I moved in here, I remodeled and commandeered what used to be the dining room for part of my studio. A studio I needed; a dining room was wasted space."

"Your guests probably end up in here anyway," he said, shrugging out of his leather jacket and hanging it over the back of one of the stools as he looked around at the bright, spacious French Country kitchen.

"Usually," she agreed.

He sat down. "I'm not surprised. This is a wonderful room."

She eyed him while measuring what looked like freshly ground coffee into an honest-to-God percolator. "I would have figured you for a different style. More classical, maybe."

He was only a little surprised; she was an artist, after all, and undoubtedly given to summing up personal style fairly quickly. "Generally speaking, that is more my style. But I like a lot of what's popular now. Like this room — French Country, but more French than Country."

Maggie smiled. "I'm not overly fond of roosters or sunflowers, to say nothing of chintz. This works for me."

John watched her more intently than he realized, wanting to take advantage of this time to gain a better understanding of Maggie. It was becoming more important to him, and he didn't bother to ask himself why.

With the coffee started, she got milk from the refrigerator and put it on the work island, then went to get two cups from the cabinet, saying abruptly, "Back at the station, when you were singing the praises of Quentin and Kendra, I notice you didn't mention their psychic abilities."

"No, I didn't."

"Still an unbeliever?" she asked, half mocking and half not.

"I don't even think that was it. Maybe I just wanted to keep everything . . . grounded."

"Grounded in reality?"

"No. Just grounded in the ordinary. The expected. Andy is pretty open-minded, didn't even blink when he found out about you, but I wasn't sure about Scott and Jennifer."

Maggie did understand. Despite his desire to keep "things" grounded, what she sensed in him was doubt and uncertainty . . . and the dawning, reluctant seeds of belief. She had caught a bit of that earlier, which was why she'd decided to talk to him, at least about some of it. Maybe show him the painting . . .

Slowly, she said, "But that's the point, isn't it?"

"What do you mean?"

"You say you want this investigation to be . . . grounded. Grounded in the ordinary, the expected. Only that isn't where it is. That isn't where it is at all."

CHAPTER
TWELVE

"Maggie —"

"Think about it. An ordinary investigation? The best lead we have to date as to how this animal is choosing his victims is found in police files nearly seventy years old. Is that the ordinary, the expected?"

"No," he admitted.

"You yourself brought in an avowed psychic — two, actually — because you knew they could help. And even before that, you wanted my help. Not the help of a police sketch artist. The help of someone with a . . . knack. A paranormal knack." Again, her smile was wry. "Hell, John, you've known from the beginning there was nothing in the least ordinary or expected about any of this."

He thought about that while she stepped away to pour the coffee and had to admit, somewhat ruefully, that she was right. He himself had always had an instinctive knack for choosing the right people for the right task; it was one of the reasons he'd gone so far and achieved so much in business. Why wouldn't it apply to this situation as much as any other?

"Okay, point taken," he said as she pushed his coffee cup across the island to him.

"But are you willing to go beyond the point? To accept the extraordinary and look for the unexpected?"

"I don't know," he admitted honestly. "I'm ready to try, if that means anything."

Maggie had already made up her mind to do this, but she still had to be careful, very careful. She sipped her coffee, watching as he added milk to his, then said, "I guess it'll have to be enough, won't it?"

"I hope so."

She nodded, then drew a breath. "I have a brother. Half brother, really; we had the same mother. But he's a seer, like Quentin, and he's helped me to make sense of some things in my life. Certain . . . instincts. Dreams. The things I feel, and the images burned into my soul."

"What kind of images?"

She hesitated, then shook her head. "That's — I'll get to that later. Anyway, my brother and I both inherited Mother's artistic tendencies, to differing degrees. Beau got the genius; I got . . . just enough for what I needed to be able to do."

"Which is?"

"Draw the face of evil."

John looked at her searchingly. "Andy says you could be any kind of artist you wanted to be, that you have talent to spare. Judging from the sketch of Christina, I agree."

"I probably could have been pretty good if I'd worked at it." She shrugged, dismissing something obviously unimportant to her. "But what I needed to do required less skill than . . . intuition."

"You mean your empathic ability?"

"Yes."

John frowned, remembering the terror, pain, and shock he had seen her endure. "You had to suffer to draw the face of evil?"

She hesitated, then said, "I don't think I could draw it otherwise. I don't think anyone could. For some things, knowledge isn't enough. Imagination isn't enough. You have to feel to understand."

"Only evil?"

"Particularly evil."

"Then . . . you've drawn the face of evil?"

Maggie laughed without humor. "Again

and again. But there are degrees of evil, just like anything else. The lesser face of evil is . . . the man who kills a bank guard in cold blood to get the money. The man who rapes his own wife every single night because he thinks he has the right to. The woman who poisons her child because she craves the sympathy and attention it brings to her. The minister who molests the boys who come trustingly to him. The nurse who murders her patients because she thinks the resources being used to care for them could better be used somewhere else."

"Christ," John muttered. "Lesser evil? Maggie, are all those examples of past investigations?"

"Yes."

"Investigations you were involved in?"

"Yes."

He couldn't even imagine what she must have gone through, and even as that realization crossed his mind, he suddenly understood what she meant about experiencing evil. Even with the skills of an artist, he couldn't have drawn it. Not even a knowledgeable and imaginative mind could wrap itself around some things enough to understand them, simply because they were beyond all knowledge and comprehension, beyond even the imagination's ability to transcend understanding.

Some things literally did have to be felt to be understood.

He gazed across the width of the island at her calm face with its haunting eyes and finally understood why compassion and perception were literally stamped into her regular, not quite beautiful features. Because she suffered. Because she understood the worst men and women could do to themselves and each other and their children in a way that he would never, could never, comprehend.

It was a long moment before he could speak, but finally he said, "If all that is . . . lesser evil, then what in God's name is greater evil?"

"Evil that doesn't die."

John shook his head. "I don't understand. Everything dies, eventually."

Maggie hesitated for a minute, obviously struggling, though whether for words or the decision to go into this with him he couldn't have said. "If the universe is . . . balance . . . then evil is the negative force, always opposed by a positive force, always kept in check, at least to some extent. But what if a particular positive force in a particular place and a particular moment doesn't do what it's supposed to do, what it's intended, designed to do. There's a . . . glitch somewhere, a hesitation, a mistake. And that evil isn't balanced, isn't negated by anything positive. Nothing stops it from growing, and growing more powerful, more sure of itself."

"Until?"

"Until not even the death of the flesh can destroy it."

"The body dies — but the negative force within it survives? Is that what you're saying?"

"Yes. It survives. Finds itself another vessel so that it's reborn in the flesh. And destroys again. It becomes an eternal evil. So the universe fights to restore the balance, because balance is its natural state. The positive force meant to negate that evil is reborn as well, sent once again to do what it was meant to do the first time around."

"You're talking about reincarnation."

She shrugged very slightly, her eyes never leaving his. "I'm talking about balance. A negative force has to be opposed by a positive force in order to maintain — or restore — that balance. We see it in science all the time. For every action, there is an equal and opposite reaction."

John nodded. "I remember that much. And it makes sense. But we were talking about evil."

"Yes. We were."

"Eternal evil. That's the greater evil you have to draw? An evil that won't die?" John really hoped disbelief didn't echo in his voice, but he was very much afraid it did. This was just a bit more than he had bargained for.

Hell, who was he kidding? It was a *lot* more than he had bargained for.

Maggie looked at him for a long moment, then set her cup down on the island. "I can't show you the face of that evil, because I can't see it yet. But I can show you . . . what it sees. What it does."

This, he realized, was what Maggie had brought him here to see. "Okay."

She came around the island and gestured for him to follow as she led the way to her studio. It was a very large room, obviously though skillfully added to the original house, and it looked the way most artists' studios looked, with a big worktable holding supplies, and shelves on one wall containing various props and bolts of material. There were bins holding canvases of various sizes, a number of completed paintings leaning against the walls but angled so that they weren't clearly visible to him — and one on an easel in the center of the room.

She didn't warn him. And the shock he felt when he looked at that painting was cold, overwhelming, visceral.

"Jesus Christ," he heard himself say hoarsely.

"I wish I could destroy it." Leaning back against the worktable, arms folded tightly as if she were cold, Maggie stared at the painting with a fixed intensity that was almost painful. "I want to destroy it. But the ironic thing is, it's the best work I've ever done. I seem to be too much an artist to destroy my best work. No matter how horrible it is."

He tore his gaze from the painting to look at her for a moment, then moved closer to the easel and forced himself to study it as calmly as possible.

Maggie was right, it was horrible. But she was also right in saying the work was technically superb, with an extraordinary, savage power he'd never seen equaled. It was almost impossible to believe such force had come from Maggie, had emerged from that slender body, from a spirit so sensitive it could literally feel the pain of others.

Trying to get past that, he concentrated on studying the dead woman, barely able to ignore his nausea at what had been done to her.

Maggie said, "This is how I knew she was dead, John. You wondered about that, didn't you? This is how I knew. Because I painted this. Last night, I painted this."

He looked at her quickly. "Who is this, Maggie?"

"Samantha Mitchell. And I've never seen her, so how could I have painted her if this wasn't real?"

John studied the painting again, this time more carefully, then turned and went to Maggie. "It isn't her."

"What?"

"I saw the photograph of Samantha Mitchell, remember? In the case file. Maggie, she looks completely different from this woman. She has short reddish hair and freckles, an upturned nose."

Maggie stared at him. "Not — Then who is she?"

"I don't know. But I think we'd better find out."

It was already dark by the time Jennifer got to the Fellowship Rescue Mission, and since the night promised to be a wet and chilly one, half the available beds had already been claimed by people in need. She only glanced into the two large dormitory-style rooms downstairs, one for men and one for women, where cots were lined in neat rows literally wall-to-wall; with the poor description of the man she was looking for, she doubted her ability to recognize him by sight and so went in search of somebody in charge.

She found Nancy Frasier, the surprisingly young and extremely placid director of the mission, just coming out of an upstairs room with an armful of blankets.

After peering shortsightedly at Jennifer's badge, the director listened to what she had to say and frowned. "David Robson? It's not a name I know, but then most of them don't offer names, especially if they're just passing through. You say he was arrested the other day?"

"Yeah, for causing a disturbance, but nothing serious. He was out within twenty-four hours." She offered the brief description that was all she had.

"And you're trying to find him —"

"Because he may have witnessed a crime or seen something that could help us solve one."

"I'd like to help, Detective, but I

couldn't say if he'd even been here before, not by the name or description. You're welcome to ask other staff members, or even some of our regulars — though I will request that you not disturb those already resting for the night."

"I understand."

Frasier nodded, then added, "Oh — and I should tell you that we tend to have at least a few new people here most days of the week, so if you don't find him tonight you might try again in a day or two."

"I'll do that," Jennifer said, hoping she wouldn't have to.

But by the time she had talked to nearly a dozen men who had no clue who David Robson was, and another three who weren't sure of their own names, she was more or less resigned to not finding him tonight.

She left her card with Nancy Frasier, saying, "It's a long shot, but if you should hear his name, I'd appreciate a call."

The director accepted the card and frowned, asking abruptly, "Is it about that rapist? I know they found one of the women only a few blocks from here."

Jennifer nodded. "Yeah. This David Robson may have seen something. Probably not, but we're pursuing every lead."

With a nod back toward the women's dormitory, Frasier said, "Our female population has more than doubled in the last few weeks. Lot of scared women out there. And even the men are nervous, I'd say. Look, I'll ask around, okay? Some of them may talk to me when they wouldn't say squat to you. If I find out anything, anything at all about this man, I'll call you."

"Thank you." Jennifer made her way back out to her car, depressed as always by the homeless, rootless, or just plain mindless people, most of whom certainly deserved more out of life than a narrow cot in a room full of strangers.

She unlocked her car, gazing absently toward the mission as she watched a couple of bearded men dressed in ancient army jackets standing outside, smoking. She grimaced when one of the men stooped to pick up a discarded cigarette from the sidewalk and then put the filter end between his lips without hesitation.

It was only then that she realized she was rubbing the nape of her neck. She stopped, aware now of the tingling, uneasy sensation. Moving her head no more than necessary, she shifted her gaze to sweep the area, trying to see whatever it was that had put her instincts on alert.

There weren't many people about, and those were grouped near the mission, unthreatening as far as she could tell. A damp, chilly breeze had sprung up, and she could hear it stirring trash in the gutter on the other side of the street and rattling a loose street sign nearby.

But as far as she could determine, there was nothing else. Nothing to make her feel so uneasy.

"Jumping at shadows, Seaton," she muttered.

She got into her car, locking the doors immediately, and sat there for a moment. She was tired and more than a little bit unnerved to find her thoughts drifting toward Terry. She glanced at her watch, wavered for just a bit, then swore under her breath and started the car to head back to the station.

Later, she thought. There'd be time later for Terry.

"It sounds like Tara Jameson," Andy reported. "According to descriptions and the photo we have, she's very delicate, almost childlike. Dark hair, long and straight; almond-shaped dark eyes; high cheekbones; sensitive mouth."

"You're still at the apartment?" John had

called Andy on his cell phone.

"Yeah."

"And?"

"Forensics turned up a few human hairs in the laundry chute, so you two were probably right about that being the way he got her down to the basement. From there, it looks like he took her out of the building through a service door that was *supposed* to be securely locked; it wasn't forced but picked by somebody who knew what he was doing. We still don't know how the bastard managed to avoid getting his picture taken by the security cameras, but I've got my people looking at all the tapes and checking out the computer that runs this place's electronics system. Her door wasn't forced, the apartment's security system was deactivated with her own code — all par for the course for this guy."

"Have you had any luck trying to find whoever sent the ransom note to Mitchell?"

"Not so far." Andy lowered his voice. "So if your FBI buddy finds anything, let me know pronto."

"I will."

When he closed his phone and dropped it into a pocket, Maggie said steadily, "It's her, isn't it? The painting is of Tara Jameson?"

John half turned on the couch to look at her where she sat curled up at the opposite end. "From the description Andy gave me, yes."

She drew a breath and leaned her head back against the couch, looking at him. "I thought it was Samantha."

"No, it definitely isn't her. And knowing that, do you still believe Samantha's dead?"

"Yes." Maggie didn't hesitate.

John was trying his best to understand this but couldn't help wondering if at least some of what he was hearing now was nothing more than symptoms of a mental deterioration Quentin and Kendra had hinted was possible. What if Maggie had simply suffered too much?

"I'm not losing it, John." Her voice was very quiet, and she smiled faintly when he gave her a startled look. "No, I can't read your mind. But I do have a sense of how you're feeling, and I know you're worried about me. Don't be, at least not about this. I'm okay."

"Are you?"

"Yeah. Tired and unnerved, I won't deny that, but otherwise okay."

"And the painting? How were you able to paint something that didn't yet exist?"

She drew a breath and let it out slowly. "I don't know. I mean, I don't understand it myself. All I know is that if he hasn't done that to her yet — he will. Unless we stop him."

"But you can't see the future?"

"No. I can't see the future." She managed a faint smile. "I did ask if you were ready to accept the extraordinary and look for the unexpected."

"Yeah, but . . . this? You talk about an evil that won't die, about balance that has to be restored, and then show me a painting of a tortured dead woman you say you painted even before she was abducted? I don't know, Maggie. I just don't know how to make sense of this."

Maggie couldn't really blame him.

"And what about your connection to it all? If you can't see the future, and your psychic ability is . . . limited . . . to feelings, then how can you be so certain this bastard we're after is some kind of eternal evil? Because you feel it?"

"Yes. And because I've felt it before."

"When?"

She hesitated, wondering if there was any chance at all he could accept this. "In 1934."

After a long moment of silence, John

said, "I really wish you had something stronger than coffee in the house."

"Yeah. Me too."

He drew a breath and let it out slowly. "You're saying you lived then? That you were another person — living another life?"

"That's what I'm saying."

"And you knew this . . . eternal evil then?"

"He was attacking women then the way he is now, I know that. When Andy and the others showed us those pictures of women killed back then, I knew it was him. Not a copycat killer borrowing somebody else's rituals, but him."

"Because you felt it."

She nodded. "I don't know anything that could help the investigation, nothing that could help us find him, catch him. I don't know what he looks like, what his name is. I don't even know why he's picking women who look like the ones he killed back then. All I know is that the evil inside him has been alive a long, long time. And I know it's my fault."

"What?"

"Balance, remember? A positive force intended to oppose a negative one? Somehow, I was supposed to stop him. Back in

300

the beginning, before his evil grew too strong, I was somehow in a position to change whatever happened then. To stop him, destroy him. Or maybe just turn him in a different direction. I don't know for sure. I don't remember. I just feel."

"And if what you feel is wrong?"

"It isn't."

"How can you be so damned sure? Maggie, what you're talking about is . . . incredible. To say the least. You failed to stop a killer a lifetime ago, and because of that he became some kind of unstoppable evil?"

"He isn't unstoppable. He just hasn't been stopped — up to now."

"And you have to stop him — now?"

She nodded. "I have to stop him. Because I didn't before. I can't . . . move on until I do what I'm supposed to do. And I have a very strong feeling this is my last chance to correct that mistake. Maybe we only get so many chances, I don't know. Maybe if I fail this time, someone else gets a shot at restoring the balance and I get sent back to learn the lesson a different way. I just . . . I just know that it's my responsibility this time around. I have to stop him."

"Karma."

"If it makes more sense to you to put it that way. Fate. Destiny. We're connected, he and I. Tied together by a mistake. If there's anything I know, anything I'm absolutely certain of, it's that once you've touched evil — I mean really touched it — you're forever changed. In a way, you are bound to it, tied to it, so that it becomes a part of you."

"There's nothing evil in you," he said immediately.

"Oh, but there is. It's not my evil, but I carry it inside me. That painting proves it. His evil. I carry his evil in my own soul . . . and I have for a long, long time."

Suddenly, John understood. "That's why you do it. That's why you surround yourself with victims, suffer right along with them. It's atonement, isn't it, Maggie?"

For the first time, she avoided his steady gaze. "Consciously? No. Not at first. But I've always been drawn to people in pain. Always felt a kind of relief if I could help them in some way. Gradually, over the years, I realized there was . . . something I was trying to fix, some mistake I wanted to correct. I didn't know what it was, not then. It wasn't until Laura Hughes was attacked that I began to understand the truth."

"Truth?" Unable to be still any longer, John rose and began wandering around the room, not quite pacing. "Christ."

"I know it all sounds unbelievable."

"You could say that, yeah."

"It is the truth, John. I wish it wasn't. I wish this was all about one evil man doing evil things in a single lifetime, something we could both accept, even if not understand. But that isn't what it's about. That's never been what it's about."

"Jesus, Maggie."

"I'm sorry. But you had to know the truth about it."

He swung around to stare at her. "So is this where you also tell me the truth about Christina?"

Maggie was honestly startled. "How did you —"

"I don't have to be psychic to know there's more to her death than what you've told me. Why do you think I kept after you about it? What do you know about her death, Maggie?"

His cell phone rang before she could formulate an answer, but Maggie didn't feel much of a sense of reprieve; from the determination on his face, she doubted he would accept anything less than the truth this time.

"Yeah, hello." He listened for a moment, then went to a notepad Maggie kept by her living-room phone and quickly jotted something down. "Okay. Yeah, I've got it. I'll call Andy and tell him. You won't do anything stupid, will you?" He listened a minute longer, then said, "Well, listen to Kendra and stay put, okay? Let Andy and his people take care of it. Yeah, I will."

When he ended the call, Maggie said, "I take it Quentin and Kendra found whoever sent that ransom note?"

"They have a name and an address." He called Andy's cell phone and repeated the information, adding, "Quentin says the information is solid, and he's pretty sure this Brady Oliver either knows where Samantha Mitchell is or knows someone who does. No information on whether she's alive or dead. Yeah. No, I'm at Maggie's. For a while probably; call me on my cell in case I'm in transit, okay?" He listened a moment longer, then said, "Yeah, I'll tell her." He closed the phone.

"Tell me what?"

"He said he just called in to check for messages and found one from Hollis Templeton. She wants to see you as soon as possible."

"He doesn't know why?"

"No, just that she needs to talk to you."

Maggie looked at her watch. "Visiting hours will be over for the night by the time I can get there."

"Andy said he's cleared it with the hospital if you want to go tonight. But if you're too tired, tomorrow is probably soon enough."

Maggie wasn't so sure. "Hollis wouldn't have called if it wasn't important. I'd better go now."

"I'll drive," he said.

CHAPTER
THIRTEEN

It didn't take Scott and Jennifer more than half an hour to find Brady Oliver at the address provided and bring him in for questioning. He turned out to be a small-time crook with delusions of grandeur and crumbled almost before Andy could even begin to get hard-nosed about the probable legal consequences of passing oneself off as a kidnapper.

"I never took her, I swear! I just found her is all, and why shouldn't I try to make a few bucks on a lucky chance? Her old man would never miss it, and she don't care no more, right?"

Andy stared at him, thinking once again that it was a helluva world they lived in. And feeling a chill. From the sound of it, Samantha Mitchell was already dead. "Where is she, Brady?"

Bloodshot eyes shifted nervously. "First, we gotta talk about this kidnapping rap. 'Cause I never took her, I just found her."

Andy leaned toward him and said gently,

"Well, I'll tell you what, Brady. What say I invite Samantha Mitchell's husband in here to meet you? And you can explain it all to him."

"Oh, hell, no, don't do that!"

"Where is she?"

"I just wanted to —"

"Where is she?"

"Alls I'm asking is —"

Andy rose to his feet.

"Okay, okay! There's a dump not too far from my place, an old abandoned building. City wants to tear it down, but there's no money to rebuild, something like that. I go there sometimes and look for stuff I can sell." He rattled off the address, looking acutely unhappy. "First floor, back room."

"She's dead, isn't she, Brady?"

"I didn't do her, I swear!"

Andy felt very tired. He said, "My people are going to go check out the address. You'll wait right here."

"I want a lawyer," Brady whined.

"You haven't been charged with anything. Yet."

"Oh. Well, then, I want a Coke."

Andy left the interview room without responding and before he gave in to the temptation to rid the human gene pool of one extremely stupid and vicious little possible breeder.

As soon as he shut the door behind him, Jennifer came out of the observation room and said, "We heard, Andy. Scott's rounding up the rest and putting forensics on alert. Do you think that piece of scum in there really just found her?"

Nodding, Andy said, "If Brady had killed her, he would have been hiding in the deepest hole he could find and wouldn't have opened his trap, except to ask for a lawyer. Since he just found her, he figures he's safe. Stupid bastard."

"So she's dead?"

"Yeah, she's dead. Come on — let's go. You and Scott can ride with me."

They collected the others from the bullpen and went out to their cars. On the point of getting into his own car, Andy noticed Jennifer still on the sidewalk; she was looking around with a frown, obviously disturbed.

"What?" he asked.

"Did you hear something?"

"I heard a lot. Traffic, voices, a horn blowing a couple of blocks away."

She shook her head, moving toward the passenger side finally but still frowning. "No, something else."

Scott said, "I didn't hear anything weird, Jenn. What'd it sound like?"

"Just . . . I could have sworn somebody said my name, that's all. My imagination, I guess." She shivered visibly and got into the car.

Andy paused a moment to look around carefully, but he didn't see or hear anything unusual. Even so, he didn't dismiss Jennifer's uneasiness, especially added to the fact that someone had apparently gotten into her locked car not so long ago.

He looked around a final time, then got into the car, making a mental note to do something about security around the station. But that resolution was pushed to the back of his mind by the time they reached the address Brady Oliver had given them.

Loath to disturb any evidence, Andy stationed most of his people around the building with instructions to tape off the entire thing for forensics, while he went in with only Scott and Jennifer as backup.

Their flashlights showed them a dirty, ramshackle place that had long ago been stripped to its bare bones. The floor creaked underfoot, and as they entered they could all hear faint scratchy whisperings and scurryings.

"What the hell's that?" Scott demanded,

jumpy and not apologetic about it.

"Rats," Andy told him. "You two stay behind me. We'll check out the room Brady said he found her in first."

With sudden realization, Scott said, "Rats . . . If the lady's here and she's been dead very long —"

"Don't think about it," Jennifer urged him, her own voice a bit thickened.

Andy hesitated, wondering if he should have left the two of them outside. Both had witnessed scenes of homicide before, but he knew they were very involved in this case and that their emotions were heightened because of that. Still, even that was part of being a cop. He moved on, slow and careful.

The long hallway led to the back of the building, where there were half a dozen rooms, their doors long gone, and empty doorways with broken casings leaned drunkenly open. Andy wondered why the whole building hadn't collapsed long ago. He paused, shining his light around, then moved suddenly toward the doorway to the room on the far left corner.

He could smell the blood.

There was no need to go more than a step into the room. His flashlight found her immediately.

"Oh, Christ," Scott muttered.

Andy said nothing, but he heard Jennifer give a little sigh and didn't have to ask to know what both of them were feeling. Because he felt the same. Horror. Revulsion. Pain. And an overwhelming sadness.

Samantha Mitchell lay spread-eagled on a bloodstained mattress in the far corner. Her naked body was bruised and battered. Her eyes were gone, and her throat was cut almost ear to ear. The rats had indeed gotten to her body.

Even more horribly, a deep slash opened the lower curve of her rounded belly.

And between her thighs lay the pitifully small, curled body of her dead child.

Still connected to her body by the umbilical cord.

"From the moment we met, there was an unusual bond between Christina and me," Maggie said. "Maybe it was because she was the first of his victims to survive the attack, I don't know. Whatever the reason, we both felt it, that closeness."

"She mentioned your name a couple of times when I flew up to visit her," John said, keeping his eyes on the road as he drove. "Didn't say much, just that you were the police sketch artist and that you'd been kind to her. That's one reason I asked Andy about you after she died. And I saw you at the funeral."

Maggie was a little surprised by that; she had made a point of keeping back and being unobtrusive. "I didn't know you saw me then."

"I just caught a glimpse near the end. Didn't know who you were until I recognized you last week in that interview room." He didn't add that something about her had stuck in his mind so that all these weeks later he had remembered her the instant he had seen her at the police station.

"I didn't get to spend much time with Christina," she said. "Just a couple of visits in the hospital, then three or four more after she went home. So much of her energy was just taken up with healing and with getting ready for all the surgeries she knew would follow."

John glanced at Maggie quickly, but he couldn't see her face clearly in the now-and-then glare of passing streetlights. "She talked about the plastic surgery?"

"Yes. She was realistic about it; she knew nothing would make her look the way she did before. But the acid had done so much damage, and she just wanted to look as normal as possible. She said . . . she didn't want to frighten children when she went out in public."

John was silent for a moment, then said, "That's one of the reasons I've been so sure she didn't kill herself. She wanted to live, Maggie, I know she did. She wanted to heal and go on with her life. She was strong."

"Yes, she was. Stronger than you know."

"What do you mean?"

Maggie drew a breath. "Once she got home, she had that elaborate computer system her husband had set up, and that new voice-recognition and reading program you arranged since she couldn't see the screen."

"Yes. I didn't want her to feel cut off from everything even if she wasn't ready to go out in public yet. Are you saying she used it for something else?"

"It probably shouldn't surprise you," Maggie said. "She was your sister, after all. She wanted answers, John."

"Answers? Are you saying she tried to find the man who attacked her?"

"She had all the information she'd been able to find on Laura Hughes, and of course she knew her own situation and background better than anyone else. She was convinced there was a connection somewhere, that the rest of us had been — blinded — by so many of the details that we couldn't see what was actually there."

"And she believed she could? Blind and virtually alone in that apartment, she believed she could find something everyone else had missed?"

"She did have a unique perspective. And she'd spent hours on end thinking about it. There really wasn't much else she could think about." Maggie sighed. "Please believe me, if I'd had even the slightest suspicion that what she was doing could have put her in danger —"

John abruptly pulled the car to the curb and stopped. He turned in the seat to stare at her. "Are you saying it did? Maggie — did Christina kill herself?"

"No."

"No? Why the hell didn't you tell me this before? Christ, tell somebody —"

"Because I can't prove it, John." She kept her voice level. "Every speck of evidence in that apartment proves that she did kill herself. Andy and his people went over it with a fine-tooth comb, you know that. They even went over it twice, because you asked them to. You yourself went through her computer files, according to

Andy; did you find anything?"

"No," he replied slowly. "At least, nothing out of the ordinary. Nothing unexpected. There was nothing about the investigation, the other victim. No hint at all that she was trying to investigate on her own."

"That's what Andy said. He even had the department computer expert check it out when I asked him to, but there was nothing. If there was any evidence before she died, it was certainly gone afterward. Nobody found anything to point to an intruder or even a visitor. Security records for that night show no one entering the apartment, and even the fact that she'd given the nurse the day and night off seems to point toward suicide. The medical examiner was absolutely positive it was suicide, no reservations at all. I read his report. You read his report. According to everything they found, Christina wrote that suicide note on her computer, then put a gun to her head and pulled the trigger."

John drew a breath. "I hadn't even known she had that gun until afterward."

"Not surprising, since according to the registration, she'd bought it years ago, when she first lived alone in L.A., for protection. And since it hadn't been registered here in Seattle, none of us knew about it beforehand. But if you've been blaming yourself for not knowing, don't. If there hadn't been a gun, he would have done it another way."

"How the hell do you know that, Maggie? With all the evidence pointing the other way, how do you *know* Christina didn't kill herself?"

"I told you we had a connection, a bond." Maggie turned her gaze to the windshield, still working on holding her voice level and calm. "The night she died, I woke up . . . hearing her scream in my mind. Feeling her pain. It was just a flashing instant, but clear. So clear I'll never forget it. And what she was screaming was terror — and protest. She didn't want to die. The gun in her hand, pressed to her temple, wasn't under her control."

Jennifer was alone in the conference room, looking over the arrest report she'd requested from the Central precinct on David Robson, when Andy came in, looking harried and tired.

"Sanctuary," he muttered. "My kingdom for an hour or two of sanctuary."

"I'd grant it if I could," she said sympathetically. "But you know the minute the switchboard doesn't find you at your desk, the phones in here will start ringing."

"Yeah, I know." He sat down with a sigh. "You should be gone. How many hours have you put in today?"

"I'm off the clock."

"That's not what I asked you."

Jennifer shrugged. "Look, I didn't want to go home and figured I might as well be busy."

"Doing what?"

She tapped the report with a finger. "Following a very unlikely lead, trying to track down a transient who might have seen something helpful."

Andy grunted. "Where's Scott?"

"Gone for a pizza. We were hungry and he wanted some fresh air." She watched him, worried by the circles under his eyes and the tense line of his jaw. "I guess you haven't heard anything from Maggie? I mean, about her talking to Hollis Templeton?"

"No, nothing yet. And whatever she's got to say might not be relevant anyway."

"Do you really believe that?"

"Hell, no."

"Yeah. Our entire world does seem to have narrowed down just to this investigation, doesn't it?"

"You'd think." He sighed again. "The M.E. has promised to work on Samantha Mitchell ASAP, but neither one of us thinks he'll find anything new. One glance told him what it told the rest of us: She was alive when her throat was cut, and died from blood loss."

"Then that with the baby was done . . . after?"

Andy's jaw tightened even more. "A minute or two after, the M.E. thinks. The baby was probably still alive."

Jennifer hadn't expected that — or the jolt she felt hearing it. "Christ."

"Needless to say, we're going to try to keep that fact out of the media's hands."

"Does Mitchell know?"

"No, and if I have my way he never will."

She stared down at the arrest report. "Andy, is there something we're missing? Something we should have done and didn't?"

"Nothing I can think of. Don't beat yourself up about it, Jenn. We've had virtually no evidence, no witnesses able to give us a description, and no predictable pattern to the attacks — so far, at least. The closest we've come to a lead of any kind is thanks to you and Scott."

"Some lead," she said, sounding as discouraged as she felt. "We have a few sketches and photos of victims from a string of murders in 1934, and *maybe* our guy somehow got access to them, but so far the only thing we can be reasonably sure of is that he's going after look-alikes."

Before Andy could respond, the phone rang, and he picked up the receiver with a resigned grimace.

"Yeah?" He listened for a minute, absently watching Jennifer continue going through the file in front of her, then said, "Okay. Tell him I'm on my way."

When he hung up the phone, Jennifer said, "Our Luke again?"

Andy used the table for leverage to push himself to his feet. "Yeah, dammit."

"He's still refusing to ask the FBI for help?"

"He'd refuse to yell help if his pants were on fire, Jenn, you know that." He sighed. "But I think we need to bring John's friends in, and I mean officially. I'm about a breath away from calling the chief directly myself."

She shook her head. "Don't do that. We both know Drummond would never forgive or forget, and he could do your career a lot of damage."

"And maybe I don't give a shit."

This time, Jennifer smiled. "Yes, you do. And so do the rest of us, in case you didn't know that. We need you right where you are, Andy. But I agree it's time something drastic was done. I don't have to hear a shrink explain it to know that now that he's started killing his victims outright, this bastard is only going to get more vicious with every day that passes. We have to stop him, and we have to stop him soon. Is there another way around Drummond? A way to bring pressure to bear on him without any of us sticking our necks out?"

"Maybe. I hate not being able to handle this ourselves, though."

"Um . . . isn't that sort of the way our Luke is thinking?"

He stared at her. "Christ, you're right. You'd think I'd have learned by now to yell for help when I need it."

"John could help, I'll bet," she suggested. "I think Maggie could as well, the way the chief feels about her. And you know both of them would in a heartbeat if it means we'd have a better chance of stopping this monster. I'll bet neither one has yet only because they don't want to step on your toes."

"Yeah, probably."

"I don't know if these agents can help

us," Jennifer said steadily. "But from all John said, they have a hell of a lot of experience in tracking monsters, and both of them are profilers. They may be able to tell us something we'd never come up with ourselves. I think we need to hear whatever they've got to say."

"I think you're right." Andy nodded and turned away from the conference table, adding, "I might try Maggie first, mostly because I think both the chief and Drummond would take that a bit better. But we'll see."

Jennifer didn't want to admit either to him or to herself how relieved she felt. It wasn't that she didn't feel herself or her coworkers capable of solving a string of brutal attacks, it was just that she was afraid that without help the solution might well come at a very high price.

And with six women attacked so far, three of them dead, the price was already too high.

Maggie knew she had no business talking to Hollis, not tonight. The previous day had been an emotional ordeal, and today had not been much better; discussing the unbelievable, even the unthinkable, with John had demanded such absolute mastery of her own emotions that the aftermath left her feeling drained and incredibly weary.

So she was feeling more than a little vulnerable when she knocked, pushed open Hollis's door, and went into the hospital room where the other woman was sitting as usual in one of the two chairs near the window.

As soon as Maggie came in, Hollis said, "The nurses are pissed at me. They want me in bed, or at least ready to be there. Can't understand why I won't at least get undressed."

"Why won't you?" Maggie asked, sitting down and absently opening her sketch pad to a clean page.

"Because I don't feel so defenseless, I suppose." Her hands were gripping the arms of her chair, knuckles whitened tensely. "Or maybe just because I'm sick of that damned bed."

"I can't say I blame you for that. You must be sick of being here at all. Will your doctors let you go home after the bandages come off on Thursday?"

"They aren't saying, but I gather it depends on how the operation turned out. If I can see, I'll be ready to go home. If I can't . . ."

Maggie didn't need to hear the rest. If she remained blind, then Hollis would need further medical help to adjust to that fact, especially after having her hopes raised by the operation. She hesitated, then said, "I don't know how you feel about the so-called paranormal —"

Hollis gave a peculiar little laugh. "Funny you should say that."

"Why?"

"I'll . . . explain later. I feel fairly open-minded about it, all things considered. Why?"

"Because someone I trust, someone who happens to have the ability to see the future, told me that whether you see again is entirely up to you."

"That sounds fairly enigmatic." Hollis didn't sound either convinced or unconvinced, merely neutral.

"I know. I didn't understand it myself, but the more I think about it, the more I'm convinced he meant that while the operation could be an unqualified success, there's a lot the mind has to accept before everything works as it should."

"These borrowed eyes in my head, you mean?"

"Not borrowed. Gifted."

"The eyes of a dead woman."

"The eyes of a woman who wanted someone else to see if she couldn't."

Hollis drew a breath and let it out slowly. "Yeah, I keep telling myself that. But I wonder what it'll feel like if the eyes do work — and when I look into a mirror a stranger looks back at me."

"Still your face. Still you."

"But I'm not who I was the last time I looked into a mirror. I've changed — so much. With all that and someone else's eyes as well, how will I even know me?"

Hearing and responding to the lost note of pain in the other woman's voice, Maggie leaned forward and put her hand over Hollis's tense one. "You'll know who you are, Hollis. Your mind will look through those eyes."

"Will it?"

"Yes." Maggie almost withdrew her hand, but then something flashed into her own mind, a quick, sharp image that caused a strange jolt of pain and even an aching sadness. The image was gone before Maggie could identify it, but she was left with the odd and inexplicable feeling that there was someone else here in the room.

"I hope you're right," Hollis murmured.

Maggie looked around quickly, uneasy,

then said, "Hollis, why did you want me to come here tonight?" She felt the hand beneath hers tense even more.

"What you said about the paranormal sort of touched a nerve," Hollis said slowly. "I've been more open-minded about it lately because of something that's been happening to me ever since the attack."

"What?" Again, Maggie felt that flash of something, so vivid that it was almost as though for a split second she caught a glimpse of someone standing just behind Hollis. It was eerie and definitely not anything she had experienced before, yet somehow not really frightening.

"I thought it was my imagination at first." Hollis laughed under her breath. "Hell, maybe it is. It started when I was — it started right after the attack. A voice in my mind urging me to keep trying to pull myself out of that building where he'd left me. It knew my name, that voice. It helped give me the will to live, might even have saved my life. They told me afterward that if I hadn't pulled myself out of the building just then, it probably would have been hours before anyone found me. And I would have been dead."

"That doesn't sound like your imagination."

"No. I don't think I ever believed that, not really. She has such a distinctive voice, it's easy to feel she's a separate and distinct personality."

"Does she have a name?"

"Her name is Annie. Annie Graham."

It didn't sound familiar to Maggie — and yet it did somehow. Again, she caught that flash of an image, a slight figure standing behind Hollis, and this time thought to herself, *Dark hair, sad face.* But then it was gone.

"Maggie?"

"Sorry. I was . . . thinking."

"Thinking I'm out of my mind?"

"No — far from it. Do you know who she is, Hollis? Or — who she was?"

After a moment, Hollis said, "You figured it out more quickly than I did. I guess it's not easy to accept the fact that a ghost is talking to you."

"I would imagine not. I've never had any mediumistic abilities, so I don't know how it feels." Except that she could feel it now. She could feel Hollis's uneasiness and doubt, feel the slight chill of being touched by something inexplicable, the peculiar sensation of gazing into an open corridor linking the living and the dead.

"Mediumistic? The ability to talk to the

326

dead, I suppose. Odd, somehow, that it has a name." She barely paused before saying, "But you do have paranormal abilities, don't you, Maggie?"

Maggie hesitated, then said, "They call what I can do an empathic sense."

"Empathy. You feel the pain of others. And, sometimes, you blunt the edges of the hurt or even take some of it away, don't you?"

"If I can."

Hollis's hand turned suddenly and gripped Maggie's. "If I'd known that, I never would have talked to you. Never would have forced you to feel so much of what I felt."

"I know. That's why I didn't tell you."

"I'm sorry, Maggie."

"Don't be. You didn't *force* me to feel anything. It's what I do, Hollis. What I'm . . . meant to do."

"Suffer?"

"Understand suffering." Maggie sighed. "It's all right, really. Right now I'm more interested in Annie and what she said to you. Is that why I'm here?"

"Yes. There are . . . things she wants me to tell you. She was the one who told me to ask for you in the first place. She didn't say why, just that I needed to talk to you."

"I had wondered how you knew my name. The police usually keep that quiet."

"Annie told me. And a few hours ago she . . . she pleaded with me to help her."

"Help her do what? Contact me?"

"Bring you here. Tell you."

"Tell me what?"

"Tell you about the next victim."

CHAPTER
FOURTEEN

John waited for Maggie where he had before, at the doorway of the waiting room on the floor where Hollis Templeton's room was. The area was as quiet as it always seemed to be, and no one disturbed his thoughts.

He almost wished someone would.

It should have been a relief to be told that his sister had not killed herself after all, that he'd been right about that much. It had been one thing he'd been determined to prove. But he still couldn't prove it. And even if he believed Maggie —

Did he believe Maggie?

It all seemed so . . . incredible. And yet he had seen with his own eyes her intense physical and emotional reaction to places where violence had occurred. Had seen how she suffered right along with the victims she tried to help.

And he had seen a painting of a brutally murdered woman, a woman he was certain was Tara Jameson. Yet the missing woman had not yet been abducted when Maggie had painted her horribly mutilated image while in the grip of some frightening virtually unconscious nightmare state that chilled him to even imagine.

Maggie had not been pretending or performing, he was certain of that. Even if there had been a reason for her to feign such an incredible ability — and he couldn't think of a single one — why would anyone go to the extremes Maggie so obviously suffered just to maintain an inexplicable pretense?

No, he was sure Maggie and her abilities were genuine. With every minute he spent with her, he was more and more convinced of her basic honesty and apparently karmic need to help people. And if she was telling the truth about everything else, why would she lie about Christina's death?

He realized, after considering it carefully, that he believed she was telling the truth about that as well. Something in her voice, in her face, even in her reluctance to tell him all this time what she felt, what she knew, had convinced him. He believed she had on some level shared, even felt, the moment of his sister's death.

And because he believed that, believed in Maggie's abilities, he had to also finally admit to himself that he believed several other distinctly disturbing . . . facts:

Someone else, possibly the man who had attacked her, was responsible for Christina's death and had, in fact, murdered her in cold blood.

Quentin really could "see" the future.

And this bastard they all wanted caught and caged, this man who preyed on women out of some obscene need no sane mind could understand, this evil beast with a human face — had lived before. And killed before.

Christ . . . what could a man do with that kind of knowledge?

His entire life, John had believed only in what he could see or touch or feel with his hands, what he absolutely knew to be real. Never a religious man, he had viewed faith as superstition and the so-called paranormal as nothing more than mysticism dressed up by wishful thinking and pseudoscience to look rational.

But faced with this — all this — he was beginning to appreciate just how little he genuinely understood the very nature of reality. Because if the world he lived in could produce seers and empaths and human monsters reborn to torment victims in life after life only because someone had failed to stop them when fate decreed, then all the certainties of his own life had been built upon shifting sands.

It was a sobering realization and yet . . . surprisingly exhilarating as well. He honestly hadn't thought there were any mysteries left to be explored, not for him. With his business empire virtually running itself these days, his goals and ambitions long ago reached and even surpassed, his life had taken on a predictable and unexciting routine he had not quite defined as boring. But boring it undoubtedly was.

He couldn't remember the last time he had felt so alive, so caught up in a unique and challenging situation.

He also understood for the first time why Quentin had joined the FBI when he had. Not because he considered himself a traditional cop, a notion John had always found unbelievable given his friend's brash, thoroughly independent, and often reckless nature — to say nothing of his occasionally cockeyed sense of humor. And not because he had a law degree he didn't quite know what to do with.

No, he had joined because Noah Bishop had been quietly recruiting qualified people with paranormal abilities for a very specialized unit of investigators, and that had appealed both to Quentin's innate curiosity and sense of justice and his need to make use of a unique talent the rest of the world found incomprehensible — and even frightening. If they believed in it at all.

"Some friend I've been," John muttered beneath his breath.

It said a lot for Quentin's nature that he had remained a loyal friend, both humorous and unoffended all these years despite John's patent disbelief. John wasn't so sure what it said about his own nature. That he was incredibly stubborn, perhaps?

Perhaps.

"John."

He straightened away from the doorjamb, surprised that he'd been so preoccupied he hadn't heard Maggie approach. As soon as he saw her face, he took a quick step toward her almost instinctively.

"What is it? What's happened?"

She tucked her sketch pad under one arm and reached for her phone, her smile a little strained. "Hollis thought she might have remembered something, but it's nothing we didn't already know." The lie came easily to her lips, but she went on immediately just in case John's acute perception where she was concerned told him more than she wanted him to know. "I'm worried about her, though. She and Ellen

Randall are the only surviving victims so far; Ellen's still blind and no threat to this animal, but Hollis might be able to see again, and I'm afraid that would disturb him enough that he might try to come after her again. Even though the surgeon and the staff here have agreed not to publicize the operation, the news is bound to get out sooner rather than later. I think she should be guarded, just in case he finds out about it."

"Sounds like a good idea."

"Yeah. Andy? It's Maggie. Are you guys making a night of it? I know, I'd just as soon work as try to sleep too. Listen, do you have somebody you can post here at the hospital, outside Hollis's room? I don't want to scare her, but I think she should be protected. No, but if this bastard finds out she might be able to see again — yeah, she could be a threat to him. Clear it with the hospital, okay? Thanks."

She listened for a moment, then closed her eyes briefly, and they were bleak when she opened them again. "I see. So he's not giving them even a chance to survive now. And not wasting much time between victims. He must have grabbed Tara Jameson within hours of killing Samantha Mitchell. Yeah . . . a whole new ball game. No,

John's still with me, so we'll come together. Right."

She listened a moment longer, then frowned and said, "Is that Luke I hear?" Her face tightened, and she said in a voice John remembered from their first meeting, "Do me a favor, and tell him I'd appreciate it if he hung around until I got there. I want to talk to him. Yeah. Thanks, Andy."

Watching her drop the phone back into her pocket, John said, "Do you think Drummond will listen to you?"

It didn't even occur to Maggie that John hadn't needed to ask what she had in mind. "I think he'd damned well better. Stubborn is one thing, but this has gone way too far to keep bumping up against Luke's pride."

"Even he has to see that much now. I gather they found Samantha Mitchell's body?"

"Yes. He'd killed her outright." She drew a breath. "Cut her throat."

John watched her steadily. "Then I'd say it's way past time to pool our resources and manpower and work together."

Maggie nodded. "Definitely. Whether Luke Drummond likes it or not."

"You've got my vote. And I have a hunch Andy is going to agree with you too."

She nodded. "I'll make sure first, okay it with Andy, and then I've got a few home truths for Luke. If I have to, I'll go to the chief — and I'll make sure Luke knows it."

"Blame me for the fact that Quentin and Kendra are already in town," he told her. "He can bitch at me all he wants without hurting any of the rest of you."

"Are you sure?"

"Positive. And if you need any extra ammo, you might try telling him the governor owes me a favor that I've been very hesitant to call in. So far."

"Is that true?"

"Yeah. I was saving it in case Drummond got nasty and tried to shut me out of the investigation entirely, but we might as well play every card we've got."

Maggie nodded again. "Okay. I'll use it if I have to."

John put an arm around her, partly because she looked exhausted and partly because he needed to touch her, and said, "Let's go."

Scott came into the conference room and sat down in a chair across from Jennifer. "Beats me what's going on, but it looks serious. Andy's in a huddle with John at his desk, and Maggie is in Drummond's office. The door is closed — but you can still hear Drummond."

Jennifer grimaced. "If he's pissed enough to be yelling at Maggie, it must really be serious. He's more careful with her than he is with any of us."

"Because the chief is so high on her."

"Yeah." Jennifer looked at her watch. "Nearly eleven. Andy said we should put ourselves back on the clock if we're planning to hang around."

"Suits me," Scott said. "All I do at home is stare at the walls trying to figure this thing out."

"I know what you mean."

"Any luck finding that transient?"

"Not so far. I called some of the other shelters in the area, but they don't have anybody matching his description or claiming the name David Robson."

"You don't really think this guy saw a ghost, do you, Jenn?"

"I think he might have seen something. At the very least, something that shook him up."

"Because Terry Lynch says so?"

"He's a good cop, Scott."

"Sure he is. I'm just wondering what a drunken transient could possibly have seen to make him believe he'd seen a ghost.

Smoke? Light hitting a patch of mist just right? Somebody dressed all in white?"

"All good possibilities," she admitted. "But maybe he saw something else, Scott. From what little we do know, this bastard may be wearing a mask at least while he's with the victims — one of those hard plastic masks. I'd think that would look plenty creepy even if you were cold sober."

"I guess."

Jennifer sighed. "I know it's a long shot, but what have we got to lose checking it out?"

Scott sighed as well. "Nothing."

"Exactly." Jennifer reached for the phone. "I have a couple more shelters on my list that should be taking calls even this late. Besides — even long shots finish first every once in a while."

"Not when you bet on them," Scott replied in a voice of wry experience.

"I don't like being threatened, Maggie." Drummond's voice was level, a distinct change from his roaring of only moments before.

On her feet in front of his desk, she leaned forward and planted her hands squarely on his blotter. "No? Then stop making it necessary, Luke. This thing has gotten way out of hand, and if you were honest with yourself instead of so bullheaded you refuse to see reason, you'd admit it."

"My people can —"

"Your people are out of their league. They're damned good cops, every one of them, but they've never had to deal with this kind of monster before. Nothing in their training or experience has prepared them for it."

"If you'd just produce a sketch —"

She straightened and half laughed. "Fine, blame it on me. I don't give a shit. Say your sketch artist just couldn't do her job, and that's why you can't catch this animal."

He had the grace to flush, but his eyes remained angry. "We're doing everything in our power, everything that can possibly be done. And the chief agrees with me; why call in the FBI when we don't have so much as a piece of conclusive evidence for them to fucking investigate?"

"Listen to me. You're a hunter — think about it. What's the logical thing to do when you're after a particular kind of animal? You look for experienced hunters. When you have a bear problem, you damned well find somebody who knows how to hunt bears."

"Cops hunt criminals. And — hey, surprise! — we catch them too."

Maggie deliberately dropped her voice to a conversational tone, unthreatening, even unemotional. "Yes, you do. But this isn't just another criminal, Luke — that's where you're misjudging the situation. This is an animal, a human monster going to inhuman extremes to hide his evil face even from his dying victims. And when you go after a monster, you need somebody who knows how to hunt them."

"Like the FBI."

"No, like a very specialized unit *within* the FBI." She allowed her voice to sharpen. "A group of highly skilled, trained, and dedicated people who don't care what the headlines read after they've done their job and gone. They don't care who gets the political points. All they care about is putting monsters in cages where they belong."

Again, Drummond flushed slightly, this time at the biting comment about his political aspirations, but all he said was "I've never heard of this specialized unit."

"No, you probably haven't. Like I said, they don't seek publicity — the opposite, if anything." She watched that sink in, and added, "But if you'll check back through the law-enforcement agency bulletins the Bureau sends out, I'm sure you'll find them mentioned a few times. They're the Special Crimes Unit — SCU. Formed to assist local law enforcement to handle unusually challenging violent crimes. Their success record is quite impressive. They have a mandate never to interfere with local law enforcement, only to advise and provide support and assistance — when requested to do so."

"How come you know so much about them?"

"Someone I know nearly joined that unit a couple of years ago." She shrugged. "What I can tell you is that they're good, Luke. They're very, very good."

"I still don't see what they could do that we can't," Drummond muttered.

Maggie knew he was going to give in — however grudgingly — so she kept her response matter-of-fact. "Like I said, they've hunted monsters before; maybe they'll have a take on this the rest of us would never think of. But even if they don't, the murder of Samantha Mitchell raises the stakes, doesn't it, Luke? People are going to be asking what *more* you're doing to stop a sadistic rapist who has now become a brutal murderer. Call these expert monster hunters in, and you've got an answer for them."

"Shit." He leaned back in his chair until it creaked, scowling.

"You know it's the right thing to do. Even more, it's the smart thing to do. Luke, a few days ago you asked me to try harder to give you a picture of this monster. Now I'm telling you that I can't do it alone. I can't do it just by talking to blinded victims. I need help. I need people who can help me to understand the way he thinks."

"Is that why you're so cozy with Garrett these days?" he asked sourly.

Ignoring the implication, she said, "As a matter of fact, John decided a few days ago that if you couldn't use the resources of this FBI unit, then maybe he could. You know how determined he is to find the man who attacked his sister, whatever it takes. He happens to have a friend in the unit, and the friend is here in Seattle along with his partner, on their own time and off the books. We have them to thank for how quickly Samantha Mitchell's body was found."

She had been reasonably sure that last would keep him from exploding, and she was right. But she nevertheless didn't give him time to start sputtering.

"Nobody's stepping on your authority, Luke, and all of us have only one goal in mind. We just want to stop this monster before he kills again. Give us all the tools we need to do that. Be a smart politician as well as a smart cop and call the unit in officially. Give Andy the okay to open up the investigation to them. I promise you won't regret it."

"I'd better not," he growled. "Send him in."

Maggie didn't allow a shadow of triumph to show and didn't waste time leaving the office. The bullpen was less busy than usual at this late hour, but she was still aware of considerable covert attention as she made her way to Andy's desk, where he and John waited. Not that she was surprised by the interest — Drummond's voice had rattled the windows, so it had undoubtedly been heard out here.

"He wants you," she told Andy. "He'll probably bluster a bit, but bottom line you'll get the okay to bring Quentin and Kendra in officially."

"Did you have to promise your first child?" Andy asked dryly as he rose.

"No. But I may be pouring brimstone out of my shoes tonight."

He grinned at her, then headed for Drummond's office.

"Well done," John said. "Here — sit down." He decided not to add that she looked very tired and he was worried about her.

She did, taking the other visitor's chair. "I think I'd almost rather interview a dozen witnesses than argue with Luke. He's about as bullheaded as they come."

John smiled faintly. "You convinced him. That's the important thing."

"Let's hope so." She smiled in return. "Are Quentin and Kendra likely to be up?"

"Oh, yeah, they're both night owls, especially during an ongoing investigation. Are you sure enough of Drummond to call them in right now?"

Maggie nodded. "I don't think we have any time to lose, do you?"

John reached for the phone.

WEDNESDAY, NOVEMBER 7

By the time they were all assembled in the conference room, it was after midnight. Drummond had left for home some time before, saying he'd meet "those agents" the following day, and many of the detectives who had been working on the investigation were also absent, either off duty and home or else out doing what they could to find the latest missing woman, Tara Jameson.

So it was what had become the core of the police investigative team — Andy, Scott, and Jennifer — who were introduced to Quentin and Kendra. And they wasted no time in getting to work.

Quentin prowled around studying the photos, sketches, and descriptions pinned to the bulletin board, while Kendra reported that their search of every available database for similar crimes going back more than six months had turned up nothing even remotely close anywhere in the country, indicating that he had indeed begun attacking women only six months ago.

"But there's this," Quentin said, tapping one of the bulletin boards. "Absolutely amazing. Who took the intuitive leap and dug these up?"

Andy nodded to Scott and Jennifer. "They did."

Scott explained their thinking about a rapist with a too-developed ritual.

When he was finished, Quentin was the first to speak, saying thoughtfully, "You colored outside the lines when you were a kid, didn't you?"

Scott stared at him for a moment, then caught the twinkle in the agent's eyes and grinned reluctantly. "Well, yeah."

"I'm not surprised. Very creative and intuitive thinking. And it is a perfectly rational explanation given the facts as we know them. Copycats are getting depressingly common these days. So maybe the guy did decide to borrow someone else's ritual and used a series of old, unsolved crimes to learn from."

John glanced at Maggie, but she was listening gravely and showed no inclination to interrupt. And he wasn't about to. Even if she was right in her incredible claim that they were dealing with an evil mind reborn, John didn't see how that knowledge could do anything except confuse the investigation. Assuming it was even believed.

No, they were after a flesh-and-blood killer now, whatever else he was, and that was the quarry they had to hunt down.

Andy said, "Jenn's trying to run down a witness who might have seen something in the area where Hollis Templeton was found, but he's a transient, so finding him won't be easy. The only other new point we have is Maggie's belief that this bastard knows the latest victim, Tara Jameson."

Jennifer frowned at her. "What makes you think that?"

Maggie glanced at Andy, hesitated, then shrugged. "Sometimes I feel things. A sixth sense, if you will. They call it an empathic sense."

"Which explains a lot," Andy said to the other two detectives after a moment. "That's how she gets those incredibly accurate sketches, how she . . . communicates . . . so well with victims. Isn't it, Maggie? When you tell them you know how they feel, you mean it literally."

"Usually. It's stronger with some people than others. But most victims of violent crime are . . . they're traumatized, their emotions much more powerful than normal. I pick that up pretty easily."

"Do you know what we're feeling right now?" Jennifer demanded.

Maggie shrugged. "In a general sense, yes. That's all I get without physical contact, just a faint impression — not much more than I'd get anyway from watching your expressions or listening to your voices."

"Tell them the rest," Quentin murmured.

She looked at him, then at the others. "Violent emotion is just another kind of energy. And it . . . lingers in some places, almost as if it soaks into the walls and floors, at least for a while. Sometimes, if I walk through a place where something violent has happened, I . . . connect with the victim or attacker. Feel a lot of what they felt at the time."

"Which is why you picked up on the arguments and stuff at the Mitchell house," Andy said and, when she nodded, quickly listed the impressions Maggie had gained from walking through that house, so that his detectives understood what they were talking about.

Maggie said, "In each case, one or both of the Mitchells were experiencing emotions more intensely than usual. The argument about the parrot was pretty fierce, as was the one Thomas Mitchell had with his father-in-law. And the broken mirror cut Samantha's hand, which caused her a lot of pain."

Jennifer said, "There've been a lot of violent emotions in this building; do you feel that?"

Grimacing slightly, Maggie said, "Until recently, all I felt was a kind of . . . skin-tingling sensation, like the way you feel when there's too much static electricity in the air. But it's getting more intense as time passes. At the hospital too."

"You didn't say anything," John said,

not quite accusingly.

"What could I say?" She shrugged. "It's almost like background noise now, a low hum of energy just beneath the level of consciousness. Usually, anyway. Sometimes a particular impression gets through more strongly."

"For instance?" There was a challenging note to Jennifer's question.

Maggie glanced at Quentin, who said wryly, "Gotta jump through a hoop or two. It never fails."

"Yeah." Maggie saw a bit of color creep into Jennifer's cheeks, but she answered the other woman's question as if she didn't see the gauntlet thrown at her feet. "For instance . . . you had someone you suspect of burglary in here really early today — I mean Tuesday. The detective working the case — Harrison? — is convinced this guy has been breaking into some pretty high-class homes in the city. Problem is, you've searched his place, and you've staked out the known fences, and so far found nothing."

"Yeah," Andy said. "So?"

"So when he was in here today, your suspect was really worried you'd find out about the storage building he rents under his brother's name."

Scott said, "Jesus. I want to run tell

Mike Harrison, but I'm afraid I'll miss something."

"Tell him later," Andy ordered. He eyed Maggie. "Any other little tidbits you want to pass on?"

"Well, that elderly woman you suspect of killing her husband didn't."

"No?"

"No. But she did dispose of his body. Buried him in the woods behind her house."

"Christ," Andy said. "Why, if she didn't kill him?"

"He wasn't insured, and she needs the Social Security checks to keep coming. So she tried to pretend he was still alive."

Into the silence, Quentin said, "Sometimes I really hate working for the government."

Scott drew a breath and said, "Well, I say we hire Maggie to sit by the front door all day."

She smiled at him. "So I can get bits of info you guys would have found out on your own anyway?"

"I'm not so sure about that," Andy said. "But even assuming you were willing, we'd have to figure out some way of making your . . . impressions . . . sound like legitimate leads, and I have a hunch that wouldn't be easy."

"Take it from me," Quentin said, "it wouldn't be. And if what you were doing became public knowledge —"

"There'd be privacy issues," Maggie finished. "At the very least. With the possible exception of cops with difficult cases to crack, nobody would be at all happy to think there was someone reading them like a book every time they walked through the door and so invading their privacy without permission or legal justification."

She shrugged. "Anyway, that's how I know that the rapist knows Tara Jameson. There was a strong sense of familiarity when he grabbed her, much more than there would have been if his only knowledge of her came from watching her."

Andy looked at the others, then nodded. "That's good enough for me. I know it's late, but I say we start pulling together everything we know about Tara Jameson's life. Family, friends, neighbors, coworkers. We all know the drill. Wake people up if you have to. If there's any chance at all we might be able to find her before this bastard can play his twisted games, I say we pull out all the stops and go for it."

Nobody disagreed.

CHAPTER
FIFTEEN

It wasn't at all unusual for Beau to be working in his studio after midnight, but it was rare for him to be working with his eyes closed.

It was also something he wasn't happy about and wouldn't have willingly been doing except by urgent request. The last time he'd tried it, the resulting painting had given him nightmares for weeks. And it was the only example of his work he had ever destroyed.

"It's not just spatters, is it?" he asked, less hopeful than resigned.

"No. Not just spatters."

"I wish it was."

"I know."

"You know too damned much."

"One thing I *don't* know is how you're able to use the artistic version of automatic writing and talk coherently at the same time."

"I don't know that either, and it freaks me out to think too much about it. Reminds me of that old horror movie about the pianist who got himself a new pair of hands. Someone else's."

"Now you're freaking me out."

"I'd like to think I could. But you've seen too much to be bothered by anything I can do."

"Don't be so sure of that."

Beau half turned his head, eyes still closed and paintbrush still moving skillfully, and frowned. "Am I going to want to look at this thing when I'm done?"

"No."

"Oh, Christ. Can I stop now?"

"I don't know. Can you?"

"No. Dammit. There's still something . . ." Beau gritted his teeth and kept painting. He hated this. It was infinitely preferable to have a vision, even if it made his head ache for an hour afterward. Preferable to have bits and pieces of knowledge or information just pop into his head, unbidden. Either of those he could deal with.

But this . . . this was major-league creepy. He'd wondered more than once if it was really his own mind, his own skills, guiding his hands when he painted this way. Considering the finished products, that was a scary thought. But even scarier was the possibility he wasn't in control in any sense, that someone else was "speaking" through his skills, using them to get a message out.

Out of hell, he sometimes thought.

"Am I the only one you know who can do this?" he demanded. "Is that why you come to me?"

"You're the best I've found. Artistic expertise matched by psychic ability. But in this case, it wasn't either skill that brought me here, you know that."

"Then why ask me to do this?"

"I use every tool I can get my hands on, you also know that."

"And to hell with the cost to me, huh?"

"You can pay the bill."

"You're a bastard, Galen — do *you* know that?"

"As a matter of fact, I do."

Beau was silent for several minutes, then said, "Maggie's just beginning to find out what she can do."

"Yes. I saw the painting."

"So you've been breaking into her house too, huh?"

"You should both invest in a little security."

"Obviously." Beau painted for several more minutes before the brush finally wavered and his hand fell. He turned his back to the easel before opening his eyes and walking to the worktable where Galen leaned to clean the brush and his palette.

"It's almost over, Beau."

"If you're trying to make me feel better, that won't do it."

"Sorry. Best I can do."

"Yeah, right." Beau cleaned his hands on a rag, paying close attention to the task, then said, "I'm going to put the coffee on."

"Late for caffeine."

"Well, if you think I want to sleep tonight, you're crazy. Cover that thing when you're done looking at it, all right?" Without waiting for a response, and without so much as a glance at the painting, Beau left the studio.

Galen looked after him for a moment, then straightened and approached the easel almost warily. He stood back some distance from it, powerful arms crossed over his chest as he studied a painting so complex and skillfully done it was almost impossible to believe the artist's eyes had been closed the entire time.

Almost impossible to believe.

Far from Beau's usual and rather famous impressionist work, this painting didn't shimmer with light but rather with darkness. Bold strokes of black, deep shades of maroon and slate gray and brown made up an indistinct yet oddly unnerving background lightened only by the amorphous flesh-toned faces and forms in the foreground.

Galen considered one face in particular, one of the few that was clearly recognizable. It wore a twisted expression of pain, wide eyes already going empty as life left them. His own rather hard mouth twisted.

"Shit," he said very softly.

Maggie had never been a nervous woman, but by the time John dropped her off at her home very early in the morning, it took all her resolution not to ask him to come inside with her. She told herself it was lack of sleep, but that didn't help much except to remind her he needed rest as well — and did not need to be worrying about her safety.

Worrying never did any good, she knew that.

Besides, if he knew the truth, he'd want to be with her every moment, watching over her — she knew that too. And as comforting as his presence was, she had to be able to spend at least some time alone and without the distraction he presented, recharging her energies while she tried to think this thing through.

At least that was what she told herself when she went into her silent house and cautiously checked all the doors and windows before taking a long, hot shower and trying to get some sleep. But sleep didn't come easily. She dozed, waking several times with a start to find herself tense, listening for some alien sound. But there was nothing, of course.

Of course.

After only a few hours, she finally got up and got dressed, not much rested. She ate only because she knew she should, then checked her garage and car as warily as she had checked her house hours before. Even when she was in the car and moving, doors locked, she didn't relax.

She wondered if she ever would again.

When she walked into Beau's studio a few minutes later, she was a little surprised to find him lounged back with his feet up on the table rather than working. The commissioned portrait of a Seattle businessman's wife that he'd been working on for days reposed on his easel, but from all appearances he hadn't picked up brush or palette today.

"I'm taking the day off," he announced before she could ask him. "Have some coffee — it's a fresh pot."

Maggie fixed herself a cup and sat down across from him, studying his angelic face with a frown. "Not that it really shows, but I could swear you'd been up all night too."

"I didn't sleep," he admitted. "Called your house pretty late and figured you were at the station."

"I was. We had a sort of war council just before midnight and ended up staying there until dawn." Briskly, she filled him in on everything that had happened since they had last talked, as usual not sure just how much he knew without being told, and finished up, "I went home a few hours ago for a nap and a shower, like most of the others."

"Most?"

"Andy's up for the duration, I think. And Quentin and Kendra seemed wide-eyed and energetic when I left."

Beau, who knew most of the detectives Maggie worked with at least by name, since she talked about them, nodded and said, "From what you've said about Andy, that isn't surprising. As for the two feds, unusual endurance is probably the rule rather than the exception for that unit."

Eyeing him thoughtfully, Maggie said, "You never really told me why you turned

Bishop down when he asked you to join up a couple of years ago."

"Didn't I?"

"No. And don't try to sidestep now. Quentin and Kendra haven't said anything, but I'm willing to bet they've known about the connection between you and me for days. You said yourself Bishop more or less told you that the plan was for him and his agents to keep track of the psychics they're aware of outside the unit, just in case of need."

"That's what he said."

"So they've probably known about you since they got here." She shook her head. "I'll give them full marks for discretion; far as I can tell, they haven't said a word to anybody, even John."

"Knowing Bishop, he'd see discretion as necessary. One of his goals was always to build the unit and earn a solid success record long before the public found out anything."

Maggie nodded. "Makes sense. So — why did you decide not to join up?"

"I don't have a law degree."

"Which wouldn't be necessary, if you went on the books as technical support for the field agents. That was another of Bishop's goals, wasn't it, to build a support team made up of people with psychic abilities *and* other talents that could prove useful in investigations? I'd say an artist might come in handy, especially one with a name so well known it would provide excellent cover for any federal snooping he was doing."

"You've been around cops too much. You're beginning to think like them."

"Don't try to distract me. Why'd you say no? It's certainly the kind of thing you'd enjoy doing."

Beau shrugged. "Let's just say the timing wasn't right."

Maggie frowned at him. "It wasn't because of me, was it?"

Honest as always — at least when pressed — Beau said, "Not entirely. Anyway, you're the one Bishop would have loved to have on his team. An empathic sketch artist already accustomed to working with the police? Perfect. But I knew you had a pretty big job to finish here, and because I knew, so did he."

"He must be a powerful telepath."

"Oh, he is. Even more so these days, I hear, since he teamed up with and married another equally powerful psychic."

"And how did you hear? The psychic newsletter? Because I don't get that."

Beau grinned at her disgruntled tone. "I keep trying to tell you there are lots of connections in life."

"Yeah, right. That degrees-of-separation stuff?"

"Sure. So I know you — and by extension everybody you know as well. It adds up."

Maggie was never entirely certain if these interesting theories of Beau's were theories — or universal facts he understood simply because he was unusually plugged into the universe.

"Um . . . okay."

He grinned again. "Never mind. So what's the plan for the day?"

"I'm going to interview Ellen Randall again in about an hour. I want to check on Hollis, make sure she's all right. Then back to the station and meet up with the others, see what if anything they've managed to find out about a possible connection in Tara Jameson's life to the man who abducted her."

"You shouldn't be out alone."

"I work best alone, you know that."

"Not this time, Maggie. This time, working alone is dangerous for you."

"I'm being careful."

"Are you?"

She conjured a smile and hoped it was reassuring. "Of course I am. Besides, you know only too well that hiding won't do me any good. I have to do what I can to stop this animal. I have to."

"Yes. But not alone. You have to use all the tools you've been given this time."

"Some of them are no help at all." Broodingly, she looked down at her closed sketch pad. "The irony is that this is the monster I'm supposed to stop, the reason I'm here — at least this time around — and even though I've been given an ability that's helped me stop others, it isn't helping me the least bit with him. I can't see him. I'm as blind as his victims are."

"And there must be a reason for that."

"The universe wants to piss me off?"

He smiled. "Maybe. I've always suspected there's a real cosmic sense of humor out there."

"If so, it's a twisted humor, Beau. This is not funny."

"I know. But there's something you have to keep in mind, Maggie. As much as you're focused on stopping this man, the universe is a huge and complicated place. The patterns all around us are made up of uncounted threads, woven in complex designs, and every thread is important to the whole. It isn't just about him. It isn't just about his victims, or the cops."

"Or me."

He nodded. "Or you."

She drew a breath, then said dryly, "Thanks, Master."

"You're welcome, Grasshopper."

Maggie had to smile. "Well, while I keep the immensity of the universe firmly in mind, I have to go on working in my little corner of it. Any advice — this time?"

"Brush after every meal."

"You know, you're not nearly as funny as you think you are."

"No? Ah, well. One tries."

"One fails."

"You're just grumpy because you don't get the psychic newsletter." His smile faded slightly. "Maggie? I was right about John Garrett, wasn't I?"

She got up and for a moment just looked at him. Then her mouth twisted, and she said, "Yeah. You were right."

"Fate."

"Fate. See you later, Beau."

For a long time after she left, Beau sat there staring into space. Then, so reluctant that every movement was slow and careful, he got up and went to the big painting leaning against the wall, covered with a piece of heavy material so that Maggie hadn't even noticed it.

Beau propped the still-covered painting on a secondary easel and stepped away for a moment, trying to prepare himself. Then he drew a deep breath and flipped back the material.

A detached part of his mind noted the technique and skill displayed, seeing and accepting the unsettling fact that this was arguably the best work of his life. But that wasn't all he saw. He saw the vague yet identifiable faces and forms of what he recognized as tormented women trapped in a dark hell of suffering, their arms reaching out desperately for help, most of them with empty eye sockets wide, open mouths pleading.

He saw the hands that had destroyed the women, hands clenched into fists, hands wielding knives and holding ropes, and hands reaching out for the women, as though to pull them back down into hell.

For a long, long time, Beau didn't move. He stared at the painting, absorbing every brush stroke, every nuance. Ignoring the nausea churning in his gut, he stared until he was certain every dreadful detail was burned into his mind.

Then he went and got a tool designed to

cut canvas and very methodically shredded the best work he'd ever done.

"Not this time," he muttered into the silence of the studio. "Goddammit, not this time."

"I always end up working in boring police conference rooms," Quentin said somewhat sadly to the room at large. "And with a great hotel this time too."

"It'll keep you humble," Kendra told him.

"Yeah, right."

John came in then and immediately asked, "Anybody heard from Maggie?"

"Not since you have," Quentin told him. "She was going to interview Ellen Randall and then stop off at the hospital to see Hollis Templeton, right?"

"So she said."

"Hasn't had time to do both, I'd say. And where have you been?"

"Letting Drummond vent some of his spleen."

Quentin grimaced. "Yeah, I thought when he was so painfully polite to us this morning that he was itching to explode."

John shrugged. "I thought it'd be better for all of us if he got it out of his system."

"We appreciate that," Jennifer said dryly.

"I won't say it was a pleasure — but you're welcome." Obviously restless, John looked at his watch, then sat down at the conference table. "Andy's still trying to hurry the medical examiner, but it'll probably be late this afternoon before we have the results of the postmortem on Samantha Mitchell."

"I'm not surprised," Quentin said absently, prowling back and forth in front of the bulletin boards. "According to the police scanner we were listening to yesterday, there were a couple of really bad fires in the city, with fatalities. The M.E.'s probably got more than he can handle."

"Still," John said.

"Still," Quentin agreed. He prowled a while longer, but when Kendra gave him a very direct look, he finally sat down across from John. Half under his breath, he said, "For somebody with a uniquely flexible mind, she gets very irritated by the smallest things."

"Even I was getting irritated," John told him dryly.

Jennifer added, "Me too, but I wasn't going to mention it."

"Then why did you?" Quentin demanded.

"Everybody else did."

Quentin sighed. "All right, all right. Can I help it if I'm restless? I hate this part of the job. Basically just sitting around going through papers and scratching our heads while we wait for the bastard to make another move." He watched John look at his watch again and added, "And I'm not the only one who hates it."

Ignoring that, John said, "Scott's out talking to Tara Jameson's coworkers, right?"

Quentin nodded. "Kendra's been running background checks on every name we've got, but so far everyone in her life looks clean. The fiancé definitely is, with a strong alibi to boot. No family here in the city. Andy has a couple of detectives canvassing the building again, and I just spent the past two hours going over the security videotapes."

"And found nothing, I gather?"

"Nada. I have a hunch the tapes don't show anything because he monkeyed with the cameras, but I'm no expert."

"Then we need to send them to someone who is."

"That's my thinking."

Jennifer said, "The security company will raise hell, most likely. They swear their cameras have not been altered in any way, that it would have been impossible for any unauthorized person to do that. Of course, they also can't explain how Tara Jameson vanished from her supposedly secure building. The egg on their faces isn't pretty."

"Has Andy made an official request for the cameras?" John asked.

She nodded. "He's doing that as we speak. And we have technicians standing by to take the things apart as soon as we get our hands on them."

"So we wait," Quentin said with a sigh. "I hate waiting." He stared at the bulletin board. "Kendra, any luck from the databases on that 1894 date?"

She shook her head without a glance at the humming laptop before her. "Not so far. Hardly surprising, considering we're going back more than a hundred years. Most records that old haven't been digitized yet."

"If it comes to that," Jennifer said, "we aren't even sure the 1894 date is part of this. Even if it *was* on the note, it doesn't have to mean anything. Maybe our mysterious tipster just wants to make us waste time looking."

Quentin looked at her for a long moment, then said matter-of-factly, "You wrote the note, Jenn."

She stared at him. "What? No, I didn't."

"Look in your notebook." His voice remained steady, even gentle. "You'll find a page torn out. The page you found in your car will match it."

At first it seemed she wouldn't do it, but finally she opened her small black notebook on the table and slowly flipped through the pages covered by her neat shorthand notes. They all saw her pause. And they all saw her rub her finger gently across the ragged remains of a torn-out page.

By the time Maggie left Ellen Randall's house just after noon, she felt drained. She drove only as far as the nearest recreation area and stopped there, carefully parking her car in an open space where she could see anyone approach her, and warily leaving the engine running even as she double-checked to make certain all the doors were locked.

For several minutes, she sat there studying her surroundings, senses probing. Nothing. The place was virtually deserted on this dreary weekday. Still, Maggie couldn't quite relax and kept glancing up from time to time even as she opened her sketchbook and looked at the still-incomplete sketch of the rapist/killer.

Ellen hadn't been able to add anything to what Maggie already knew, and her continuing pain and anguish were still so intense it was difficult for Maggie to feel anything else right now, but she tried to concentrate.

Longish hair. Roughly oval face — maybe. Difficult to be sure, since he always seemed to wear a plastic mask of some kind. Eyes? Who knew what shape or color. Who knew if his nose was straight, or his mouth thin-lipped or full. Who knew if his ears were set high or low.

None of the women had seen him. Not so much as a glance. They had only felt what he did to them. Felt his body against theirs, felt his hands touching them.

His hands.

Hardly aware of what she was doing, Maggie turned to a fresh page and began slowly, tentatively drawing. Her eyes were half closed, remembered voices soft in her mind while remembered suffering made her ache.

. . . felt his hands holding my wrists . . .

. . . he pushed my chin up, as if he wanted to look at my throat, and then he touched it . . .

. . . he was holding my legs apart . . .

. . . strong, so strong. The grip of his fingers was so strong, his nails bit into my skin even through the gloves I know he was wearing, dug into my very bones . . .

. . . he cupped my cheek with this obscene gentleness, and then I felt his teeth . . .

. . . he was squeezing my breasts and I could hear him breathing, panting . . .

. . . his nails dug into me . . .

. . . he slapped me, and I felt —

— the ring he wore tore her flesh, laid it open along her jawline. She could feel the warm wetness of her own blood trickling down over her throat, feel him hanging over her like some monstrous creature out of her nightmares. Part of her was glad he'd wrapped the nightgown around her head in a blindfold, because she was terrified to see his face, to see the animal he'd become. But she was even more terrified of what he was going to do to her now that he had her helpless. She felt his hands roughly tying her wrist to the bedpost just as he'd tied the other one, and a low moan of protest and anguish throbbed in her bruised throat.

Bobby . . . don't, please . . . Bobby, I'm sorry, I'm sorry, I didn't mean —

Maggie came out of it with a start, hearing an odd little whimper that at first she didn't even recognize as coming from her own throat. With shaking hands, she wiped at the tears on her face, looking around her to make certain there was no one near as well as to ground herself once more in the here and now.

A peaceful scene. A park mostly deserted on this Wednesday afternoon in November, a bit damp and chilly, but unthreatening. Quiet.

Safe? Probably not, but for the moment she was safe, surely. For the moment.

But it was nevertheless several long and unsettling minutes before the overwhelming terror and strange sense of guilt finally left her, before her breathing steadied and the hot pressure of tears eased.

Before she could nerve herself to look down at what she'd drawn.

Hands. A man's hands reaching out for something or someone, raw-boned in their brutal strength. Awful in their sick, grasping hunger. Large, sinewy, ugly. With sparse black hairs sprinkled across the backs and even onto the fingers. Nails that were surprisingly long but ragged because he bit them.

Because he bit them . . .

The fleeting memory, wispy as smoke,

drifted away, and Maggie was left staring down at the hands she'd drawn. So unique she knew she'd recognize them instantly if she saw them in the flesh. But otherwise there was nothing to identify them — except the rings.

On the right hand was a big gold ring, inset with some kind of stone.

On the left hand was a wedding band.

Maggie stared down at the sketch for a long time, her gaze locked on the hands that had tortured and maimed and murdered so many women.

"Bobby," she whispered.

CHAPTER
SIXTEEN

"But how could I have written it without knowing I had?" Jennifer protested. "I swear to you, I don't remember anything except finding the note in my car."

"Of course you don't remember," Quentin said soothingly. "I'm not saying you did it consciously, Jenn."

She scowled at him. "How else could I have done it?"

"It's called automatic writing. It's a way to free the unconscious mind, to tap into our own memories or abilities."

"You're saying I *remembered* those dates?"

"No, in your case I'm saying it was a latent ability you tapped into." He traded glances with Kendra. "We're not entirely sure where it comes from, but automatic writing sometimes shows up during stressful situations, especially in cases of extreme need. You tend to be intuitive, don't you?"

"Yeah, sometimes."

"That's usually the case. Someone with good intuition can often tap into unsuspected, latent abilities."

"Are you saying I'm psychic?"

"No, I'm saying that with the right trigger some time during the early years of your life, you might have been. There's a theory that most humans have some sort of extrasensory ability if we only know how to tap into it. Maybe left over from more primitive times, when we needed an edge just to survive one day to the next."

"I've heard that," Jennifer admitted.

Quentin nodded. "In this case, you badly wanted an answer, or at least something to point you in the right direction, so your subconscious tried to help, opening itself up — sort of like an antenna. Thoughts are just energy, after all, the electrical impulses of the brain."

She was still frowning. "My mind picked up somebody else's thoughts?"

"Caught the gist of them, let's say." He frowned as he thought of those two dates. "The bare gist."

"And those thoughts just happened to come from the rapist?"

"There are few coincidences in life, I've found. You're looking for him, and have been for months. He's . . . embedded in your consciousness. Science is only beginning to understand the way our brains work, but suppose the electrical energy of our individual minds has a signature as distinctive as a fingerprint. That's entirely possible. And maybe there's a part of our brains that can recognize those signatures, even if we can't do it consciously."

"So my subconscious sort of tracked his?"

"Maybe. It's certainly a possibility. In any case, we've found that the source automatic writing taps into tends to be surprisingly both specific and accurate."

She eyed him. "Has anybody ever told you that you are a very weird FBI agent?"

"Frequently."

"I'm not surprised."

John said, "But he is making sense. At least, I think he is. And none of us has been able to come up with any other explanation for how that note got into your car."

Jennifer sighed. "Great, that's just great. Now I not only talk to myself, but my subconscious mind is listening in on other minds."

"Only under extreme stress," Quentin reminded her gravely.

She got up. "I'm leaving now. I'm going out on the streets to talk — out loud — to some of the uniforms who patrol the area where Hollis Templeton was found."

"Still looking for your transient?"

"I'm going to find him, dammit. With absolutely no help from my subconscious."

Kendra asked, "Mind if I come along? I don't know if I'll be any help, since this is your territory rather than mine, but God knows I could use the fresh air and exercise. If I stare at this laptop much longer, I'll either go to sleep or go nuts."

Jennifer barely hesitated. "Sure. I'd welcome the company."

"Don't get into trouble," Quentin told his partner.

"Without you along," she responded politely, "how on earth would I?"

"Ouch," John murmured.

"She's mean when she loses sleep," Quentin told him.

Kendra wiggled her fingers gently at her partner and followed a grinning Jennifer from the room.

Quentin sighed. "I don't think Jennifer quite bought the automatic-writing explanation. Sometimes I forget how hard this sort of thing is for most people to accept."

"But you do believe that's where the note came from?"

"Oh, yeah."

"Then am I wrong in thinking the

chances are the rapist was somewhere close by when Jennifer . . . tuned in on him?"

"You caught that, huh?" Quentin smiled. "Yeah, probably. Distance is usually a factor, so it's likely he was nearby. That's why Kendra's tagging along with Jenn. We don't figure this is the sort of guy who hangs around police stations because cops fascinate him; if he was here, it was because he was watching someone."

"Jennifer?"

"Maybe. He might well consider grabbing a cop to be the ultimate challenge."

"But it could have been any woman entering or leaving this building?"

"Of course. Or any woman in the general area, for that matter. There's no way to know for sure."

"Figures." John looked at his watch again and said restlessly, "I know there hasn't been a lot of time and virtually no new information, but are you two profilers getting a handle on the way this animal's mind works?"

Quentin tapped a finger on the legal pad in front of him, where his neat printing filled most of the top page. "Maybe."

"And?"

"And the bastard likes his work. A lot."

"Yeah, I got that. Answer me this. Why

have victims of his attacks survived when those in 1934 didn't? I mean, if he's copying the crimes."

"Good question. I'd guess he expected them to die; he took care always to leave them in out-of-the-way locations where they were more than likely to remain undiscovered, certainly long enough to bleed to death or die of exposure, especially this time of year. The fact is, those women fought to stay alive, maybe harder than he expected. And after three straight victims survived, he made damned sure Samantha Mitchell wouldn't, by cutting her throat."

"If he expected them to die, why bother to blind them?"

"To keep them from seeing. Maybe his face, or maybe something else. He didn't want them watching him, didn't want them to see what he did to them. Maybe didn't want them to know he enjoyed it."

John's mouth twisted. "Christ."

"Yeah. Not a nice boy."

"Massive understatement." John was silent for a long time, his gaze moving over the photos and sketches on the bulletin boards. Then, slowly, he said, "Quentin, do you believe in fate?"

"Yep."

"That was quick."

Quentin chuckled. "John, when you do the sort of work I do, you get most of your own philosophies and beliefs figured out early on. You bet I believe in fate. I also believe in reincarnation — and the two are definitely connected. Is there a karmic pattern to our lives? You'd better believe it."

"What about free will?"

"Oh, there's that too. I never understood why people think they're mutually exclusive. Ask me, our entire lives aren't planned out for us — just some things. Specific events along the way, crossroads we're meant to come to. Tests, maybe, to measure our progress. But we always have choices, and those choices can send us along an unplanned path."

"And change our fates?"

"I believe so. Still, if you listen to Bishop and Miranda — and I certainly do, though don't tell them I admitted that — there are some things that are meant to happen at a certain moment and in a certain way. No matter which path you choose, which decisions you make along your own particular journey, those pivotal moments appear to be set in stone. Maybe they represent the specific lessons we're meant to learn."

"Set in stone. Things we have to face. Things we have to learn. Responsibilities we have to fulfill. And mistakes we have to correct." John continued to stare broodingly at the bulletin board.

Quentin watched his friend for a moment, then said quietly, "So that's it. That's why Maggie does what she does. Atonement?"

"She says . . . she's responsible for the continued existence of this bastard. Because she didn't stop him once before, as she was meant to."

"I see. No copycat at all, just the same twisted, evil soul reborn to do his thing one more time."

John looked at him. "You don't seem surprised."

"This isn't the first time we've encountered something along these lines."

"A reincarnated killer?"

"That's right." Quentin's smile was a bit wry. "Reincarnated, resurrected — or just plain dead and still kicking. An amazingly resilient thing, evil."

"You're saying Maggie really is responsible for this?"

"I'm saying the universe might be holding her accountable for it, or for some part of it. Maybe that's why she was put in this particular place at this particular time and given the abilities she was born with."

"To suffer? To pay in agony for a mistake she might have made a long time ago?" John was dimly surprised by the harsh sound of his own voice.

"We all pay for our mistakes, John. In this life — or the next. But if you believe that, you also have to believe we're rewarded when we get it right. Yeah, Maggie's suffering in this life. She's also helping other people, easing their suffering. Whether she's here to correct a mistake or just living another stage in her own spiritual development, I'd say Maggie is earning major bonus points this time around."

John had to smile, albeit reluctantly. "So she'll be rewarded in the next life?"

"Hey, maybe she'll be rewarded later on in this one."

"If she corrects her past mistake?"

Quentin shrugged. "Maybe. Then again, Maggie might already have balanced her books with the universe, John, despite the sense of responsibility she still feels. We have no way of knowing what's expected of us."

"Not even seers?"

"Not even seers."

After a moment, John said, "That really sucks."

"Tell me about it."

Long after Maggie left her, Hollis sat as she usually did, her face turned toward the window. She wondered idly if, after tomorrow, she'd still be able to hear as acutely as she did now. She could hear the cop out in the hall shift in the chair where he sat. She could hear the elevators at the end of the hall as the cars passed this floor on their journeys up and down. She could hear the murmur of somebody's television. Outside and several floors down, she could hear the busy *swish* of traffic.

Would she be able to hear so well if, tomorrow, she could see again? Probably not. But that wasn't what bothered her. She would happily trade the sharper hearing for the return of her sight. But would she, alone of all the victims so far, survive his attack still able to see? And if so — why? If Maggie was right about fate and destiny, there had to be a reason. What had she done to earn that?

Or . . . what was she supposed to do?

Quietly, she murmured, "Annie? Are you there?"

I'm here.

The voice was faint, hardly louder than a whisper, but at least it was a reply after many hours of silence.

"There's a lot you haven't told me, isn't there?"

Yes.

"Why? Don't you trust me?"

I had to be so careful, especially at first. Other times . . . other times, those I tried to warn could never accept me. I . . . frightened them. I didn't want to frighten you.

"I'm not frightened."

I know. Now.

"Then tell me what I can do to help Maggie. She helped me, more than she knows. She took away so much of the pain and fear. And . . . she's fighting for all of us. I have to help her. Tell me how, Annie." At first, she didn't think there'd be any sort of answer. But finally, even more distantly and fading into silence, the answer came.

Soon. Soon, Hollis. . . .

When John finally reached Maggie on her cell phone, he had to force himself to speak calmly. "Where are you?"

"I'm leaving the hospital after checking on Hollis." She sounded as calm as always, though John fancied he could detect a note of strain. "I just turned the phone back on."

"Then you're on your way back here?"

"I was. But there's one more thing I

think I should go ahead and do today."

"What?"

"A walk-through of the building where they found Samantha Mitchell. Maybe I can get something useful. Can you give me the address?"

Immediately, John said, "You don't need to do that alone, Maggie. I'll meet you there."

She barely hesitated. "Okay, fine. What's the address?"

He found the Mitchell file on the cluttered conference table and read off the address to her, finishing with, "If you get there first, wait outside for me. All right?"

"I will. See you there."

John closed his cell phone and said to Quentin, "She shouldn't do it alone."

"Did I say anything?"

"You wanted to."

Quentin smiled slightly, but said very quietly, "She has to do this her way, just like I warned you days ago. But you already knew that, didn't you, John?"

"Let's just say I figured it out. I've gotten to know Maggie, to understand what makes her tick, or at least I think I have. You said all along that her motivation for feeling the pain of all those victims had to be deep, powerful. Maybe even . . . set in stone. Atonement. Whatever the . . . judgment . . . of the universe, in Maggie's mind there's only one way to truly correct the mistake she believes she made. Stop this bastard, here and now. And she means to do everything in her power to make sure that happens, no matter what the cost to herself."

"I'd say so. I'd also say you won't do her any favors by trying to protect her, and you won't stop her from doing what she feels she has to do."

"Are you sure about that? Can you be?"

"Are you asking me if I know what the future will bring?"

Visibly bracing himself, John replied, "I guess that is what I'm asking you. Can I protect her?"

"No."

After a long moment, John drew a breath and said lightly, "You won't mind if I try?"

"I wouldn't expect anything else."

John nodded, then turned without another word and left.

Alone again in the conference room, Quentin murmured into the silence, "Fate doesn't expect anything else of you either, John. I wonder when you'll realize that."

When Andy came into the conference room a few minutes later, he found

Quentin slumped in his chair, feet propped on a closed file on the conference table and fingers laced together across his middle. He was frowning.

Andy didn't know the agent well, but he knew preoccupation when he saw it. "Worried about John?"

"Hmm?" He looked at Andy and blinked.

"I asked if you were worried about John. I saw him leave a little while ago, and he looked a bit . . . upset."

Absently, Quentin said, "Yeah, he isn't hiding his feelings too well right now, is he?"

"He's going after Maggie?"

"Yeah."

Patient, Andy said, "And you're worried?"

Quentin blinked again, then shook his head. "No, not about that. No sense worrying about something set in stone a long time ago."

Andy started to ask what he meant by that, then decided he really didn't want to know. "Then what?"

"Did you ever get the nagging feeling there was something you'd overlooked?"

"Occasionally."

"And?"

"And I usually find I've overlooked something."

"Yeah. Me too." Quentin stared at the cluttered table. "Somewhere among all this stuff is a detail I should have paid closer attention to."

"Can't narrow it down any more than that?"

"No. Dammit." He took his feet off the table and sat up, opening the closed file rather grimly. "But I intend to, because it's bugging the hell out of me."

Andy shrugged philosophically. "Let me know when you find it."

When he reached the abandoned and deserted building where Samantha Mitchell's body had been found, John wasn't surprised to find the entire area all but deserted. It wasn't an especially inviting day — cold, cloudy, and dreary, and misting rain from time to time — and the neighborhood wasn't what anyone would have called appealing. Far from it. What few buildings within view hadn't already been condemned or scheduled for demolition wore the barred-window, iron-grated-door look of desperate fortresses holding danger at bay.

Maggie's car was parked in front of the building where Samantha had been found, and she got out as he parked his car, waiting for him on the sidewalk.

"This is not what I'd call a cheerful place," he noted as he joined her.

"Hardly," Maggie agreed. She was hugging the sketch pad to her breast as she often did, as though it were a shield. The chill breeze made the tip of her nose pink and stirred her long hair so that it seemed to have an independent life all its own. "It's almost as if he chooses the places where he leaves his victims partly for their desolation. As if he wants the women to feel . . . abandoned. Alone."

"Maybe he does. Maybe it's all part of his twisted game to isolate his victims in every sense of the word."

She shivered visibly. "Yeah."

"Maggie, maybe you should wait to do this."

"We need all the information we can get, you know that."

"Yeah, but it's hardly fair — even of a demanding universe — to expect you to keep putting yourself through this."

"Didn't anybody ever teach you that life isn't especially fair?"

He looked at her for a moment, then said lightly, "I'm learning that all the time."

Suddenly a bit self-conscious, Maggie

went to put the sketch pad inside her car. "No reason to take this in with me," she said. "I never can sketch anything while I'm walking through anyway."

When she rejoined him, John touched her arm. "Are you sure you're up to this? After our all-nighter at the station, you can't have gotten much rest."

"I doubt anybody got much rest. Did you?"

"No — but I'm not an empath carrying around the weight of other people's pain."

Maggie smiled suddenly. "Can you imagine yourself even saying that a week ago?"

He had to laugh, however briefly. "No. In fact — hell, no."

"We live and learn." She started up the uneven walkway to the front doorway of the building.

John followed. "And you didn't answer me. Should you be doing this today?"

"We don't have a lot of time left."

He caught her arm just short of the front steps and stopped her. "Something you feel? Or something you know?"

"Both." She met his intent gaze as steadily as she could. "Tara Jameson could already be dead, but even if she isn't, she's suffering right now."

"That isn't your fault, Maggie."

She didn't try to argue with him. "If I don't do everything within my power to try to find her, to stop him, I'll blame myself for the rest of my life. Do you understand that?"

He hesitated, then with an oddly tentative movement as if he couldn't really help himself, he reached up and brushed back a strand of her hair that had blown across her cheek, his fingers lingering only a moment against her skin. "If I don't understand anything else, I do understand that," he said. "But there's something you have to understand, Maggie. I lost my sister to this bastard. Andy and his detectives have lived with the investigation for months. Quentin and Kendra put their lives on the line every day trying to put monsters of every kind in cages where they belong. Maybe we don't feel the pain of the victims as intensely as you do — but we feel it."

Maggie drew a deep breath and let it out slowly. "You're right. I'm sorry. I'm just not used to . . ."

"Being a team player?"

"Don't tell me you're used to it."

He smiled. "Usually a team leader. So this isn't so easy for me either. But as long as I can feel I'm contributing, I can handle not being the one in charge."

Dryly, Maggie said, "I have a feeling you've been in charge since you got here. One way or another."

"Don't tell Andy that. Or Quentin, for that matter."

"If you think they don't know, you're wrong."

Realizing he was still holding her arm, John forced himself to let go of her. "Then they've been very gracious about it. So — we're going in there, huh?"

"I don't know if it'll help. Maybe he spent as little time here as he did all the other places he left his victims. Maybe I won't find anything new. But I have to try."

"Okay. Hang on a minute — it's so overcast out here, we're bound to need flashlights inside."

Maggie waited while he returned to his car for a couple of flashlights, and then they entered the building.

The flashlights helped them see a place very like the one where Hollis Templeton had been left — a dirty, ramshackle building that had long ago been stripped to its bare bones. The floor creaked underfoot, and they could both hear the whispering scurry of rats.

"Yuck," Maggie said. "I hate rats."

"I'm not crazy about them either. And there's no blood trail to follow this time; according to the report, she was found down that hallway, a room at the rear, on the left side of the building." John kept his voice matter-of-fact.

Maggie stood there for a moment, collecting herself, slowly opening the door to those inner senses. Almost immediately she could smell the blood, and it was no easier to bear than before, thick and cloying in her nostrils. But this time, she forced herself to push past that, to let her senses probe beyond the sickly sweet odor.

"Maggie?"

"I'm okay. It . . . feels different somehow."

"In what way?"

"I'm not sure." She began moving slowly down the long hallway toward the back of the building, where there were half a dozen rooms, their doors long gone and broken casings leaning drunkenly like a child's drawing of doorways.

"Creepy place, even with only five senses," John muttered.

Maggie wanted to tell him it was infinitely creepier with extra senses, but her attention was tunneling, fixing on the particular slanted doorway to the left that was drawing her toward it. The blood smell was growing stronger, and with it came flashes of darkness, much as she had sensed where Hollis had been left. Flashes of darkness, and pain, and terror, and — Why was it getting harder to breathe? Why did she feel an odd sensation, as if some great weight or . . . presence . . . hung over her, bent toward her —

She didn't even hear John's cell phone begin to ring.

CHAPTER
SEVENTEEN

Scott joined Quentin in the conference room, tired and dusty but triumphant, to add to the bulletin board two more photos of victims killed in 1934. "Dug these out of a file box over at the North station," he reported. "Victims number three and seven in that year."

Quentin stopped frowning over files on the conference table long enough to study the photos. "Resembling Samantha Mitchell and Tara Jameson, respectively."

"Yeah. That's six victims so far, and they match up with our six. Call me crazy, but I'd say that was fairly conclusive evidence that our guy is a copycat."

Andy, who had come in virtually on Scott's heels, nodded. "I'd say so."

Quentin said, "We're reasonably certain there were eight victims that year, right?"

Scott nodded. "According to that book Jenn found, yeah. But so far there's no sign of the police files for the remaining two victims. I've got two more possibles to check, including a hell of a big box of old miscellaneous files that somehow ended up at City Hall."

"Our tax dollars at work," Andy muttered. "Well, we don't know that finding photos of the last two victims will help us — but we don't know that it won't, either. Keep at it, Scott."

"You bet." Energy renewed by success, Scott hurried back out of the conference room.

Andy sat down at the table and rubbed his face with both hands. "I'm barely ten years older than he is, and it feels more like twenty. Jeez — what happens to stamina after thirty-five?"

"It's still there," Quentin told him. "It just has to be tended a bit more carefully. I like catnaps, myself."

Andy eyed him. "How many of those have you had today?"

"I'll get one later." Quentin frowned at the cluttered table. "I'm still in search of whatever it is that's bugging me."

"Still no idea what it is?"

"Not yet. But I know it's here somewhere." He reached for another file. "Something a friend or family member of a victim said in an interview? Something in an autopsy report or crime-scene photo? I just don't know."

Before Andy could respond, Quentin's cell phone rang, and as the agent answered, Andy could hear the excited, booming voice distinctly even across the table. It sounded like a big bear in a very small cave.

"Quentin? Hey, Quentin!"

"I hear you, Joey." Wincing, Quentin put a prudent few inches between the phone and his ear. "What's up?"

"Listen, Quentin, I got to thinking maybe I could help you find that rapist you cops are after, so I been asking around, and I think maybe I got a lead."

"Joey —"

"Guy I know swears he seen an old black Caddie like my dad used to drive parked weeks ago near where they found one of the ladies after he got done with her, and he thinks he seen it more than once since then. In the neighborhood, you know, around, 'specially at night."

Quentin untangled that as best he could. "All right, Joey, but, listen, don't —"

"The guy I know, he thinks he seen the car again just the other night, you know, where that poor Mitchell lady was found? So maybe it's the bastard you're looking for. I'm gonna check it out, Quentin, see if maybe I can find that Caddie for you."

"Joey, we can —"

"I'll let you know soon's I find something, Quentin — and I'll be careful, I promise."

"Joey? *Joey?*" Slowly, Quentin turned the phone off. "Shit," he muttered.

Andy said, "I gather that was the source who gave us Samantha Mitchell's fake kidnapper?"

"Yeah."

"You think he might be on to something?"

Quentin rose and went to a large city map on one wall, where several small red flags marked the locations where victims had been found. "Weeks ago, he said. Probably around the time Hollis Templeton was found. And if the car was seen again the other night near where Samantha Mitchell was found . . ." He indicated the two flags closest together. "Not more than three miles apart. Definitely what Joey would consider in the neighborhood. Yeah, he might be on to something."

Andy rose. "Then I say we check DMV records for a black Caddie. What model, do you think? *Old* covers a lot of territory."

Quentin came back to the conference table, still frowning. "Joey's dad was killed twenty-five years ago. As I recall, he drove a 1972 Caddie. To be on the safe side, I'd cover 1970 to at least '76."

"Right." Andy grimaced slightly. "There can't be too many thirty-year-old black Caddies still on the road, surely, at least not in Seattle."

"Let's hope not."

On the point of turning away, Andy said, "You look worried again."

"Yeah. Let's just say that Joey has all the subtlety and caution of the proverbial bull in a china shop."

"So if he finds that Caddie —"

"He's apt to find a hell of a lot more than he can handle," Quentin finished grimly.

"Then we'd better find it first." Andy left the room.

Quentin was left alone with his thoughts, and none of them was pleasant. He had no idea where Joey had been calling from and knew he had little chance of finding him before Joey quite possibly found trouble. Bad trouble. As much as Quentin wanted to find and catch the rapist, he really hoped Joey's lead at the very least failed to point Joey in the right direction.

All Quentin's training and experience told him that Joey's simple cunning and brute strength would be no match for the evil he was trying to find. Bad as he was, Joey wasn't nearly bad enough to successfully fight something he could never understand. Unless he was very, very lucky, he would lose that fight. Problem was, Joey had never been lucky.

And there were too many deaths on Quentin's conscience as it was.

"Shit," he said again, softly this time. He sent a restless glance toward his phone, wishing Joey would call again but certain he wouldn't, not because of any premonition but because he knew Joey was hellbent to find the rapist and so do something to help Quentin and repay an old debt. A debt Quentin had not hesitated to use in the ensuing years to keep Joey in line and out of trouble.

He was really beginning to wish he hadn't done that.

Trying not to worry about what he couldn't change, Quentin drew another file toward him and tried once again to figure out what was bugging him. But before he could get too deep into that, Andy returned to the room.

"The M.E.'s report on Samantha Mitchell," he told Quentin, not without satisfaction. "A few hours earlier than expected."

"Anything we didn't know?" Quentin asked, accepting the folder and opening it.

"Nah, not really. At least, not that I can see."

Quentin began reading the report, and almost immediately stiffened. *"Shit."*

Alarmed by the tone, Andy said, "What?"

"She died there? Samantha Mitchell died where her body was found?"

"Yeah. But we knew that."

Quentin grabbed his cell phone and began punching in a number, saying grimly, "Not all of us knew it."

John couldn't have said why he felt uneasy. Maybe it was simply because he still had trouble even imagining what Maggie was doing, what it was like to literally feel the sensations and emotions experienced by another person days and even weeks before, simply by walking through a place where they had occurred. Maybe it was this dark, chilled, and definitely eerie building. Or maybe it was just his own increasing sensitivity to emotions. His.

And hers.

"Creepy place, even with only five senses," he offered, more to maintain contact with Maggie than anything else.

He saw her turn her head toward him for a brief instant, but then she was gazing toward that dark doorway at the end of the hall, moving toward it.

John had the strongest impulse to stop her, to get his hands on her so that he could — could what?

His cell phone rang, and he jumped as the strident sound broke the silence. Maggie didn't even seem to hear it, still walking toward the room, going through the doorway. He followed, though he was still behind her as he dug his phone out and opened it. And he heard even before he could get the phone to his ear.

"John? Get out of there." Quentin's voice was sharp, imperative.

"What? What're you —"

"Listen to me. Get out of there. Get Maggie out. Now. She died there, John. Samantha Mitchell died there, in that room. And if Maggie gets too close —"

John heard a thud, saw Maggie's flashlight hit the floor, and quickly pointed his own at her. He was still behind her and at first saw only the cloud of her hair, long and a little wild. But then she turned slowly, making an odd choking sound.

Her hands were at her throat, the face above them very pale, and her mouth was open as though she wanted to say something to him.

For an eternal instant, John was frozen, just staring at her. Then she took her hands from her throat, looking at them as though they belonged to someone else.

Her hands were covered with blood.

So was her throat.

Jennifer rejoined Kendra beside the car and shrugged wearily. "There are an awful lot of transients in this area, so I guess I can't blame the uniforms for not noticing one in particular. Dammit."

"We can check the shelters again."

"I know. But they won't start filling up until tonight."

Kendra nodded. "And I noticed that a few likely people to question sort of melted away when we got here."

"Yeah. The uniforms say everybody's jumpy as hell around here. And, of course, some of the transients figure if we can't find the actual rapist we'll make do with one of them." She sighed. "Really can't blame them for the distrust, but it doesn't make the job any easier."

"No." Slowly, Kendra added, "Didn't your patrolman friend say Robson was picked up for creating a disturbance?"

"Yeah. According to the arrest report, he was accosting people coming out of that liquor store just down the block, babbling something about how the ghost of his old enemy was coming after him. And he kept looking toward the building over there where Hollis Templeton was found." Jennifer shook her head, suddenly uncomfortable under the other woman's steady, clear-eyed gaze. "At the very least, this is turning into a real wild-goose chase. I don't know why I thought it could be a legitimate lead. Just a drunk rambling, probably."

"There must have been something that drew your attention. Something that alerted your instincts."

Jennifer fumbled for a toothpick and made herself say, "Maybe it was just desperation. Maybe I'm imagining leads where none exist."

Kendra smiled faintly. "I doubt that. You're too good a cop to imagine something like that. You trust the friend who gave you the tip, right? That was why you followed up on it initially."

"Yeah."

"But there was something else, wasn't there? Maybe something you read in the arrest report?"

Jennifer almost denied it, but then as she recalled details of the report one by one, she realized what had caught her attention. And felt the rush of adrenaline she always felt when a puzzle piece fell into place. "Yeah, there was something. Most of his ramblings didn't make sense — he's more schizophrenic than bipolar, if you ask me — but Robson did say something that struck me."

"What?"

"He said the ghost of his old enemy was carrying a sack over one shoulder — a sack with puppies in it. Robson was certain the ghost was going to drown the puppies, then come back for him."

Kendra nodded slowly. "There was something alive in the sack, that's what he saw. Something moving."

"Yeah. That, plus the fact that this ghost of his was carrying anything at all, seemed to me just a bit too detailed to be completely delusional."

Turning to study the building in the distance where Hollis had been found, Kendra said, "I'd guess at least a few transients use that half-demolished warehouse there on the corner for shelter when the weather's bad. It was cold when Hollis was found, wasn't it?"

"Yeah, very."

"Am I wrong, or can the rear of that building be seen from at least one side of the warehouse?"

"Let's go find out."

Ten minutes later, the two women stood gingerly on a rusted old catwalk still connected to a single interior wall of what remained of the warehouse. There wasn't much inside the building, but what was there was clear evidence that at least a few people had been using the place as shelter recently. There was some old furniture — a mildewed sofa and ragged chair — grouped in one corner with a threadbare tarp providing a third wall to help keep out at least the worst of the wind, and a fire had been kindled in an old trash barrel in the center of the area, obviously for warmth.

With the toe of one shoe, Jennifer nudged a pile of newspapers and old rags that had clearly been used as a bed up on the catwalk. "Scary place to sleep, I'd think."

"But maybe safer than down there," Kendra pointed out, gesturing toward the concrete floor below. "At least from the viewpoint of a paranoid schizophrenic. The way this thing creaks, it would certainly provide a warning if company came."

"Yeah. And maybe he slept underneath the window for the same reason — because he was paranoid and wanted to keep an eye on things." Jennifer looked at the window just above the makeshift bed; it was the only one that still had opaque frosted glass in most of its panes, but two of the panes were missing. And through the openings, she had a dandy view of the rear of the building where Hollis had been found. "And take a look — you were right."

Kendra leaned in to glance out the window. "Far as I can tell, this is probably the only vantage point in the area where that entrance would be clearly visible. Isn't that a streetlight just off the corner there?"

"Yeah. So even on a dark night, Robson — if it was him up here — could have seen someone go into the building and could have been able to tell he was carrying something wrapped in a tarp or in a sack, something that moved."

"A ghost. Maybe masked, eerie in the light. Or maybe even someone he really did recognize from his own past." Kendra looked at Jennifer with a faint smile. "If you ask me, this is no wild-goose chase we're on. I say we keep looking for David Robson."

Conscious of the familiar adrenaline

rush, Jennifer nodded. "I agree."

It was only a few minutes later, as they got into the car, that she added, "How did you know there was something in the report that could have been important, anyway? You never saw the report, did you?"

"No."

"Well, then?"

Kendra smiled. "Call it a hunch."

"Christ, John, I'm sorry," Quentin said into the phone. "Since this bastard always just dumped the women and left, doing his torturing and maiming elsewhere, I assumed he'd done the same thing to Samantha Mitchell. That he'd cut her throat and abdomen *before* he carried her to that building and then just arranged her body for maximum shock effect. If I'd paid closer attention to the crime-scene photos, I would have seen it; that mattress was soaked with blood, especially around her head and shoulders. I should have realized that he must have killed her there, in that room."

"It isn't your fault, Quentin." John sighed. "We were all a bit distracted trying to deal with the less . . . physical details of all this."

"No excuse, not for me. How's Maggie?"

"If you want the truth, she's doing better than I am. The bleeding stopped as soon as I got her out of the building, and by the time I got her in the car and wiped some of the blood away, there was just an angry-looking red line where before it was . . . open."

"Where is she now?"

"Sleeping. The moment the shock wore off, it seemed all she wanted to do was sleep. So I brought her back here to her place and put her to bed."

"Then I'm sure she'll be okay. She wasn't in there long enough to connect completely with what happened to Samantha Mitchell."

"And if she had been? Are you telling me it could have killed her?"

Quentin hesitated, then said, "It's possible, at least in this instance. I don't think she's quite there yet, but if her sensitivity continues to increase, I believe she might eventually become an absolute empath."

"Absolute?"

"Yeah. Her system, both physically and emotionally, would become so sensitive it would literally absorb the injuries or illnesses of someone else. If you cut your hand and she touched you, the cut would heal on you — and appear on her. A real, bleeding cut, pain and all, identical to the one you'd had."

"Jesus."

"Yeah. What I'm not sure about is whether she's a healing empath or a sharing empath. If she's healing, any injury she absorbed — at least, short of a mortal one — she would also be able to heal. So your cut would vanish, and the one on her would disappear as soon as she was able to heal it, probably within minutes."

"That . . . can't be possible," John protested. "To heal someone else's physical injuries with a touch?"

"Oh, that part of it's definitely possible, believe me. I know of a healer so gifted she literally brought a man back from the dead after he was shot. With her, though, it's a distinct ability, not empathic but simply healing; it takes a great deal of her own energy, her own life force, to heal, but she doesn't absorb the actual wounds of whoever she's trying to help."

"But Maggie would. If she's a healing empath."

"That would be my guess."

"And if she's a sharing empath . . . she wouldn't heal? She'd just absorb the injuries, the pain, and suffer with them?"

Quentin hesitated again. "I don't know for sure, John. We've never encountered an absolute empath, just theorized about one. But considering the slash on Maggie's throat 'healed' as quickly as it did, I'd say she'll probably be a healing empath. The only real question is whether it'll be an automatic ability, triggered simply by touch, or one she'll have to concentrate to use. We'll hope for the latter, so she'll have some control."

John drew a breath. "Now tell me how she absorbed a slashed throat from an empty room, will you?"

"Samantha Mitchell died in that room. Recently — and horribly. Suffering a hell of a lot of pain and anguish, to say nothing of terror. Those emotions, that energy, lingered there in the room. Maggie was able to connect to that, to actually begin to experience some of what that dying woman went through." With a sigh, Quentin added, "Whether she evolves into an absolute empath or not, I think Maggie's system is especially sensitive to these particular deaths because she's connected to them, linked to them in a very . . . basic way."

"Fate. Destiny."

"Yeah. Whether these victims are all

souls Maggie's known before or it's his slimy soul she's connected to is impossible for me to say. Maybe she knows."

Sitting in Maggie's quiet living room, gazing at the painting above the fireplace, John said, "Maybe I'll ask her. But I'm hoping she'll sleep for hours yet. Look, I don't think she should be alone, so I'm going to stay here. If anything happens, anything changes, or you guys come up with something we need to know, call me, okay?"

"I will. Considering the worsening weather, I'm expecting Kendra and Jennifer back anytime now, and Scott as well. If nothing else, we'll at least have the DMV list of black Caddies to go over. Something's about to break, I know that much. I have an itchy feeling on the back of my neck, and that usually means we're close to the end of things."

"One way or another?"

"Yeah. One way or another."

After they'd said goodbye and hung up, John wandered over to the fireplace and gazed up at the painting. The signature on the lower corner was a scrawl, but he could read it. Rafferty. Beau Rafferty. Her brother's work.

No wonder the style of the painting had

412

been familiar to him; he owned two Raffertys himself. Young as he still was, the man was considered one of the most talented artists this country had produced in the last hundred years, almost single-handedly bringing impressionist-style painting to the forefront of twentieth- and twenty-first-century art.

One artist who painted masterpieces for the world to enjoy, and another who talked gently to traumatized victims of crime and then sketched uncannily accurate images of criminals so the police could bring them to justice.

Two talented artists who shared a mother and who both possessed other unique abilities. It really made him wonder about their mother. A powerful psychic as well as a gifted artist? Or were psychic abilities in any way hereditary?

Deciding that he was doing the inner equivalent of whistling in the dark because he was feeling unsettled, John glanced out at the increasingly gray, dreary afternoon and set about making himself comfortable. He turned on the gas logs in the fireplace, and when the cheery fire was crackling, also turned on the television, low, to a news program, more for company and background life than any desire for news.

He'd had enough news for a while.

He made coffee, having little trouble with Maggie's old-fashioned percolator, then explored her freezer and found a large package of what looked like homemade soup. It seemed an ideal meal to prepare and allow to simmer until Maggie woke up, so he did that.

While the soup was heating, he checked all the doors and windows a second time, making certain everything was locked and secure. He wasn't normally so security-conscious, but what had happened to Maggie had shaken him more than he wanted to admit even to himself, and he intended to be as careful as possible.

Maybe he couldn't protect her from "psychic vibes" that could cause her pain and injury, but he could damned well make certain nothing more tangible could hurt her.

Such as a serial rapist who might have been watching the police station and so might have seen Maggie as easily as he could have seen Jennifer or Kendra. A rapist and murderer who could well decide to eliminate the threat of a sketch artist who, given enough time, might well be able to see him as his victims never had.

Restless, John went to Maggie's bedroom door and eased it open. The room was quiet and still; the lamp on her nightstand was turned low and showed him that she was still sleeping, apparently peacefully.

He stood in the doorway for several minutes, just watching her, listening to her breathe. He had removed only her jacket and shoes and covered her with a blanket when he had carried her in here. She had been too drowsy to protest and terrifyingly slight and defenseless in his arms. As far as he could tell, she hadn't moved so much as an inch since he had left her here.

He stepped into the room and picked up her flannel jacket where it lay across the padded bench at the foot of the bed. He could see the bloodstains even in the dim light, and when he brushed his thumb across them they were still damp.

Blood. Real blood. He could smell it.

He had seen the gash in her throat, all too horribly real, and though Maggie had not cried or made a sound afterward, he had also seen the suffering in her eyes.

Slowly, John lay the jacket back across the bench, then went out of the room, easing the door nearly closed. He checked the rest of the house again, methodically, checked the soup. Then he returned to the

living room, drinking coffee and broodingly watching a weather report that promised a wet and blustery night for Seattle.

CHAPTER
EIGHTEEN

Even though the weather had worsened by late afternoon, Jennifer and Kendra elected to keep searching for David Robson rather than return to the station. They stopped at a small café for coffee and checked in with Andy and Quentin by phone, pleased to discover there was another possible lead in the search for the old black Caddie that might or might not belong to the rapist. Even though Quentin sounded more frustrated than hopeful when he reported to his partner what little information they had so far.

"Nearly fifty old black Caddies in the city, dammit. It's going to take time to run all the names through the computer even to give us a place to start."

Kendra, who knew her partner, merely said, "It isn't your fault Joey decided to take matters into his own hands."

"Yeah? Then whose fault is it?"

"He's a big boy, Quentin. A very big boy."

Quentin didn't laugh. "And he never

would have gone looking for this bastard if I hadn't pointed him in that direction."

"You asked him to find out who claimed a kidnapping that never happened, that's all. Anything more is Joey's doing, not yours."

"Yeah, yeah." Quentin sighed. "Listen, you and Jenn be careful out there tonight, okay? Watch your backs."

"You know something?" Kendra asked bluntly.

"No. I just have a very bad feeling about tonight." He sounded restless.

Kendra, who had almost as much respect for Quentin's "feelings" as she did his premonitions, nevertheless thought he was probably letting his worries about Joey get the best of him. But all she said was "We'll be careful. Two transients we talked to about an hour ago swear they know David Robson and that he'll be at the Fellowship Rescue Mission tonight, so that's probably where we'll be."

"Okay. Keep checking in, will you?"

"You bet." Kendra turned her phone off and returned it to her shoulder bag, then filled Jennifer in on the relevant details.

"Your partner sounds a little antsy," Jennifer noted.

Kendra nodded. "Yeah, I give him another hour or so, and he'll be out here himself looking for Joey."

"They're friends?"

"That I couldn't tell you. All I know is that Quentin feels responsible for the guy, maybe because they knew each other as kids."

"Baggage from the past. We all have that, I expect." Jennifer sipped her coffee.

"True." Kendra looked out at the dreary streets and added, "It's already getting dark. I figure the shelters are getting busy about now."

"Yeah. We'll give it a few more minutes, then go on over to the mission, okay?"

"Suits me."

It was raining when they left the café, the wind fitful as it gusted one moment and died off the next, and the temperature had fallen to hover only a few degrees above freezing. So it wasn't surprising that they found the Fellowship Rescue Mission to be a very popular place.

"We'll have a full house, all right," Nancy Frasier told them. "I've already opened the rooms upstairs and put out all the cots and sleeping bags we've got."

"We're still looking for David Robson," Jennifer said. "Mind if we wander around and talk to people?"

"It's fine with me, as long as things stay polite. Some of these people are a little . . . uneasy around cops, remember."

"We'll keep it low-key," Kendra responded with a smile.

"Thanks, I'd appreciate it." Frasier sighed. "We've already had a couple arguments today. I knew it was tense out on the streets, but the nerves are coming inside now."

"Because of the rapist?" Jennifer asked.

"That's a big part of it. Because two of the victims were found in this area. Because the women are frightened and the men are getting tired of the way the women are looking at them. Because we're heading toward the holiday season. Because the weather's really lousy." She sighed again. "Take your pick."

Somebody down the hall yelled for Nancy to come help get something unstuck, and she left the two cops with an apologetic grimace.

"If we split up," Jennifer said, "we can get through here faster."

Mindful both of her partner's warning and the reason she was with Jennifer, Kendra said, "Maybe, but I say we stick together. If these guys are as tense as the director says, some of them might be in a more confrontational mood than usual."

"And they'll be less likely to take on both of us?" Jennifer nodded. "Yeah, you're probably right. Want to start down here or upstairs?"

"Down here, I guess. It looks like the main room for the men is already full." They heard a sudden burst of laughter and a few colorful curses coming from that room, and Kendra added, "Rules or not, somebody always manages to smuggle in a bottle."

"My favorite pastime," Jennifer muttered sardonically as they moved toward the men's dormitory. "Arguing with a drunk or two."

"Maybe we'll get lucky and find David Robson quickly," Kendra offered.

But nobody was more surprised than she was when they did, in fact, find him ten minutes later, after another man told them Robson had gone upstairs to find himself a more private area of the house.

"Thinks he's too good for the rest of us," their informant sniffed, sounding quite insulted.

The man sitting on the next cot disagreed. "Naw, he don't think he's better'n us, he's just skittish as hell. Somebody dropped a shoe on the floor a while ago, and he damn near ran back out the door."

"Why's he nervous?" Kendra asked.

The man gave a thick chuckle. "Says a ghost is after him. So you'd better not say boo to him, ladies." He cackled happily at his own wit.

Jennifer and Kendra exchanged glances, then thanked the men and made their way back out of the dormitory and to the front stairs.

"After all this," Jennifer said, "if the guy turns out to be completely delusional, I'm going to be really pissed."

"I know what you mean."

They climbed the stairs to the second floor, encountering the director in the hallway. When they reported what the men downstairs had told them, she said, "If he's looking for more privacy, he may have taken one of the small back bedrooms; several of them haven't started to fill up yet."

They looked into two such bedrooms, finding one occupied by a snoring man who didn't come close to matching the description they had and the other still empty. In the third room they checked — the most isolated bedroom in the house — they found David Robson.

Jennifer realized instantly why Terry's description had been so unhelpful. Robson looked like two-thirds of the men presently at the shelter, virtually interchangeable with them. He could have been any age between thirty and fifty. He was hunched and thin, wearing shabby clothing too lightweight for the weather, and both his rather wild hair and his thick beard were a nondescript brown with threads of gray. His eyes were heavy-lidded, a muddy brown color, and more than a little bloodshot.

Also like so many of the men in this place, he was uneasy in the presence of police, literally backing himself into a corner of the small room and clutching in front of him an ancient canvas duffel that apparently contained all his worldly possessions.

Working together instinctively, the two women separated a bit as they came in, with Kendra moving a couple of feet to one side to lean casually against a low chest and leaving Jennifer to step closer to Robson. It was a tactic designed to make him feel less threatened, but it only half worked; his eyes moved nervously back and forth between them almost continually.

"I didn't do nothing," he protested as soon as Jennifer told him who they were.

"We know that, David," she replied

soothingly. "We'd just like to ask you a few questions, that's all. About that ghost you saw a few weeks back."

He stiffened and pressed himself even tighter into the corner. "I didn't see nothing. Whoever said I did is a liar."

Jennifer hadn't expected it to be easy but nevertheless stifled a sigh. "You aren't in trouble, David, I promise. Nobody wants to hurt you. We'd just like to know what you saw that night. You were on the catwalk, weren't you? Sleeping in that old warehouse? And you looked out the window?" Not being in a courtroom, she didn't have to worry about leading her witness; all she wanted was something — anything — that might help her find or at least identify the rapist.

He swallowed visibly and made a little sound in the back of his throat, a frightened sound. "He went to drown the puppies. I know he did. He went to drown them, and now he's looking for me."

"We won't let him find you," Jennifer reassured him. "You're safe here. Did he have the puppies in a sack, David?"

He nodded jerkily. "Yeah, a bag. Carried it over his shoulder."

"And you saw them moving?"

"Poor things. Poor little things. He'd already hurt 'em, cause they was bleeding. I saw the blood on the bag. He never liked dogs. Never liked 'em at all. Probably cause they didn't like him. Dogs know who's good. Dogs know."

Jennifer tried not to let the excitement she felt alter her relaxed and unthreatening tone. "It was night, David, and you weren't close; how did you know it was blood you saw?"

"I saw it! I smelled it!"

Wary of getting him too agitated, she tried another tack. "Did you see him when he got to the building, David? Did you see his car?"

Robson clutched his duffel closer to his chest with one arm, while his free hand plunged into the bag and brought out a ring of rusted keys. "D'you think he dropped these? I think he dropped these. I'll give them to him when he comes to get me, and maybe he'll leave me alone. D'you think he'll leave me alone? He likes keys."

Jennifer glanced at Kendra, finding the agent studying Robson with a faint frown, then returned her attention to the man as she wondered if she was asking the right questions. You never knew, not with a witness like this one.

"The car, David. Did you see it?"

425

He stared at the keys in his hand, then dropped them back in the bag and began rummaging again. "It was here. I know it was right here . . ."

"David, did you see the car?"

"What? Oh. He took the puppies out of the trunk."

"You saw that? What color was the car, David?"

"Black. Black as the inside of hell. Big sonofabitch too. Maybe a Lincoln, I don't know."

Jennifer drew a breath and probed carefully. "So he carried the bag of puppies into the building. Did he have the bag when he came back out, David?"

"Had the bag. But it was empty. He'd drowned the puppies and left them in there. I told you that!" he snapped suddenly.

"I'm sorry, David, I'd forgotten." She paused, then said, "You know who he was, don't you? You know who the ghost was?"

He made another of those frightened sounds in the depths of his throat. "Dead. They said he was dead, but the devil can't die. I know he's the devil. I know it! I saw him one time. Saw him looking at her, and there was nothing in his eyes. Nothing. Why was that?" he demanded of Jennifer suddenly, desperately. "Why was there nothing?"

"I don't know, David. Maybe if you told me who he is —"

"No! If I tell you, he'll know! He always knew, always. Always watching, smiling. Always knew when I messed up the code." The muddy eyes shifted between Jennifer and Kendra, worried, fearful, increasingly anxious. "I'm a good programmer! I am! He knew that, even though he got me fired."

"David —"

"You're going to tell him I'm here, aren't you? You're going to help him get me!"

"No, David, we just want to —"

It happened with horrifying suddenness. The duffel bag fell to the floor, and Robson was holding a pistol, his hand shaking so badly that it was pure chance it was aimed toward anything at all when it went off.

Jennifer was moving, reacting instinctively as she lunged toward him, dimly aware that Kendra was moving as well. But both of them were just a little too far away and just a heartbeat too slow in reacting.

The bullet tore through the sleeve of Jennifer's coat and slammed Kendra back against the wall.

★ ★ ★

Some time around eight John heard the shower, and by the time Maggie came out he had the soup ready for them. She looked more fragile than he'd ever seen her, faint purple shadows under her eyes despite the sleep and far too much tension in the set of her shoulders.

He could still see a thin red line across her throat.

"You didn't have to stay," she said at one point.

"Finish your soup."

Maggie looked at him for a moment, cat-like golden eyes grave, then silently did as he ordered.

"Now I understand why you never walked through Christina's apartment after she died," he said suddenly. "Because she died there. Because you would have felt it."

"Yes. I wasn't sure it would happen, that I'd feel all of it, but there was a chance, especially since I — I felt some of what she felt when she was shot. Even though I was nowhere near there when it happened. And even without the connection I felt to Christina, what I was sensing had been getting so much stronger, so much more . . . intense with every day that passed." She shrugged a bit jerkily. "I'd started being careful about crime scenes even before she died, just to be on the safe side."

"You should have told me that."

"You wouldn't have believed me."

John knew that was true, so he could hardly deny it. He remained silent while they finished the meal. He cleared up afterward, sending her to the living room with coffee, and joined her there a few minutes later. She was curled up on one end of the couch, the overlarge black sweater and dark sweatpants she wore making her skin appear even more pale than usual and her hair more vibrant.

When John joined her on the couch, she was looking at her hands, and said absently, "I feel like Lady Macbeth. All that blood on my hands. I can still smell it."

Steadily, he said, "All I smell is lavender soap."

She tucked her hands down between her knees and shifted her gaze to his face. "It's supposed to be soothing and relaxing, that scent. Usually, it is."

"Maggie, maybe you should go back to bed."

"No. I . . . don't want to be alone. Do you mind?"

"Of course not. But you didn't get enough rest."

"Enough for now. It was the first time in days I was able to really sleep. Probably because I knew you were here. Have I thanked you, by the way?"

"For what? For staying? I wanted to, Maggie."

"For staying. And for pulling me out of that building. I don't know if I could have gotten out if you hadn't been there."

"Promise me you won't ever do that again. Go into a place like that alone."

"No, I won't." Her smile was a little shaky. "I wouldn't dare, not after this. That was very scary."

John would have chosen a stronger word, but all he said was "For me too."

"I'm sorry." She lifted her hands and looked at them again as if she couldn't help herself.

"The blood's gone, Maggie."

"Yes. I know." She allowed her hands to fall, to rest on her thighs, but kept her gaze on them.

He hesitated, not at all sure if he was ready for this. For any of this. "We don't have to talk about it."

Maggie smiled again, wry this time. "Okay."

"I didn't mean — Maggie, it's not that I doubt what you can do."

"I know. You're just . . . very uncomfortable with it."

Trying to keep it light, he said, "Stop plucking my feelings out of the air, will you?"

She looked at him finally, that little smile lingering. "One of the major drawbacks of . . . getting too close to an empath, I'm afraid."

"It's not something I expected," he confessed.

"I don't mean to invade your privacy. I'm sorry."

He shook his head. "I don't have any no-trespassing signs, not where you're concerned. It just takes some getting used to, that's all."

"I know. I know it does."

He wasn't saying any of what he wanted to say, and his own inadequacy disturbed him. All too aware that the wrong words would hurt her, still unsure if he was ready for this, he watched her turn her restless gaze to the muted television.

"More rain," she murmured. "Always rain. People in Seattle don't tan —"

"They rust," he finished.

"I keep forgetting you grew up here."

"I've thought about moving back. Oddly enough, I miss the rain."

It picked up outside just then, drumming against the roof of Maggie's small house, and she nodded. "I think I'd miss it too. It's a very soothing sound."

The silence that fell between them wasn't particularly soothing, and John didn't have to be psychic to feel that. There was too much left unsaid, and yet he knew they were at a turning point, a crossroads come upon so suddenly that neither one of them had been prepared for it.

"Maggie —"

"We really don't have to talk about it," she said. "About any of it. Too much has happened for either of us to be sure of anything right now."

This time, he didn't hesitate. "I'm sure of what I feel. I'm just not sure of what you feel. I mean —" He shook his head as she looked at him, wryly aware that he was as awkward as a teenager facing, for the first time, the girl who was so desperately important to him that every word spoken took on terrifying significance. "Maggie, you feel so much of other people's emotions, other people's pain. I can't help wondering if you even have the energy left to . . . feel for yourself."

She was obviously surprised, a little puzzled, even uneasy. But she didn't duck the question. "Sometimes it's easier to be alone."

"Because there's been too much of other people's feelings? Because when you're alone, you can find peace?"

"Is that so wrong?"

John hesitated, then reached over and brushed back a strand of her hair, allowing his hand to linger against her face. "God knows I can't blame you for making that choice. But it's an unbalanced existence. You said it yourself, Maggie — life is about balance. How can you go on giving and giving of yourself, your energy and compassion — and empathy — without at least sometimes taking something for yourself?"

"Because it isn't that simple." Her eyes were steady, the curve of her mouth a little vulnerable.

"I'd ask you to give as well as take."

She half nodded agreement, but also an obvious pleasure in the touch of his hand against her skin as she moved. "People do. It's only fair. I just . . . don't know how much I can give right now."

"And if I said whatever you can give will be enough?"

"I don't think I'd believe you." She drew a breath. "Anyway, it doesn't matter. This wouldn't even be happening if you hadn't been shaken up by today."

"The hell it wouldn't." John didn't give her a chance to argue, just pulled her into his arms and kissed her.

Maggie had told herself almost from the day she had met John that if this happened she'd be able to stop it. Really easy — just say no. Tell him she didn't want this, didn't want him. Tell him she wasn't the slightest bit interested in acquiring a lover, thank you very much. Even if it wasn't love, even if it was only desire. Passion was very clearly and very certainly something she didn't need in her life.

She had been very sure of that.

She had been very wrong.

To her astonishment, it was about warmth as much as it was passion, about the simple, necessary human lifeline that was the touch of flesh on flesh. Her body, racked so often and so long with the pain of others, craved the healing warmth of him, the pleasure he created just by touching her. And her weary spirit longed for the closeness, the intimacy he offered.

There was no pain in this, no fear, no darkness. There was nothing but elation and the certain knowledge that some things really were meant to happen.

Without knowing if she had moved or he

had moved her, she found herself on his lap, her knees on either side of his hips. She felt his hair, silky between her fingers, felt his mouth hungry and insistent on hers. She felt his hands slip under her sweater and touch her skin, felt them slide upward slowly until they could close over her breasts, and heard a little sound escape her, so eager it almost embarrassed her. Almost.

John drew back just far enough to look at her, his eyes darkened to emerald and so intense she couldn't look away. "Just give what you can, Maggie," he said roughly. "I swear I won't hurt you."

She touched his face with both hands, almost as if she were blind and needed her sensitive fingertips in order to see. She touched his mouth, and then her lips followed, teasing his, taking his. "I never thought you would."

THURSDAY, NOVEMBER 8

As promised, the rain grew even heavier after midnight and the wind began to whine and moan like something lost and lonely.

Maggie didn't mind. Her lamplit bedroom was warm and tranquil — at least for the moment — and she was discovering how good it felt to lie close to someone else in an intimate and peaceful bed. It felt very good. She wanted to hold on to this, to make the moment last, and knowing it couldn't made it all the more achingly sweet.

John shifted position slightly and rose on an elbow to look down at her. "You're very quiet."

She smiled. "Listening to the rain. Wishing the night could last a little longer than it will."

"There's that fatalism again," he said, intentionally light.

"Sorry. Character fault, I'm afraid. But . . . the morning will come, John."

"And then the next morning, and the one after that. Mornings don't mean endings, Maggie."

"Sometimes they do."

"Not this time." He shifted again, pulling her closer so that his forearms were beneath her shoulders and his fingers could tangle in her long, thick hair. "I don't intend to lose you."

Maggie responded as she had to when he kissed her, her arms going up around his neck and her mouth every bit as urgent as his. It was rather terrifying, she thought dimly, that he could have this effect on her when she had known him barely a week. Then again, sometimes a week was a lifetime, and sometimes knowledge had nothing to do with time.

There was nothing of the normal awkwardness of new lovers between them. No fumbling or uncertainty. He knew without asking what would please her, just as she knew what would please him. Yet even as Maggie knew that to glide her fingertips up his spine would elicit a shudder of need, there were also the still unfamiliar sensations of this particular body against hers, unexpectedly hard and powerful.

She knew he was a silent, intense lover, yet there was also the discovery that her voice murmuring his name had the power to affect him like an actual physical caress. And just when she was certain he couldn't possibly make her feel more than she already had, he did.

"It's obvious to me," she murmured a long time later, "that you didn't spend *all* your time building a business empire."

John chuckled and drew her a bit closer to his side. "A man has to have hobbies."

"Ah. And, naturally, you applied yourself to those *hobbies* with all the energy and dedication at your command."

"Naturally."

"Well, none of it was wasted."

"Thank you. You're not so bad yourself." He hesitated only a moment. "Maggie?"

"Don't say it, okay?" She kept her voice quiet.

He was silent, then murmured, "Because you already know."

"Because I don't need to hear it. Not now. Later . . . when it's all over. Tell me then, all right?"

John didn't answer aloud, just wrapped both his arms around her and held her, wide awake as he listened to the wind moan outside.

CHAPTER
NINETEEN

"I should call John and Maggie," Andy said.

"No, let them sleep." Quentin glanced up at the big clock on the wall, then shifted restlessly on the uncomfortable couch in the hospital's waiting room. "It's nearly three. Besides, there's nothing they could do."

Andy watched him. "She'll be all right. You heard the doctor. Stable enough for surgery, and he didn't anticipate any complications."

"So why's it taking so long?" Quentin looked at the clock once again, frowning. His face was drawn, the anxiety in his eyes obvious.

"He said it could be hours, Quentin, you know that."

"Yeah. Yeah."

Jennifer came into the waiting room and immediately asked, "Any news?"

"Not yet," Andy told her. "Still in surgery. What about Robson?"

She sat down beside him on the couch

across from the one Quentin occupied. "Under restraints and sedation. He won't be any help anytime soon, at least not verbally. But when we ran his prints, we did find out that about four years ago he was employed by one of the electronics companies in the city, a big one. They run three shifts, but I had to get the personnel manager out of bed so he could give me a list of employees working for the company at the same time. We're comparing it to the list Kendra had put together of every person even remotely connected to the victims or the investigation."

"So maybe this *ghost* he was so afraid of will turn up."

"Maybe." She shrugged, her gaze moving to Quentin. "He did specifically say the ghost had gotten him fired and mentioned being a programmer. And I do believe he saw somebody go into that building, somebody who was carrying something in a sack that was moving. So maybe it'll turn out to be a worthwhile lead after all."

Quentin stirred slightly and said, "It was a worthwhile lead. Stop blaming yourself."

"I should have at least checked to make sure he wasn't armed," she responded, her voice tight. "We knew he was paranoid, jumpy as hell, and the way he was clutching that duffel I should have at least taken it away from him."

"You couldn't have known."

Jennifer looked as if she wanted to continue protesting but just shook her head silently.

Quentin repeated, "You couldn't have known. No one can be on guard all the time against the unexpected. And there were two of you there, don't forget that. From what you told us, it was pure chance Kendra was the one who got hit."

"He's right," Andy told Jennifer.

She grimaced. "That doesn't make it easier."

"Yeah, I know." Andy looked back at Quentin. "Shouldn't you report in, call your boss? We tried to keep it quiet, but you know as well as I do that by morning the media will know an FBI agent was shot while questioning a witness."

"I'll call it in when we know something. Where the hell's that doctor?"

"He said he'd talk to us as soon as the surgery was finished," Andy answered patiently.

"Yeah. Right."

A silence fell that none of them was willing to break, and the clock quietly ticked away the minutes. It was just after three-thirty when the doctor finally came into the waiting room, tired but satisfied.

"We're not out of the woods yet, but everything looks good," he told them. "We were able to extract the bullet and repair the damage. She'll have to take it easy for a while, but there should be no complications. And we have an excellent trauma therapist on staff to help her through the emotional aftereffects of having been shot."

"Can I see her?" Quentin asked.

"Not until she comes out of recovery, and that'll be hours yet." He looked at all of them, adding, "My advice would be for you to get some sleep and come back later in the morning. Believe me, there's nothing you can do here, and we'll call if there's any change."

"Thank you, Doctor." When they were alone again, Andy said reluctantly, "We should all be back at the office. The search for that Caddie is narrowing, and the lead Jenn and Kendra were following could pay off at any time."

"I know." Quentin shifted his shoulders as if to ease tension that refused to leave him despite the good news. "And with every hour that passes, we're less and less likely to find Tara Jameson before he kills her. You two go on back to the station. I want to have another word with the doctor before I call Quantico and report in."

"You're sure?"

"Yeah, go ahead. I'll be along in a few minutes."

After they left him, it took Quentin less than five minutes to find the surgical recovery area and Kendra. Between the lateness of the hour and his inborn ability to slip into places unnoticed, he was able to reach her bedside without being challenged.

She was either still sedated or sleeping deeply, and he didn't try to wake her. He just stood looking down at her for a long time, without moving, his face bleak.

"Sir? You shouldn't be in here." The nurse's voice was low but authoritative.

Quentin looked at her, saw her take a half step backward, and made a conscious effort to tone down the savagery he was afraid she had seen and smile reassuringly. "Yes, I know. It's all right. I'm leaving now."

Hesitant, the nurse said, "She'll be fine, sir."

"Yes. Thank you, Nurse." He sent a final look at Kendra, then left the room without another word.

He went directly to his rental car in the parking lot near the emergency room and started the engine but didn't move the car. It was a long time before he reached for his cell phone and punched in Bishop's familiar number.

Jennifer poured herself another cup of coffee, afraid to stop and try to figure out how much she'd consumed in the past couple of days. It was barely six a.m. on this cold, dreary Thursday in November, and she had enough caffeine in her system to stay awake until Christmas.

Not that she expected to sleep between now and then anyway.

Scott came into the room, looking as tired as the others but considerably more dusty. "If I never see another file again," he announced, "it'll be too soon."

Jennifer felt a stab of guilt. "I should have been helping you, Scott. Sorry."

"Don't worry about it." He grinned. "I'll get even later."

"The question is," Andy said, "did you find anything helpful?"

Triumphant, he said, "I found out what happened in 1894. Well, sort of."

Sitting at the conference table at Kendra's laptop, Quentin looked at him in respect. "How in hell did you do that? The computer databases haven't coughed up a damned thing."

"Punch in Boston," Scott advised.

"Kendra's the expert with this beast," Quentin said as he scowled at the laptop. "But I'll try."

Andy said, "What'd you find out, Scott? And how?"

He grimaced. "How is simple enough. That box of miscellaneous files I've been going through. I found the police report of the seventh victim from 1934." He opened the folder he was carrying and produced a photograph of a young woman with dark, curly hair and striking dark eyes.

It didn't take more than an exchange of glances to confirm that she was completely unfamiliar to all of them.

Andy sighed. "Why did I hope at least one of us might recognize the face of the next possible victim so we could do something about it before he grabs her?"

"Wishful thinking," Jennifer said. "It was always a real long shot, Andy, you know that."

"Yeah." He watched Scott pin the photo on the bulletin board in its proper place in the line of 1934 victims, then said, "But she was killed here, right, in Seattle? So how did you find anything about Boston and 1894?"

"One of the investigating officers in 1934 put a note in the file, apparently out of frustration more than anything else. Said he'd tried everything he could think of to find the bastard killing Seattle's young women, even thoroughly checking out all the family members of the victims despite their lack of motive — because his father, who had also been a cop, had told him about some murders that took place in Boston forty years before, murders that sounded eerily similar to the ones here, at least as far as what was done to the victims."

Quentin frowned at him. "So why did the cop focus on family members?"

"Because in the Boston murders, it was apparently the brother of at least one of the victims who committed the crimes." Scott shrugged. "He was vague on the details, just said these killings were different in some ways but he was desperate, willing to try anything, so he checked out family members."

"And?"

"Well, nothing more in that file. I still have more to look through, and we don't know anything about the eighth victim.

Maybe there'll be more info in that folder — assuming I can find it."

Quentin looked at the humming laptop. "It'll take this thing a while to check the historical databases again, even with a specific city and date."

"I'm going to keep looking for the file on the eighth victim," Scott said. "Maybe there'll be more info that might help us."

"Get a shower and breakfast first," Andy told him. "And maybe sleep a couple hours, at least."

"I will if you will," Scott said dryly, and left the conference room before Andy could respond.

With a sigh, Jennifer said, "We're all going on caffeine, adrenaline, and nerves. Much longer, and none of us will be worth a damn." She got up. "I'm going to go see if we have anything useful yet on that company Robson worked for."

Andy's phone rang as she left, and he answered it with a hopeful expression that very quickly turned to grimness as he listened. Finally, he said, "Okay, yeah, tell 'em we're on our way." He cradled the receiver and muttered a curse under his breath.

Quentin lifted a questioning brow. "They found Tara Jameson?"

"No." Andy hesitated, then said, "But they found somebody else, Quentin. At least, it sounds like . . ."

After a moment, flatly, Quentin said, "Joey."

"Yeah. I'm afraid so."

Quentin didn't say anything during the trip with Andy out to the waterfront location, and after a glance at his face Andy didn't try to open a conversation. He thought fleetingly that the seemingly easygoing, humorous man beside him would be a very, very dangerous enemy, and he was glad they were on the same side. It wasn't the first time he'd thought that.

So he said nothing until he parked the car near a cluster of other police cars not too far from where I-90 crossed over Lake Washington from Mercer Island. It was a fairly congested area, so it wasn't surprising that the body had been discovered so early by an unlucky jogger.

Andy said, "Given the tides, there's no telling where he was dumped into the water. The southern end of Lake Washington, probably, but that covers a lot of territory."

Quentin nodded but said nothing as they approached the taped-off area near the water's edge.

Andy stopped to talk to the detective in charge, but Quentin went on until he could look down on the body sprawled on the rocks half in and half out of the water. Faceup.

Cause of death was obvious. There was a gunshot wound to the center of the chest and another between the eyes. Quentin didn't have to hear the medical examiner explain it to know that the first shot had been to the chest — and had failed to stop Joey. Quentin hadn't known many men capable of withstanding what should have been a mortal injury, but he had no doubt it hadn't stopped Joey. It had taken a second bullet to do that.

"Ah, Joey," he murmured.

Andy joined him. "He had your card, which is why they called me." He shrugged when Quentin looked at him. "Word's got around already that the Bureau is helping out on the rapist investigation, so they knew who to call."

"How long's he been dead?" Quentin asked matter-of-factly.

"Preliminary estimate is eight to ten hours, give or take a couple. Some time last night."

Quentin turned his gaze to the lake before them, frowning. "So it didn't take him long to find whatever he found. Maybe he was near the water when he was shot, and maybe not."

"Yeah. Doesn't narrow the possibilities much."

"Not unless we can place an old black Caddie fairly close to the waterfront."

"You think he found it?"

"Don't you?"

Andy grimaced. "I think it'd be stretching coincidence too far to think somebody uninvolved killed him right after he started looking for the Caddie."

"Agreed." Quentin's mouth was a thin, grim line. "So let's find that goddamned car."

Jennifer met them back in the conference room, still obviously wired with caffeine, and announced, "Maggie just called; she and John are on their way in. And the computer's sifted through the information on that electronics company, but so far nothing. No name matches up to any on our list of family, friends, or acquaintances of the victims. Now I'm going over the list myself. I don't trust these damned machines."

The damned machine on the conference table beeped just then, and Quentin went to study the laptop's screen. "Okay, we have a couple of very brief articles from a Boston newspaper, 1894. A man named Robert Graham is suspected of murdering his entire family." He looked up suddenly. "Seven sisters. And his own wife."

"Any more details?" Andy demanded.

Quentin nodded and looked back at the screen. "A few. It was a fairly big story at the time, especially since nobody had a clue why he did it and because he'd already vanished when they found the bodies. In those days, it wasn't at all uncommon for even a large family of siblings to continue living together in the family home, especially if they remained unmarried. Apparently, none of Graham's sisters — all under the age of twenty-five — had married or had jobs, and he was supporting them. Their parents had died . . . just the year before, as a matter of fact, in what was probably a flu epidemic.

"They believed the killings were spread out over a period of at least three days. That he probably tied up or in some way restrained and gagged all of them, then took his time killing them, beginning with . . . his twin sister. They believe the wife was last; from the looks of it, he had tied her to their bed early on and left her there while he killed the others. She may or may not have been conscious and aware of what was going on."

"Christ," Andy muttered.

"Yeah. No descriptions of the victims, and precious few details of what he actually did to them — but they were all found with something covering their eyes, either bits of their own clothing or sheets, towels, something like that."

Jennifer drew a breath. "So he killed his own family — not what happened this time, with the victims all unrelated to each other. But he didn't want them to see or watch him — which is definitely like our guy and, apparently, the killer in 1934."

Quentin sat down at the table, rubbed his face briefly with both hands, and said, "Family members. Maybe the cop in 1934 was on to something."

Andy objected, "But our victims are unrelated, like Jenn said."

"Unrelated to each other, yes. But maybe at least one of them was related to her attacker."

"All the relatives have alibis for at least one period of time in which we *know* this guy was either snatching another woman or spending a few hours torturing one," Jennifer pointed out. "Every single one of them. We triple-checked that."

"What are we missing?" Quentin muttered. "There's something . . . a fact or question so all this will make sense."

Andy looked at Jennifer. "The list of the electronics company's employees was screened, but the computer was only looking for connections to family, friends, or acquaintances of the victims, you said?"

"Yeah."

"What about the victims themselves? Were their names included?"

"Sure. The computer said there was no connection."

He sighed. "Shit."

Quentin rubbed his face again and said, "You said you were going over the list yourself, Jenn, and I say it's a good idea. Maybe you'll see something that escaped the mathematical logic of a computer."

"Right." She immediately bent to the task.

"Andy, do we have a copy of that DMV list of black Caddies in the area?"

"Yeah — it's right here."

"Let's see if any of those names jump out at us."

"We can't possibly be that lucky," Andy said, but handed over half the list to Quentin.

They were all tired, too tired to be doing what they were doing. Not that it stopped them, of course. But the weariness did make Andy question what he thought he was seeing nearly half an hour later. "Reported stolen," he murmured.

Quentin looked at him across the table. "What?"

"There was a black Caddie reported stolen two years ago. Never found."

"Probably not so unusual," Quentin noted.

"No, not that part. It's who reported it stolen. Who it belonged to."

"Who?"

Before Andy could answer, Jennifer said, "Hey. *Hey.* Do you know who used to work for the same electronics company as David Robson? Who was, in fact, his boss in the software design department?"

Slowly, Andy said, "Simon Walsh."

She stared at him. "How'd you know that?"

"Lucky guess. He reported his father's old black Caddie as missing and probably stolen just over two years ago. I love a good coincidence, but this can't be one."

"Christina's husband," Jennifer said. "Christina's husband was David Robson's boss *and* had him fired, just like Robson said. And he used to own a black Cadillac?"

"Yeah."

"But he's dead."

"According to the record, yes." Andy looked at Quentin. "Which would explain why the computer didn't come up with a match. We didn't even have his name on our lists, since Christina was — or was supposed to be — a widow. It was a sailing accident, wasn't it? That supposedly killed him?"

"Yeah. In fact, since I knew Christina and John, I came to his memorial service." Quentin shook his head. "He was a sailing nut, often went out alone even in bad weather. This time, the storm won. And there were witnesses, of a sort. Another boat near enough to see Walsh struggling with equipment, see the boom swing and hit him. And over he went. The other boat pinpointed the area, there was a pretty massive search, and they recovered his boat mostly intact — but he was never found. As I remember, John hired experienced mariners and rescue people to search even after the official search was called off, but they had no better luck than the Coast Guard."

Jennifer fumbled for a cinnamon toothpick and thought longingly of a cigarette. "But, Andy — she was his *wife*. You're saying he did that to his own wife? The rape? The acid?"

Softly but with a distinct note of loathing in his voice, Quentin said, "Vows don't mean much to sociopaths, Jenn. After what you've seen him do, how can you doubt he'd balk at brutalizing a loyal and loving wife?"

Andy said, "And wasn't Walsh some kind of computer genius?"

Quentin nodded. "Electronic security systems would have been child's play for him."

Jennifer was still protesting. "If you're right about this, Christina was his second victim. Why marry her, then fake his own death a few years later — and not attack Laura Hughes until a year and a half after that?"

Quentin said, "He might have been drawn to Christina without really knowing why and believed himself in love. Sociopaths don't feel the way we do, but they often pretend to feel, to live normal lives. He could have married her, intending to live that normal life. Then either felt too confined or just got tired of the game. Faking his death was a nice dramatic way out of all the ties binding him, gaining him his freedom without any messy emotional confrontations.

"Then he sees Laura Hughes one day," Quentin continued, "and something about her face triggers his psychosis. We can be pretty sure it's the way these women look that makes him single them out, even if we're not entirely sure what it is. He sees Laura — and goes after her. Once he attacks her, once he begins to explore and satisfy his needs, his hungers, whatever restraints he felt before would melt away. He not only has the taste of it but possibly understands now why he was drawn to Christina, why her face attracted him in the first place. And she becomes his next victim."

It sounded all too horribly likely, even to Jennifer. She stopped protesting.

Andy drew a deep breath. "Okay, we've got to start looking for a dead man. And we have to do something else."

"Yeah," Quentin said. "We have to tell John."

Hollis adjusted the sunglasses on her nose. They felt oddly loose somehow. Looser than the bandage had been.

"We'll keep the lights out in here, Hollis," the doctor said, his voice both soothing and disappointed. "We don't want to add any unnecessary strain. It may just take a little time, that's all. The muscles are working properly, and the pupils. The optic nerve looks fine. The eyes themselves are very bloodshot in appearance, but that's perfectly normal."

Hollis thought he minded more than she did. "It's all right, doctor. We both knew the odds."

"I don't want you to lose hope, Hollis. In optical surgeries, there's often a period of adjustment when the bandages come off. Give it a little time, okay?"

"I don't have any pressing appointments," she said lightly.

He sighed. "I'll come back in a few hours, and we'll check again."

"Sure."

When she was alone again, Hollis turned her face toward the window. The blustery night had been followed by a miserable day, according to the nurses. Wet, dreary, cold. So she wasn't missing much, at least as far as the view out the window went.

But she would have liked to see it.

She really would have liked to see it.

Hollis?

"Hello, Annie. Were you around when the doc was here? I'm still blind, you

458

know." Her voice was the same as it had been with the doctor, even and calm, almost placid.

Hollis, listen to me. Are you listening?

"Sure. Sure I'm listening."

You have to see.

"I can't."

Yes, you can. The eyes are yours now, Hollis. They belong to you. They were a gift, so you could see. You must see.

"But I can't. Just darkness. That's all I see."

Do you want to help Maggie?

Hollis sat very still, her fingers curling on the arms of the chair to grip hard. "You know I do."

Then you have to see, Hollis.

"But —"

You have to see.

CHAPTER
TWENTY

John didn't say a word in protest as it was all laid out for him. But something changed in his face, and Maggie, watching him, could feel the pain.

"I'm sorry, John," Quentin said. "We could be wrong."

With a twisted smile, John said, "I hope you are. But somehow . . . it makes sense to me. It would explain so much, wouldn't it? How he got into high-security places, for instance. A snap for a computer genius."

Reluctantly, Maggie said, "John, it could also explain Christina's death."

He looked at her, and she felt another flash of pain that was quickly and ruthlessly shoved aside. "Yes, it could. Of all his victims, Christina was the most likely to be able to identify him, given enough time. He must have known that. Must have realized, when she survived the attack, that he couldn't let her live. Especially if he got into the apartment and saw the work she was doing trying to find her attacker. It could also be why he didn't bother to go after Hollis Templeton or Ellen Randall a second time when they survived the initial attacks; he wouldn't think they had any chance of identifying him, so they were no threat to him."

Maggie thought that if they both survived this, she would have to do something about this tendency of his to repress pain. But for now, all she could do was say, "If I'd been able to walk through her apartment afterward, maybe I could have seen all this."

"It would have killed you," John said flatly.

Andy, who had been mostly silent until then, said, "John, I swear to you I believed Christina committed suicide."

"I know that, Andy. You have nothing to apologize for."

"Then why do I feel so rotten about it?"

"Never mind. What we have to do now is figure out where Simon could be."

Quentin said, "We've started on that. Given that he had access to quite a bit of money before his presumed death, it seems logical to assume that he planned carefully. I think we'll find evidence that he liquidated some assets and investments and possibly sold property as well before he took that boat out to die."

John frowned. "Thinking back, I was a bit surprised there was so little money. Plenty for Christina to live comfortably, but given what he'd been earning with those cutting-edge software programs of his, I expected to find more."

"There was more," Jennifer announced as she came into the conference room. "While some of the guys are looking for property he might have sold, I've been on another computer, checking out his financial records in the months before his supposed death. Quentin was right — Simon Walsh was moving around a lot of money. No one amount large enough to raise any flags, but taken together it's pretty obvious he shifted a sizable portion of his net worth somewhere I haven't been able to trace."

"He put it in another name," Quentin said. "He laid all the groundwork for disappearing long before he did."

Andy said, "I still don't get why he went to so much trouble to hide his face when he'd already blinded his victims. I mean, I could see him being extra careful with Christina, but the others? None of them knew him, right?"

Quentin said, "I think wearing a mask

and wig is tied in with why he blinds them. He doesn't want them to see but, even more, he doesn't want them to know it's him. And he's convinced they would know, if they were able to see him, touch his face, even get a whiff of his natural scent. Because he recognizes their faces somehow, or believes he does, and because he believes he knows them, he believes they could know him."

"It makes sense, I guess," Andy said. "As much as this twisted bastard makes any kind of sense."

"So how do we find him?" Jennifer demanded.

Maggie half listened without offering comment as the others discussed various ways they might find Simon Walsh's secret torture chamber. What would it take, she wondered, to push a precarious mind even further into insanity? Maybe even . . . break it for good? Was that an effective way to destroy evil, by splintering it so that not even its own will could hold it together any longer?

"Maggie?"

She blinked at John. "Hmm?"

He leaned slightly toward her, his hand coming to rest warmly on her thigh. "Are you all right?"

"I'm fine." She managed a smile. "Just . . . wondering why I couldn't see this. Couldn't see him. Christina had pictures of him, of course. She showed them to me."

"You couldn't see him because none of the victims ever saw him. He made sure of that."

"I know. Still."

He squeezed her thigh gently, then leaned back and looked across the table to meet Quentin's gaze. "Do you think we'll find him by figuring out what properties he sold before he faked his death?"

"I think we've got a fair shot at it. To do what he does requires isolation and privacy. And he's got to feel safe there, certain no one will find him."

Andy said, "You know, he could still have Tara Jameson at that place. We haven't found a body yet, and he's had her barely forty-eight hours. Plus we think he may have been interrupted if Quentin's source actually found him or at least got close enough to draw his attention. So he could still be . . . working on her."

Maggie, remembering the painting, said, "I don't think she's alive . . . but she could be."

"Which means," Quentin said, "he could have a hostage. So assuming we do find a likely place where he might be holed up, we'll have to be damned careful approaching."

Grimacing, Andy said, "Yeah. No fucking S.W.A.T. team. If we blunder in and a victim dies because of it . . ."

He didn't have to finish that sentence, because all of them could do it for him.

Half an hour later they had a printout of a list of properties Simon Walsh had sold in the months before his death. It was a long list. And they found Tara Jameson's name on it. She had been the realtor involved in one such deal.

"You were right," Andy said to Maggie. "He did know her."

Maggie nodded, but said only, "Anything else helpful on the list?"

"So far," John said, "it looks like different buyers. But at least half a dozen were sold to what look like holding companies. It may take some time to find out who actually owned them."

"Of all of us, you're most likely to be able to find information on businesses without wasting time," Quentin noted.

"I can make some calls," John said. "I still have plenty of contacts here in Seattle." He carried his copy of the list to the phones at the other end of the room.

"I'll go get a map," Jennifer said. "We can start pinpointing all these."

Maggie studied the list, waiting for something to jump out at her. Even so, she was very surprised when something did.

She knew this city, knew it well. But she wasn't certain why the address of a waterfront warehouse should leap out at her the way it did. Why? It was one of half a dozen other warehouses, at least three of them fairly remote or isolated. So why did this one feel so . . . right?

Because Quentin's friend Joey had been found at the waterfront?

Or . . . because of the sound?

. . . I know I heard another sound, a sound that bothered me somehow. Because I recognized it, or thought I should have . . .

Hollis had said that. And Ellen had said the same thing. Even Christina had mentioned hearing something, something she hadn't been able to remember. What had they heard?

Maggie half closed her eyes, concentrating, trying to bring that faint, half-heard, and half-understood sound out of the hodgepodge of impressions and sounds and scents stored in her own subconscious after all the interviews with the victims.

Water.

Water lapping against pilings.

Maggie looked around the room. John was on the phone, jotting down notes on a legal pad. Jennifer, Andy, and Quentin were bent over a map spread out on the table, carefully marking locations from possibilities on the list.

Maggie looked at the list, then laid it down atop her sketch pad. There was only one waterfront location remote enough to provide the privacy and secrecy he needed. She should tell them. She knew that. There was really no excuse not to tell them.

Her car was here at the station, John had driven her back there to get it this morning, both of them surprised to find the car not only intact but apparently untouched, her sketch pad safely inside, and she had driven it here, where it was more likely to remain safe.

She got up and went to pour herself some coffee, having already noticed the pot was empty. Picking it up with a shrug, she left the conference room, ostensibly to get more water.

On her way out of the station, she left the pot on top of somebody's filing cabinet.

"Well," Jennifer said, staring down at the

map, now marked with numerous little red flags, "if we eliminate all the places that aren't remote or isolated enough for his . . . needs . . . we end up with six possibles. All warehouses or storage facilities of some kind."

John joined them and said, "Only three of the addresses on this list are no longer in use, at least according to my sources." He bent over the map and pointed them out. "Here. These three. Supposedly either empty or storing bits of equipment and machinery forgotten long ago."

Quentin frowned at the map. "Two warehouses and one storage building. But only the two warehouses are remote enough to satisfy his requirements, I'd guess, and they're miles apart."

"So which one do we check first?" Jennifer asked.

Before anyone could offer a suggestion, Scott spoke from the doorway, his voice strained. "Where's Maggie?"

John looked around swiftly, realizing only then that she had been out of the room far too long. "She's . . ." He steadied his voice, something in Scott's face sending cold fear through him. "She went to get more water for coffee, I think. Why?"

"I found the file on the last victim from 1934."

Quentin was frowning at him. "And?"

Scott opened the folder he carried and silently held up a photo all of them could see clearly. All too clearly.

The last woman killed in 1934 could have been Maggie's twin.

"Christ," John breathed. And he knew, even before they looked for her, that Maggie was no longer in the building, that she knew or guessed where Simon would be and had slipped away to face him.

Responsibility. Atonement.

"She's gone after him," he told the others, hearing the hoarse fear in his own voice.

"Alone?" Andy stared at him. "In Christ's name, why?"

John shook his head, unable to even begin to explain any of it right now. "Just — trust me. That's where she's gone."

Quentin didn't waste time with questions, just said, "She hasn't got much of a head start on us, but if we're to catch up to her in time we'll have to split up to check both warehouses."

"No S.W.A.T. team," John said immediately, repeating Andy's earlier statement. "If a bunch of cops show up and she's there, he could —" He couldn't even finish the thought.

Quentin said, "I agree."

Andy groaned. "Shit."

"Do *you* trust anybody else to go in, with Maggie in the line of fire?" Quentin asked him.

"No. Dammit."

"Then it's us. John, are you armed?"

"In my car."

Andy scowled at him. "Goddammit, John."

John shrugged into his jacket. "Don't worry, Andy, I have a permit to carry. And I'm a good shot."

"Listen to me. If you shoot the man who killed your sister, there'll be a lot of sympathy, but —"

"If I shoot him, it'll be because I have absolutely no other choice. It won't be for revenge. Trust me on that." He looked at Andy steadily.

"Shit. Okay, Jenn and Scott will come with me." He stared at the map, at the two remaining flags. "Want to flip a coin?"

Quentin studied the map for only an instant. "John and I'll take the waterfront warehouse."

Andy looked at him. "Because of Joey?"

"Yeah. Because of Joey."

"Let's go," John said.

It didn't occur to Maggie until she got there that the warehouse might have been wired for security. But as she approached the place on foot after leaving her car nearly a hundred yards back along the rutted road, she also realized that he would have done nothing to draw undue attention here. The isolation alone would protect him, that and the fence Maggie had scaled just after parking her car.

It was still a gray, dreary day, cold, not raining but almost, and nothing dry crackled under her foot to give away her approach. The warehouse she neared was a huge, hulking old building, part concrete and part rotting timbers, with a slate roof and very few windows. Maggie found the door easily enough but paused with her hand on it, her eyes closing briefly.

Useless not to admit she was terrified. Because he was in there. And because there might be a dying or dead woman in there with him, a woman Maggie wanted desperately to save if she could. If she could.

What she couldn't do was open the door to those inner senses. They could give her an edge — or destroy her. They could help her find him — or kill her with another woman's mortal injuries long before he could get his hands on her.

So she did her best to keep those inner senses firmly under control, shut deep inside herself and as inactive as she could possibly force them to be. It required almost as much focus and concentration to *not* use the senses as it did to use them, and she was all too aware that she would not be able to do it indefinitely. A few minutes, maybe.

Maybe.

She drew a deep breath, then slowly pulled the heavy door open. The hinges didn't creak. Inside was darkness, but as she stepped in and eased the door shut behind her, her eyes quickly adjusted. She could smell old machinery and dust.

And blood.

It stopped her, but only for an instant. She picked her way carefully among splintering crates and looming pieces of rusting equipment, gradually getting a feeling for the size of the place. And seeing, finally, a light in the distance.

She moved toward it cautiously, becoming aware that he had not enclosed the space in which he . . . worked. Perhaps he

472

was claustrophobic. He had been before, she remembered. Hated enclosed places, just hated them.

When had that been? 1934? At the very beginning, in 1894? She wasn't sure. Her memories of other lives were only instincts, flickering bits of knowledge, precarious certainties. The universe refused to make it easy for her.

He had picked a warehouse with soaring spaces above and arranged his . . . working space . . . within walls made only of old crates and unused equipment in an area near the waterside end of the building. A worktable with various tools and ropes and bottles of unidentifiable liquids. A gurney off to one side, presumably so that he could wheel his victims out to whatever transportation he used.

And in the center of the space . . .

It looked obscene. A double bed with carved oak head and footboards. And beside it, a chair. A beautifully upholstered, wingback chair. With a footstool.

From her angle, Maggie could see a woman's wrists raised and tied to each side of the headboard, but she couldn't see if Tara was alive or dead.

And even with her inner senses closed off, she could feel pain. Pain from this victim and those who had gone before her, distant whispers of agony so acute they had soaked into the very matter of this place, the particles that made it real. Maggie had to stop for a moment and press her hands to her mouth, concentrate on blocking, closing out, holding within.

When she finally opened her eyes again, she saw him.

He had come out of the shadows and was doing something at his worktable, and even from here she could dimly make out a wordless humming, almost a crooning sound. When he turned toward the bed, she saw that he wore a plastic mask, not a horror mask, but one with perfect, smoothly polished features, like those of a statue, white and lifeless. Female features. And the black wig he wore swept down on either side of the white mask, so that he had the creepy look of a mannequin.

She also saw that he was holding a knife.

Maggie took a quick step forward, then froze as a shadowy figure emerged from between two large crates near her, paused only to make a beckoning gesture to Maggie, and then flowed toward the work area. A slender, childlike young woman with a heart-shaped face and delicate features and long, dark hair.

Annie.

"Bobby . . . Bobby . . ."

He jerked to a stop, the eerily pretty white face turning quickly.

"Bobby . . ."

Understanding, Maggie eased her way to one side so that she would be approaching from a different direction and then moved toward him, hoping her own voice wasn't shaking too badly, and sounded as eerie as Annie when she called out, "Bobby . . . I'm sorry, Bobby, so sorry. I didn't mean what I said . . ." She didn't know where the words came from. Memory. Instinct.

The knife he held clattered to the stone floor, and he backed up another step, his physical posture one of tension and uneasiness while that white face remained expressionless. He fumbled behind him on the table, then held out a gun in one black-gloved, shaking hand.

Maggie wondered if it was the gun he had used to kill Quentin's friend Joey.

"Bobby," Annie murmured sadly, "you hurt me, Bobby. Why did you hurt me?" She glided into the circle of light, facing him. Confronting him. The nightgown she wore was fine linen, and thin, and her feet were bare. "Why did you hurt me, brother?"

He made an odd, harsh sound.

"Bobby," Maggie called, moving toward them slowly. "Bobby, I didn't mean it when I said you weren't a man. I didn't mean to laugh at you." She cast a quick glance toward the bed and flinched at the blood-soaked mattress, the pale, thin body that was bruised and battered. The missing eyes.

She couldn't tell if Tara was dead or alive.

For an instant, her control wavered, and she felt a jolt of pain so intense it nearly doubled her over. Desperately, she struggled to shore up those inner walls, to close out the suffering she couldn't afford to share this time.

"Bobby." Annie glided another few steps toward him, holding out her hands beseechingly as she drew his attention away from Maggie. "I've been trying to find you, Bobby. I miss you so much . . ."

He made another choked sound and this time ripped off the mask and wig. Maggie recognized him from the pictures Christina had shown her. He was an ordinary man with brown hair, a high forehead, and pale grayish eyes. Slender but with wide shoulders and those oddly incongruous, outsize hands, their power ob-

476

vious even gloved. Especially gloved.

But otherwise an ordinary man.

"You're dead," he said hoarsely to Annie.

Maggie moved into the light. "We're both dead, Bobby. You killed us. You killed us a long time ago." She was terrified she was wrong about this. Terrified of not being strong enough to destroy his evil. Terrified of dying.

He swallowed hard, staring at her now. "Deanna . . . I killed you. Why won't you stay dead?" His voice cracked. "Why in hell's name won't you *stay dead?*"

Annie uttered a sweet laugh. "We're stronger than you, Bobby. We always have been. Didn't you know that?"

Shattering the quiet, he fired two times directly at her.

The bullets hit the crate behind her, splintering wood. She smiled at him. "We're stronger, Bobby. We'll always be stronger."

"No! I'm stronger! I can kill you! I can kill you all!"

"You didn't kill me, Bobby," Hollis said as she stepped out of the shadows a few yards to Maggie's right.

He let out a sort of wail and backed up until he was up against the worktable and could retreat no farther. "No. No, I can kill you. I *did* kill you . . ."

Without planning to, Maggie said, "And it doesn't do any good to blind us, Bobby. We see you. We always see you."

"Always," Hollis echoed as she took another step toward him. Her eyelids were reddened and the marks of the attack were only half healed on her face, but blue eyes gazed at him, clear and steady, and she wore a small, contemptuous smile. "Did you really think you could take my eyes, Bobby?"

"I did," he muttered. He laughed suddenly, his own eyes gleaming with tears or madness. "I did. I took them. I cut them out. I did. I know I did. I put them in a bowl and watched them float. I took your eyes, Audra. I took — they were brown eyes. I remember that. Brown eyes. And I took them. And you couldn't see me."

"I see you now." Her voice was flat, cold. "I see you, Bobby. We all see you. You'll never be able to hide from any of us ever again."

"No," he mumbled, the gun wavering, his wide shoulders hunching. "No, please."

"We see you," Annie repeated.

"We see you," Maggie echoed.

He laughed — a strange, high sound —

and watching him, Maggie saw his eyes change. In those flat gray depths, something was coming apart, disintegrating. She felt a peculiar sensation, as if some force, some energy, had blown past her, pressure more than air, nearly causing her ears to pop.

It all happened within the space of seconds, and then, before she could move or react, that wavering gun pointed at her, steadied, and he whimpered, "No —"

Maggie had a split second to gaze into eyes that now held nothing but a kind of dumb hatred, and then a third shot echoed through the warehouse.

She expected pain, waited for it. But the pistol in Simon Walsh's hand clattered to the floor, and he crumpled almost soundlessly.

It was over. It was finally over.

Before Maggie could do more than catch her breath, John was there, holding her hard with one arm while the pistol in his free hand remained pointed toward Walsh.

"Maggie —"

"For a minute there," she heard herself say with astonishing calm, "I thought you were going to be too late."

"He nearly was," Quentin commented, moving out of the shadows near where

Annie had been. He went to warily check for a pulse in Walsh, keeping his own gun at the ready but relaxing when he found no heartbeat. "I didn't have a clear shot from my angle, so it was all up to him."

"Tara —"

But Quentin was already moving toward the bed and seconds later looked at them with grim eyes. "She's alive, but just barely." He took out his cell phone to quickly summon an ambulance, while Hollis joined him at the other side of the bed, helping him to gently untie Tara Jameson's wrists and murmuring soothingly to the terribly injured woman.

"You two took a hell of a chance," John said, his voice jerky. "Jesus, Maggie —"

Maggie sent a fleeting glance around, unsurprised to find Annie gone, then smiled up at him. "I know. It was just something I —"

"Felt you had to do. Yeah, I got that." He flicked the gun's safety on, then stuck the weapon inside his jacket and put both hands on her shoulders. He didn't shake her, but the desire to do so was evident in the way his fingers tightened. "Want to tell me how you thought you could win this little confrontation without so much as a big stick?"

She shook her head. "I knew my face gave me an edge, that it would catch him off guard to see me here. It gave *me* the control, at least for a little while. I thought . . . maybe the only way to fight his evil would be to shatter it — or at least the mind holding it. To have one of his victims face him, knowing all his secrets. It was the only thing I could think of to do. I had to try, John."

"Just don't ever do anything like that to me again."

"No, I won't." She looked at him searchingly.

"I won't have nightmares about killing him," John assured her. "And no regrets. When you put a mad dog out of his misery, you're only doing him a favor."

"You had no choice," she said anyway.

"I know." He pulled her into his arms. "Are you all right? Even I can feel the pain in this place."

Maggie considered, then smiled at him. "When you touch me, all I feel is you."

"Good," John said, and kissed her.

Nearly an hour later, Andy stood outside the warehouse with the others waiting for his forensics team to arrive and said, "So that was what evil looked like. I wasn't impressed."

"No," Maggie said.

He gazed at her with lifted brows. "No?"

"No. That was just the shell evil lived in for a while."

"You mean because he's dead now?"

"Because the evil was destroyed this time before the flesh was."

Andy blinked, looked at John and Quentin, then shook his head. "Never mind. I don't think I want to know what it was all about."

"Wise of you," Quentin murmured.

Scott joined them, saying, "The Caddie is parked in that shed over there. A '72, looks like. Just what your friend Joey described, Quentin."

He smiled faintly. "Yeah, he always did know cars."

Jennifer asked, "How the hell did Hollis Templeton get here?" Since Hollis had left in the ambulance with Tara Jameson, she asked the question of the others.

Maggie shrugged. "She said . . . a little voice told her she should be here. So she came. Didn't say how."

"Jesus," Scott said.

Andy looked at him, seemed about to say something, and then obviously thought better of it. He settled his shoulders with the air of a man deciding things.

"Well, as far as we're concerned, Simon Walsh raped and killed women. He was the Blindfold Rapist."

"Nobody's arguing with you, Andy," Quentin said mildly.

"No?"

"No."

Andy heaved a sigh. "Good. Now, will somebody please tell me what the fuck I'm supposed to put in my report?"

Quentin grinned at him. "You can try the truth. Of course, the truth is a bit complicated. I mean, what with Maggie and Hollis being here, to say nothing of Annie."

"Annie?"

"The little voice Hollis heard," Quentin explained solemnly. "She was here. Well, sort of."

John looked at him. "So you saw her too?"

"Oh, yeah."

"Good. I was afraid it was just me."

Andy stared at them both for a moment and, again, very obviously decided he didn't want to know. They all heard the sounds of sirens approaching, and he groaned. "I'll either get a medal or get committed."

"Welcome to my world," Quentin said.

EPILOGUE

Sitting up in her hospital bed to better talk to her visitors, Kendra said to Hollis, "So Annie was Robert Graham's twin sister, the first one he killed."

"Apparently. I'd had her voice in my head since the attack, but it was only the last few days that she told me who she was. And what she needed me to do."

"I'm glad you were there," Maggie told her. "I think you were the clincher. Standing there looking at him even though he'd thought he had blinded you for good."

"I wasn't sure what I was doing," Hollis confessed. "Just . . . saying whatever popped into my head." She shook her head. "Annie had told me I had to be there, that it was the only way to help you. When she told me that, told me I *had* to see or else he'd be free to go on killing, I just — all of a sudden I could see. It was easy to distract the cop guarding my door, easy to slip out. And I knew, somehow, where to go."

"You and Maggie," Quentin said. He looked at Maggie. "Thanks for sharing."

"Don't you give me a hard time," she warned him with a faint smile. "I've already heard enough about it from John. I'm sorry I didn't tell you what I knew — or thought I knew. It was just that so much of it was vague or unclear. I was afraid if I said too much I'd cause things to go even more horribly wrong."

"We've been there," Kendra told her ruefully. "Sometimes we walk a very fine line between what we think we know and what's actually going on."

Maggie nodded. "It can be a challenge. I mean, there were flashes of memory or bits of information I wasn't sure I could trust, but all I really *knew* absolutely for certain was that I had to be there at the end, confronting him."

John said, "Because you'd been his wife long ago and weren't able to stop him from killing."

Maggie looked at the others with slightly lifted brows. "He's having a hard time with this."

"No, I'm not," John denied. He was

stared at politely, and finally sighed. "Okay, I am."

"He'll get used to it," Quentin assured Maggie. "Between us, we've nearly worn away that high gloss of logic and rationality he used to wear."

Hollis looked at John. "Aren't you grateful?"

"Oh, immensely. The world's beginning to look almost normal standing on its ear."

"It's all about balance," Maggie murmured.

John took her hand with a determined air and said to the others, "If you'll excuse us, we have things to discuss."

"Thanks for the visit," Kendra said, smiling.

"We'll be back tomorrow," Maggie told her.

"I'll look forward to it."

As they left the hospital room, they heard Quentin saying to Hollis, "Listen, our boss should be here any minute, and he's sort of anxious to meet you —"

Maggie said, "Do you think she will? I mean, join Bishop's unit?"

"You know her better than I do," John replied. "But from what I've seen, I'd say Hollis Templeton is very aware of having a brand-new life stretching in front of her, and I doubt that after this she'll be eager to . . . embrace the ordinary."

"Very poetic."

"Thank you."

"And probably true," Maggie added. "There are certain corners that, having once been turned, change your view of the world forever."

As the elevator doors closed and the car started downward, John looked at her gravely. "I'll say."

She smiled faintly. "You're seriously considering it, aren't you? Helping to build some sort of civilian resource organization similar to Bishop's unit?"

"Quentin's had worse ideas," John admitted.

"Admit it — you're just beginning to enjoy seeing the world standing on its ear, that's what it is."

"Well, that's part of it. And there's you, of course. You're not about to stop doing what you do best just because that greater evil got buried this time around. And much as I respect Andy and the other cops, I think we both know that your talents deserve . . . a broader canvas."

"So do yours, for that matter," she said. "Building the kind of organization Quentin was talking about won't be easy. Lots of strikes against it, beginning with the uneasiness most people feel about psychic ability."

"Which is why I'm perfect for the job. I know how to build organizations from the ground up, and I'm about as nonpsychic as they come."

They left the elevator and walked down the bustling hallway toward the doors, and it wasn't until they were outside in the clear, chill air that Maggie stopped, looked up at him with a smile, and said, "It's all about balance."

"So I can say it now?" he asked, smiling but intent.

"You still don't have to." She slipped her arms up around his neck as he pulled her close, both of them oblivious to the people walking past them. "We balance perfectly. I love you, John."

Just before his lips touched hers, John murmured, "That's all I needed to hear."